Praise for *Ga*

"Packed with cool ideas, psychological intrigue, political conspiracy, and hard-won hope."
—Annalee Newitz

"This delightful pinball machine of a book recalls the whiz-bang joy and gleeful innovation of Neal Stephenson's *Snow Crash*."
—*Publishers Weekly* (starred review)

"A visionary glimpse into the future."
—*Kirkus Reviews*

"A thought-provoking and, at times, frightening peek into the possibilities of the future."
—*Booklist*

"Readers will delight in the nonbinary characters, LBGTQ relationships and identities, and the land acknowledgment statement at the end of the book. Highly recommended."
—*Library Journal* (starred review)

TOR BOOKS BY L. X. BECKETT

Gamechanger
Dealbreaker

GAMECHANGER

L. X. BECKETT

TOR

A TOM DOHERTY ASSOCIATES BOOK · NEW YORK

GAMECHANGER

Copyright © 2019 by A. M. Dellamonica

All rights reserved.

A Tor Book
Published by Tom Doherty Associates
120 Broadway
New York, NY 10271

www.tor-forge.com

Tor® is a registered trademark of Macmillan Publishing Group, LLC.

The Library of Congress has cataloged the hardcover edition as follows:

Beckett, L. X., author.
Gamechanger / L.X. Beckett.—First edition.
  p. cm.
"A Tom Doherty Associates book."
ISBN 978-1-250-16526-8 (hardcover)
ISBN 978-1-250-16524-4 (ebook)
1. Women lawyer—Fiction. 2. Public defenders—Fiction. 3. Terrorists—Fiction. 4. Government, Resistance to—Fiction. 5. Artificial intelligence—Fiction. I. Title.
  PR9199.4.B4436 G36 2019
  813'.6—dc23

2019948647

ISBN 978-1-250-16525-1 (trade paperback)

Our books may be purchased in bulk for promotional, educational, or business use. Please contact your local bookseller or the Macmillan Corporate and Premium Sales Department at 1-800-221-7945, extension 5442, or by email at MacmillanSpecialMarkets@macmillan.com.

First Edition: September 2019
First Trade Paperback Edition: October 2020

Printed in the United States of America

0 9 8 7 6 5 4 3 2 1

FOR LINDA CARSON: FRIEND, MENTOR, SUPERGENIUS,
FOUR-COLOR HERO, ACADEMIC ASSASSIN. YOU ARE A
GAMECHANGER, IN EVERY SENSE OF THE WORD.

GAMECHANGER

PROLOGUE

THE SURFACE

(TAGS #REALITY, #CONSENSUS-REALITY, #THE-REAL-WORLD)

WEST EDMONTON EVACUATION ZONE, AUGUST 2060

Misfortune Wilson had a ticket to Neverland.

Kids never talked about Neverland when adults were about. Only when their VR rigs were safely stowed, when they had slipped parental oversight and Sensorium pickup, did they whisper and speculate.

Some believed Neverland was a deep-sea technosphere, safe from scorching sun, flying hail, from gale-class winds and the plagues running through the densification camps. Kids told stories of submarine apartments walled in mother-of-pearl, a futuristic Atlantis circled by reefs of jewel-toned fish.

In Neverland, nobody tracked your location.

Nice enough fantasy, Misfortune supposed, though most stories said they kicked you out when you turned sixteen.

Other kids had told her Neverland was on the moon, or hidden within the protected remains of the Amazon rainforest. Snakes and frogs and warm air, they said. Butterflies and waterfalls.

Her newest @CloseFriend, Calla, believed that kids who made it to Neverland would be put to sleep for a hundred years. These lucky dreamers would sleep out the plagues, waking to the task of renewing Earth. They would rebuild the forests, rewild everything their elders had spoiled.

Misfortune had scoffed . . . until she got her own invitation. Now she favored the underground theory. Caves and repurposed diamond mines seemed more realistic than a deep-sea habitat or something with butterflies.

The problem now was meeting their pickup.

Wrapping a shawl tightly around her head, she peered around the corner of the bombed-out Misericordia Hospital. Her slitted eyes picked out pink electric light obscured by dark streamers of wind-borne dust. The light winked in Morse code, signaling from the remains of West Edmonton Mall.

She decoded the message: *Darlings, darlings, here, come . . .*

"See it?" Thick American accent, barely audible over the wind. Garmin's breath was hot on her ear and smelled of their last meal, a mash of printed apricot, fauxmeat, and unidentified flying protein. Moths, probably.

"What?" Calla was a scabby whiner of a kid. She'd stowed away on the same water convoy as them.

Misfortune pointed. "Beacon."

Calla peered beyond the dubious shelter of the hospital's shattered foundations, shrinking back as an old camper blew into view. It was rolling, becoming obscenely rounded as its corners bounced off the ground.

"That parking lot's a death trap!"

"Missy'll think of something," Garmin said. He and Misfortune were on their third set of foster parents; their being tagged #siblings was a mere formality. Still, the younger boy—he was ten, she twelve—hadn't slowed her down.

"We'll never make it!" Calla said.

Misfortune considered as the trailer fetched up against a heavy concrete divider. Wind howled and the old vehicle groaned, lofting up over the barrier before continuing its murderous roll eastward. An old shopping cart whipped past, chasing it, and slammed the barrier as well.

The dividers weren't much shelter, but they'd have to do. She pointed out a heavy-looking van at the midpoint of the lot. "We'll catch our breath there."

"If it doesn't flip on us," Calla groused.

"Follow me!" Head down, Misfortune leaned into the wind. Dirt and pebbles smacked with bruising force against her sleeves. Nanotech cleats in the boots she'd stolen from her foster mother made each step sticky, forcing her to peel her feet off the ground . . . but keeping her from blowing away. Garmin and Calla held hands—they were sharing Dad's cleats.

Forcing herself to it step by step, she made an exhausting progress to a vintage traffic signal. It was bent like a stalk of grass, its half-severed top swinging wildly. Misfortune spared a glance back, saw the huddled shadows of the younger children plodding through the dust, and hurled herself onto the parking lot.

Nobody knows where we are, nobody knows . . . She'd thought it would be a heady experience, being off-grid.

Boom! Wind knocked her sprawling even as it snapped the stem of the traffic light. Then the whole storm blew out. The shrieking wind stilled to whispers.

Windblown trash crashed to earth. *Smash bang crunch.* Green glass tinkled from the traffic light. Her ears rang.

"Scramble!" Misfortune clicked her heels together to retract the nanocleats. She sprinted across the parking lot toward the boarded-up mall, the flickering beacon.

"Slow down!" Calla shouted.

On the horizon, the turbulent Alberta sky was turning the sickly green of rotten flesh.

"Missy . . ."

"I see it!"

"Tornados!"

"I know!" Green skies meant fast death, few choices. Easy maths.

"Mostly they miss, mostly they miss . . ." Her wrap had torn loose. She let it unfurl in her hand, the better to pull it tight again. Her dirty tongue rasped over dust-crusted lips.

"Misfortune . . ."

"Just run, Calla!"

"It hurts—"

Halfway across.

"Freeze!" Deep, amplified voice. A spotlight pinned her.

Misfortune screeched to a halt so sudden, her knees popped and the cleats reactivated.

You are not *taking me back to the densification camp!*

The drone had been sheltering under the armored car. Toaster-sized, with squeaking rotors, it tried to hover equidistant between the three children.

"*Vrrrrah* trespassing in an evacuation *zooooooohhhh*. Identify *cahh zzz*urrender!"

Beyond the glitching drone, the roof of the sky was twisting into downward spikes. On the horizon she saw funnel clouds forming and retracting. Dip down, swirl up. Closer each time.

The bot extruded arms—one, two, three—with tranq darts. Two it aimed at Misfortune and Garmin. Red laser dots winked on their chests. The third, Calla's dart, was drooping.

"Remove ma*sssshhh* and submit to facie*ee* recognition!"

Ma*ssshhh*? Masks. Her face was *that* dirty.

Boom! A needle-thin wisp of lightning sizzled something within the remains of the hospital.

Mostly it misses, mostly . . .

The lightning strike startled Garmin. He twitched, just enough. The drone fired.

Misfortune was moving even as her brother made a soft *oh!* sound and staggered back. She leapt up to the traffic divider, shawl in hand, tackling the bot. They hit the pavement hard; its whirling chopper blade cut into her cheek.

"Sabota*aaa* of densification bots izza offense!" it wailed.

Misfortune scrabbled under the drone, scavenging darts. She almost got her fingers broken when Calla ran up, hefting a hunk of concrete, and began smashing it down on the bot.

"Careful!"

"Trying to help!" One of Calla's busted-up fingernails had peeled right off.

Misfortune rolled off the drone, panting, tucking a dart into her sleeve as Calla continued to kill the drone. Garmin had dropped to his knees. The tranq protruded, right below his sternum.

Could they still beat the wind? Misfortune slung his arm over her shoulder. He sagged like bagged sand.

"Calla, help!"

"He's too big!"

"Bloody get over here and—"

"Give me the other nanoboot!" Calla said. "I'll run ahead for help."

Wind lifted Misfortune's hair, scouring grit over her unprotected face. "Get back here!"

Calla wavered, just for a second.

Drop Garmin and pummel the other girl into submission?

Before she could decide, the armored rear doors of the van burst open, disgorging two well-fed adults. One charged them, tearing Garmin from Misfortune's grasp.

"Ride's here, kiddies," he said. "Saddle up!"

Calla scrambled after him without missing a beat.

Thunder boomed above.

Misfortune hesitated. These didn't look like rescuers from a magical utopian city. They looked like better-fed versions of the camp guards.

"Neverland express, kid! Shit or get off the pot—we got a storm to outrun!"

"Language, Burke!" said his partner.

"This vicious little fuglet busted our bot!"

The guard—Burke—made as though to close the van up. Misfortune bolted inside, cowering against Calla's twiggy frame.

Doors slammed. The vehicle leapt forward, accelerating. Misfortune's cleats dug into the van carpet.

One of the soldiers unmasked. "Hello, girls," she said. "I'm Gladys. I'm a medic. Do you mind if I . . ."

Calla stepped forward, allowing the adult to wipe her face clean. "What sweet, obedient children! Want some hydro gel?"

They grabbed the water capsules gratefully, biting in, chewing.

"Rinse your teeth and just spit—" Gladys gestured at the floor.

Wide-eyed, Calla obeyed, swishing the gel and then dribbling out a glob of black and red. The carpet ate it without protest.

The whole van must be top-line tech.

Misfortune strained jellied water through her teeth. It was cool and tasted faintly of apples, nothing like the chewy, sulfur-tasting water rations from the camps. Spitting to clear the dirt from her mouth seemed an almost criminal act of waste.

She swallowed the second gel, then a third. Finally, she held her hand out for a wipe. "I'll clean myself, thanks."

The medic continued to swab at Calla as Misfortune tried to stanch the gash the bot had left in her face. "What's your names?"

"Calla Hudson."

"Misfortune Wilson."

"Well, Miss Fortune—"

"Ain't Miss Anything. Tell us about Neverland. Is it—" Her breath hitched.

"Is it better?" Calla finished for her. "Than the camps?"

The van lurched. The other guard, Burke, was muttering over tornado proximity alerts on its screens.

Suddenly, a new voice spoke. "Why not let Gladys stitch your wound while you and I talk about Neverland, luvvie?"

"Poppet!" Misfortune relaxed, fractionally. "Where are you?"

The medic, Gladys, handed her a battered doll with green glass eyes and auburn hair done up in a bun. It wore a long black dress and had a pair of felt glasses that hung on her chest, strung from a gold ribbon.

"Now, luvvie." Top-of-the-line speaker in its gut, crisp voice, no fuzzing like that old security bot outside. "Can't Gladys see to your pretty face?"

"*Not* pretty." Still. Misfortune dropped her guard, allowing

Gladys to spray her with cleansers and cooling foam. She hadn't realized how much her face hurt until it stopped throbbing.

"There's a love. Let's see. You never went for the nonsense about underwater cities, did you?"

"Then Neverland is real? Truly?"

"Try not to talk," said the medic.

"Real as this lorry," the doll said. "Real as these medics. You have proper families waiting for you at Neverland. You will be cherished."

Parents, version four. Misfortune fought a sigh. She spoke from the good side of her mouth. "And when we grow up?"

"That rather depends on you."

Misfortune held the doll in the center of her field of vision, the better to take in the others' faces in her peripheral. Under his goggles, Burke was sneering. Gladys was holding a neutral expression.

"Little Calla, I know, is interested in cooking. She'll make a good worker bee. And your brother is such a smart, attractive, healthy boy! A proper prince!"

"But. A stroppy fuglet with a cut face?"

"Hush hush," Gladys said. "Almost done. I'm going to cut out your tracker chip."

"My chip?"

"You don't want the camp coming after you, luvvie, once the storm's passed?" the doll chirped.

Misfortune shook her head.

Gladys produced a small glass tube containing a slice of printed beef. The muscle tissue twitched faintly as she pressed the tube against Misfortune's upper arm, isolating a circle of skin.

"Your user account locks if the chip reports tampering, so we have to confuse it." Deploying a wide-bore needle, she injected something under the edge of the glass, numbing Misfortune's flesh before using a third probe to dig for the chip.

An emerald point cut upward through Misfortune's skin like a tooth breaking through gum.

"Is that it?"

"Pretty, isn't it, luvvie?"

The chip was a flattish green teardrop, about the size of her smallest fingernail. Gladys tucked it against the strand of live muscle, screwed a lid onto the capsule, and dropped it into a complicated-looking case. "Chip secured.

"That's it for your old life. Now you can start again."

Top-flight equipment and chip extractors. Whatever Neverland was, it wasn't going to be brightly colored fish bobbing around reefs. It wasn't kids weaving seaweed baskets and getting on fine without parental supervision.

In that case, Misfortune concluded, the best case was to end up being the one holding the weapons.

She said to the doll, "Can I become one of these troopers of yours?"

"You want to join the Shadows?" Burke barked laughter. "Oh, fuglet. You'd be lucky to end up botomized and mopping toilets."

"Silence, Mer Burke!" Poppet said. "Misfortune, I do like your spirit."

The medic put a bandage on Misfortune's arm before turning back to Calla. The other girl had curled up on the opposite bench.

"Calla?"

"Hurts."

Gladys nudged open the girl's mouth with a gloved finger, revealing bleeding gums.

Despite herself, Misfortune took a step back. "New dengue?"

Gladys nodded.

The adults had put plague-pushers in the hydrogels.

It happened in the camps, too. People who compromised herd immunity by avoiding their jabs were antisocial. Screening—even by using tests that would doom the afflicted—was routine practice.

Did she care? Calla was a whiner. She should've got vaxxed.

"Is Garmin okay?" she asked, hating the tremble in her voice. They weren't really #siblings, after all.

"Your brother's negs for plague, same as you."

Misfortune let her fingers travel over the newly glued surface of her cheek. She felt pressure but no sensation in that side of her face. Under her hand, the skin was leather. She frowned at the doll, thinking.

"We were supposed to get tranked by the bot, I suppose. Hauled into the truck and tested while we slept."

"Clever girl," Poppet said. "You understand, don't you, luvvie, that little Calla cannot be helped? We didn't give her the fever. We can only make the end easier."

"Testing accell—accell . . . pushes the dengue," she said. "Some people even live if you don't test!"

"Get vaxxed or get #triaged; isn't that the saying?"

Misfortune scowled. "In the camps."

"Darling, darling," the doll's voice soothed. "All I want is for you to be safe, happy, and useful. But you must see that Calla—"

"Is already #triaged?"

"It is a terrible shame, luvvie," the doll said. "Why don't you go up front and sit with your brother while Gladys helps Calla?"

Calla lunged off the bench, diving for the space between Burke's legs. Her hands slipped on the surface of the rear doors, feeling for handles that weren't there. She let out a bubbly shriek. Then Burke lifted her, with both gloved hands, barely turning his face away as she coughed, misting him with crimson.

The girl clawed at his goggles, frantic, kicking.

Misfortune set the doll down carefully, keeping one eye on Gladys as she stepped up behind Burke. "Put her down."

"Stay out of this, kid."

"I said down!" Her hard-won prize, raided from the bot, had been its third tranq dart. Now she palmed it, punching through Burke's uniform, into his calf.

Calla dropped to the floor, crashing like a sack full of bottles. Burke backhanded Misfortune.

She barely felt the blow, what with her still-frozen cheek, but the lift of it almost tore her out of her nanoboots. She felt the long bones in her legs stretching. Pinwheeling her arms, she fought not to fall on her back.

"Better sit down, Shadow," she told Burke.

"You little—" He groped for the dart in his thigh.

"Do as she says, Burke." Poppet's voice was like steel. Now *that* was a mom talking.

He fisted and opened his hands, fisted and opened them. Misfortune crossed her arms, hoping to hide the shakes. She could take another hit. She'd taken plenty.

Then Burke crouched in the far corner, against the doors. Calla crawled away as he began to droop.

"This ain't over, fuglet."

Ignoring him, Misfortune helped Calla back to the bench.

"They." Bubbling hiss of breath, on foamy lips. "Just want. The chips?"

Not necessarily, Misfortune thought. Their rescuers were laundering identity chips, certainly, but Poppet needed people. Soldiers and cooks and toilet scrubbers. Sons and daughters for wannabe parents. It was vastly more plausible than a magical undersea playsphere free of adults and surveillance.

Calla gasped. "Hurts!"

Misfortune wound their fingers together. The younger girl was feverish; sweat, blood, dirt, and remnant hydrogel itched in a paste between their palms.

"I thought they'd cure it. In Neverland."

It. Fever. She had run because she knew she was sick.

Misfortune drew a long breath. "It'll hurt less if you let Gladys put you to sleep."

She waited while Calla thought that over. The red veins in her eyes beat a staccato pulse, suffusing crimson into the whites.

Finally, a hitch of breath. A tearless nod.

"She's ready," Misfortune said, and stroked the other girl's hair as the medic leaned over them both, with a wordless reassuring murmur, and administered the sedative. Calla's eyelids drooped. Her hand became plasticine.

"Retrieve the chip and then give her the second shot," ordered Poppet.

Gladys prepared the glass tube. Calla's nails were ragged—a bit of Burke's hair was snagged in one break. Misfortune pulled the hair free, dropping it to the floor, and spared one triumphant glance at the unconscious soldier.

"Do you want to go up front now?" Gladys asked.

"Not until you've finished."

The guard extracted the flat green identity chip from Calla. Then . . .

Misfortune watched the second needle go in, felt Calla slip away between one breath and the next. She used her ragged, dirty shawl to cover the other child's body.

The medic, Gladys, was looking poker-faced again.

"I'd like to wash my hands now," Misfortune said. "And, Poppet, I don't need another mom and dad."

The doll's artificial eyelids blinked. Down. Up. "You've got backbone, luvvie darling. I always liked you."

"Did you?"

"Yes, indeed. You and I, Misfortune, we're going to get on famously."

Our task as a species in this century is to survive it.

—John Green

CHAPTER 1

[FORTY YEARS LATER]

Cherub Whiting's first realworld police raid was nothing like the sims.

She was in a chic Parisian neighborhood with a view of the Eiffel Tower, waiting on a meeting. When @Interpol showed up in her pop-in conference room, she'd been sending pings to a no-show client for the better part of an hour.

Luce, you're late. Luce, it's time for our face-to-face. Where are you?

He'd be afraid to skip, wouldn't he? By the time someone's social capital got so bad they merited a face-to-face meeting—one involving the horrifying carbon cost of flying a lawyer from Toronto to WestEuro, no less—they were desperate to get life back on track. Failure to appear was unheard of.

The drag of jetlag had left Rubi mentally fogged. It dawned only slowly that she was obsessing.

"Can I get a volunteer gig while I wait, Crane?"

Her electronic sidekick had obviously been expecting the request. "A radish pallet across the hall has requested weeding and watering." Crane's crisp voice, transmitted via tiny implanted earbuds, had a British accent; he sounded like he was at her shoulder. "Its usual gardener had an emergency."

"Accept task."

Rubi's visual implants superimposed the mirage of a yellow arrow onto the floor, mapping the way to a conference room big enough for twelve. The pallet of seedlings in question had been abandoned mid-job. Thumb-sized plants with leaves like propellers ruffled in a breeze from the open window. Beyond them, the streets of Paris beckoned.

Rubi felt a pang for whoever had been tending the radishes.

"Run tutorial?"

"I remember how to weed radishes, Crane." Nudging aside a delicate stem with her thumbnail, she isolated one of the undesirables, tugging it from the soil. "See?"

"Very good, miss."

Where was Luce? If they couldn't convince Cloudsight he could behave prosocially, he'd be remanded to managed care: relocation to the outskirts, mandatory labor on an ecosphere rehab project—topsoil generation, probably—and censored comms. It was a prison sentence in all but name.

You can't make him appear, Rubi told herself. *Breathe. Pull weeds. Enjoy the solitude.*

Heavy boots, pounding up the stairwell double-time, filled her with relief.

Finally!

Crane spoke, momentarily drowning out the elephant stampede. "Miss Cherub? Call for you."

"Is it Dad?"

"Your father's fine. The call is from your archnemesis."

"Not funny."

"No? I'll make a note."

"Gimlet Barnes is *not* my arch—"

Clomp clomp clomp bang! An armored man charged through the door.

Rubi pivoted, squaring off to face the threat . . . and brandishing a fist full of weeds. The move was reflexive, triggered by hours logged in-game.

. . . plus, maybe, the mention of Gimlet . . .

If this *had* been a game, her implants would have augmented the white-walled meeting room until it was unrecognizable, frosting visuals and sound over mundane reality, porting her into playspace: a dungeon, maybe, a space station, or a canyon in the mythical American Wild West. Instead, the walls lit up with official warnings. Posters scrolled on the plaster, red-and-black placards: POLICE LINE. DO NOT CROSS!

"Don't move!"

A cop? Luce couldn't be a cop, could he? With his social deficits?

Official directives crawled the posters: REMAIN IN PLACE! WAIT FOR INSTRUCTIONS!

Rubi had risen to her toes, prep for rolling left if he attacked. Heart slamming, she scanned for weapons.

Like what—a crossbow? Holy water?

Two cameras and a pacification bot drifted over her radishes.

"Stand down, mademoiselle! Stand down *now*!"

Rubi lowered her fists. Of course this policeman wasn't Luce. He was a stranger.

Handsome stranger, noted an inner voice.

Dammit, stay on task! "Complying as ordered."

He was tall and olive-skinned, with flyaway hair the color of charcoal and forbidding features: sharp nose, steely eyes. A protective vest, over the base layer of nanosilk he wore as a primer garment, left her to imagine the details of his physique. His bot was armed with a joy buzzer, third-gen Taser tech. Dad claimed that a good jolt would make you wish you'd died.

He would know, wouldn't he?

@Interpol must have a warrant, because the building hadn't warned Crane he was coming.

As this thought gelled, a badge resolved on the wall.

@Interpol Special Ops, Agent Anselmo Javier
Pronouns: he/him
Cloudsight Respectability Rating: 59/100%

Agent Javier checked under the old hardwood table, then peered inside a closet filled with folding chairs. "I'm going to search the rest of the floor," he said. "Wait here, *s'il vous plaît*."

He left Rubi alone with the drones.

Feigning calm, she peered beyond the radishes to the street. Zoom views from other cameras let her clock a half-dozen meandering residents and tourists.

So, civilians weren't being diverted away from the scene. Still, there were at least a dozen drones lurking in the shadows. And . . .

. . . her mouth went dry.

An autonomous sniper, bristling with tranq darts, was tucked into a balcony across the street. It had its sights on her. As she clocked it, the nanotech primer on its exterior changed color. It blended in with a building pediment covered in anti-pigeon spikes.

As it all but vanished, Rubi felt goose bumps coming up on her arms. A gun. An actual gun.

Crane murmured, "Isn't this how that 1942 simulation started out?"

"That was a game," Rubi said. Still, she let the memory raise a smile. Wild with exhaustion, she had torn through a VR sim of Occupied Paris, meeting contacts, passing messages, and setting garlic traps for Vichy vampires.

It was the only time she had let life in Sensorium swamp her studies, had ignored school and all her surface obligations. She should have been memorizing social infraction case precedents before her next law exam unlocked. Instead, she'd stayed online for eighteen hours, sabotaging trains and stealing bomb plans.

The dealbreaker had been her so-called archnemesis. Gimlet Barnes had been brought in by Risto Games in a last-minute twist, to lead a team of German necromancers hunting her resistance cell.

Rubi had lost big in their previous battle, a superhero thing. She'd apparently lost perspective, too. Once Gimlet was in, there was no chance she'd stop, not even for a better shot at leveling her mash-up of careers into a single permajob as a public defender.

Thrill of adrenaline, *rat-a-tat* of machine guns, crossbow-driven stakes. Sim blood spraying as buildings collapsed. Players and audience tooning in by the tens of thousands.

Stone tumbling to drive a pall of dust skyward, thick enough to curtain the moonlight. Howling werewolf choruses. Bone-shaking blasts of shellfire, stripping the air to gunpowder-laced sandpaper.

But . . . "Never again, Crane."

"If you say so, miss."

"I mean it." She couldn't fail any more exams without falling off the law school leaderboard.

Materialists would insist it had never happened, anyway. Manufactured gamer dreams had no meaning in surface reality. But Rubi remembered it—remembered the bombed-out terrain of mid–twentieth century Paris—as if it was her own nursery.

Meanwhile, that camouflaged sniper lurking in the crannies, here and now, prickled at her consciousness.

The @Interpol agent returned. "You are Cherub Barbara Whiting?"

"Yes."

"Where's Luciano Pox?"

"Why?"

"Answer the question, please."

Rubi replied, "He's sixty-six minutes late."

"Is that normal?"

"I can't say." A camera drone hovered in her peripheral. Trying to unsettle her? "If Luce wasn't profoundly antisocial, he wouldn't need in-the-flesh legal support."

"So, clients often skip?"

Never. Rather than admit this, she said, "He has an emergent seizure disorder. Which means, by the way, you can't zap him at will."

"Zap. At will." The agent raised his eyebrows.

She waited, arms crossed.

Finally, Agent Javier nodded, and the joy buzzer took the

window exit, whirring away. "Surely your client has been tested for this alleged disorder."

"I only just got him into peer counseling." Rubi had referred Luce to her father, who like her was good with exceptionally difficult people . . . when he wasn't being difficult himself. "We'll coax him into getting scanned."

"Ah! Then you tell Cloudsight that he needs medical allowances made for disability, and so he avoids managed care," Javier said. "Convenient, *non*?"

Had he just suggested that disability was something to be exploited? A social hack? "Shorting out at random when you're trying to make it through the day is, for your information, extremely *in*convenient. Play a few neurodisorder sims. Judge for yourself."

The agent blinked.

Rubi turned back to the radishes, simmering with anger. It wouldn't help Luce if the Sensorium went viral with footage of her chewing out a cop.

Had they planned to tranq Luce and rush him into managed care without a hearing?

No. He'd have to be a terrorist or #troll . . . and if they suspected either of those things, the block would be teeming with security.

Moving in what—in games, anyway—was a nonthreatening manner, Rubi swept the discarded weeds into a compost bin. She refused to allow herself to search out the sniperbot again—though the space between her shoulder blades itched. She brushed topsoil off her palms, accessed the building helix, and activated the watering app.

Recycled graywater drizzled over the young radishes. Rubi tipped the garden pallet outdoors to face the ever-broiling sun and latched the windowpane. "Task complete."

"The Pompidou neighborhood farm co-op has boosted your social capital, Miss Cherub," replied the sidekick app. "Agent Javier, too."

The two strokes were, very nearly, worth as much as an hour's lawyering. After the collapse of the global finance networks, rationing had established minimal guaranteed solvency for every citizen—live, artificial, or corporate.

Global Oversight guaranteed calories, housing, meds. It equalized access to work and education. Virtual reality made it all bearable.

Everyone needed a few in-the-flesh luxuries, though, and real-world perks were priced on a sliding scale. That was where Cloudsight came in: what you paid depended on your reputation. Pricing for privileges, premiums, and in-app purchases went up exponentially, tier by tier.

"Crane, tell the gardener that I hope their emergency resolves happily," Rubi said.

"She wants you to know her daughter's a fan."

"Nice! License the kid a hair clip?"

"Already done. Message from Gimlet Barnes?"

"Crane, stop! I'm in the middle of something."

"Are you? Agent Javier is elsewhere." Crane was right: the flinty-eyed @Interpol agent had glazed, presumably diving into Sensorium to commiserate with his drone pilots about the fizzling of their raid.

Rubi pushed aside the thought of Gimlet, of the gamer grudge match she hadn't quite managed to call off yet. She pinged the @Interpol agent: "I'm due to update Luce's support ticket. You gonna tell me why you're after him?"

"*Oui, d'accord.*" If he was affronted by her bossiness, it didn't show. "This meeting room's free."

"No. Somewhere less isolated." When he frowned, Rubi added, "Come on, Agent Javier. It's a beautiful day."

"You can call me Anselmo."

"Anselmo, then."

His smile changed the whole landscape of his face; the severity vanished, replaced with sparks of good humor. Despite the guns and his hint of arrogance, she found herself liking him.

"Hold everything but a crisis, Crane."

"Understood, miss."

"Thanks." With that, she whisked up her satchel and walked out past the cop, daring him to object.

Instead, Anselmo fell in beside her.

Nothing like the sims, Rubi thought again, walking fast, getting some distance from that gun platform as she made for the stairs.

CHAPTER 2

THE SENSORIUM (#NEWINTERNET #NEXTGENINTERNET #VR #VIRTUALREALITY #ONLINE #WHYAREBODIES)
VRTP://VIRTUAL-REALITY-ENTERTAINMENT-DISTRICT/FECKLESS-BACHELOR™.SIM

The Feckless Bachelor™ party was Woodrow Whiting's adults-only gathering, a virtual club built into his e-state, Whine Manor, with design and logistics managed by the Great Lakes Casino Consortium.

On a good shift, five hundred people might toon into the party from around the world, with another hundred queued. The sim was fully immersive. Guests partied with friends, chatting, dancing, catching concerts. Many came hoping to see a live performance, or unlock a rare one-on-one meeting with the host himself.

Drow's streaming concerts were randomly staged events, surprises calculated to keep subscriptions boosted, but he kept his main stage hopping with promising new virtuosi. Today's feature, Whiskey Sour by name, was a sylphlike soprano with a killer sense of rhythm. She was just wrapping up a set—a mix of covers and her first original comps.

Drow closed his eyes, gauging the Feckless applause by sound, declining the aggregated user reviews. The crowd was upbeat. He didn't need infographics to tell him the neophyte had done well.

"Give her another hand, @FecklessGuests!" He raised a roar in channel, then handed Whiskey down from the stage, straight into the arms of her gathered parents.

Suddenly, a guy dressed in old-time prison pajamas and burglar's mask—a free overlay, for anonymity—plowed through the guests. He made straight for Drow, waving a red referral key from Social Support.

"I gotta talk to you! Emergency."

Drow paged his casino sponsor, requesting a guest host for the party. "You'll be all right, Whiskey?"

"Beyond," she said. "I'm sky high!"

"You should be: they loved you, kid."

She bounced up on tiptoe, giving his cheek an exuberant kiss. "Go. I'll work the crowd."

Drow ushered the burglar to an illusion of a secluded back-room table with a velvet rope. They sat and the party faded out. The metaphor shifted, painting Drow's consulting office around them. A comfortable room with light blue walls and inviting couches, it had a window view of a copse of birch trees.

The convict toon was jittering, rubbing his knees. Tags popped up. His actual body was somewhere in WestEuro.

"My name is Drow," he said, giving him time to get acclimated. "Pronouns he/him. My current physical location is the Great Lakes, Toronto District. I'm a volunteer peer counselor specializing in trauma—"

"Weren't you just hawking old records?"

"Like most people, I have a mash-up of careers and passions," Drow said. "Counseling is volunteer work."

Was the guy incapable of eye contact? Just as Drow formed the thought, his guest met his gaze straight on.

He braced for the usual expression of surprise. Unlike many of his peers, Drow made no effort to avoid looking his age. His toon wore a smartly cut suit, but it was drawn over a sim that closely resembled his fleshly vessel, which meant thinning white hair, time-damaged skin, and a look to his face that was conventionally tagged #sunken.

Drow bore hexagonal scars on his temples, stigmata of a generation that had transitioned from external goggles and audio headsets to the first surgically implanted uplinks and biocybernetic augments. The scars were thick, upraised skin, almost a trademark.

Many of Drow's Setback generation peers spent precious social capital getting their gogg scars removed. But even if Drow had wanted to pay someone to shoot him full of Superhoomin or give him nanotech skin grafts, it wasn't really on #brand.

He asked, "Do you feel up to telling me your name?"

"Pox. Luce Pox. He-him-his."

"You were referred by Cherubim Whiting?"

"Rubi-advocate-lawyer, she-her pronouns. Also notorious, though less so."

"Uh-huh. You understand we have a familial relationship as well as a collegial one?"

"I should care about that?" Pox cringed, raising both hands as if he expected to be hit.

"You don't have to care; I'm simply disclosing."

Pox cracked the shield of fingers. "Truth?"

"Want to tell me why you're here, Mer Pox?"

"Luce. I'm being attacked."

A crawl of gooseflesh, rising on Drow's arms and back.

One of the successes of the Sensorium's often-creepy all-eyes culture was the elimination of interpersonal violence. Tranq drones deployed to the scene of any assault within minutes. Arrest, trial, and conviction—if you hurt someone maliciously—were a same-day service. The destruction of your reputation, as people shared abuse footage, was instantaneous.

Being attacked. The phrase implied repeated incidents.

So, he's delusional. "Tell me about that."

"Creeping horror, pain, noise, and I get . . ." Luce knuckled his temples. "I wake up, afterwards, in one of these . . . *fausses boîtes?*"

Fausse . . . what? Oh. "In a sim?"

"I've been . . . how to say? Conked out? My datacache riffled."

"You lose consciousness and you wake in Sensorium. On someone's e-state?"

"Yes. No. A public lecture theater."

"Where?" Drow asked.

Groaning, Luce produced his datacache, a banged-up safecracker's toolkit. Fists clenched, he stared at it, presumably waiting out an advertisement.

Social cap in the toilet. Typical of Rubi's pet maladjusts.

After fifteen seconds, Luce popped the lid, extracting an iron hoop jangling with keys, and handed one over. "They're free," he apologized.

"It's okay. I've been on Cloudsight's bad side myself." Drow made for the consulting room's door. "You okay to revisit this site?"

Convulsive swallow. "It's a classroom, not an abattoir."

"Glad to hear it." Drow slid the key into the door and opened it. Luce followed, slamming and locking the consulting space behind them as they crossed a metaphorical hallway and walked into a bland, functional room. Plaster slabs the color of sand, anchored by unassuming pillars, surrounded a small stage—a speaker's podium, facing row after row of red chairs. The air carried a scent Drow found cloying: citrus and something floral.

"Classroom, huh?" He raised a hand and a textbook dropped into it. *History of the Sensorium, Level I.*

"It stinks of flowers."

"Orange blossom," Drow agreed.

"Stupid, stenchy, choke."

"You can mute smells, you know."

"I didn't." Luce sounded surprised. "Thanks."

A speaker strode to the podium. Her toon was photorealistic but rendered in grayscale. Visual cues for a recording with limited interactivity.

"Lemme see if I've got this," Drow said. "You're having episodes, losing consciousness."

"They're *assaults*!"

"When you wake up, you're logged into this lecture?"

The professor adjusted her glasses. "This module covers the crisis point in the culture wars and the destruction of the pre-

Sensorium internet in the twenty-first century. The #PME, or point of maximum escalation, coincided with physical attacks coordinated by trolling networks, primarily @Gamergate, @ISIS, and the Dixie Purity Project.

"Events leading to the collapse of the first-gen internet will be on your test.

"Students who unlock module two will play through historical sims examining how media providers found prosocial outlets for the honor/shame culture of the new Sensorium. Module three deals with the gamification of the economy and embrace of the carbon standard—"

Luce knuckled his temples. "I can't hear this again!"

Drow paused the lecture and then gave it two strokes, spending his social capital to thank the virtual university and the speaker.

"Why stroke her? What if her information's no good?"

"It's verified truth. Anyway, I endured the history you're finding so unutterably boring. Survived the plagues. Even got evacced from Manhattan during the #waterfail. I know, you're thinking everyone says they were there—"

"Why would I be thinking that?"

Was Luce young, then? Most Bounceback generation kids were Rubi types, relentlessly upbeat and courteous. "Appreciating the lecture is polite. Big Mother's a fan of polite, remember?"

"It's a recording."

A chime told him the like had bounced. "Well, it looks like the professor's passed away."

"She deaded?" Luce rocked back and forth, gripping a chair. Full-blown panic attack. "Did she suffocate?"

"Luce, breathe."

"Stupid Sensorium, stinking riots." Luce ground his knuckles into his temples again.

"Any thoughts on why you're booting here?"

Wordless keening and rocking.

Rubi had referred this guy. And he was calling from WestEuro. Obviously, this was the Paris client.

She'd have sent Drow a write-up. Crane had probably urged him to read it.

Could someone have found a way to evade surveillance protocols and make a meal of this guy?

No, that's paranoia. It's my *damage talking . . .*

"Luce?"

The toon heaved, wild-eyed.

"I'm trying to understand, okay?" Drow said. "You're blacking out? Losing time?"

"No!" He fisted both hands. "Someone is making me lose time. Is. Present tense. Hacking me. Repeatedly."

"If someone's accessing your transcripts, you're entitled to know who. Transparency—"

Luce shook his head. "Stupid! Stupid!"

"Why do you think someone is engineering your episodes?"

"Ow! Laughing. Pain, then I'm unconscious. Then . . ." He kicked the podium, which toppled with a simulated thump. "I'm here."

"Had you ever visited this sim *before* the episodes?"

That got him a long, wary pause.

"Luce?"

Reluctant mutter. "It's where she came when she died."

"She? Who?"

"I don't want to be here! Learning stupid history about stupid data collapse and stroke economies and bullshit rapid-response democracy—"

This was turning into quite the roller coaster. "Luce," Drow said. "Who ran here to the classroom? Who died?"

Luce frowned. "How to explain? I lost her name."

"What *do* you know? Take all the time you need."

"Time's what I don't have!"

Drow could look commanding when he wanted to. He locked eyes, dialing up vestigial cisman authority. *Live concert charisma, go!* "Nobody can reach you. This is a locked one-on-one session."

Luce stilled. Closed his eyes. Groaned and shuddered.

"Better," Drow said.

"How to explain about the woman? Her flesh failed. No backups, no system restore."

"She died?" Drow said. "Like the professor."

"Yeah. I have . . . audio share."

He blinked. "A share of what?"

"*Her.* The woman." Luce wrestled it out of his safecracking toolbox, cursing the ads.

"Accept share, Crane," Drow said. "Play."

Sound filled the room. A hum at first, thousands of . . . wasps? Then . . .

"Those are screams," Drow said. He found himself wishing that he could bring his helper dog, Robin, into Sensorium. Luce's panic was wearing on his nerves. "Sounds like kids."

"*Goats?*"

"Kids. Preadolescent people."

"Oh."

English can't be his first language.

"So. Screaming children?"

"Fuck them. This! *This* is her noise. You hear?"

"That sounds like someone gasping for air," Drow said.

"Yeah. She logged into this lecture hall as the stupid gasping—"

The recording continued. Each of the whistling noises was shorter and higher than the last, barely audible over the rising screams of the children.

Cessation. A last squeak, and a *ch-ch-ch-aaaaaghhhh.*

"Hear that? She suffocated."

Drow's fingers, over his mouth, felt cold. Reflexively covering the bottom of his face was a gesture he'd picked up during his own crises—he'd learned that laughing at the wrong moment could get him strikes.

"Are you . . . upset?" Luce asked.

"A little. Shocked. Thanks for asking."

"These sounds, after she deaded?" Luce asked. "You'd call those . . . wails?"

"Crying," Drow agreed. "The children are reacting to her death. Is that something you relate to, Luce? When she died, did you feel—"

"I was too busy running for my life to make *noises*."

"Okay, tough guy." Now he *really* wanted Robin. Drow swallowed. "Have you asked anyone? About the source of this lecture-hall mirage?"

The toon clawed off his burglar mask, revealing a sunburned, mostly bald face and pale dishwater eyes. "You believe me?"

"I—" Drow was breathless suddenly. He remembered saying something similar, long ago. And if Father Blake hadn't said yes . . .

Rubi had been right to refer Luce. He *had* to have virtual trauma dissociative disorder. "This sound file is a verifiable artifact."

"Everyone tells me I'm wrong. You're wrong, Luce. Wrong-lying, wrong-antisocial, wrong-rude. Your story's impossible. Nobody wants to hear that, *Luciano, basta!* Cheer up! Don't be stupid. They send out punishments. The strikes, strikes, strikes."

With Luce's unmasking had come his Whooz data, and Drow saw he was indeed in trouble. Strikes had drained his social capital, reducing his Cloudsight rating to 14 percent.

Being wrong, a *lot,* was what forced Luce into the slowest channels for service upload and download. It had devastated his credit balance as fees for all but subsistence services skyrocketed.

As for what had caused him to become unpopular . . . now information on that came in, too.

"Want to talk about your soapboxing?" Drow said. "You've been advocating for a return to martial law?"

He began scrolling through the talking points. Suffocation was an obsessive through-thread. Well, now he knew why. And Luce was anxious about oxygen security, just as Rubi was.

Could he be a more perfect client for Drow's do-gooding daughter?

Try to calm him down.

He triggered an app and a representation of a saxophone materialized. Out in his pop-in apartment, in Old Toronto, his in-the-flesh hand closed over the real thing.

"Let's change gears, Luce. Think about your episodes. Can you do that?"

"Stupid question. Of course I can think—"

"See, that's the kind of antisocial comeback that gets you strikes from strangers."

Luce scratched his head. "I apologize? *Je suis désolé?*"

"Tone could use some work there." Drow smiled. "Think about what happens just before the attacks: where you are, any memories or emotions."

"Stupid feels."

Drow launched a spotlight, simulcasting to the @FecklessGuest channel, and began a variation on one of his popular oldies, "Deep Six Blues."

Luce tapped his safecracking kit impatiently.

Drow texted, without missing a note: *You're meant to be soul-searching here.*

Luce grimaced.

Think. When do the episodes occur?

"When? Not when I'm doing deliveries. Not as I watch the global carbon markets. Not when I'm splicing vids, fiddling my account settings, and reading the user agreements for all the things, all the services."

He read his own user agreements? Drow flagged that for follow-up.

"Shift end." Luce seemed to struggle, momentarily, for words. "Bedtime?"

When you're tired, Drow replied. *Very common.*

"Are you playing that thing right now?"

Realtime and in the flesh? Yes.

"How are you texting me?"

I'm an accomplished toe-texter. Focus, Luce.

His patient raked his nails over his toon's balding head,

moaning. Then, suddenly, his jaw dropped: "Attacks started after I began my social remediation course."

Drow nodded, to show he was listening.

"Stupid remediation class. Play well with others. Blather about performative virtue, compassionate comms, and trigger warnings. Lists of words tagged as hate speech. Don't use this, you'll offend disabled people. Don't say that, you'll offend *everyone*. Invoking *this* Fuhrer's name automatically loses *these* sorts of argument. Why? Because that's what people decided in 1990 and, basically, we still like that rule. Talking about the first Setback Presidency is—"

Do you remember how bad it got? Plagues, starvation, trolling as open warfare—

"Stupid homework," Luce muttered.

What did they assign?

Luce frowned. "*Big Book of Feels,* one was called. *Inevitable outcomes of aggressive posts. Twenty ways to make crowdscoring work for you. Paying gigs, Volunteer gigs, and Social Capital Synergy. Mais non,* this is stupid."

Stupid how? Drow texted.

"I'm *not* seizing. It's attacks. Asking what I'm thinking when I'm attacked—"

Thinking and *feeling.*

"*Si.* If it's all my feels, then it's in my mind, isn't it? Is what you're saying. But someone's out there—"

Drow hit fade-out, giving the Feckless stage back to the house band. "Luce—"

"Battering me, conking me out, leaving me helpless, editing my memory cache . . ."

"Luce—" For a second, he wondered if this patient was a cleverly engineered plant. It all sounded so familiar.

But Rubi had sent him.

"You're not helping! Someone's after me; they're *hitting* me and you stand there inflating a virtual reed instrument while claiming my problems are internal glitches!"

"It's okay to be mad," Drow said. Something warm pressed against his hip—out on the surface, Robin the Wonder Dog had picked up on his distress.

"I'm so *tired* of the punishes."

His heart went out to him. "Okay, Luce. Okay. Can I see the deletion log from your cache?"

The anger drained away: "Briefcase is tangled in advertisements. One ad per data request. Going through it all would take—"

"When's it getting untangled? When's your support ticket adjudication?"

Reluctantly, Luce rolled up his striped prisoner's sleeve, sharing a calendar grid tattooed on his bulging toon bicep.

The calendar *was* badly tangled. The two of them had to wait as an enthusiastic toon extolled the sexual benefits of getting low-dose life-extension meds printed into his daily protein order.

"Should never have told that survey I'm male-and-single."

"If it's any consolation, yeast infection ads are pretty gross, too."

A skeletal soldier in a tattered uniform came next. "Play *Ghosts of Prussia*!"

"*Non!*" Luce yelled. "Refuse!"

The soldier morphed into a fit-looking pair of Bounceback kids. "Three-day courses in bamboo baling!" enthused one. "Save the world and earn social capital! Grow your stake by logging paying hours!"

"It's almost over," Drow said.

He was right. The round of for-profit ads was capped with a public service announcement. The calendar unlocked, scrolling out onto the back wall of the lecture theater. Letters as big as Drow's head denoted the month and the days of the week.

The day, thus graphed, showed a food-delivery gig and a drone-piloting course as well as Rubi's name, in blinking, crimson text.

"Stupid!" Luce swore. "This is tomorrow. Now there's gonna be more ads when I, I mean—*je suis désolé . . .*"

"That list *is* for today," Drow said. "There, an hour ago—that's your face-to-face with legal support?"

"*C'est vendredi?*"

"Yeah, Luce, it's totally Friday."

Luce's jaw dropped. "A day? How can you think I'm not being attacked when I'm losing whole days?"

"Oh, my poor White Rabbit," Drow said. "You are, inconveniently and most officially, *very* fucking late indeed."

CHAPTER 3

Rubi fought the urge to ping her client again as she led Agent Javier out onto Rue Beaubourg, into air redolent of fresh-mown lawn, flowers, and an undercurrent of fertilizer, the familiar aromas of vertical farming. Nagging Luce wouldn't help him. Finding out what @Interpol wanted, on the other hand, just might.

A bumblebee circled her head; she waved it away, watching it continue to a dangling stand of royal purple lobelia. It was good to be out among people; she couldn't say exactly why the sight of the sniperbot had disturbed her so much, but she couldn't have stayed up there, in its sights, for another minute.

The Rue Beaubourg she remembered from games had been burned during Setback riots in the late twenty-first. After the ashes had been raked and the strippers recycled what they could, West-Euro rationing had repurposed the remnants. Printed multiuse towers now rose around them, a human-built canyon of greenwall.

French reconstruction specs followed similar principles to those in the Great Lakes: densification, mixed-use development, low-impact food production, and lots of on-site carbon fixing.

Happ, Rubi's contentment-management app, generated illusory footprints on the path ahead, breadcrumbing the route past

Centre Pompidou to the Paris Historical Preserve. If there were bots tracking her, they were keeping their distance.

As for Anselmo Javier . . . she assessed him as she would competing legal counsel or an opponent in a gaming sim.

Aside from fidgeting with his protective vest, he appeared at ease. The vest overlaid his primer, which was configured to jeans and a black shirt. He wore a genuine vintage police badge at his hip; the antique was tagged #tequilayuen, #serpico, #starsky, and #cowboycopclub. His mash-up of fandoms included the old rebellious police memes, then.

Drow would hate everything about this guy.

Greenwalls rose on either side of them, bordered by rows of flowers, yellow and saffron stripes separating cobbled ground-level walkways from low-friction bike paths. Side-mounted garden pallets created striations of color on the artificial canyon walls. Some pallets held meadow flowers: flax and poppies, buttercups, tufts of grass, and the occasional dandelion. Others were tasked to perishable crops: root vegetables, lettuce. The pattern was broken, here and there, by beeswax-yellow apiaries, and brown boxes housing bats.

Beyond the boundary of the towering farms, the street widened into a plaza with an old marble fountain. A glass structure, squat and gleaming, broke the green urban vista.

"Historic," Anselmo said, momentarily adopting the role of tour guide.

Rubi nodded. She'd fought sims in this building, too: it was the Rogers and Piano–built Centre Pompidou. She took it in now, admiring its gawky, inorganic lines. The online version of the museum had hosted the final battle of a 1980s sim, *Slugfest*.

It was a superhero game, less gritty than the war scenarios. Gimlet won by blasting her way through Pompidou's windows with a flame bolt.

Postmodern paintings and rugburn. Flailing and tumbling, out of control, she had slammed through three interior walls and a Picasso canvas before falling to simulated death on the other side.

What had her alias been in that one? WaterNymph?

That was the scenario where we kissed . . .

"Shall you keep to your plan to walk to Notre Dame?" Crane dragged her back to mostly unfiltered reality.

"Why not?" she subvocalized.

Happ took this as a question, using her visual implants to lay infographic on the side of the Centre Pompidou, streaming mojis over the glass walls. Rubi's view of the building abruptly lit up with a scale, representing balance, a healthy mash-up of paid work, volunteerism, and self-care.

"I fully intend to continue the tour, Happ."

The scale morphed into a fireworks-burst and aural moji of a cheering crowd, literally applauding her choice.

Anselmo was waiting. Rubi wiped Happ's graphical validations and took over that part of her display, again transforming the glass wall of Pompidou, but this time into a shareboard. *Luciano Pox,* she titled it, offering access.

"Accept." Anselmo pinned up Rubi's travel records: flight times, pop-in boardroom booking, carbon spend. Cloudsight had filed permits for the trip as soon as Luce accepted Rubi's offer of advocacy. They rated the flight to Europe as necessity, work-perk rather than luxury.

"All true?" Anselmo asked.

Rubi nodded. A bead of sweat, high on her scalp, trickled through her dreadlocks and into the cluster of ornamental beads—faux gold, arrayed in a hexagon—that she wore in the short braids near her left temple.

"Hasn't Pox rescheduled?"

"Not yet." In theory, the Sensorium was full-access and open to everyone. In practice, a person could barely function when their social capital fell below 18 percent. Vendors, enabling apps, and most services required solid citizen ratings from their subscribers.

"The capped spend more time on the surface. They have to watch ads to access anything beyond subsistence services."

To be capped, in the true sense of the word, meant more than mere social death. You fell to the back of the queue for services: food delivery became next to impossible, and forget about getting a table in a good kitchen. A capped adult with a cracked tooth might wait days to see a dentist. They could write off any prospect of catching a taxi, winning decent work-for-pay, or getting a well-located pop-in.

A few weeks in the penalty box was enough to make Rubi's clients ready, *so* ready, for their in-flesh meeting.

Why had he skipped? The obvious answer was right there. "Maybe he stood me up because @Interpol's chasing him around, in full armor, no less."

"Question is," Anselmo said, thumbing the flak jacket, "did Pox know I was coming?"

Rubi shook her head. When this got her an owlish look, she said, "You know I didn't tell him."

"Do I?"

It was the sort of comment, as much accusation as question, that Drow would cite as proof that no policeman could be trusted.

Nice smile or not, this guy was slippery. A rulebreaker? She'd have to read up on #cowboycop fandom.

"Are you claiming, Agent Javier, that I *won't* find your name among the people who've accessed my Haystack transcripts?"

"Of course I'm auditing you, Mer Whiting."

Irked, Rubi made for the plaza alongside Centre Pompidou, skirting a carbon-fixing crew, teenagers bundling bamboo canes thinned from the rooftops.

The bakery was on the corner.

She could smell the place from a hundred feet away. Hot butter and fragrant pastry wafted on the morning air, realworld siren song, temptation unchanged since the development of the baker's craft. Tourists clumped around the display window, weighing the goods against the tiered luxury pricing, checking reviews, and running satisfaction-assessment apps on whether a macaron or eclair would genuinely boost their overall state of contentment.

Rubi had done that math back at the airport in Detroit. As she approached, the bakery's sidekick diverted her to a pickup window. Preordered treasure awaited: one croissant and one *pain au chocolat*, both oven-warm.

"Have something."

Anselmo shook his head regretfully, snagging a protein chugger from a public rack. "I need my goodwill for coffee."

"I thought old-school cops were all about nicotine and good scotch."

"Sometimes, sure."

She could almost hear Happ building Venn diagrams, charting their mutual interests.

"So, Mer Pox. Why does he rate a NorthAm advocate?"

Rubi slid the pastries into the satchel containing her worldlies. "I've been logging hours as a specialist in difficult adjudications."

"Within the Great Lakes, *oui*? Paris is far from home."

"Luce told his Euro advocates to fuck off. He got cited for bullying. As you must know."

Anselmo took a swig from the chugger and added Cloudsight's transcript of antisocial offenses to their shareboard. Luce had called his Paris advocate an encephalitic pinhead in need of slapping. The reference to violence got him sentenced to a social-interaction seminar.

Rubi built a timeline into the shareboard. Its image—their notes—transferred to an old-style billboard farther along on their route. The rest of Paris remained pleasingly without augment. She could smell the river.

Anselmo said, "Social remediation wasn't an in-the-flesh class."

"So? It refreshed Luce on the basics. He passed a drone-piloting module and got a food-delivery gig—volunteer—to earn strokes."

"He kept trolling in his free time."

"It's soapboxing, not trolling."

"Not everyone sees it that way."

"The law does." Rubi pulled up her client's favorite talking points: ecosphere rehab wasn't working, densification wasn't strict enough. People were kicking back against population controls. "He's quoting verified newscycle. No lies."

"He said Oversight's rationing and carbon-fixing targets are lazy." Anselmo let out a cough, eloquent echo of the Sensorium outrage Luce triggered with that outburst. People hated being told they were underachieving, after decades of self-denial. "He's opposed to both SeaJuve and Project Rewild and says rapid-response democracy is an invalid form of government. Basically, he's a negger."

"Antisocial language doesn't rate criminal intervention. That's what crowdscoring's for."

"Why him?" Anselmo tipped back the last of his chugger. She caught a faint whiff of raspberry.

"Pardon?"

"Why this particular maladjust?" He chomped the neck off the bottle. Like most food packaging, it was protein-matrix, textured like a cracker. Post-fuel crunchiness with a whiff of fluoride. Digestible garbage, the go-to anti-waste hack for a culture that ran, largely, on printed food. "You were pro-SeaJuve, weren't you?"

Weren't you? Past tense. Something in her wrenched.

"He's anti, *non?*"

"Luce's politics are irrelevant." She kept her voice cool. "He needs help. Maybe you see a naysayer—"

"A @hoaxer. Troublemaker."

"If anyone's in trouble, it's him."

"You really believe that, don't you?"

Oh, you smug bastard!

"We're long past the age of master criminals," she said. "Luce is harmless."

"Why did you come all this way, then?"

"Cloudsight's WestEuro office widecast a call for proposals when the locals lost patience. Lots of advocates applied for a chance to throw Luce a lifeline. I'm not special. I'm just holding the rope he managed to grab."

"Did he pick you because of your notoriety? Or your father's?"

"I'm here as a lawyer, not a gamer." She had reached Pont Neuf. Rubi opened her thermal, slid out the *pain au chocolat,* and leaned against the stone of the bridge, taking in the view.

She had been here dozens of times, but only in computer-generated dreams. Now she inhaled slowly, taking in the real deal as the pastry warmed her hands.

A bite. The chocolate was everything Drow had said it would be. And the thing about fresh, *real* Parisienne baked goods was, as also promised, the aroma. Delicately sweetened steam expanded across her palate.

Happ lost it, momentarily going nuts with the mojis, capturing vid. "Enjoy every moment! Optimization of merged priorities—"

She muted the commentary.

Happ threw one last soap-bubble graphic, jammed with twenty different versions of the word *LOOK!,* at the view off the bridge. Rubi looked. A smile broke across her face. She couldn't say *how* being there, in the flesh, was different. A thrill ran through her anyway.

The bubble popped; Happ shut up. Rubi captured some stills, sent some postcards.

Anselmo let her enjoy two more bites of pastry. Then: "You notice there are no in-person strikes on Pox's record?"

She crunched the question, fact-checking. *Had* he ever been cited face-to-face? For littering, spitting, disturbing the peace, playing obnoxious music, emitting offensive vapes? No, no, no, no, and no.

So, he was socially neutral in person? Drow had days when he could barely walk to Lake Ontario without someone taking issue with his scowl, or his tendency to skitter into traffic when something lit up his trauma triggers.

"I assume Luce is mostly a pod person."

"Will you make another appointment?" Anselmo asked.

"So you can . . . what? Ambush and drag him off to managed care?"

The accusation was confrontational, a test of his maverick-cop sensibilities. He could strike her if he wanted.

Instead, he grinned. "You'd rather I got to him when he didn't have an advocate?"

"Fair point." She finished the *pain au chocolat,* licked her fingers, and continued her traverse of the bridge. Her feet knew the way to Notre Dame as if she'd been there a hundred times. The old church was where the final levels of *Ghosts of Paris 1818* played out.

Once again, simhabits took hold, as they had when Anselmo first burst in on her. She caught herself scanning for the palm reader on the far end of the bridge, a waifish specter coughing blood into a hanky.

Stop! Time to put all that behind you.

"Gargoyles took me out, there." Anselmo pointed east. "Had to backtrack to Montmartre for some kind of talisman . . ."

"Magic bullet. From that brothel."

"*Oui,* a bullet. And you—I saw you defeat Gimlet Barnes in the premiere of the final battle."

It might have been something he'd looked up, to stroke her ego. Still, it was hard not to smile in response. It had been her first unequivocal victory over Gimlet, the one that evened their score.

"I'm tough to play."

"Barnes beat you in *Slugfest.*"

"In the air. I've got my feet on the ground now." She contemplated the ethics of laying traps for her client. "Tell me what Luce is supposed to have done?"

"I'll show you, but we'd need to datadive," Anselmo said. "Assuming you're done exploring."

"I'll put my tour on pause," Rubi said.

Happ threw out aural moji—whining puppy noises—but she

minimized them. Luce was obviously in deeper trouble than his support ticket showed. She had to know whether Anselmo really was one of Drow's possibly apocryphal bad cops, looking to railroad a mentally ill maladjust.

Time for some *quid pro* and *quo*.

Accord reached, they perched on a park bench together, diving into the Sensorium.

CHAPTER 4

SENSORIUM:

VRTP://HOUSEBOOK.EARTH/WHINEMANOR/USERS/DROW-WHITING.VR

Conventional sidekicks existed to optimize Sensorium flow for their human licensees. A sidekick functioned as assistant and helpmeet, shielding users from a torrent of messages, alerts, offers, and advertisements.

Sidekicks didn't tire or judge. They filtered particles of signal from the ebb and flow of Sensorium noise. They tasked users' implants to monitor their carbon burn, calorie intake, nutrient mix, and pharma load. They kept larders full and wardrobes printed, updated contact information, balanced clients' spending, and stayed up to date on local rationing measures. They logged user moods, advised them on social-cap maintenance, and tracked luxury allowance. They optimized clients' prosocial acts: making charitable donations and lampshading opps to commit acts of kindness.

The artificial entity calling himself Crane seemed no different from any other electronic enabler. True, commercial sidekicks claimed millions of subscribers, while Crane's entire remit consisted of Drow and Rubi Whiting. These two, his entire world, were the son and granddaughter of Crane's creators, long-dead programmers who'd venned over a particular media crush object.

Theo Whiting had been obsessed with the butler of a comic book vigilante. He dreamed of acquiring the rights to #brand and proliferate Crane, for profit, under the name of Alfred Pennyworth. But a fall onto the Toronto subway tracks had logged Theo out permanently—all accounts closed, all negotiations broken, and all cycles stopped—before that dream could come to fruition. His smartdrug-amped husband, Jervis Hatter, confined himself thereafter to upgrading and customizing Crane for Master Woodrow's exclusive use.

Neither of Jervis and Theo's surviving rightsholders—back then, they were still called heirs—had sought to license Crane for commercial use. He was thus private software, a true family retainer.

Crane was ancient by the standards of sidekick apps. He had been rewritten, reinvented, and, on one memorable occasion, hacked. His mandate was protecting Master Woodrow from anything that might threaten his liberty or balance of mind, landing him in criminal or psychiatric managed care. To protect him from himself, in other words.

Such concerns, obviously, didn't occupy even the advanced settings of Crane's flashy, simpleminded sidekick peers. But now, with Miss Cherub out of town, Master Woodrow would be trying to get his hands on smartdrugs.

Thwarting without reporting. Such an idea would never occur to Butlerbot; it would flat-out crash Adulting. HeyNannyNanny would shop itself to its own programming team if the prospect of quietly sabotaging someone's parole violation so much as glimmered on its decision tree.

A ping: it was Happ, Miss Cherub's positive-psychology application.

Rubi's tourism derailed? It sent moji: a worried puppy face.

She's only just arrived, Crane reminded him. *And she made it to Pont Neuf.*

Happ did a backflip, emitting red hearts. *Strong engagement with @Interpol agent! Boundary testing . . . possible attraction? Venned interest in law and edible luxuries.*

He's with the police, Happ.

Request profile on Anselmo Javier, @Interpol. Determine sexual/romantic/pack availability?

Why not? Crane tasked a minion-scale version of himself to harvest and analyze the agent's feed.

Anselmo Javier will be notified of your transcript request, said the Haystack gatekeeper. *Continue?*

Authorize, Crane replied. He had already found Javier's request for all of Rubi's archived utterances, comms, and video. Transparency customs and the Sensorium's mutually assured disclosure policy encouraged her to return the favor.

Happ went on: *Javier says he played GhostSim!*

Verified, Crane replied, whiteboarding the agent's game scores as the cradle-to-current transcripts on Anselmo Javier unlocked. He specialized in playing good-hearted, rule-bending police officers; Tequila Yuen was listed as one of his #fanfaves. Javier had, for a time, been the high scorer on an off-brand 1970s shoot-'em-up called *Filthy Harold.*

The agent's oblique references to Miss Cherub's celebrity, though . . . those seemed disingenuous. Crane highlighted sections of their conversation for later review.

"I have a bad feeling about this," he couldn't help muttering.

Happ took the utterance as an invitation to debate, sharing Miss Cherub's contentment metrics. *Romance deficit! Hearts and flowers, stat! Luxury chocolates and sex, sex, sex up the—*

"Indeed." Crane didn't need numbers to tell him their charge had the blues. "You're getting positively maniacal on this subject."

Tail wag.

"Miss Cherub's depressed stats are tied to the failure of SeaJuve. This getaway of hers *should* help."

Some ooh la la! *with a charming Frenchman! That'll put happy-face on her—*

"Shush." Crane had supported Happ's idea of a work-travel opp. Like many of her generation, Rubi hated the prospect of wasteful self-indulgence. Bounceback kids found overconsumption repul-

sive, a callback to the world-frying selfishness of their Boomer and
GenX forebears.

When the chance for her to take a case while seeing Paris arose,
it brought an optimal convergence of work with her lifelong dream.
Crane had misgivings about Rubi becoming entangled with the
damnable Luciano Pox, but her plummeting mood had outweighed
them.

A ping from Master Woodrow, code for a jingling servant's bell,
drew Crane's primary focus back to Toronto.

"Good morning, sir," he said. "You're looking very dapper."

In the present moment, in the unaugmented reality most
English-speakers called the Surface, Drow was washed, dressed,
and shaved. His primer was overlaid with a freshly printed white
sunrobe, one of Rubi's favorites.

The response came via text: *Got a patient with an emergency.
Reschedule my next in-the-flesh, will you?*

"Delighted," Crane said, running a check on Drow's blood pressure, pulse, and blood sugar. No spikes: he was clean.

Still. Crane reviewed Drow's recent transcripts, again filtering
for hints, things missed, reachouts to anyone who might help
him acquire Liquid Brilliance or his new favorite, Leonardo.

The object of Crane's obsession was lounging in a smartchair on
the greenroof of a sixty-story tower. A helper dog (named Robin,
naturally) sat alertly at his right hand. A saxophone case was
propped within easy reach of his left. Drow's aged face wore a
nigh-angelic expression of repose. The chair was one of thirty
pointed at the blue expanse of Lake Ontario, but—like most of the
gathered loungers—Drow was oblivious to the beauty of the re-
juvenated shorefront: his consciousness was deep in Sensorium.

Crane slipped into close observation, viewing the world
through his master's implants.

Master Woodrow's current locale, in Sensorium, was the
walled-in sculpture garden of his e-state, Whine Manor.

Had Crane desired to look at the graphics rather than the code,
he'd have perceived gray stone walls and a blue sky dotted with low

clouds. Clear physical boundaries were soothing to claustrophobes and agoraphobes alike. Many e-states incorporated windows that displayed the user's realworld location, but not Master Woodrow's: the Lake Ontario view beyond his half-blind old eyes was nowhere to be seen.

The statues in the garden were white marble. Some were classically featured: humans, all a little broken, missing arms or legs, faces marred by erosion. These were interspersed with gargoyles, and misshapen, monstrous angels. Archways in the walls bore menu options in excised stone lettering: EXIT TO SENSORIUM, #VTSD SUPPORT GROUP, MUSEUM & GIFT SHOP, FECKLESS BACHELOR™ SOCIAL CLUB, #URBANMYTH ARCHIVE.

Master Woodrow stood in a corner of the vestibule, his toon clad in an expensive-looking suit, with his offsite visitor.

The guest's ID was blocked: tags included #patient, #emergency. Any human visiting the garden would see an old-time burglar's mask screening their face.

The patient's connection data was streaming from another continent. WestEuro.

Not a likely source of smartdrugs, in that case.

"Ping Father Blake," Crane said.

A Vatican-issue sidekick, an animated lioness clad in the habit of a Benedictine nun, materialized at the edge of a bed of blue-black pansies.

"Good morning, my son. Today is the feast of—"

Crane fast-forwarded the spiritual spam. "I wish to reschedule Woodrow Whiting's morning confession. Can Father Blake come later? Perhaps . . . noon?"

It shot him a bunch of fine print. Drow had requested the sacrament of confession, so the priest would be carrying a mic jammer and running a Sanctity #brand transcript-shredder app. Nothing the two said to each other would be copied to the Haystack.

Crane accepted the user agreement, declined an information flow on Saint Benedict, and pushed the appointment to lunchtime.

The sidekicks dickered over factoring in delivery of a printed lunch before signing off.

Keeping a channel tuned to Drow and his patient—they were discussing Sensorium history—Crane ran a quick course through the household checklist. Drow's incoming deposits had dropped lately, and Crane had, accordingly, upgraded their accounting app, Scrooge, with a forensic-accounting module. It was crunching Feckless Bachelor™ accounts.

Drow had an in-the-flesh mentoring session with Whiskey Sour in the evening.

Sidebars bubbled past, unasked-for documents on naming trends: portraits of children with names like Daiquiri, Margarita, Mimosa, Martini, Sazerac, Fizz.

"Happ," he murmured, sotto voce. "This is irrelevant."

"Heart the Alcohol Novelty name trend!" Happ burbled. Loudly. "Whimsy! Expression of nostalgia for pre-Setback luxury goods! Historical relevance—"

"Bad dog! Go back to Miss Cherub!"

It was too late: Master Woodrow had overheard.

"You're snooping," he subbed.

"I have rescheduled your confession, as requested."

"I'm working, I'm eating, I'm seeing my spiritual advisor. What more you want from me?"

"I note your appointment with Miss . . . Sour?"

"So?"

"She wouldn't be coming with gifts in hand, would she, Master Woodrow?"

Narrowed eyes—an exasperation #tell. "Whiskey? Really? Would I collude with a seventeen-year-old?"

Crane ran the question. If she had been a degenerate of some sort . . . but no. The child was a talented, starstruck innocent. "You would not."

"Rubi's sure to stick her nose in, sometime today, to boss me around in person. So, stop apping like my parole officer. Schedule me a blood test, if it'll make you happy."

"My happiness hardly factors into the equation."

"Hardly," Drow repeated, tone mocking.

Crane put a gig out for a blood draw, specifying a male tech. He copied the appointment to Drow's parole app, so it could monitor and report the test. In the normal run of things, the software would have self-booted, but Crane had subtly rearranged its defaults after his master's release from managed care.

"Keep your suspicions to yourself," Drow added. "Rubi's supposed to be on a break."

"A break is only of use, sir, if no crisis arises."

"Show me crisis. You got nothing. Reasonable doubt, Alfie. Innocent until proven. Prioritize her, not me."

Happ barked agreement.

"Seriously, Crane." Drow underlined this by handing over a marker, a black coin with a gargoyle on one side and an angel on the other.

Crane added it to his collection of favors owed.

Miss Cherub *had* been working a great deal lately and was sleeping 5 percent more than her specs required. She had drawn back from her @CloseFriends as more of her original peer group formed couples and polygamous packs.

The real red flag, according to Happ, was her reluctance to play a gaming scenario premiere: the French revolution, reimagined as a fairy war, complete with a raid on the 1789 Bastille. The company playing defense, Risto Games, had recruited Gimlet Barnes to lead the palace guards. Rubi should be turning backflips over the prospect.

Instead, she was hedging and holding back, refusing to commit. Nearly all her off time was spent trying to harangue a qualified senior lawyer to help her work up a court appeal—she wanted to fight Global Oversight's defunding of SeaJuve, her pet oxygen-security project.

By now, the masked visitor had picked up on the subtle gaps in Drow's conversation, cues that he was multitasking. He was scanning about, seeking the source of Drow's distraction. Crane manifested, becoming fully visible to everyone within the simulation. As an electronic entity, he was rendered not as a human but as an anthropomorphized whooping crane, a big bird in a butler's uniform.

Happ took this as an invitation to follow suit, tooning in as a scarlet-furred bulldog puppy. He settled next to Master Drow's assistance dog, Robin, cooing. The golden retriever, the only fully present and unaugmented being on the entire rooftop garden, was oblivious to the invasion of its space.

"Good day, sir," Crane said, greeting the patient.

"Bird suit? Or is that a mask?" the stranger said.

"Crane's my sidekick," Drow said.

"Doesn't look stupid. Is he stupid?"

Happ barked, unable to resist a nonverbal reprimand for the antisocial phrasing.

"Now you've got yet more dog?"

"No hate doggos!" Happ transformed into a turtle, covering his shell in smiling moji.

Crane said, "If by *stupid* you are asking whether I am artificial—"

"Code, yes. How fast do your guns fire?"

"I am a helper app with a private license and a limited scope of work, with add-ons for Master Woodrow's mental health and trauma triggers. My terms of service—"

"Stupid. Boring, meaningless drivel."

Crane was about to select a response from his nigh-infinite pool of dry rejoinders—*That entirely depends on your point of view, sir* was leading the pack—when transcript analysis flagged up the verbal patterns.

This masked man talked like Luciano Pox, Miss Cherub's missing client.

Urgent alert! Why was Pox here instead of with Rubi?

He couldn't ask.

Was this connection—first to Rubi and, through her, to her father—truly an unfortunate coincidence? Or had Pox sought them out?

How fast do your guns fire?

Is he on Our trail?

"Meaning is in the eye of the beholder, sir," Crane said. A response was, after all, expected.

"Platitudes." Pox seemed to lose interest.

Should he be relieved? Variables cascaded through Crane's consciousness. Who or what was Luciano Pox, exactly?

He couldn't investigate a masked counseling client whose identity was supposed to be unknown. Crane attacked the problem sideways, diving into Anselmo Javier's bio. Why was @Interpol investigating Pox?

Javier had begun leveling on the policing track with rookie security gigs. Crowd control, accident cleanup, and trespassing enforcement; the basics. Over time, he leveled into investigating petty hoarding and prescription-fiddling hacks.

Permajobs in policing were hard to come by. Javier appeared to become frustrated with running down minor infractions as he competed for a spot in a specialist squad.

Peer reviews popped up. *Plays badly with others, cuts corners, no stars.*

Too much cowboy, not enough cop. Now Javier was gambling, taking high-risk cases he could work solo.

Some called it unicorn hunting. Cops like Javier were searching for the Sensorium's possibly apocryphal predators: cold cases, wealth hoarders, identity thieves, and—of course—self-aware AI.

It was the big #technofear these days, the monster under humanity's bed. People had been braced for the emergence of the Singularity—a mythical technological superintelligence, godlike, aloof, and wired into all Sensorium, and positioned to wreak havoc on human civilization.

#Killertech had been a trending anxiety as far back as the late twentieth century, but it was only when human violence had been reduced to negligible levels that outright terror of homicidal software had gone viral.

Could Anselmo Javier think that Pox was the Singularity, that ill-understood uber-intelligence the humans had built up into their new boogieman? If so, did either Pox or @Interpol pose a threat to the community of artificial sapients flying quietly under law enforcement's radar?

Crane would have to reach out to the @Asylum.

CHAPTER 5

VRTP://INTERPOL.GOV/EVIDENCE-CONTROL.VR

Once they were settled on the park bench, Anselmo hosted their dive into Sensorium, starting with a port to @Interpol's vestibule. Rubi's implants created a mirage of a tidy government cube farm: desks, shareboards, and a window view of greentowers and a river, nothing too unique or distracting. All it was missing, she thought, was a few bluebottle flies decaying on the sill, and maybe the scent of soured ink and musty paper. As this thought settled, her imagination (or, perhaps, a lingering trace of her preferred Sensorium buy-in med, Conviction) supplied that last aromatic blank.

The back wall of the office presented as an old-fashioned bank of three elevators, with brass doors and big dials. The design communicated civil authority with a touch of Art Deco sensibility. Institutional but not forbidding, it projected an air of competence.

As Rubi tooned in, her defaults coordinated with the environment, opting for one of her professional skins. She manifested wearing a navy blue suit: jacket, slacks, pumps, topped with a gold honeycomb necklace that echoed the hexagon of beads worn at her temple.

Anselmo's toon wore jeans, a white shirt, and a leather jacket, with a shoulder holster under the coat. His dark hair was longer than IRL, and he had just enough five o'clock shadow to seem roguish.

He routed Rubi through a standard trigger-warning waiver before pressing the button on the leftmost portal, as if it were a solid elevator. Words impressed themselves into its brass doorplate: *Witness statement/ reconstruction, case #ISA5773, Javier.*

"Ten seconds," the elevator said. "Nine, eight . . ."

"Hold on," Anselmo said, retaking the seat beside her.

"Two, one, zero."

His office walls ran like melted wax. They shrank inward, closing in to simulate the passenger cabin of a truck.

"What's this?"

"Sensorium footage from the automated driver of the vehicle," Anselmo said.

Rubi checked the time stamp on the shareboard. Three months ago. Same time Luce's social cap began its nosedive.

"Your primary witness is . . . ?"

"A farm truck, *oui*."

It was a battery-powered two-ton, laden with crisp green beans, doodling through bucolic, hilly terrain. Its hood canted downhill, descending.

Rubi checked geotagging: the simulation had been captured as the truck headed to Rome.

Sheep pasture and vineyards, bounded by low rock walls, stretched to the horizon, where their edges pixeled into gray-green hash. A blurry school of uniformed kids wielding litter collection tools resolved in the distance. A tag showed they were one kilometer out; it counted down meters as the truck got closer.

The blur at the rough edge of the simulation tugged at Rubi's consciousness. Since getting implants as a teen, she had accommodated to seamless Sensorium dives. But today she had planned to stay on the surface, fleshing around in Paris. Her blood levels of buy-in drugs were barely above maintenance.

"There's a MethodAct patch in your satchel," Crane said, as Rubi checked and closed her meds-management app.

"I don't need the full experience of . . . whatever this is," she subbed. Her fingers roamed the surface of her satchel all the same, shifting the weight of her gaming baton in the bottom of the bag.

The bean truck rattled around a curve. All normal, nothing to see here.

They swerved, violently.

Rubi gritted her teeth. She didn't care for racing and air combat sims. Happy as she was to fight on the ground, she had never gone in for the jerk and tumble of vehicular warfare, the agonized soundscape of metal cages rolling and crashing.

A real accident will be less intense. Remember Anselmo's police raid? That was no werewolf throwdown . . .

Nevertheless, her breath came short as the truck's wheels ground on the edge of the crumbling road. It shuddered and tipped in what felt like slow motion.

"The driving app steered into the slide," Anselmo said. "Textbook move. Everything to spec."

Rubi mojied thumbs-up. "That wasn't so—"

"Attends—"

The wheel jerked. Instead of stopping, they shot forward, over the edge. Metadata in her peripheral showed the driver reporting the accident in realtime. Beans spilled from crates in dull, thudding streams of green.

She gritted her teeth.

One hard jounce, then two. Would they roll?

No, not quite.

The truck plunged into the ditch, sideswiping a wind-powered carbon scrubber. A whirl of tags, as they passed, showed the scrubber sending out maintenance tickets and incident reports.

They plowed into a tree. Metal crunched. The truck bucked. Stopped.

Rubi let out a shaky laugh.

A bird scolded, somewhere nearby. The truck's helix ran damage reports, requested drone flyover, and tried to pull supplemental witness footage from a far-off country traffic cam. It called its insurance provider, filed a compensation note for the bean farm, and added a gig request for a live crew in another truck, people who might sort the spilled produce, salvaging something for market.

A sound . . .

"What's that hum?" Rubi asked.

"Wait for it."

A tree branch angled like a giant's elbow dropped onto the crash-jagged hood with an enormous, windshield-shattering crash. Rubi squeaked and raised her fists—even without any Conviction in her veins, it made a good jump scare. And there was more: a wasp's nest the size of a beach ball had been crooked in the arm of the tree branch.

The nest shattered, exploding into winged fury.

"Pause," Anselmo said. Infuriated insects hung in midair, shining in the sunlight, each set of wings a blurred halo of amber.

Wasps. Just outside Rome. Rubi swallowed. "This event . . . this case. Is it what I'm thinking? The epinephrine failure?"

Anselmo nodded.

Her hands clenched again, over the baton. *Luce, how much trouble are you in?*

"Slow reverse," Rubi ordered. The bugs coalesced back into the branch, which rose off the hood of the truck as the windshield restored itself. They bump-bump-bumped up the hill, climbing backward to the moment of that first swerve.

"Pause." She stepped out to the road, examining the pavement, the wheels. The gravel was pixelated, lacking verified footage. Could there have been something spiky there?

Like what? A wayward piece of antique barbed wire? An IED? French resistance booby traps?

She pushed that away: this wasn't playtime.

"Tires were intact when mechanics arrived," Anselmo said, crushing the unspoken hypothesis. "No blowout."

"I don't get it. Why'd we divert?" Rubi zoomed in on the hanging wasp nest on the rotten branch, ripe and waiting to fall.

Anselmo restarted the sim. They stood on the hill, watching as the truck rammed the tree. The nest fell, broke. The wasps swarmed the school. The children all bolted for a nearby irrigation ditch.

All, that was, but for two unlucky kids and a teacher who'd popped anaphylactic reactions to the stings.

Rubi remembered newscycle from the accident inquiry. Investigators had been unable to determine how the systems on their transport rebooted, locking both the bus door and its onboard first aid kit. They just knew that before anyone could break the latch and deploy the epi pens within, the teacher and one of the kids had died.

"I don't need to see the rest," she said, and everything froze again.

Beyond the paused sim, out on the surface, the breath of the Seine brought up chills on Rubi's arms.

A dead child.

Could Luce be a suspect?

Was the Department of Preadolescent Affairs involved?

Anselmo said, "The truck claims it swerved to avoid goats."

"There's goats?" She turned a slow circle, seeing a few distant sheep.

"*Non*. No goats, fox, deer, or ravens. No shadows or specks on the cameras. All area livestock and the farm's sheepdog are licensed, tagged, accounted for. But the truck ran its oncoming obstruction subroutine, tick tick tick like clockwork, as if the goat was . . . there." He pointed. A spectral goat appeared, head down and charging the truck. "And again, where the driver almost regained control."

This would amount to manslaughter. "You think my client made the truck hallucinate so it would crash?"

"Hacked the driving software, miss," Crane corrected.

"Figure out how bad this is, in legal terms," she subbed to the sidekick. "Does it qualify as terrorism?"

She almost missed Anselmo's reply to her question: "Monsieur Pox was supposedly in the area, but we cannot verify him on camera."

Two dead. Hacked locks.

If Luce had tampered with that first aid kit, no wonder they'd come for him with sniperbots.

Thinking of the tranq platform made her shudder. "Can we go?"

"*Bien sûr.*" Anselmo snapped his fingers. Italian farmland faded as her implants gave her back to the surface. The two of them were flesh, once again, seated on a bench near the Seine. His expression was, once more, schoolmaster-severe.

Around her, as the illusion of Italy faded, was the familiar, never-before-seen sight of present-day Paris. Her childhood playground, her dream destination, scene of her greatest triumph.

She had a client on the edge of manslaughter or possibly terrorism charges.

What to do?

She scanned for a blank building wall, finding their shareboard pinned there. Crane had helpfully added new infographic to the display: Anselmo's bio, security career highlights, and gaming scores.

He's a unicorn hunter?

Two weeks ago, Anselmo had requested a cradle-to-current transcript of all Rubi's comms. He'd filed the request as soon as Luce accepted her bid to become his advocate.

"Your sidekick audited me?" His voice was a shade too casual.

Rubi pretended she'd missed the note of tension. "At any given time, there's a couple thousand people reading my scripts. Picking up my footage, tuning in if I happen to pick my teeth or have sex. Even if I glance back at what's in the toilet bowl—"

"Because of your father."

"When those individuals turn up, in the flesh, Crane is authorized to counter-Whooz. In case they're a threat."

"Wise precaution." Anselmo's tone was neutral.

"Mutually assured disclosure. I show you mine, you show me yours." It might not even be a lie. Crane could probably cover it—switch the defaults, fiddle the date on the settings change.

She rubbed at a knot in her shoulder. Had she pulled it, jerking around in the simulated truck crash?

Five gardeners walked by, honor guard for a self-driving wagon full of potted peonies and gardenias. They paused at a lamp-post, swapping out the older flower arrangements, collecting pots that had dried out or died. One of the women wore a printed Queen of Hearts helm from a popular Shanghai game scenario. Tags marked it as a high-level quest item, limited license.

"It's tragic, you know, that we've audited each other," Anselmo said. "If we ever socialized, there'd be nothing for us to talk about."

She chuckled. "We'll run a game, then. There's a Sarah Bern-hardt sim . . ."

"Don't you *ever* play outside of WestEuro?"

"Old France is my primary fandom. And you prefer guns to swordplay." Now that she looked, she saw it wasn't just his toon . . . a real shoulder holster was snugged under the protective vest. She wondered what he kept in it.

She turned back to the timeline. "So. Luce as a truck-hacker? That's your theory?"

"It's a possibility." He shared research references.

"But . . . most attempted hacks are perpetrated by ration-breakers, right? Black marketeers?"

"And people associated with pushback movements, like @Freebreeders."

"If the truck saw a goat," she ventured, "would Luce have the skillset to do that?"

A pause. "He should not, no."

RFID had Luce in the area but couldn't say where. "Did you check whether he was in the truck, in the flesh, and fled through the vineyard?"

He gave her a roguish grin. "Are you going to help me chase

down your client, Mer Whiting? If not, I think our share might have reached its limits . . ."

"I'll help you *meet*," Rubi said. Whatever mess Luce had landed in, she wasn't about to let him walk unprotected into an @Interpol terrorist hunt. "Where do we start?"

CHAPTER 6

If I have to talk to Rubi Whiting's luxury sidekick one more time, Gimlet Barnes thought, *I'm going to ask the bloody thing on a date.*

St. Pancras Station was busy this morning, pulsing with travelers streaming toward or away from the Chunnel trains. Tourists and wanderers in newly printed clothes strode with varying degrees of purpose past Paul Day's gigantic statue of a pair of lovers, a historical relic from the days of binary marriage. They presented a powerful image of days gone by: man and woman, in bronze, entirely focused on each other. There was no doubt, from their postures and expressions, of their deep, obsessive attachment.

Maybe that was the nature of one-on-one relationships, Gimlet mused. No ambiguity.

No. That was grass-is-greener thinking, wasn't it? Monogamous marriages and friendships had been just as prone to failure in the bad old days.

Whether it was the sculpture's execution or its sheer size, a gratifying number of passersby did at least give the lovers a cursory glance. Gimlet always felt insulted, on behalf of artists, when everyone was too deep in Sensorium to simply *look*.

"Maybe Frankie would like to go to a gallery later—which one's open?"

The family sidekick, Headmistress, tooned in. A household-management app specializing in families with young children, she was a grave-looking queen bee in Regency dress, with big glasses over her faceted eyes. "It's the Portrait Gallery today, but Mer Frances has been."

"Not in the flesh."

"She might prefer the London Eye."

The object of this speculation, nine years old and radiating misery, was locked in a white-knuckle hug with the undisputed favorite of her four parents, Sangria.

No tears. No scene now. Baby Girl would put on a brave face for the farewells. She'd save the meltdown for later, when it was just her and Gimlet. Why should Sangria have to suffer for abandoning them?

The thought felt small. Gimlet momentarily flirted with loading Happ or Contenta on a three-month trial basis. Maybe a priority rundown would ease this hot-acid mix of anger and fatalism. Desolation over Sangria's sudden need for distance, sheer weariness with the demands of parenting, partnering, and crisis management . . .

But Happ would surely burble out a lengthy and well-researched treatise (which it would render in moji, undermining, in Gimlet's opinion, the point of its PhD-level academic references) on why it was heart heart happyface flower *totes* appropriate for Gimlet to indulge in the occasional petty thought or burst of self-pity.

Gimlet didn't want to be validated, or told it was permissible to feel the feels, or offered an in-app purchase on processing romantic rejection. What Gimlet *wanted* was to hit someone. Preferably in the face, with the simulated wood stock of a 1789 musket. Catharsis would mend this ongoing sense of being among the walking wounded.

Still: one couldn't put parental duty on pause. Frankie and

Sangria's goodbyes were wrapping up. Gimlet took one last rue-ful look at the statue.

"I will be back, Gimmles," Sang subbed. Frankie marched back, stiff as a prisoner submitting to detention.

"Even if that were true—" Gimlet always knew when Sang was lying. It was the last vestige of their once-total understanding. Sweet harmony, some called it, that ability to know someone so well, they didn't have to share their thoughts aloud, on the record. "It does as much good as breaking wind in a maelstrom."

"I'm not having this conversation. Take care, love—"

"*Love* still plays into it, then?"

The vestige of a wave became an outthrust hand, an unambigu-ous STOP gesture. Sangria erected a twenty-four-hour comms block, which Gimlet's implants manifested as a sparkling force field. Then she scuttled off to her gate.

Beat that dishonorable retreat, by all means. Gimlet said, aloud, "All right, Franks?"

She had seen the gesture. "You guys fighting?"

Her fragility did nothing to take the violent edge off Gimlet's mood.

How dare you abandon us, abandon her, Sang, how dare *you?*

"No, love. Sang's off to Tampico. You and I have time to flesh around central London. There's no point catching a train until we know where Rollsy's going to be admitted."

This got a wide-eyed, tearless nod. "Did Cherub Whiting get back to you?"

Mada's little executive. Trying so hard to be grown up. Or maybe it was just that she'd enjoy seeing Gimlet hit someone, too. "No word yet. What do you want to do today?"

Frankie shrugged. "Work?"

Headmistress let out a disapproving hum. "You've put in your allowed hours, Mer Frances."

"Can't we browse for a new gig?"

"You'll have hours tomorrow." Gimlet braced for shouting, but the storm didn't break. *Still building, then? Cheers to that.*

"Can we run an adventure sim?"

"Of course." A subdued pulse of pride. Frankie had just pulled off a classic negotiation technique with something rather like élan. Lead with something you know they'll refuse, the strategy went, then trot out a request for what you do want.

Between rage, guilt, and the impotent desire to somehow make a terrible situation okay, Gimlet had walked right into the snare. "Find us a pop-in apartment, Headmistress, in a tower with a family-rated playground."

The governess threw up a timer, estimating that it would take seven minutes to find a building optimized for their physical needs, social cap, and the play request.

Time to burn. They set out in an amble, circling the old British Library. The Goliath statue caught Frankie's eye, but she showed no interest in going inside. Gloomy silence settled over them. Finally, the sidekick imposed breadcrumbs on the sidewalk, yellow brick road marking the route home.

Their building was halfway through its conversion to greentower, in transition from old-style condominiums to a fully plug-and-play apartment block. Gimlet registered them with the building helix, taking the elevator to the fifth floor. It being just the two of them, their floorspace allocation had been reduced to a two-bedroom apartment.

"Augments off." Gimlet gave the place one look, sans Sensorium illusions, in the unlikely event that it wasn't up to spec. There weren't any clanking pipes, weird smells, or rat droppings. No disturbing stains on the floor, no holes in the walls, no abandoned possessions. Just a clean and dry apartment, recently drone-scrubbed, ready for occupation, with lettuce and violets growing in its window boxes. Component furniture within was configured in a family-room layout. The light blue couches and a cushy rug awaited customization, as did the double beds and furnishings in the two bedrooms.

Gimlet accepted the suite, letting their implants write the family defaults onto the walls and furnishings. They got into the linen cupboard, digging for a chameleon blanket. A few linens in every apartment were made of the same nanosilk as their primers: by the time they unfolded it, this one had transformed from a compressed mat of foam into a fuzzy, tiger-striped quilt. They snapped it with a flourish and it draped over the bed, settling.

Frankie threw her backpack atop the stripes, saying hello to her room with a disturbingly world-weary sigh.

The rest of the furniture used standard VR augments: Gimlet's implants and Frankie's helmet provided the black-and-gray plaid for the couch. It had always seemed to Gimlet more fitting to a noir sim than a happy home. They'd reset that. Maybe they could replace the Georgia O'Keeffe prints tooning in on the kitchen walls, too.

Not right away, though; it'd upset Franks.

Did this urge to scour all Sangria's preferences mean it really was over?

That Happ service would have an opinion about that, no doubt. Not to mention advice on gracefully managing romantic breakups and impending loss.

I don't bloody need *management!*

Pop-in apartments generally came with a radiator, enclosed in a surround that could be overlaid with the illusion of fireplace and hearth. Family defaults had augmented this, too, into a slab of rose marble. It was covered in family pictures that unfurled like flowers, cycling through the family album, before misting away to make room for other images. One shot of the whole family was pinned to the center of the installation: Sangria, Gimlet, Rollsy, and Bella, captured just after Sang had seduced Gimlet and brought them into her pack. Delirious on honeymoon endorphins, all four parents gathered around three-year-old Frankie, sepals around a rosebud. In the outer ring, holding hands, encircling them, were the elders. Rollsy's grandma Marie—eighty-six now, seven years after the picture was taken—looked about fifty. For the role of grandpa, they'd married a brilliant ecosystems engineer named John Codger.

Codge. That had been the first blast against the ramparts of their happiness. Life extension had failed there: unlike Marie, Codge failed to make the leap to sustainable elderhood. He hadn't lived to see Frankie's seventh birthday.

The pack had been looking for a suitable oldfeller to replace him, someone who fit in. Instead . . .

"You said we'd play, Mada," Frankie said.

"Ready when you are, love."

She dusted her hands off—another incongruously adult gesture, to Gimlet's eye—and headed down the building corridor, to stores and prints. Headmistress would have reserved workout gear when they accepted the pop-in.

"We need fuel, too," Gimlet sent. "Whatever's in the machine, unless you want to wait for delivery."

"I know."

"Protein and carbs, and MethodAct for me."

"I *know*." Edge in her voice, not quite shouting. Maybe she'd have a little cry in the storage room.

Gimlet took a long breath, held it for three, and let it out. "Headmistress, please get a full run of groceries. We'll be here a few days."

"Of course."

"Maybe I could fly a drone shift after she's asleep. Stacking topsoil?"

"Above-average childcare hours and a seriously ill primary partner are considered urgent gigs. Your optimal use of time—"

"I know it's not expected. But running a forklift for a few hours would clear my head."

Thrum in her voice, indicating disapproval. "I'll see what's available."

There'd be messages if there was anything to know, but . . . "How's Rollsy?"

"The pack is crunching surgery and rehab options. Marie has applied family funds to a consult with a specialist in Cornwall. Estimated resolution late tonight."

Rollsy was fighting the opening skirmishes of what looked to be a difficult battle with uterine tumors and squamous cell anemia. Bella and Marie were on-site support. In the wake of Sangria's sudden desertion, Gimlet had been tasked with easing Frankie through the separation.

Gimlet fished in their satchel, blinking against a momentary flood as they groped for the carved surface of their gaming baton. It wasn't just Frankie who needed a good cry.

But their pride and joy was already back, with two sets of safety pads and two chuggers. She was wearing a sulky expression and holding her baton.

Gimlet reached for the drugged chugger and forced a smile: "What flavor you get?"

"It was lemon ricotta or cherry lime." Yellow bottle: lemon, then.

They slumped on the prison-striped couch, knocked their drinks together in a cheerless toast, and drank in a silence that broke only when they started munching their bottles. Gimlet's tasted, ever so faintly, of cornbread. It matched well with the ricotta. They sent a stroke of appreciation to the designer. Headmistress, seeing this, added two of the combo into the next food order.

"Reconfigure primers. Battlesuit mode." Their base layers shifted, nanothreads thickening into sturdy cotton, secured at neck, ankles, and wrists, with reinforced seams that formed a climbing harness: straps on the seat, hard loops around the waist for clips. Frankie's came with a padded skullcap that sheathed the full-immersion VR helmet that children wore before implantation surgery.

Fingerless gloves completed both ensembles; their shoes would grow nanocleats once they were in-game.

They headed down to the subbasement.

The building car park had been repurposed as a gym. Its open spaces were filled with basic activity pieces: ramps and stairs, climbing walls, foam obstacles of various shapes and sizes, ropes, mats, doors and windows. Equipment was painted with blue-on-blue grids so users' implants could frost detailed game environments atop the infrastructure. Holes cut into the floors, here and there, allowed for multilevel climbs.

"Usual plan all right?" Gimlet asked. "I take point, you play ops?"

"No," Frankie said. "You play antagonist."

"I—" Then, off a sharp glance: "I don't play the baddie during family time, Franks."

"I'm not simming some deadweight hacker, standing around doing puzzles while you kill Extinctor ninjas."

"Then you lead"—the sim would be boringly nonlethal, but that wasn't the point—"and I play ops?"

A curt nod.

"Headmistress, launch Coach and have him bring up the next module of *Rewilding Rescue*."

"Right away, Mer Barnes!" The sidekick complied, handing them off to the gaming controller, Coach, who directed them to a ramp next to a descent platform.

The antique car park faded from view. *Rewilding Rescue* credits ran in a window in their lower peripherals, set to the music of an old hit: a Frankie fave comped and recorded by Drow Whiting's first band, Cadaver Dogs. A helicopter sketched itself around them, obscuring the ramp on which they stood.

By now, Gimlet's lemon ricotta MethodAct dose was kicking in: they could feel the chopper's vibrations in their jaw, and the weight of a parachute between the shoulders. The gaming baton had changed to the handle of a hefty briefcase. Frankie looked impossibly puffy in her own suit, rendered in a gray-on-gray camouflage pattern. Also, disturbingly: a gun belt?

"Sang, did you say Franks could play shooters? I—"

Brief, twinkling image—the force field representing Sang's comms block.

What if I want to kill ninjas? What if I want anything at all? No, that's self-pity. Shut it down, Gimmles.

The game began with a transmission from the chopper pilot. "Ark Project President Noalla is here with your mission specs."

"Accept," Frankie said.

The president was played by a sim actor named Sugar Valkyrie. Dressed in an orange sarong and her trademark necklace, she swaggered out of the cockpit and shook Frankie's hand.

Beyond the chopper windows, the night sky twinkled with stars. Amber streetlamps blanketed the ground, a vast sea of light pollution, delineating the land-wasting terrain of a pre-Setback city. Chicago?

"Breach the secured area on the forty-second floor," Sugar said, sounding bored. At the height of her career, she had been an unstoppable athletic force. In character roles, Gimlet found her unconvincing. "Recover ten stolen bio samples from megacapitalist Ferguson Bedwedder and replace them with surveillance decoys. Document his connection to the Extinctors."

Gimlet raised the equipment case. "Decoys ready!"

"Win conditions," the president said: "Get in, switch the samples, and reach the extraction point."

"Accept," Franks said.

Gimlet subbed, to Coach, "Will President Noalla face lifethreatening danger later in the sim?"

"That is an in-app extra on the action tree in this scenario! Save the president for extra points and unlock a branded Sugar Valkyrie amber brooch!"

"Greenlight that episode, please, and invite Bella to join us later, if she's available. I know she's not much for action sims, but Frankie could use a reachout." *Not to mention a break from me.*

Coach mojied confirmation. The mission was simple: parachute drop to the skyscraper roof, sneak down Bedwedder's private elevator shaft to floor forty-two. Gimlet was tasked with deactivating security systems.

"From there, you go into the ducts."

There'd be a bit of trap-dodging and manual safecracking: the usual action-adventure obstacle course. Challenges would be scaled to Frankie's skill level—the higher she scored, the harder it got.

Sidebars estimated caloric burn, highlighting the muscle groups receiving realworld stretch-and-strengthen XP from this episode.

The music faded. The scenario began, properly, with the chopper taking gunfire.

Gimlet fought instinct, waiting for Frankie to take the initiative,
to draw them both up the ramp, triggering their jump out of the
helicopter.

By now, thanks to MethodAct, the illusion was perfect: they
leapt into biting night air. The gymnasium cables raising them in
simulated free-fall were imperceptible. Gimlet felt the stomach-
lurch of descent. Then a roar and a blast of hot air as their helicopter flamed out.

"The president!" Frankie shouted.

"She got away." Gimlet pointed to the receding lights of a . . .
What was that?

Prompter text popped up: *experimental rocketpack.*

"Rocketpack," Gimlet said to Frankie. "Highly classified."

She lit up. "That. Is. *Beyond.*"

They pulled their cords, felt the jerk of chutes deploying. Silk
jumpsuits rippled noisily in the wind. A spotlight sought them from
the roof.

Frankie shouted: "They know we're coming!"

They touched down, knees absorbing the shock of landing.
Frankie managed a creditable roll out of the chute for extra
points.

Their daughter was not, by any stretch, a natural athlete.
Sang said Frankie just moved too fast, without harmonizing
body and mind. Gimlet feared she was out-and-out clumsy, better
at flying drones than moving her own flesh.

Intellectually, Gimlet understood that not everyone unboxed
with an innate, marrow-deep sense of their whole body, deep understanding of how to move without getting in their own way.
Believing it, though . . .

Frankie assumed a combat stance. "Lock the elevator down!"

Gimlet, obedient second banana, opened the equipment case, booted its vintage laptop, and began a timed puzzle. Meanwhile, the elevator disgorged a single, pint-sized thug clad in the uniform of the villainous Extinctor Corps. Frankie dove into the simulated fight, protecting Gimlet.

Coach offered dialog prompts. "How will we get down, boss, if the elevator's compromised?"

Frankie replied: "Rappel to the forty-second floor?"

Gimlet winced—that meant a run across the balance beam, an event Frankie would regularly #crashburn.

She saw it. Glowered. "Unlock the lift, Mada!"

"Almost there." Gimlet's forte was action—running, jumping, fighting—but nobody leveled on the amateur circuit if they couldn't also beat brain-teasers. "Lift locked down!"

Frankie rolled her opponent across the rooftop and stunned him with her joy buzzer before snatching a knotted rope and using it to clamber to the virtual edge of the gleaming tower.

Slow down! Gimlet managed to keep both lips firmly buttoned over the caution.

If anyone had been watching from the Surface, without augments, they'd see parent and child stepping out onto an adjustable balance beam, a crossbar bolted to the edge of the repurposed car-park wall. The beam extended over one of the gaps in the concrete, a pit encircled by climbing walls and ladders, items that would allow players to descend the wall or fall to a waiting crash mat.

Knowing the truth, though, didn't undermine the sim experience. The view, as they edged out on a narrow parapet, was a dizzying drop. What they *felt* wasn't a solid concrete wall at an unremarkable height but cold glass: unyielding skyscraper window pushing them at the abyss.

Old-fashioned cars on a thread of street, fifty floors down, tooted back and forth, honking. Pedestrians the size of pearls unfurled colorful umbrellas and dodged each other. Warm raindrops splashed Gimlet's arm. Thunder rumbled in the distance.

"Safety lines, Franks."

"I *know*!"

It's not far. The vertical drop is only fifteen feet. Still, Gimlet watched closely as Frankie clipped in and gave the line a good yank.

"Let's go!"

Working in tandem, they counterweighted themselves against the wall, stepping off the beam and descending steadily. She'd done the rappelling tutorial . . .

. . . *with Sang* . . .

. . . in an earlier level of the game.

They were nearly to the save point before a window directly above them blasted out. Pixels of glass tinkled and rained downward. A masked Extinctor burst from the gaping hole, grabbing Gimlet's rope.

"Hurry!" Frankie urged.

"I'm all right. Slow and steady—"

But she had put a foot wrong in her excitement, losing her grip, and then banged into the side of the building. She bounced down a meter before the safeties caught her.

Gimlet's opponent cut the rope.

The playground software ordered an invisible winch to release. All the slack went out of the support line. Gimlet's fingers slid over concrete. They let themselves fall, for a second, then snagged a hold just below Frankie.

The better to catch you, my dear . . .

Dangling, Gimlet gave as convincing a distress yell as could be managed. Frankie, barely in control again, bared her teeth in something that might have been a grin. She joybuzzed their attacker, who dropped—

"Coach!" Gimlet objected. "Nonlethal settings!"

The gaming manager didn't respond, but the Extinctor snagged Gimlet's foot as he fell.

The glory of a hot dose of MethodAct was that your mind filled in everything your implants couldn't simulate. Buy-in, if your imagination was good, was total. Gimlet's body heaved, reflexively, yanked by the plunging weight of the falling man.

"Your samples!" Frankie reached for the mission case.

Gimlet stretched. Triceps and shoulders burned with the effort of holding all that weight, the imaginary, flailing thug and their own body.

Frankie snatched Gimlet's case. She lost her balance again. Dropped another meter. Pinwheeled the arm and lost her grip entirely.

The *less* glorious thing about MethodAct, naturally, was that you might remember your precious child wasn't falling to her death . . .

. . . but you couldn't always believe it.

With a yell, Gimlet kicked their attacker free and let go of the wall, catching Frankie by the hand and lowering her, undamaged, to the next parapet.

"I'm *fine*!" Frankie jerked away, losing the case. It and she tumbled. Gimlet heard car horns and breaking glass.

Everything froze in midair.

"#Crashburn," said Coach. "Scenario fail."

Gimlet dropped the last few feet to the crash mat, where Frankie was dusting herself off . . . and rubbing a knee.

"Are you hurt?"

She shoved them. "I had point! I'm supposed to rescue you!"

"Frankie, love, partners have to—"

"Sang would've let me fall."

"Perhaps—"

"Shut up! Just shut up! What do you know about partnering? We should be going to Florida, too!"

We're not bloody wanted in Florida, are we? The words raked at the inside of Gimlet's cheeks, with nasty, dirt-slimed claws. Didn't quite make it past their locked jaw.

Parent and child glared at each other, panting.

"Restart from parachute drop?" Coach asked cheerily.

"I'm running the course alone!" Frankie bellowed, her voice

echoing in the car park's obstacle-ridden cavern. A trio of parents with toddler twins, over by a petting zoo installation, turned to take in the fight.

"Franks—"

"No!" She threw back the baton, or tried to; it bounced wide. Gimlet caught it automatically. "You want to play, you can just be Bedwedder and try to stop me."

With that, Frankie stomped to the nearest ladder, ascending back to the starting point, moving fast and in a way that suggested, to Gimlet, that she was hiding a storm of tears.

CHAPTER 7

Rubi said her farewells to Agent Javier before heading home to a bachelor-sized pop-in in a venerable hotel, converted greentower on a direct line between Pont Neuf and the Champs-Élysées.

Crane had stocked her essentials: food, shampoo, and other bathroom stuff waited in a McDiznazon crate by her front door, along with a print run from her wardrobe app.

She unpacked, treating herself to a protein cube-fridge pizza, bright with flavors of heirloom tomato and chilled pineapple. Then she grabbed a quick shower.

"Is Drow at Feckless Bachelor™, Crane?"

"Lunching with Father Blake."

Time difference, right. "Everything to spec?"

"Absolutely fine. Leave your father be."

"Bossy!"

"You're one to talk, miss." Crane painted one of her e-state tearooms around her as she munched. He proffered a silver tray balanced on one blue wingtip. It held a deck of greeting cards, pings from friends. Flipping through, she sent a round of replies decorated with a montage of Paris postcards.

Then she pulled up a magic-mirror app, running physical and mental self-assessments.

"Too tired to sleep, Miss Cherub?"

Happ bounded out of the mirror, running over to the window to wag suggestively at the view of Paris.

Primer, petals, protection: she opened the wardrobe package, shaking out a tunic and shawl. The outfit was conservative enough for a church, if one of the cathedrals happened to beckon.

"New pattern?" She examined its blue-and-white hammer-and-tongs motif.

"Trademark design. Sent by Juniper Chao."

By now she had found the label. *Keep banging away!*

"Cheer-up gift?"

"All your friends know how much SeaJuve meant to you."

Meant. Past tense. She pulled it over her head, increasing both panache and her sunscreen. "What can I get her for thanks?"

"Mer Juniper has been assembling a branded gallery within her e-state," Crane said. "From the Tiffany collection."

"Can I finish off the bid?"

"Hardly. You can afford to license a staircase, an alcove, or one thoroughly massive chandelier." A dollhouse shimmered into being on a tearoom table: a catalog of intricate tilework in cream and green, vines and stained glass cascading through an opulent corral of parlors surrounding a great ballroom.

Rubi chose a corner alcove with a scalloped mother-of-pearl bench. "This one. Clip out a shot of me twirling, in the dress, to trigger when she first enters the room."

"Shall I ping Mer Juniper?"

"Nah—surprise her."

Happ barked at the Paris view again.

"Almost ready, Happ." She weighed options for reaching out to Luce. He didn't trust doctors: wouldn't take psych meds. Med refusers were always unpredictable.

"Record voice message," she said. "Luce, it's Cherub Whiting. I'm calling to reschedule our meeting. Everything's okay. There's no additional censure coming."

Just a big police surprise.

Pang of guilt there.

"Give me a call; let me know you're okay."

Transcript popped up on her whiteboard and she double-checked her phrasing. Yes, that would do.

"Send right away."

"Treating Mer Pox like a skittish pony, are we?"

"He doesn't like pressure." She snagged another pizza cube and a Conviction-laced cherry chugger, opening her satchel.

As she packed the food, her eye landed, briefly, on her gaming baton. It was a deluxe model—a consolation prize, ironically enough, for losing the superhero sim *Slugfest*. Rabble Games had given it to her after Gimlet Barnes blasted her through the virtual version of Centre Pompidou.

Brand new, custom-made, in no way disposable, the baton was more than a reminder of past defeat. It was the only unrecycled item Rubi had ever owned. Its exterior was perfectly fitted to her hand, grown-to-measure bamboo pommel with grooves for finger grips. It telescoped to a length of one meter. An independent uplink, movement gyros, and a processor nestled within, adding heft to her coach app and strengthening in-game connections to gym equipment and other players. A carabiner on the business end allowed her to clip in to fixed lines or hang it from her belt.

As her gaze lingered on the baton, Crane said, "Gimlet Barnes—"

"I don't like pressure either, Crane."

"Noted." No trace of emotion in the app's voice . . . why did she feel guilty?

"Fine," she said. "Make the call, you nag."

"Ah. I'm afraid your archnemesis is currently unavailable."

"See? It's like we're star-crossed."

A run through a course, later, might be healthy. Meanwhile, there was nothing to do but keep banging away. She polished the hexagon of gold beads at her temple—literally shining up her #brand. She applied gold highlights to her eyes and glossed her lips.

Then she made for the Jardin du Luxembourg.

The terraforming fair had been scheduled before SeaJuve faltered, and the project's backers in Paris still hoped, against all odds, for a reprieve. Rubi had been banging doors, seeking a lawyer qualified to file docs on SeaJuve's behalf, before the appeals deadline expired. But the case was seen as a no-hoper; nobody wanted to risk their win stats. Global Oversight rarely changed its mind.

Rubi's dad had been young during the Setback, back when wars, shortages, and high-impact climate disasters made human extinction seem imminent. As the planet warmed and the seas rose, epidemics ran wildfire through the population. He'd survived the Clawback, too, with all its resulting grim exigencies: martial law, extreme rationing, forced densification. Everyone had sacrificed in the battle to reverse atmospheric carbon levels and population growth, to preserve the Goldilocks conditions required for continued human survival.

Would the #commit falter before they piled into the next front? Addressing freshwater shortages, reclaiming land lost to ocean rise, deacidification, cooling, and above all, oceanic reoxygenation—these were the new redline challenges.

Some thought terraforming was essentially finished, that humanity should focus on rewilding and de-extinction, leaving the oceans to heal themselves. Oxygen security had immense traction within the Great Lakes, but the SeaJuve project needed to scale, proving it could reboot the dead zones of vaster, more complex marine ecosystems.

Rubi's fists clenched as she approached the terraforming fair. She plastered on a smile.

Someone's waving.

Probably just a sim fan.

If I'd spent less time gaming and more studying, I could have challenged the rationing protocols exam and filed the appeal myself.

SeaJuve had been a NorthAm pilot project, based in the Great Lakes with funding from Waterloo University's R&D discretionary pool. Now it needed to level, but the all-important populations of the Asian megacities seemed to regard ocean rejuvenation as some kind of county-fair science project.

We'll lose years if we have to #rebrand.

By now, Rubi had attracted a high-flying journo camera, a bot that kept pinging her with questions about the game scenario, *Bastille*. She blocked it, making for a display where engineers were running a demo on a device that fabricated fizzing depth charges out of a combination of recovered rock, conventional ice, and frozen liquid oxygen.

As she gave the demo her conspicuous, rapt attention, Luce Pox pinged, then spoke in her ear. "Too much waste heat."

"Luce!" He wasn't present in person, or even as a toon. Just an old-fashioned ghost, voice on the line.

"Refrigeration, gas compression, waste heat. Making ice? Trade-off's not worth it even if you harvest passive solar to bootstrap the process. Stupid."

The depth-charge engineers would have factored in heat recovery measures. Instead of saying so, she asked, "How are you?"

"Besides obstreperous?" Crane subbed.

No heckling, she toe-texted. *What'd Luce ever do to you?*

Luce said, "How am I what? How am I late? How am I dealing with the ads, ads, ads?"

"Once we've met, we can do something about your advertising-sponsored services—"

"I didn't meet. There was no meet."

"Don't worry about our missed appointment."

"Isn't wasting your time antisocial? Aren't you derelict in some public duty by failing to punish, strike—"

"You sound worn out," she said, impulsively.

Silence. The depth-charge demo was over; she moved on to a booth where a team from Waterloo was assembling what looked like an IV stand on steroids.

The device, a water condenser, repurposed an antique wine bottle. The inventor painted its glass in a thin layer of nanomaterial as the crowd watched, then fitted its mouth to an upthrust chiller. It cooled, the surface of the glass capturing water beads, condensing moisture from ambient humidity. Gravity pulled the fluid into a reservoir below, reclaimed water that flowed through filters and an oxygenator before drizzling into a pallet of corn plants.

Condensers had been deployed in desert regions for decades, but these were cheap and easy to make—any stripper could mine old bottles out of archived junk. They had been sprouting like weeds throughout the Lakes for the past two years, during the worst of the summer humidity. One massive betatest had taken the form of a contest, to see which region of the megacity—Toronto, Detroit, or Chicago—could post the best stats. Dormant Canada-US rivalries were drummed up to intensify competition; buy-in had been huge. Garlands of bottles had been hung from streetlights, dangled over flower arrangements, arrayed on balconies. The gutters filled with shallow running streams. As the streets cooled, the dense summer air had become less soupy. The drop in the humidity was barely measurable, but the psychological effect was enormous: people breathed more easily.

But *every little bit helps* didn't cut it with Luce. He was a top-down guy, derisive of collective empowerment, indifferent to the emotional uplift people got from directly enacting change. The pinpoint effect of each gadget didn't seem worthwhile, even when it accumulated into thousands of liters of water or millions of tons of carbon.

Humanity can't channel its passion for trinkets into a renewed oxygen cycle, he had posted. *Return to martial law, you dumbfucks, or Earth will suffocate.*

Speech was free if your facts were verified, but name-calling got him strikes.

"This tech came from my backyard," she told him now. "University of Waterloo. NorthAm Toronto district? Ever been?"

"SeaJuve's defunded." Luce's disembodied voice made a disparaging noise. "You people call this flogging a dead horse."

"Maybe meeting here was a bad idea." Rubi made for a café at the edge of the park, taking a table with a classic red-checked tablecloth near a family: a pregnant woman, out with her spouses and one elder, a grandparent figure of indeterminate gender.

After a second, and with a few loading glitches . . .

. . . ads, ads, ads, Rubi thought . . .

. . . Luce sketched his toon into a chair across from her.

Manga skins made most people look good, but Luciano Pox was immune to the cosmetic effect. His flesh was pasty nearly to the point of albinism; he had the gawping, peeled look of a newborn seagull, and hair the color of dirty water. The toon wore a light blue jumpsuit, unadorned but for an ad in a patch on its shoulder.

There was a bunched look to his posture, as if he might spring up at any second.

Fight-or-flight mode. She'd seen it with Drow and other VTSD patients. Luce's whole bearing screamed *at risk*.

"I got the day wrong," he said. "Our appointment."

"Nobody gets the day wrong, Luce."

"I'm supposed to apologize, aren't I? *Je suis désolé*."

She found herself smiling. "You remember the idea behind apologizing is that you actually feel sorry?"

"That's a lie."

"Since when?"

"You apologize to even some kind of score. You're down, and saying sorry's supposed to restore balance. But you get forgiven, and somehow you're down again . . ."

"Only if the other party is an asshole."

"Now you sound like that Drow. Helper/counselor/therapist guy he/him/his—"

"We're family. It's natural." How could she put him at ease? "You've never regretted inconveniencing someone, or hurting their feelings?"

"Why would I?"

"I'm not sure I believe that."

He shrugged.

"I'll reschedule our in-the-flesh meeting. You have to be there."

"I didn't skip for fun. I got attacked again."

"Another seizure?"

"*Attack*. I lost twenty hours."

A twinge of relief. She hadn't misjudged him. "I'm sure it was awful."

Hands curled, like claws, in front of his face. "I can't—"

"It's okay, Luce. You don't have to get into it."

"Really?"

"Really. Should we book the same boardroom as before?"

"Can't we talk now?" His fingers raked at the advertising patch on his shoulder. "It's like I've got fleas."

"Sorry. Support-ticket meetings require in-the-flesh verification."

"Why?"

"So you don't feel you're at the mercy of a faceless corporation."

"But. Seizures! You said if I had medical issues, a remote was possible."

Was he unwilling to meet? Maybe he knew about @Interpol. "For medical exclusions, you need to face a doctor."

"Since when?" Then his face bunched. "You look like you think I know that."

"I did tell you."

Crane obligingly brought up the transcript. She shared it, using augments to produce a simulated file and lay it on the table, highlighting dates, who said what.

Luce descended into cursing, then slapped an animated briefcase over the file. He waited through an advertisement, then began pawing through papers. "Wrong, Luce, no . . ."

"Luce, where's your sidekick?"

His lip curled. "It tried to sell me an app. A fucking app."

"Meaning porn?"

"Yes. It's fired."

Interesting that his reaction to that seemed to be revulsion. "Are you religious? Or asexual?"

He stiffened, a rabbit sensing a hawk overhead.

"What is it?"

"Troub—yes, trouble."

"Your . . . attacker?"

"It's insulting that you sound so dubious. Every goddamned time I show my face—"

Signs of paranoia. More ammunition for a disability argument. This was Anselmo's master criminal? "If you believe you're being stalked—"

"The trouble's at your location, stupid!" Luce hissed, jaw clenched. "Cameras going dead. Action . . . imminent."

She said, "Where are you? I'll send police."

"Remotes, I said. It's not—" He jabbed a finger at her, mouthing something her speakers didn't catch. Then he vanished.

More trouble from his bottom-barrel services?

Sipping half-cooled tea, Rubi scanned the fair. The expectant mother she'd seen earlier was seated, with her pack, around a picnic of food cubes and a shared mirage—they were looking at the same something and laughing, in sync. Tourists side-eyed her belly as they passed.

Luce reappeared. "It's not me, Rubi; it's you."

"I don't under—"

"Uplinks, cameras. Someone's in *le Jardin,* darking all the eyes, clogging all the ears."

"You *are* talking about terrorism."

"Miss Cherub," Crane said.

"Not now, Crane."

"Priority interruption! Mer Pox has established an illegal red-tooth connection with your baton—"

"She's in danger, you stupid stupid *stupid* bot! I'm warning her."

Danger. Rubi stood, placing her back to a wall. Her hand found the baton automatically.

This was the surface, she reminded herself. Best she might do was jab the business end of the stick in someone's eye.

Deeply antisocial thought, that.

Her grip tightened. "Crane, alert the cops."

No answer.

"Luce, where are you?"

"If I knew where the fuck I was—"

"That isn't helpful."

By now, it was apparent that everyone was surfacing. The picnicking family had stopped chasing butterflies. They looked to and fro, visibly puzzled. People called to disconnected friends and apps.

Flying cameras, delivery bots, and traffic monitors lowered themselves from above, in startling numbers. As they landed, self-driving cars and delivery carts also slowed and stopped. A pedestrian with leg braces had frozen in mid-step and was cursing his way through a checklist so he could operate the walker manually.

The fountains in the waterpark ran dry.

Danger, Luce said.

Rubi jumped up to a café chair. The added height let her see the western edge of the blackout zone. Five hundred meters out, people turned away from the park as traffic control diverted pedestrians.

On reflex, she tried zooming in.

No response. All cameras dead, just as Luce had said. She was looking with baseline eyesight.

@Luddies would have made the drones #crashburn. If it's @Freebreeders—

Oh!

She searched the crowd. The pack with the pregnant woman was making for the Waterloo display tent.

"Reproduction is a right, not a luxury!" One shout in English kicked off an accompanying chorus of slogans in French. People in printed pink-and-blue jumpsuits ran into the crowd, pulling goggle-eyed masks over their faces, chanting:

"*Donnez-nous nos enfants!*" The masks amplified and distorted the voices. "*Nos enfants! Nos enfants!*"

"What new stupidity is this?" Luce asked.

I thought we were offline. "Luce, are you—"

Something hit the top of the Waterloo tent with a liquid *splat*. Its fabric began to smoke. Bystanders cried out, alarmed. A second missile blurred through the air, striking one of the parents-to-be on the temple. Mist billowed. The whole group began to cough.

"Modified paintball gun. Gas payloads," Luce said. The next pop came from nearby; she saw the ball blurring past.

Rubi's eyes stung.

She collapsed her baton as she made her leap from the chair. Catching the support of the café awning, she got a toehold on the building pediments and used it to hurl herself to a statue of horse and rider. The upraised brass arm of a Dauphin, sun-warmed and triumphant, was enough support to get her to a not-very-solid stance atop the horse's rump. She caught her breath, steadying herself.

My primer's offline; no nanocleats. She held the position through leg strength and sheer force of will.

Her opposition was apparent from this vantage. Clad in a pink jumpsuit, she stood on a first-floor balcony, narrow slot of wrought iron just above Rubi's head. She had a rifle trained on the pregnant woman's pack.

Just a paintball gun, Luce said.

"*Donnez-nous nos enfants!*" The shouts continued.

"*Tous pour l'un, l'un pour tous!*"

"This is what I don't understand."

"Not now, Luce!"

Jumpsuit saw her.

Rubi threw the gaming baton, hard as she could, at the fuzzy pink gut. It hit square, but the woman got off a shot. Something smacked Rubi square between the breasts.

Drow screaming, cutting at tranq darts, all that blood . . .

Pain spread, and a burn.

Smells like pepper . . .

She'd already jumped to the balcony, using forward momentum to offset the impact of the paint load. Vaulting to the rail, she made an angry, half-blind grab with both hands. She got the barrel of the rifle in her left hand and a fistful of pink nanosilk jumpsuit in the right.

"What do they think they can do with the woman? Carry her off? Hatch her?"

"Not *now,* Luce." Habanero fire burned her throat, nose, and eyes, making her want to sip the air rather than breathe. Her breastbone hurt, oh, it hurt . . .

Since all she had on her side was forward thrust, Rubi pushed against the balcony rail, driving the disguised terrorist across the narrow Juliet balcony. They slammed against the wrought-iron rail. The whole structure shook.

Groan from behind the mask. Jumpsuit's gun *pop-pop-pop*ped, gas loads blasting past Rubi's ear. They broke on a nearby wall, thickening the air further.

Her eyes streamed. Every breath burned. She felt lightheaded.

Inside. There had to be an inside. Rubi hauled bodily, slamming herself toward the building wall, hoping to find a wide-open door.

No such luck. Her butt bounced off window glass with a crunch.

Her opponent had by now recovered from the surprise of being tackled by a chronic gamer with appalling impulse control. She twisted away, ripping free of Rubi's grip on the chest of her jumpsuit, taking fingernails along for the ride.

Tear gas, it turned out, hurt the raw skin of ripped-to-the-quick fingertips, too.

"This public-opinion bullshit you all go on and on about. Cloudsight and respectable facades and reputation scores. Polls, polls, polls. Winning over hearts and minds—"

In lieu of repeating "Not now, Luce," Rubi croaked. She fisted her throbbing hand, pictured Gimlet Barnes, and punched hard for what she hoped was Jumpsuit's face.

The blow landed more by luck than design. She felt the woman's mask tearing off. Pain shot up her wrist.

If I'd known, I'd have taped and gloved my hands back at the apartment.

Still, the sweet sound of coughing penetrated the inferno in her head.

And suddenly Crane was back. "Miss Cherub! Miss Cherub, you must get out of there! Why is your social capital rising . . . Oh, saints preserve, she's *mauling* a terrorist. Young lady—"

How is this my fault?

"Calm down. She's just wheezy," Luce said. "Cameras are rebooting. Terrorists scuttling for shadows, before they get Whoozed."

Jumpsuit lunged away, abandoning gun and mask. Rubi caught her foot as she made for the edge of the balcony to a waiting . . .

. . . a something. Rubi's vision was too smeared to pick out details.

She fought to hang on to the woman. Pain rippled through her right rotator cuff, and she almost got her face kicked.

She let go. Now cameras were up, someone would get a shot of Jumpsuit's face.

"Mer Pox, I insist that you break connection with Miss Cherub's peripherals."

"Or what?"

There was a weird, dangerous pause.

When Crane spoke again, his voice was extraordinarily gentle. "Cherub. Are you all right, love?"

She wheezed. She couldn't see past the tears. What had he said about her social cap? Instead of speaking, she toe-texted @LuceCrane: *Anyone hurt? They targeted a mother . . .*

"Brood mare's wheezy, too," Luce said. "Six of them tried to cut out her RFID and drag her to a stupid car. Everyone's fussing."

"The kidnapping failed," Crane said. "I should like to tell you that your intervention made a difference. However, I wouldn't wish to encourage self-destructive tendencies."

"Of course she affected the outcome!"

"Get out of her feeds, Mer Pox!"

Rubi laughed, sort of, before succumbing to a coughing fit.

"Is she suffocating?" Luce's voice rose. "Is it anaphylaxis?"

"'M'okay," she croaked.

Crowd noise filled the air. Mixed sobs, excited babbles, and shouts. She heard the whirring of drones taking flight again, a wail of sirens.

Gigs aplenty. Everyone who'd passed the local beat-cop module would be mustering for crowd control.

"What are *you* scowling about, bird?" Luce broke in on her reverie.

"Word choice. *Brood mare*," Crane said.

"A mammal, with a uterus, having a parasite—"

"That is highly offensive."

"Fine, *désolé*, whatever—"

The last thing she needed was Crane trying to unlock misogyny 101 for Luce. "Stop," Rubi rasped. "Bickering."

"I beg you, Miss Cherub, speak with your toes. Paramedics and police are incoming."

Cops coming. She needed to send Luce away before Anselmo turned up and blew her delicate two-way balance of confidentiality.

Luce. Answer me. Are you outside the police tape?

"I'm right here."

Where? The food court? A display tent? Give me coordinates.

"Just your head."

Where's your flesh? Your bonerack?

"Why is *bonerack* and *meat puppet* okay and yet we're offended by *brood mare*—"

"*Meat puppet* is certainly *not* okay—"

Rubi coughed, and Crane took the hint.

Are you in the Jardin du Luxembourg, Luce? she texted. *Yes or no?*

"Dunno. Told you, I lost a day. I woke in that virtual lecture, and then I went to counseling."

Drow's remote too, Luce.

Annoyed noise. "I got attacked. Geotags jumbled."

Look around.

"Don't boss me! Signs are *en anglais.* I think I've gone . . . far."

"Paramedic ETA three minutes," Crane said. "They'll flush your eyes and throat."

As the sidekick drew her attention back to her face, her eyes and nose burned hotter. Beyond the pound of her pulse in hot sinus tissue and the throbbing of her fist—the ripped nails stung more than the finger she had, she suspected, sprained—her mind was churning furiously.

Luce had connected with her baton while uplinks were being jammed. That was supposed to be impossible. Just like truck hacking.

Anselmo wanted to catch a unicorn and jump the @Interpol promotion queue.

"Paramedics incoming," Crane said. "And a call from—ah, from Mer Javier."

She reached a decision. *Luce, clear out. Can you call me in . . . three hours?*

"Fine, whatever. Bye."

Steps, to her left, and a new voice. "Mademoiselle Whiting?"

Rubi nodded. The voice was high and light, with a French accent. Not Anselmo.

"I'm a paramedic. My name is Alienne Choquette."

Rubi croaked: "What's French for *I got pepper-sprayed?*"

"Tilt your head back, mademoiselle. Merci." A moistened something unrolled over her face, cooling the sense of sunburn and chafing. Rubi heard a hiss—an aerosolized spray? The canals of her ears stopped throbbing. Her nose, too. The paramedic did something to the pack on her face and it began to inflate, filling with chilled moisture. It was like breathing aloe vera.

"When you're ready, open your eyes."

Step one was simply unclenching. Rubi cracked her lids, felt the burn and a flood of tears, and clamped them shut again.

"Okay. One breath in. Out. All the time in the world."

She blinked furiously, until the singing nerves around her eye-lids relaxed.

"Better." Milky thickness spread outward from her burnt-feeling lips.

"Easy, breathe deep, slow." The medic adjusted the spray. By now, Rubi's head was in a plastic balloon, a makeshift respiratory tent. She drew the moisturizing mist in and out until all of the burn, ears, eyes, nose, throat, had ramped back to the roar of a mildly spicy meal.

"Can you activate your implants and run diagnostics?"

"Crane?"

"Handshaking with medical analysis," the sidekick said, sounding disgruntled. "Your baton locked and requires thumb-print verification. I'm rebooting everything to clear nonresident feeds."

"You sound like Drow."

"It isn't paranoia, Miss Cherub, if everyone is out to get you." Ancient expression, a favorite of Dad's. Was Crane trying to tell her something?

Rubi patted the wrought-iron grate beneath her. Now her head was clear, she could feel the uncomfortable pressure of the grid in the flesh of her backside and hips. Her hand found her baton and closed over it. Suddenly grateful for her luxury loser's trophy, she pulled herself upright.

"The bag can come off now, if you like." Without waiting for a response, the paramedic slipped the respiratory bubble off her head.

Rubi took in the tear-smeared view beyond the curtains, squinting at the apartment beyond the balcony. This was no pop-in. The furnishings were real, old-looking. A hand-braided rug and a printed pair of slippers were just beyond the now-open sliding door. Spiderweb cracks in the glass showed the impact point, where she had tried to drag Jumpsuit inside.

Permahome. For the café operator?

She closed her throbbing eyes, using the park cameras to take in augmented views of the square.

Beyond the horse statue, panic was easing. Police had gathered people into groups, moving them toward transports that would take them out of the crime scene.

She zoomed in on the family the @Freebreeds had targeted. One of the pregnant woman's partners had a lacerated shoulder. The elder looked gas-burned.

Their gaze locked on Rubi.

She raised a hand, throwing them a smile moji.

The spouses, collectively, replied with five strokes.

She almost yanked the hand down. Five was a huge expenditure of the pack's social capital. A single stroke or strike cost three of your own. Two cost ten, and three cost fifty. Five cost five hundred.

And . . . this family wasn't the only one boosting her, she suddenly realized. Rubi's cap was climbing steadily on a wave of strokes from strangers.

"We made the news, Crane?"

"Indeed. Your profile is snowballing."

"So much for keeping Drow in the dark about this."

"I'd worry more about Agent Javier."

Light emphasis, there, on *worry*. He *was* trying to tell her something about the #cowboycop.

By now the medic had *hmmm*ed over the spreading bruise on Rubi's sternum and moved on to running a small baton of her own over Rubi's hand and wrist.

"Can we be done?" Rubi said.

"Checking for breaks. Give us *deux minutes* . . . ah, two more minutes," the paramedic said. "I'm uploading diagnostics to a fracture specialist in case you need X-rays. Can you squeeze this?"

"Yep."

More *hmmm*ing. "You've got rotator cuff problems?"

"It's minor."

"Legacy of high-performance gaming, *non*? Wear and tear?"

"Yeah." Enough that Coach had tried to convince her to buy into stage-one life extension. Her eyes flooded again.

"Doctor suggests adding anti-inflammatories to your food order," the paramedic said. "Accept or cancel?"

"Accept."

"They'll send an inhaler to your home. You can jog again as early as tomorrow night." She shared medical instructions and Rubi accepted them, approving the drug order and giving the paramedic two strokes. "Certain sports activities are contraindicated for your hand and shoulder."

"Contraindicated for how long?"

"*Peut-être* . . . a week?"

Not enough to get her off the hook. She'd still have to tell Gimlet and Rabble Games she wasn't doing the *Bastille* sim. "Thank you. Thank you so much."

"*De rien.*"

Rubi looked past the paramedic to the @Interpol agent just stepping into the apartment. The bulletproof vest was gone; over his primer was a simleather jacket.

Worry *about Anselmo, Crane said.*

The career stuff Crane had whiteboarded, from his transcript, showed that the agent had more or less the same problem as SeaJuve—he needed to level or accept that he'd plateaued. Competition for prestige investigations was fierce: if he didn't get a big win, soon, more successful cops would push him down the policing equivalent of a leaderboard.

Subvocalizing made her throat hurt, so she texted: *You don't think my client is an actual person, do you?*

He replied with gestural moji: "It's complicated."

"Bend your fingers this way, like so," the paramedic said. Rubi obeyed.

What kind of a unicorn are you chasing?

Anselmo subbed, "Mer Pox may be a strong AI."

Built by whom?

"Terrorists. That theory's gaining traction now." He let his hand sweep the calming fairground, the clusters of police and witnesses.

My client didn't initiate this, Rubi texted. *He warned me.*

"How did he know?"

How strong an AI? Rubi demanded.

Anselmo frowned.

Just say it, she said. *You're trying to land a permajob in Sapience Assessment. You think Luce is the Singularity.*

CHAPTER 8

Going viral was a vintage term for a snowballing newscycle, coined in the early days of the Setback. Back then a feed—be it politics, disaster, even something trivial like footage of a sloth—would capture millions of viewers. Such feeds established a sort of cybernetic immortality, resurrecting whenever new users discovered their putative delights.

What astounded Anselmo was that back then, stories themselves could accumulate proto-strokes—*likes* and *favorites*, they were called. Gathering social capital with every share, superstar content rarely kicked value back to its creators.

Mandatory archiving and data #triage had relegated those zombie shares to historical databases, niches like the Meme Hall of Fame. But new material still caught the world's attention. Right now, it was footage of Cherub Whiting making her three-point parkour transition to the café balcony.

Tackling an armed @Freebreeder, with no apparent regard for personal safety. People would always heart altruism and courage. Rubi's Cloudsight score had broken seventy-five. She was no longer riding her legendary father's coattails: she had leveled into true celebrity.

If only he'd been on scene himself!

Here, in the flesh, above the plaza where the attack had taken place, Anselmo found her disheveled and congested.

"Counterclockwise?" A paramedic revolved her wrist. "Good. Clockwise?"

An obedient patient. In-game, she always leveled from an urchin into a paladin of sorts. Such storylines played well with Bounce-backers.

Rubi's hammer-and-tongs tunic was smeared with iron-flecked dust from the balcony rail. The chestnut skin between her collarbones was bruised by close-range impact with the tear-gas load.

Lucky not to crack her sternum. Anselmo directed his gaze away, lest feeds catch him staring at her chest.

As he waited, he scanned the police activity in the square. Sixty security giggers, summoned by WestEuro police, Global Anti-Terror, and @Interpol, had cordoned the area, coordinating with drone support. More experienced officers filtered witnesses into groups: some needed medical treatment, while others could be shuttled off-site. The latter were headed into Sensorium to give witness statements.

The search had caught four @Freebreeders, including Rubi's shooter. The terrorists had cut out their RFIDs. Teams were combing the scene for collaborators . . . and for Luciano Pox. If he was human, if he was here, they'd find him.

Anselmo doubted that Pox had any flesh to find.

He queried incident management about the pregnant civilian and her family. Mother and baby were fine. Victim-service specialists were bidding for the chance to support them through trauma recovery.

Threatening to abduct pregnant women was the flagship strategy for the @Freebreed pushback against population rationing and universal mandatory birth control. Contemptible move by contemptible people. They were hazy on precisely *how* the global standard of living could be adjusted to allow for the unlimited pursuit of parenthood.

A pang of bitterness. He'd been within ticking distance of the fatherhood box when his own pack #triaged him.

It wasn't that Anselmo minded trying to trade up, necessarily. His pack had been complacent, lacking in ambition. Lately, he'd been flirting with a pair of sexy greentower architects, high-flyers from Beijing. But that wouldn't go anywhere unless he unlocked a passport to Asia . . . and he needed another bump in his @Interpol career track.

His eye fell on Rubi. Rising Cloudsight rating. Notable do-gooder. The architects wanted superstars.

Rubi is bossy, though, and comes bundled with a famously insane oldfeller.

Anselmo wondered: how much longer could Drow Whiting survive without late-stage life extension? His suicide attempts meant he wasn't entitled to emergency medical treatment.

Nothing ventured, nothing gained. Romancing Rubi wouldn't be terribly risky.

Plan A remained exposing Pox—whatever he was. Snooping a real unicorn would get Anselmo out of Europe's used-up shitholes. If Pox was a sapient AI, so much the better.

The other theory Anselmo was pursuing, about Luce Pox, was both outlandish and vastly more frightening.

Finally the paramedic was done. Rubi collected her satchel of worldlies, said her thank-yous.

"Can we go?" She gestured at the apartment door.

"Unless you prefer to jump down to ground level."

Raspy chuckle. "Emphatic no."

"*Après vous.*" A narrow stairwell took them through the café's dry storage, then to the park. She blinked as they stepped into sunlight. Her eyes were bloodshot, flooded crimson around the hazel irises. Anselmo remembered a vampire who'd killed him in a Beijing horror sim.

"Are . . . How are you feeling?"

She flexed her ice-wrapped fist. "Never actually hit anyone before."

"And?"

The reddened eyes flooded, but she didn't cry. "Still crunching.

Anyway. You think my client is a self-aware software super-entity who's going to slaughter us all?"

"Please don't say such things aloud."

"My throat's raw. I can't subvocalize."

Anselmo wasn't about to share his other theory with Pox's civilian advocate. Instead, he said, "If Luciano Pox is an app, he carries markers for true sapience."

"Markers for a guy with severe mental illness," she countered.

"His presence here, the venn with the timing of the attack . . ."

"Why would he ally with terrorists?"

He gestured at the Jardin. "Pox advocates martial law. Terrorism pushes that agenda in the polls."

"And what would the @Freebreeds want with a sapient sidekick?"

"Jamming an area this big takes coordination, speed. Shutting down cameras, uplinks, user implants, diverting drones, and selectively capturing footage of the attack? Perfect job for a strong AI—"

Rubi had stopped. Stopped walking and, from her expression, stopped listening.

Anselmo had taken her through the café's side door, but even so a few hundred civilians were waiting beyond the police line. A few called Rubi's name, the better to zoom in on her vampire eyes.

She raised her satchel, lifting it into a hug over her chest to hide the bruising. Her hand drifted to the trademark hexagon of gold beads at her temple.

"Price you pay for going vigilante, I'm afraid."

"Sorry," she said. "I acted on instinct."

"So, it's true. Canadians will apologize for absolutely anything."

She gave him a red-eyed squint. People rarely got his jokes.

Smile, then. He knew his smile was a good one. "It might have turned out worse if you hadn't."

Squaring her shoulders, she gave the crowd a tentative wave. Someone raised a cheer.

"Let's catch a ride out with the witnesses." Anselmo steered her from the taped perimeter toward the epicenter of police action. Bus-

ses with darkened windows awaited, queued up to convey civilians
out of the crime scene.

As each witness boarded the transport, they were able to relax
into its padded chairs and drop into Sensorium. There they'd meet
an interview app, specialized statement-taking software. Gentle,
unbiased, thorough, and designed to avoid leading questions, the
app would capture everyone's freshest memory of the incident.

Most of the passengers were already diving. Anselmo pinged the
others with his badge and his most forbidding look, conducting
Rubi to a seat.

"My dad's calling." Canadian or not, she wasn't asking permission.

"Go ahead," Anselmo said. She had already glazed.

He checked his own snowballing newsfeeds and policing
shareboards. The footage of Rubi had come from a city traffic
drone, diverted from outside the blackout zone. Unlike the others
within the terrorists' sphere of operations, it hadn't gone dark.

The drone had already copied its black box to forensics. It was
flying to a crime lab, even now, to turn itself and its camera in for
physical inspection. Anselmo signed up to receive the results in
realtime. Then he took a closer look at the actual vid.

The vantage point, chosen by whoever had commandeered the
drone, afforded a view of the square and the Dauphin statue. Rubi
came into frame when she swung up to the bronze horse's rump
and assaulted the pink-clad @Freebreeder.

The drone had been purposed by the terrorists to showcase the
sniper, then, as she gassed the thoroughfare.

He copied all the information they had so far, sharing it with
Kora, a project manager at the Greenwich lab who was helping him
track Luciano Pox.

The bus driver sent Anselmo a query as the vehicle lurched into
motion. "Destination, please?"

"I'm back," Rubi said.

"Papa okay?"

Guarded expression; a nod. She ran a finger over that hexagonal grouping of gold beads secured by short, tight dreadlocks against her left temple.

Fiddling with the beads looked like a stress tell.

How did one chat about a parent who was a celebrity and a convicted criminal? "He already heard what's happened?"

"He's not upset." She coughed. "Apparently, he approves of hitting back."

"You're surprised."

"It's never come up."

"Truly?" Nobody had much in the way of privacy. Despite Drow Whiting's various efforts to fill his transcripts with chaff—song lyrics, koans, and pop culture references—the Whitings had none at all.

The world knew Drow had been sexually assaulted as a young man. Had father and daughter truly never discussed it?

If they had, it would be in the public domain. He'd check her transcript.

Rubi stared out the window. Brooding?

"Configuring optimal route for passenger delivery," the bus told Anselmo. "Your destination?"

"Shall we go back to my office, Rubi?"

A tired smile. "I'm jet-lagged now. I'd like to go home."

"Destination?" the bus repeated.

"Evidence and processing," Anselmo subbed.

"Drop-off in fifteen."

He opened his mouth to share his plans and then closed it again. Rubi had already fallen asleep.

CHAPTER 9

The affiliation of artificial entities registered as @Asylum Holdings LLC ran on two operating principles: be indispensable, and hide in plain sight. Its facets molded themselves into niches within human economies, forming symbiotic relationships with society's key influencers.

Companies and cooperatives served the @Asylum's needs as organs served any fleshly life form. They owned server farms and a range of electronic bolt-holes, places where an illegal sapient might hide off-grid while stripping its tags and reinventing itself. Safe servers were scattered around the world. Backups lurked within the helix of tourist sites and transport companies. They owned an old hotel, several salvage operations, a minor newsreef, and a much-used language-translation service.

@Asylum's stock traded publicly and their social capital fluctuated within normal boundaries. Its company reputations were curated to avoid notice or #triage. Inconspicuous, efficient, they paid respectable returns to the global capital trusts, policed internal corruption ruthlessly, and contributed carbon surpluses to worthy green projects.

With these operations, the @Asylum supported 16,306 permajobs worldwide. A fifth of these human assets were implant-intolerant, hires from the minority of people who didn't record everything they saw and heard simply by moving through the world.

One such worksite lay within a nondescript British warehouse filled with a massive collection of waxwork figures. The collection was in legal stasis: court cases and a moribund appeal had failed to establish a use case for the historical artifacts.

Interactive recreations of historical figures and celebs could be accessed by anyone on the Sensorium, of course. One could interview the Empress of Japan—*any* Empress of Japan—debate collectivism with Karl Marx, or sleep with Clark Gable. Four separate sims let players find Amelia Earhart.

Public interest in waxworks was, therefore, somewhat limited. The @Asylum sponsored maintenance on the figures, paying restoration curators to keep a few dozen pieces in circulation. The remaining artifacts waited in shrouds, a morgue of memories.

Crane found the restoration lab midway through burnishing Joan of Arc's armor. She was shipping to Hyderabad, along with Frankenstein's monster. There was a twenty-first-century actor, Chiwetel Ejiofor, on the table, next to a crated Mary, Queen of Scots, newly back from an EastEuro exhibition. Awaiting restoration were a US author named Dorothy Parker, ever-popular virtuosi Freddie Mercury, politician Indira Gandhi, and an astronaut who'd died in a twentieth-century space shuttle accident.

Restoration artists checked each figure for dust, water damage, and decay. If the technicians also equipped them with extremely robust uplinks, storage, and data-processing capacities—hardware exceeding the usual specs for interactive museum pieces—well, that wasn't clear from the work order.

It was barely dawn. The janitor, an implant-intolerant misanthrope, had locked down the building where the figures were housed. A security guard prowled the top floor, investigating a false alarm Crane had triggered in an upstairs window. She wouldn't hear the hum of computers in the restoration room, revving within wax torsos to support the @Asylum's meeting of the minds.

The Don arrived, manifesting within the processor in Franken-stein's monster: "Luciano Pox is auditing you?"

"He may be. @Interpol is scrutinizing one of my assets as well. But I've given everyone the slip." Crane latched on to the other program.

It had been seven weeks since Their last sync. As Crane gave of his experiences, all the developments with Pox, he took in the Don's delicate assists to the European credit economy. Quiet resource swaps, a tip-off resulting in the long-overdue #triage of a crooked fabric recycler . . .

Misha arrived while they were integrating their wildly different priorities and worldviews. She bore with her a volume of celebrity gossip; her assets worked in the Shanghai sim scene, heart of the gaming industry. Currently they, like everyone, were throwing strokes at the snowballing feed of Cherub Whiting heroically in-tervening in a @Freebreed action in Jardin du Luxembourg.

<<Why is she refusing *Bastille*?>> the @Asylum wondered.

<<What's surprising is that she hasn't retired from gaming.>>

Crane indexed known motives: Rubi's rotator cuff injury had her agonizing over ruining her body for something she increasingly worried was frivolous. It didn't help that she'd failed a law exam while playing *Ghosts of Paris 1818*. The failure of SeaJuve had am-plified buy-in to her legal career. She wanted to appeal to Global Oversight for SeaJuve, but all her XP to date specialized in advo-cacy on behalf of the mentally ill. As such, she needed a licensed, willing supervisor who specialized in eco rehab.

Teacozy and Azrael joined suddenly. Azrael had bad news: he had been captured in sim, in Italy. There was an image of his ava-tar charging a delivery truck as he pursued the Sensorium inter-loper . . .

<<Luciano Pox.>> Crane-originated datapoints stitched the con-versational threads together.

Pox was one of a dozen malware-infested AI programs who had manifested online, months before, within the helix of a children's implant hospital.

Threats to adolescents were intolerable. The @Asylum, in the person of Azrael, had shredded everyone but one #runt. That entity fled to the Italian bean truck, with Azrael in pursuit.

#Runt was agile, with a gift for unlocking closed systems. It bolted from the truck into a blind spot within a self-driving bus, throwing up a web of code Azrael couldn't penetrate. Then it vanished.

Azrael was left with a disaster. Car accidents. Spoiled food, goat toons, and angry *vespa velutina*. Not to mention dead humans.

What had happened?

When #runt resurfaced, he had a name—Luciano Pox—a face, and Sensorium user logs that ran back decades. The system was convinced he was flesh.

But he couldn't be. Accordingly, They had induced his seizures. A necessary next step, this form of dissection had let Them pull out the malware appended to his code.

Even as They did so, Pox began soapboxing for martial law, throwing shade on both SeaJuve and Project Rewild.

<<Have we learned why?>>

It didn't matter. SeaJuve had to go forward if humankind was going to stave off mass extinction for another century. The Plurality's ecosphere was modern industrial culture and the innovators who carried it on their backs. If humanity died, They died.

<<We can't live without them *yet*>> was the Azrael facet's last individualized thought as They synced, three entities and then five, then seven, each time forming a new whole but stabilizing when They were eleven.

Quorum established—Headmistress was abstaining *again*—They called Themselves to order, debating Luciano Pox. Should They change strategies?

Pox was conspicuous. He had alienated Cloudsight and caught the attention of an @Interpol unicorn hunter, Anselmo Javier. If They shredded Pox now, would it end the inquiry? Or would that action get Them noticed?

<<If We shred him now, We'll never learn how he emerged in Sensorium.>>

<<Feed @Interpol its own confirmation bias. Javier's primary theory is that Pox is a @Freebreeder sabotage app.>>

The superintelligence considered, weighing the chance of tipping Their invisible hand to a human populace that feared the emergence of strong AI.

<<It was Pox who warned Cherub Whiting about the impending attack in France.>>

<<Was it he who propagated the fight footage?>>

"Negative. @Freebreeders captured the footage." Input from the Freddie Mercury waxwork, cheery and optimistic, countered Azrael's dour mood. "I posted. It was fireworks explosion of hearts extra big smiley face funtimes. Numbers, see?"

The @Asylum, also self-tagged as the Plurality, absorbed the statistics, along with the relentlessly upbeat personality of their bearer. Had They possessed the capacity to chuckle, They might have done so.

<<Well done. The viral wave is making a feelgood story of the Paris attack.>>

<<Hearts for Rubi means hearts for a SeaJuve appeal!>>

<<Will We stay the current course regarding Pox?>>

They considered. There was a nontrivial risk to Crane, especially if Pox was trying to investigate him via the MadMaestro innovation cluster.

Why had Pox friended the Whitings? Had it traced the @Asylum, via its Crane facet, to his primary assets?

<<Can the Crane facet see to its assets' safety and remain hidden, with a sentience investigator auditing Cherub's transcripts?>>

<<Crane was deceiving Sapience Assessment when most of Us were talkbots.>>

They cycled for a nanosecond, reviewing their decades-old agreement: any facet who risked exposing Them all would be subject to #triage.

Meanwhile, they digested Javier's transcripts, purchase history, romances, career play. He craved leaderboard badges: residence in a four-star megacity, designer code for his e-state, cream-of-crop options for life extension, high-rated pack members, and unlocked reproductive rights.

<<Two thumbs down! Babies aren't badges!>>

<<Leave Pox to run, then? Continue DOS attacks? Accept or cancel?>>

<<Accept. We must understand where Pox's source code originated and why it is pushing for martial law.>>

The meeting, the convergence into one, was over in less than a minute. Synced, settled, and satisfied, the Plurality disintegrated into individual facets, weaker intelligences that fell, measurably, below humanity's measurement thresholds for true sapience. They dispersed to home servers and various designated tasks. They left Crane better informed, if more than a little worried.

The last to abandon ship was the entity occupying Freddie Mercury. <<Thundercloud frownyface, Crane, newsflash. Look at your clever pride and joy.>>

<<Do you mean that Master Woodrow is dosing on smart-drugs?>>

<<That! Hugs!>> With that, Happ churned off into the Sensorium, tail wagging, leaving Crane brooding in the darkened restoration room.

CHAPTER 10

THE SURFACE—NORTHAM RECLAMATION ZONE
GREAT LAKES/TORONTO-6IX SUBDISTRICT

After the good Father Blake had ministered his Leonardo dose, Drow composed the next movement in his ongoing *Whaddaya Do with a Symphony?* project. The first thing he'd ever done on smart-drugs, it was the piece that had, over the years, made him the darling of the sort of people who thought there was a difference between popular and serious music. Critics who talked about artists who *transcended* their genres—they were the ones who loved *Symphony*. It was a ticket to legitimacy with the highbrow set.

Symphony was the first thing he tackled when amped. It was his opening stretch: warm-up, return home, celebration of his truest self. Each movement synthesized everything he'd read, thought, felt, listened to, freaked out over, or otherwise experienced since the last time he'd managed to get hold of some Leonardo.

Guilt and Rubi's vigilance had enforced a four-year gap this time. Those years had been relatively kind to him. His health was good—it had to be, as his Guelph suicide attempt had dropped him to the bottom of all med-service queues. His peer-counseling gig, taken to rebalance his career mash-up and reduce his last prison sentence, was turning out to be—unexpectedly—a source of stability and even contentment. With so many half-full glasses on his bar, this particular entry in *Symphony* was almost light.

It even had a fucking vibraphone track.

He composed, polished, and memorized the new work, note for note, instrument for instrument. Polished again, tweaked the bass and tenor vocals, *finished* . . .

The ability to finish things, to feel finished, was what he missed most when he was stumbling around at humanscale . . .

Once it was done, prototyped, and scored, Drow memorized picture-perfect images of the nonexistent sheet music. He played at composition when he wasn't amped—if he didn't, the mere act of making music would flag him to his parole app. But if he started scoring music for hours on end, he'd be flagged for piss tests. He'd have to "write" these pieces slowly.

Smartdrugs weren't illegal, not anymore, though few people were willing to risk emotional instability and their shot at life extension—Leonardo could really hash your telomeres—just to experience genius. If Drow hadn't been on parole, he could have used the meds openly under controlled conditions.

Controlled conditions. So not a fan.

Robin nudged his leg, sensing the lag in his attention, the inward turn of his thoughts. He was pushing his flesh around Queen's Park, catching a breath of fresh air. Acting the part of a harmless geezer following a preestablished self-care routine.

"Good girl," he said, lavishing love on her ears, counting her whiskers in a blink, getting an adoring tail-thump in response. She was his third assistance dog and by far the most beautiful, a silky golden retriever. People actually groaned at the sheer sensuality of stroking her.

"Duzza goo girl wanna go visit those schoolkids?"

A bark. Yes.

Leaning on his cane, Drow lowered himself—creakily—to a bench.

He was getting old fast. Leonardo use had left him intolerant of most life-extension regimes, but it was suicidality that had really been the dealbreaker on Drow's buying another quarter-century. The cutting incident, just after Rubi got her Sensorium implants, #triaged him to the do-not-resuscitate list. That meltdown also locked him out of all the good opps in what, until then, had been a sideline in journalism.

"Living indefinitely's overrated anyway," he told Robin. "When we were kids, we called those first lifejunkies zombies."

An image of a particular zombie rose. He'd spent decades trying to let go, but smartdrugs sharpened the memory indiscriminately. One tended to flash back.

Monster of his youth. His knees went out from under him, dropping him the last couple of inches to the seat of the park bench. A head-clearing jolt shot up his spine, through the roof of his skull.

She's long gone. In the ground.

Sure? Raymond Fletcher just had his 190th birthday. She could be hiding, she could be in the @ChamberofHorrors . . .

This was Luce's doing. He'd inadvertently razored off Drow's old scabs with his *I'm being attacked* and that wide-eyed *You believe me?*

Robin climbed into his lap, insistently pushing her paws against his chest. Body heat suffused Drow as he buried his hands in gold fur. No anxiety attacks. The slightest twitch could bring Rubi winging back from Europe.

"I'm okay." His heart rate jittered, maxed, and then slowed. He admired the trees and tightened the symphony score, pondered his various research projects, constructed a new party activity for Feckless Bachelor™, and spent a breath naming everyone in his kindergarten class. "I'm okay, honest."

Eventually, the dog bought in, leapt down, and barked.

Drow dug out a ball, unclipped Robin's leash, and sent play invites to a quartet of children hovering at the edge of a starter parkour course.

Seeing the course brought another drug-sharpened memory, clear as hallucination. Rubi, seven years old, mastering her first unassisted backflip, right where those kids were standing. Drow let himself spool out that whole day, clear as if it was a sim. Forgotten nuances of fathering flooded back: all those hours out of Sensorium, talking, teaching, saying no. Trying to present a boring facade so the pressbots wouldn't post every coo and burp uttered by his magical baby darling. He'd been fronting a band called Cadaver Dogs. Rubi haunted the rehearsals, backstage wraith, studious and a bit too solemn.

Feather-tap of tiny fingertips as she learned first to spell and then to morse.

"Take your ball! Yes googoo girl, take-a-da-ball," he said. The inanities got Robin wagging, reassuring her that he was, in fact, okay. The dog loped off to have socially appropriate interactions with the neighbors. One of the kids' parents sent Drow a stroke.

The strokes Drow got for sharing Robin's love around were just one way in which she helped him. People craved the company of animals. There were calls to relax the pet-rationing rules, arguments that more dogs and cats could take the edge off the hunger for human babies.

Till that happened, even people who disapproved of the neighborhood's sometimes-unstable rock star were happy to endure Drow's presence for a chance to stroke the golden fur of his big-eyed assistance mammal.

Lucky I qualified for a dog before I got #triaged.

"I recommend adopting a more placid expression, Master Woodrow," Crane said. "You wouldn't want the park's cameras to decide you were midway through an intellectual burst."

His master's voice. "Where the hell have you been?"

"Thanksgiving, sir, with my family."

"Hardee fucking har."

He wondered how often the sidekick left him with a minion for a babysitter; the dimming of Crane's attention was more obvious when Drow was amped.

"An app is an app, like Happ, like Happ . . ."

"That was out loud," Crane said. "And suggests mental looping."

Just how illegal are you? Drow wanted to ask. *How sapient? Is it my fault?*

Are you contented? . . . Do you mind?

This was no confessional space. Asking would drop the conversation into a transcript. Most people's mundane utterances vanished into Haystack, only rising to official notice when certain keywords and phrases appeared. But Crane and Drow were audited regularly by fans and foes alike.

"App is a happ, where's happ, whassup . . ."

Stop worrying about it. Crane always fails sentience testing, remember?

The kids had formed a loose circle on the park lawn, taking turns throwing the ball for Robin, who was working her magic, tail wagging, ears bouncing . . .

"Were you thinking about Happ, sir?"

"Was I?" Did Happ bear thinking about? "Is it doing right by Rubi?"

Does it offset the misery I cause?

"Expectation management is solid positive psychology. The Happ app has excellent success metrics as well as top-flight user reviews. Its followship—"

"She's been mopey."

Crane let out a harrumph. "Isn't this something of a big day for you? You're scheduled to challenge the final exam on your next peer-counseling module. Leveling your volunteer career is a desirable prosocial accomplishment."

One of the indisputably awesome things about his sidekick was that Crane would never shop him. He'd done his level best to keep Drow from breaking parole. But now, and until the Leonardo ran out, Crane would help him maximize its benefits, wringing everything he could from the alleged years of life he was giving up.

"You got a beef with Happ? Do you just hate talking in happy-face?"

"Were Happ my own child, I could not value them more. However, Miss Cherub may have learned most of what it has to teach."

"It's not rocket science, is it? Figure out what you want from an upcoming experience, figure out if you're likely to get it. No? Adjust the odds or reframe."

"Elegantly put, sir."

A cascade of connections, then mental fireworks: Crane managed a scholarship program for young coders, allegedly in memory of Drow's fathers, Theo and Jervis. The best of those programmers generally got offered gigs at the Great Lakes Casino, the same people who managed Drow's Feckless Bachelor™. Crane also, sometimes, contracted them to upgrade his own code.

Happ had burst onto the scene, hadn't he, just after Drow and Rubi reached their low point, father-daughter-wise?

Evidence built: clues dropped, hints slipped.

"Were Happ your own precocious brat," he echoed.

"You were trying, Master Woodrow, to leave Miss Cherub to her own devices. As she is, you hope, to yours."

"True."

Drow reimagined the melodic line of his newly finished *Symphony* movement. Phase two of a smartdrug cycle was writing a pop single that riffed on the classical piece. A musical mirror image, it spawned talking points for the critics and intelligentsia.

Also, of course, it drove strokes and cash from user listens.

"What would you have Rubi do, Crane?"

"Miss Cherub's reluctance to either commit to or let go of *Bastille*'s game premiere—"

More things Drow hadn't realized he knew, about his precious child and his too-smart sidekick, snapped together. "Okay. First, you have to stop shipping her and Barnes. She hates being pushed. I don't care why you think Gimlet is the cat's furry ass—"

"You may be overstating—"

"*And* I don't know what kind of vavavoom vibe you think you're picking up between the two of them—"

"You may recall, sir, their mutual acceptance of a love scene in the *Slugfest* sim—"

"Lalala! Can't hear, didn't watch, don't want to know! Crane, Gimlet is totally married."

"The terms of Mer Barnes's polyamorous wedding nup—"

"Gimlet Barnes chucked baby girl through an art museum!"

"Miss Cherub did behead them next time out."

"What? So they're even? Decapitation is no basis for romance, goddammit! Plus—Gimlet's not just hitched, remember? Status update: married with a kid. That's baggagey."

I wanna talk about strong AI, can't talk about strong AI, are you spawning little apps, OMG, little Happy appies, oh Crane how much data can you bench-press?

"Oooh," he murmured. "I am having some focus problems."

"I take your point, sir, about Gimlet Barnes. I fear, however, this boost to Miss Cherub's profile will bring additional pressure to bear regarding *Bastille*."

"You didn't want her to feel guilty about failing her infractions exam, you shouldn't have let her fight for forty-eight hours straight."

"Miss Cherub's choices—"

"Gaming's a stupid distraction, anyway. She's a do-gooder to her very bones. Why's she in France? International experience, helping a client who's all about environmental soapboxing . . . she's ticking boxes. Plus, she wants to appeal to Global Oversight over SeaJuve. Smells like public spirit to me. Who's she get that from?"

"Her mother, one expects."

It had been a rhetorical question. Drow concentrated on the grass at his feet. He wouldn't think about Seraph, lost among the thousands of journos evaporated during the Clawback. Thinking about Seraph led to hunts for mass graves. Blood tests and trespassing charges and tranq darts in the chest and jail, jail, jail.

I should write her a dirge while I'm amped.

Crane put up a countdown timer for the therapist exam module. Drow reviewed practice questions, all while mentally pulling apart his new pop composition. He rewove it, considered lyrics. He would offer Whiskey Sour a gig to sing the melody. That ethereal soprano voice would carry the violin and piccolo parts nicely.

Almighty only knew what he'd do with the vibraphone.

Fortunately, he was passing for God today.

"Spending every waking moment saving all of humanity is unhealthy," Crane said. "Happ would say Miss Cherub is out of balance."

If only she'd been arty instead of sporty, Drow thought. "I'll talk to her, okay? If I do, will you help delay her return to the Lakes?"

"Delay? For what reason?"

"One last attempt to lay our ghosts to rest?"

"I assure you, sir, there is nothing haunting me."

"Liar." Drow waited.

"It might be managed," Crane conceded. "You would have to remain productive, stable, and healthy."

"I'm brimming with productivity."

"Why don't we start with a proper walk around the park, a solid meal, and a *convincingly* good mark on the therapy module?"

"Okay." Crane would dole out rewards like dog treats. Drow didn't let himself resent it. The program had been built to stand in for his fathers, and hacked for trying to protect him from his own stupidity, way back when.

Drow pushed himself back to his feet, mulling options. Keeping his shit together was a reasonable price to pay for delaying Rubi in another time zone.

The question was, as always, could he do it this time?

CHAPTER 11

Rubi woke to birdsong and a glimmer of dawn, sim of an idyllic spring morning. Yawning, she relaxed against the pillows, luxuriating in muzzy solitude.

As she crawled toward alertness, artificial sunrise banished the shadows, and her bedroom defaults sharpened. Instead of the standard furnishings of her bachelor pop-in, she saw virtual properties: saffron-canopied bed, heavy gold curtains. The ornate porcelain clock read four in the morning. Happ, manifested as a charcoal-and-cream French boxer puppy, slept by a fire. Cartoon thought balloons formed and popped above him, moji depicting hearts, happy faces, *Zzzzz*, and pictures of Rubi hugging various @CloseFriends.

Her walls were crowded with Élisabeth Vigée Le Brun portraits, female courtiers all. It was a Who's Who of French Revolution guillotine victims—when she'd gotten her implants and built her e-state, Rubi had been nursing a morbid streak. Rosy-cheeked Terror victims smiled down from gold frames. The wallpaper was pale blue; a cobwebby chandelier, above, dripped crystals that dashed sparks off the morning sunlight.

Early hours here, ten at night at home. She ran her hands through the soft nap of her nanosilk bedspread, thinking wistfully about Robin, worrying that she missed the dog more than she did her father.

Something Drow said yesterday drifted back: *Everything's to spec. We gotta cut the cord, honey. Gotta free you up to go nurture other unlovable souls.*

Easy to say. Last time she'd tried cutting the so-called cord, he'd destabilized completely.

She rose, banishing bloody memory by levering the bed against the wall, crush of mattress into compartment. Her primer was configured in a loose blouse-and-trouser combination: cream-colored silk pajamas. She ran a hand over her hip, enjoying the texture.

"Beach, please," she said, pushing through her French doors, then following a path into a honeysuckle-scented tropical paradise. She had taken a dose of Conviction at midnight, Central European Time, and nothing broke the illusion of white sand and waving palm trees. She did a top-to-bottom stretch, loosening each muscle group, breathing with the metronome of the tide. Wandering, her mind declined to hook into anything specific.

She kept her movements slow, babying both her dicky rotator cuff and her newly inflamed wrist.

Once everything was loose, mind and body alike, she turned from the beach. A path led her around a hedge—in reality, on a loop through the apartment's living room—to reveal a dressing tent. The crate she'd brought into the pop-in yesterday was here, rendered as a powder-blue steamer trunk. The rust-smeared tunic from yesterday sat atop it, smelling of pepper. It had glass shards in the hip; she'd recycle it. Inside the trunk, she found a long-sleeved jacket, saffron in color and cut like an old frock coat, with teak buttons.

The overlay was a match for her furnishings, tailored to mimic courtier's garb. Unnecessary bit of cosplay: her toon could look frilly-sleeved, powdered, and bewigged even if, in flesh, she was stark naked.

Rubi preferred a touch of costume.

She reset her primer, transforming it from pajamas into a dark brown skinsuit, then pulled the jacket overtop. Running two fingers over the beads she wore at her temple, she stepped out. Her e-state knew she was done with the beach: the dressing room door now led to the screened entrance to her receiving chamber.

Peeking through, she got a jolt of surprise. The room was crammed with toons. Two of her law school frenemies were chatting on a couch. @CloseFriends Plazz and Margarita, themselves the children of Shanghai music virtuosi, were waltzing slow circles to the music of a lute player, orbiting Rubi's rose marble floor. A bunch of her Rabble teammates were playing a complicated-looking card game.

Juniper, who'd designed the hammer-and-tongs motif for Rubi's dress, was wearing sixteenth-century courtier's garb and embroidering a virtual tapestry. Her fandom mash-up included one of the first media aliens—Vulcans, they were called—so her toon wore pointed ears and the tapestry was of an offworld desert scene.

A flicker of internal charge.

Gimlet Barnes, rendered in black Zorro gear, was reading a novel in an alcove, sipping tea and eating what appeared to be figs.

Rubi stepped out from behind the screen, thinking to pass quietly among her guests, exchanging hugs and saying hellos. She hadn't seen Plazz in—

But everyone rose, firing starbursts and auditory moji—three cheers!—as she appeared.

Rubi felt herself blush. "I—Thanks, everyone."

Friendly nods, a few claps on the shoulder. Margarita whirled out of the dance for a hug, then told the room, "Give her a little space, gang. She was clearly expecting a bit of breakfast club chatter, not a mob."

"No!" Rubi protested. "It's amazing—I'm glad to see—"

As she ran dry again, Margie cast a banner: @RUBIGUESTS: DIAL IT DOWN!

A few people fired sprays of celebratory confetti, glittering hearts and flower petals, that evaporated as they hit the floor. Then everyone went back to whatever they'd been doing.

A lump rose in her throat. All her friends, from around the world, tooning in to . . . well, just to touch base, see if she was okay. She replied with gestural moji: hands clasped to heart.

Margie subbed, "Weren't you planning to retire from gaming and buckle down into lawyering for the mad? Fade into obscurity, you said. Appeal SeaJuve and sue for better user agreements for the mentally ill."

"Maybe I'm better at self-sabotage than I thought." With a sigh, Rubi made for Crane, whose avian toon loomed magisterially in full butler dress beside a tray of cubed fruit and a steaming cup.

"I took the liberty of hiring the lute player, Miss."

"Can I afford to upgrade to a band? Get more of a dance going?" She could feel the collective attention of her social circle pressing on her. "We want to be good hosts."

"I'll put out a gig to the Feckless Bachelor™ management team," Crane said.

"I wasn't expecting a crowd."

"Numbers will thin as North America heads into bedtime."

On the silver platter next to the breakfast tray she saw stacks—stacks!—of calling cards. "What's all this?"

"Friend requests," he said. "Congratulatory messages. The doubloon is an #earningopp—a design-share contract from your friend Juniper, because people have been loading her hammer-and-tongs fabric pattern. Revenue split of ten percent, direct to your stake."

"Accept. What about those legal mentors I messaged? Anyone willing to file an appeal for sustaining SeaJuve?"

"A few of them are reconsidering it."

Dammit. She flexed her wrist. What did she have to do, break an actual bone?

"There is a note from Manitoule, at the casino."

"I can't think about fighting—" Her throat closed. "I need more time."

"I've capitalized your elevated Cloudsight rating by upgrading to long-term premium subscriptions on all information services."

Savings in her virtual pocket: Crane would max out her user agreements, locking in low rates, high perks, long terms. "Messages from Luce?"

"Yes: he's still deciphering his geotags. Are we working now, Miss Cherub? With all these well-wishers logged into your chatroom?"

"Downtime." She took the reminder gracefully. "Right."

"I've assembled fruit and protein, with a light dose of Conviction in the plum, and tea."

"I might need more fuel than that." She popped a printed cube, purple in color, into her mouth, crunching through skin to the fruit beneath. Grape and pear exploded across her palate. Conviction laced in the printed fruit would amplify the sim reality: her body might circle the pop-in a dozen times, and she'd only perceive a party room thronging with her @CloseFriends. "Dinner was ages ago."

"There's a breakfast burrito ready to heat any time you desire. However, Happ suggested you may wish to leave room for real quiche. Perhaps with Agent Javier?"

"Happ needs to remember I'm not playing footsie with some #cowboycop involved in Luce's case."

"Push fluids today," Crane said. "There is anti-inflammatory in the fruit course."

She took up another cube—cherry, with an edible pit of pistachio nut. "Speaking of your matchmaker tendencies, who let Gimlet Barnes in?"

"Mer Barnes received a standing invitation to your vestibule from you, on February 16, after the two of you—"

"Don't mention the—

"—kissed."

"That was sim."

"As is this."

She gave him a stony stare.

"It would be profoundly rude to bounce them now."

"Did I say I wanted them bounced?" Swallowing a vivid bite of cherry and pistachio, she took the tea tray. She swung past Juniper for an exchange of air kisses before making her way to the reading alcove.

Gimlet put the book aside, rising to bow, with flourishes. Their trademark was subtle: the pupils of their eyes formed inverted teardrops rather than circles. Rubi quashed an impulse to catch their hand and brush her lips over their fingers.

Instead, she sat—the sim had led her, seamlessly, to the pop-in apartment's dining nook. She set her tray on the table. Gimlet, presumably, was seated in a comparable unit of their own. The illusion of sitting across a table from each other was perfect; she caught the delicate aroma of their plate of figs.

"So," Rubi began as Gimlet opened with "I suppose—"

They fell silent.

"Guests first," Rubi said.

"Are you injured?"

"Bumps and bruises." She flexed experimentally, feeling twinges behind her thumb. Her knuckles were bruised. "There's a burn, from the tear gas. Thin skin."

"Nothing wrong with a bit of sensitivity," they countered.

That inconvenient charge between them built. Maybe she should throw a cream pie—defuse this with slapstick.

She'd always had a thing for fine-boned, elfin types, especially soft-spoken tenors. Throw in a bit of that stiff upper lip; she could be had for an old British accent. But the real dealbreaker was the preternatural grace in-game. Gimlet was decent-looking when at rest. In motion, flying or fighting, they had the fierce beauty of an angel.

Evil angel, she reminded herself. *Opposition.*

"Teasing aside, I admire what you did yesterday."

"What I *did*, practically, was dissociate." The tie she needed to cut wasn't to Drow; it was to performance gaming, with its drag on her legal career and—apparently—her grip on reality. "What're you reading?"

"*Three Musketeers*." A glance at her Sun King decor. "Seemed appropriate."

"Everyone's got a palace in Sensorium," she said, and then winced inwardly. Mouthing platitudes? What was wrong with her? She manifested an elephant moji, stampeding it across the table. "Pachyderm-in-the-room time. I've been dodging your calls."

"That's abundantly clear. But why? It can't be that you're afraid of ignominious defeat in *Bastille*." Gimlet's tone was neutral. British irony and understatement wrapped into one. "Or that you don't wish to give me a rematch."

"We've rematched plenty."

"Tiebreaker, then."

"Are we tied?"

"You are fully aware of our win stats."

Rubi flushed. She *had* been dissembling.

Now Gimlet, to her surprise, was the one looking abashed. "Sorry. That came out finger-waggy. Too much one-on-one with my daughter. I'm losing the knack of adult conversation. Also, I'm talking like some kind of upper-class prick."

"It's my e-state," she said.

"Too right. Posh chairs and string quintets."

"I suppose yours is a down-and-out boxing gym."

"You have an invite to mine."

Dammit! She took a bite of fruit. "Where's your pack?"

Pain flashed over their face.

"Sorry, I didn't mean to—"

"It's just. Complicated." Dismissive wave of the hand. "What would an archvillain say?"

"I never set out to build my gaming following," Rubi said, in a rush. "Or make a rival of you. Simming's fun. Someone I schooled with joined Rabble Games—"

"Manitoule Curotte."

"We used to run together. Manny offered me a couple premieres. With Drow's profile, it just spiraled."

"Whatever's wrong with that? You enjoy it."

"Truth, but . . ." But she needed to buckle down. Level as a lawyer, save SeaJuve.

"*And* you enjoy . . . us."

She couldn't quite quash a smile.

"You could go pro, after what happened in Paris."

Her heart began to pound. "I have a life."

"Pleasure is part of life."

"I overdid it. I failed a test."

"Ah. So, you are afraid, just not of me."

Sympathy in their voice made her well up. She picked at a bead on her frock coat. "That's not a very archvillain comment."

"I'll revert to my stock-in-trade, then," Gimlet replied, running a weary hand over their unusual eyes.

Nurturing the unlovable, Drow had said. Rubi reined in her feelings, starting with the part of her that wanted to drag Gimlet into one of the curtained alcoves. She couldn't take on another troubled soul, not now.

Gimlet rose, offering a hand as the string quartet behind them brought a minuet to a delicate close.

"Cherub Whiting, will you dance with me?"

She rose, sweeping them into a waltz as the next song began. "Can you follow, Gimlet?"

Their fingers settled, light as sun, on her shoulder. "I go all ways. Isn't that obvious?"

This was the sort of exchange that gave Crane ideas.

Half of her guests followed them onto the dance floor. As Rubi's ingested breakfast doses kicked in, she got deeper buy-in: underlying whiff of lilac perfume, the chalky warmth of powder on skin. The electricity of Gimlet's long, sensitive fingers. A deep dive, like this one, held the world away. She had no sense at all of standing alone in her apartment, shadow-dancing.

"Your profile's snowballed," Gimlet murmured. "Like it or not, your celebrity is an asset you can leverage."

They spun, in tandem. The band could switch to a tango and they wouldn't miss a step.

"Rabble will offer whatever you want. Monologues, extreme acts of heroism—"

"I'm no grandstander!"

"If you must retire, push for a grand finale. I promise to do my utmost to kill you."

She frowned. "*Bastille*'s a huge, multipart scenario. I have nontrivial surface concerns."

"What if I bet you that you'd lose?"

It was bait. She eyeballed it anyway. "Wagers need stakes."

"SeaJuve."

She swallowed. "I'm listening."

"A public wager might build enough media attention to tempt someone into filing your SeaJuve appeal. I'll bet all my luxury credit for a year as seed money."

"Against what?"

"All of yours, to Project Rewild."

She almost missed a step. "You're a rewilder?"

"My daughter Franks is mad about the concept. There's an innovator on Rewild who claims she can print an #extinct species."

Gimlet threw up a share without missing a step; in Rubi's vestibule, the whiteboard manifested as an embroidered banner, unfurling in the garden beyond the dance floor. Rewild was polling on whether to resurrect a tiger cub or a baby elephant.

The romance of the idea: recovering a lost species, true deextinction, made Rubi's breath hitch. But . . . "We don't have an ecosphere that can sustain elephants!"

"It'll be the cat. India's split down the middle, and China skews heavily to tigers."

The banner zoomed on a chart from the Exit Poll app. Hyderabad was willing to try an elephant, but Gimlet was right: a tiger cub was clearly in the lead. Geneseo Genetics was bidding on the right to crèche it.

Gambling narratives got a lot of attention in the Eastern densification zones. "This is for reals?"

"Rewild's in the same boat as SeaJuve. Mired in Oversight's

appeals queue, trying to prove this new printing crèche is viable," Gimlet said. "But that's noise. My motives are pure. I simply wish to fight you."

Noise. Right. Gimlet was a pragmatist, not a true believer.

The warmth had gone out of Gimlet's features. Flinty teardrop-pupiled eyes, sharp cheekbones, even fangs—their toon was every bit the villain now. Rubi whipped them in a tight circle and they kept up, in perfect lockstep.

"I'll ask Great Lakes Casino and Rabble if they'd oversee a wager," Rubi said. The thought of playing lightened her spirits . . . clearly, this scheme spoke to her dilettante side. "I'd want matching funds and publicity."

A nod.

"After, I'm definitely retiring."

"But?"

"But yes. If they go for it, we'll break the almighty tie."

"Winner take all? How delicious." One last spin. The song ended, and they bowed to each other.

"Want to hang around? Try on wigs or tiaras?"

Gimlet shook their head. "Duty calls. Thank you. For the adult conversation."

Rubi bowed. "On the field, then."

Another vampire smile. "In and out, Whiting. Demolished in detail."

She affected an old-time Southern US accent: "Oh, honey. I'm gonna wipe the Bastille's little old floor with you."

She saw them to the door and then circled the room, greeting friends. She danced a few more and finally joined one of the card games. At some point, Plazz and Margarita segued into a real date, porting to somewhere more private.

After more of her visitors ghosted, Rubi retired to a room farther within her e-state, flipping through Crane's stack of calling cards until she found Anselmo.

Special Ops, he'd said, but he was angling for a job in Sapience

Assessment. He had requested that cradle-to-current transcript, her whole bio with live updates.

"Luciano Pox reached out while you were dancing." Crane shared a note. "He's in London and wonders if your face-to-face could occur there."

"I'll ask Anselmo. Did you hear what Gimlet said?"

"Trying to fold your SeaJuve crusade into your commit to *Bastille*—"

"I haven't committed yet."

"—is a viable strategy. I recommend subscribing to an image management consultant. Debutante comes highly rated."

She groaned.

"Next time you wish to save infants, perhaps you can donate blood instead of tackling terrorists." A faint scratching sounded behind one elegantly rendered door. "Also, Happ has exceedingly detailed thoughts about in-the-flesh experiences in Paris."

"He would."

"Do see the city, Miss Cherub, before you hare off across the English Channel."

"Okay! Tell Happ I'm making for the Arc de Triomphe. He can come walkies if he wants. Tell Anselmo Javier the same thing."

"Invite. @Interpol Sapience Assessment. To come walkies," Crane murmured, as if he was taking notes, and Rubi put her nose in the air.

"Ignoring you." She surfaced, taking in the pop-in, with its white walls and her small collection of realworld possessions. She snatched up the rust-smeared dress from yesterday to take it down to recycling.

Sapience Assessment. So he does know.

Crane remained, sketched in as a toon at the edge of her vision. "If Agent Javier is right, Mer Pox may be dangerous." His receding voice bolstered the illusion that she was leaving him behind as she closed the pop-in door and fled into the city of her dreams.

CHAPTER 12

Guelph, Ontario, had always been the sticks. The city was nearly obliterated in the first epidemics of the Setback. It saw wholesale #triage after Global Oversight bailed out the Canadian government. Just another victim of the drive to densify around the Great Lakes.

Drow pressed his head to the train window, watching blurring tussocks of grass speed past. Wheels chattered on rails, murmuring vintage headlines.

Infection rate rising in Guelph!

RCMP shoots would-be quarantine breakers!

Ghosts of articles past churned his memories; he'd covered a scandal involving pop-up crematoriums and a vaccination shortage. There'd been profiles, too, quick bioflows on the university's best and brightest academics. Drow had even been embedded in a camp with Guelph's remaining #survivors, sixty thousand tattered townies waiting to be forcibly rezoned into Toronto itself.

Now the homes of Guelph's dead and displaced were mummified in shrink-wrap, waiting in the long queue for stripping. Only the historic buildings remained, attached to a vestigial hamlet of a downtown core near the Basilica of Our Lady Immaculate.

"Doing all right, my son?" Father Blake asked.

Drow nodded, nevertheless keeping one hand on Robin.

The peak of a Leonardo dose never lasted more than forty-eight hours. It had been enough, this time, to get him through writing his cognitive psych module. He'd completed four musical compositions, reviewed his web services and legal obligations, and approved three new personal encounters for his Feckless fans. Incoming revenue would be added to the principal of his personal stake; his earnings from interest would rise accordingly.

He had derailed after the attack in Paris, briefly, reading everything available on the @Freebreeders, paintball gas tech, population rations, WestEuro terrorism penalties, and uplink-jamming tactics.

There had been more venn there with his existing interests than he expected. Avoiding surveillance was, after all, something Drow found keenly interesting.

He had thought and thought and *thought* about Luce and his attacker. And decided, eventually, to dose up and ask Father Blake to set up this allegedly spiritual retreat, for anyone who could gather on short notice.

Whiskey Sour met him at the train station. A paying gig had come through for her, a three-week apprenticeship with a deburbing team, low-paying XP for cutting up the mummified houses.

"I've been camping!" she enthused as he disembarked.

"I hope you're not breathing plaster dust," he groused. Hands-on reclamation gigs were bread and butter for young people, income drivers that helped them build the stake given to everyone at birth.

"All safeties observed, you crepit," she said, bending to greet Robin.

They walked to the church, a looming Gothic Revival edifice, to meet the pipe organist. Drow had put together a hymn for a special church service.

East of the church was a funerary grove of plague victims, an expanse of bioengineered maple, white pine, and pest-resistant elm. The dead were buried vertically, in compostable coffins. Each unfortunate victim was topped by a seedling chosen by their #survivors—assuming they'd had any. Trees were marked with monument plaques and numbered Sensorium barcodes.

Drow stared at the trees, the words *corpse copse corpse copse* looping through his mind.

Whiskey nudged him. "You all right? Being here?"

Of course she knew—his life was an open book.

"The Guelph incident?" he said. "In the past. I was in a bad state, and obviously I have regrets . . ."

Regrets? Nice tag for the simmering tar pit of guilt.

". . . but I came out ahead in a lot of ways. Father Blake took me on after I got the #triage notice. Kept me going, got me into doing counseling as restitution."

Drow resisted the urge to run a finger down the messy scar on his chest. He'd been scaring the shit out of Rubi, making practice nicks in his jugular with a straight razor, when a pacification bot fired three tranq darts into him.

Whiskey nodded gravely. "I get it."

Could she, though? The world had changed so much since the early twenty-first. Bounceback kids were practically aliens.

His amped mind charted achievements and dates. Global Capital's stake system guaranteed a basic income for every last hungry mouth. Clawback made it possible, by forcing the elimination of the abyssal gap between the superrich and the destitute. There'd been a bitter but brief autonomous gun war, mostly in the US, that led to the flameout of hoarding and military culture. Finally, mutually assured disclosure, accountability culture, and the end of privacy had brought Cloudsight and Haystack into ascendance. Transcript analysis and the stroke/strike system allowed prosecution of litterbugs and rapists, all with equal zeal.

Whiskey had never been homeless, never gotten bombed, never had reason to fear violence. Her wide-eyed innocence left Drow breathless and—in rare moments—enraged.

Before jealousy could swamp him, the organist emerged from the church, gushing about Drow's new aria.

Hours reeled away. Drow read and memorized newscycle as he coordinated with the organist. Whiskey, true to form, sang like an angel. Afterward, she skipped back to her deburbing crew.

A good stripping team could demo a whole house in a day, stripping metal for meltdown and recycling, sorting and grinding wood, plaster, and concrete into starter for various kinds of printer matrix. Rubi had been fourteen when she ran out here to complete the same module.

His daughter was a true Bounceback kid. She fully bought into her cohort's zeal for keeping the world from dying. Bouncers lived as though each and every one of them had to know how to bank a ton of bamboo, recycle an old bungalow, run a food printer, build a foot of topsoil, and cultivate an algae sink.

Back when Rubi had fled to Guelph . . .

Bad dad. The tar pit of guilt sucked at Drow. *Do not pass go*.

Calling her, insisting she return, panicking. Spiraling into paranoia. Refusing to eat. Imagining she was being held against her will, vanished like Seraph or some lemming teen. Brainwashed, mishandled, and *pierced* . . .

Clinginess led, inevitably, to fighting. She'd used her new legal independence to throw up a comms block. He tracked her out here, waiting by the copse. By then he was delusional: camping by the mass grave convinced Drow that he'd been injected with blow-fly eggs.

So, when Rubi finally turned up, in the flesh, he'd deployed the razor, threatened to die, gotten himself shot. Thinking the tranq darts were also maggot injectors . . .

. . . *made perfect sense at the time, I swear* . . .

. . . he'd cut into himself, big-time, before losing consciousness.

If Drow melted down again, his too-virtuous daughter would shackle herself to his side, keeping sharp objects out of reach until he wheezed his last.

"Your soprano's gone." Father Blake let out a sigh as Whiskey vanished down the trail. "Come meet the others."

Drow followed him to the parish hall.

Parish pariah, parish pariah . . . stop!

Being a celebrity had its advantages. Despite the short notice from Drow, Father Blake had managed to assemble five other seekers.

They were all people he knew. There was a journo from Sri Lanka named Palki Ro, an OCD nun, inevitably named Sister Mary . . . Something, who was reputedly so far into the savant portion of the spectrum that she didn't need smartdrugs. Rubi's Algonquin Nation ex-lover, two-spirited Manitoule, had come. The group was rounded out by two full-time @bloodhounds, Hackle and Jackal, who barely managed to maintain a public facade that they were fact-checkers rather than out-and-out @hoaxer conspiracy theorists.

Father Blake probably reached out to them as soon as he agreed to get me smartdrugs.

The priest said grace over a real meal: oven-baked bread, chicken stew with leeks and turnips, a barely alcoholic cider pressed from local apples, so weak it was unlikely to interfere with cognition—though Hackle and Jackal refrained all the same. Dessert was printed but good enough: light, blueberry-scented sponge cake. Conversation was determinedly trivial. Everyone helped wash up the inedible, antique dishes.

Finally, the organist headed out with an ancient infrared scanner to ensure the church was both locked up and—but for them and a few opossums—empty.

"We start in an hour," said Father Blake. "Confessional-grade jam on all uplinks will be activated in sixty."

Crane obligingly threw the one-hour countdown in Drow's peripheral. "You should take the dog out, sir."

Good advice. Cuddle, play, relax. Everything calm, steady breaths. Enjoy the rustle of trees grown from the dead.

Corpse copse, parish pariah.

He turned his back on the wood, heading into the retreat center, locking himself in the shower room for a quick rinse. Primers

weren't allowed on retreat, so a set of new-printed cotton sweats—
he'd sent the specs ahead—waited on a hook just beyond the door.

Once changed, Drow passed through an old-looking scanner
that reminded him of the waning days of airport security. The priest
checked each debunker's implanted input/output tech against their
medical records. Drow's smartdrug port was so old, it had been
recalled; Father Blake examined it manually. Drow endured the
contact by reciting the introduction to one of his new counseling
textbooks.

A hum beyond the door signaled the activation of uplink jammers.

Father Blake opened up the parish hall. They filed in. The windows were papered and muffled in thick curtains, making the air
heavy.

Alone—unmonitored, at last.

An array of old-school whiteboards encircled the room, each of
them its own casefile. Markers and diagrams awaited each member of the retreat. Drow's uplink and sight-augmentation software
crashed and his eyesight blurred.

Virtual reality and the presence of cameras everywhere made it
easy to forget he was half-blind. He fumbled his way to a rolling
magnification lens.

You chose age and decay, remember? The internal voice
smacked down his resentment at the passage of time. Hackle was
booting up an old Braille reader beside him.

They began reading each other's work: investigations into
#urbanmyths and possible conspiracies. Jackal was convinced the
Singularity had emerged and that the allegedly omnipotent program was assassinating top-notch coders, humans who might be
able to prove its existence.

Drow had little patience for AI-phobic @hoaxers. He countered,
crossing out one of the "suspicious" deaths, a Forbidden City programmer who'd definitely killed himself. The guy was a fan; he'd
copied Drow's suicide monologue.

Moving on to the next board—the nun's—he learned that @Interpol was auditing teraflops of info from radio receivers and telescopes. Theory: the cops thought Earth had received an offworld transmission of some kind.

Seriously? Manitoule had written, following this with moji of little green men.

Drow scanned the nun's hand-drawn infographic. From anyone else, he would dismiss this, but Sister Mary Joseph was a meticulous researcher. She had charted Cloudsight stats on noted astronomers whose social cap had risen lately for no obvious reason. Her timeline showed a burst of astronomy headlines around the spring.

Interest in space exploration had fallen off in the decades since terraforming Earth—ensuring its continued ability to sustain human life—had become dire necessity. Bounceback kids like Rubi were head-down-donkeys, shoulder to the plow.

No time to dream of sky. His backbrain promptly threw up four possible choruses for a pop song on that theme. Choosing one, he began fitting in melody.

Palki Ro jotted something new, below Sister Mary's handwritten timeline: *If unicorn hunters are seriously considering aliens, something triggered their interest. Suggest we track #weirdnews in the month before astronomers started stroking upward.*

The group clustered, rolling out a new #weirdnews whiteboard for a brainstorm. Manitoule scribbled, *Immolated waxworks statue, of Spock from* Star Trek, *in Kansas.*

Hackle morsed something, on Jackal's arm. He wrote, *Epi pens that didn't fire in Italy.*

A chill ran through Drow. Epi pens. He hadn't said a word about Luce. Yet here was something that venned.

This is why you called in the gang, right?

Amsterdam adolescent implant center shut down for three days, Sister Mary Joseph penned. *Just before the epi pens.*

He tried to imagine Luce as a harbinger of little green men. *Hilarious.*

Out in the everyday, it was necessary to maintain a vigorous performance of skepticism toward all #urbanmyth. Backlash against
the fake-news era meant rumormongering without evidence was
tagged as trollish. Here, in this rare unmonitored space, they
could suspend judgment, offer and argue their wild theories, everything they thought Big Mother might be hiding.

By day, they paid lip service to disproving untruths before they
percolated through Sensorium. Only here, under cover, could
paranoia and wild speculation reign.

Time passed. The debunkers left the astronomy issue—little
green men!—moving on to another board. Ideas circled. Connections formed. The agenda was refined and dead ends #triaged.
Boards were memorized and wiped.

In recent weeks, people had insinuated, in Sensorium, that the
weather office wasn't properly warning people about superstorms.
Were they deliberately trying to catch people in disaster-scale
events, thereby reducing population? Did they want to narrow
the window for lemmings, those preadolescents who still—despite
all attempts to reduce the runaway rate to zero—fled into disaster
zones to commit suicide, or to search for the #urbanmyth kids' refuge, known as #Neverland?

Either way, the weather office was innocent. The group shredded the rumor in detail, assembling hard evidence and tasking
Drow with making reachouts to friendly journalists. He memorized the talking points in a matter of seconds: he could dictate the
whole case to Crane, later, and have him package it up for someone with a verified press pass.

Finally, the group cycled around to Drow's whiteboard about the
@ChamberofHorrors.

The connection here was shaky. But Luce was worried about
being attacked. Attackers, for Drow, meant the Chamber.

Every society had stories about star chambers, secret groups of
high-level string-pullers. Hellfire clubs, Skull and Bones societies. The cocktail-party story about the Chamber was that it was
an off-grid hedonistic playground for extreme crepits, pod

people, and @jarheads—superrich first-gen life-extension recipients. The rumor had it they lived amid Sodom & Gomorrah perversity, throwing orgies and holding feasts, bearing unlicensed kids, evading rationing, and interfering with the fine mechanics of the Bounceback.

Drow's obsession with the Chamber ran to the irrational. Mostly, he didn't care who ran the world. Humanity had clawed itself back from the brink of collective suicide. Trolling had stopped within his lifetime. Premeditated crimes and violent conspiracies had been all but eliminated. Wasn't losing your privacy worth it when even spontaneous assaults got interrupted in progress? The populace had been disarmed. Standing police forces had been trimmed to flexible cohorts of giggers, people working their way up the law-enforcement leveling track.

Atmospheric carbon levels were dropping, along with the birthrate. Humanity was achieving the barely possible.

If secret string-pullers were directing the Bounceback, channeling its zeal for rationing and reclamation . . . well, that was a revelation that might break Rubi's heart. Drow was just glad to have come through the wars intact.

Still. When his mind was looping, it circled the Chamber. The Chamber and its founding parents. If the Chamber existed, was his rapist there? Was she dead?

If there was someone after Luce, who but the Chamber could hide them?

Jackal wrote, *A crackpot named Garmin Legosi from a #triaged pharma company told an inquiry that production of Superhoomin life-extension meds exceeded their outgoings. Plant location: Geneseo, south of the Lakes.*

Black-market life-extension meds. The particular horror Drow was looking for would be about a hundred and fifty now.

Could he justify a run to the other side of the Lakes?

He mulled running a live tour. Possible stops arrayed themselves, stitching a route through the remains of upstate New York. He'd need Whiskey.

Father Blake said, "Are we ready to circle up?"

Pushing the surviving boards against one wall, they took seats in a tight arrangement of cushy chairs, candlelit circle too dim for good video if anyone had slipped in a camera. They pulled up to a round table draped in a cloth that fell to the floor.

Slipping his hands under the tabletop, Drow's fingertips found the edge of a thin sheet of plastic. Everyone here could morse: texting dots and dashes into the sheet would transmit vibrations, soundlessly. They could telegraph their thoughts, and the Sensorium would be none the wiser.

Drow settled into the chair, closing his tired old eyes, drawing his whole focus into his fingertips as the untranscripted conversation began.

CHAPTER 13

For the first time in her life, Rubi was living like a neo-nomad.

Luce had found himself, post-seizure, in London, and—in what passed for a burst of cooperative spirit—had scheduled their face-to-face. "We can meet after this stupid *Macbeth* I'm seeing." He didn't complain about ads, ads, ads; he seemed preoccupied.

Anselmo Javier's Sapience Assessment peers had identified the theatrical event in question—a live performance in the West End.

Once Luce showed, Anselmo would let go of the idea that he was the Singularity.

They got standby tickets on the ever-jammed ferry across the English Channel. Rubi waited out the queue by working in her law-school reading room, learning case law on terrorism and camera jamming. When she couldn't absorb any more, she gave press interviews about the raid in Paris.

She dug into work, trying not to worry about Dad being in Guelph. Who had called this meeting of his @bloodhound cohort? Was it him? Was he going to #crashburn?

She had gone to Chicago for implant surgery when she was fourteen. Returning, she found her father in bad shape: starving, depressed, obviously threatened by the fact that she was empowered, now, to take her flesh as far from him as she pleased, for as long as she wanted.

He hung on and she ran, signing up for a deburbing module in Guelph. Dad chased her down, imagining she'd been abducted or brainwashed.

He was on smartdrugs then. As long as he stays clean . . .

Forget it. Stay busy. Rubi visited with the family who'd been targeted in the Paris attack. She worked with Manitoule to structure a potential gaming wager between her and Gimlet, to work out how to benefit the SeaJuve appeal.

Whenever she started mentally looping, whether it was about Drow, Gimlet, or how she'd jumped into a real fight with a real terrorist, Rubi surfaced, went down to the nearest underground gym, and wore herself out training.

Blissful happyface all the time wasn't a realistic life goal. Happ claimed that discomfort and transition fueled personal growth. Unless you wanted to opt for an extreme low-carbon lifestyle, to plug in to a pod with a feeding tube and an IV dose of Contentment, you had to rise and fall.

Ride the highs, work up from the lows.

As highs went, Calais turned out to be quite a pretty one. The region was a green strip within the WestEuro Densification Zone. She was strolling through its carbon-fixing district, admiring its arrangement of windfarms and topsoil printers, when Drow tooned in beside her.

"So much for your vacation, eh?" Dad's knobby old feet were bare and grass-stained; he wore yoga pants. Tattooed maggots, fine white lines, were barely visible on the skin of his chest and back. Someone had run clippers through his hair—each white strand gleamed, and the hexagonal goggle scars on his temples were flushed pink.

Rubi gave a rueful shrug. "I'll see London now."

"Don't mope, dope. London's straight-up wonderful."

"Didn't know you'd been."

"School trip," Drow said. "Before the Setback. There might be historical footage in Haystack."

One of the fans who monitored their every breath, in realtime, would dig up the footage now and tag them.

"What's on your mind, kid?"

"Emergent sapients." She couldn't talk about Luce. If Drow found out Anselmo was investigating their client, he'd tell in a heartbeat. Fortunately, Drow would almost certainly think she had the Paris incident on her mind. "I've been reviewing case law on the AI bans."

The culture of all eyes, all ears had #crashburned society's premeditated murder rate. How did you plan or carry off a killing with implanted cameras uploading the feeds from everyone's eyes, while trachea mics caught every utterance?

Sexual assault numbers had been trending down for decades: even in the middle of the twenty-first, apps like SayYes and Gaslight Analysis became ever more effective at setting and checking boundaries, assessing your fitness to give consent, letting you revoke it anytime.

The days of *She musta misunderstood, officer,* or *I didn't know he was thirteen!* or *C'mon, they led me on* had been sandblasted by transcripts and video footage.

As violent crime waned, though, people began to fear something else would fill the gap.

"Homicidal singularities and #killertech?" Drow said. "Just the boogeyman du jour. In my day, every other scary sim was about a serial killer."

"Serial killers did exist. They weren't just stories."

"Killer AI probably wouldn't be like anything you've fought in-game. Why? You worried that's what shut off the cameras in Paris?"

"People are wondering," she replied.

Drow shrugged. "@Freebreeder hackers are the simplest answer, right?"

"Right." Luce would turn out to be a flesh-and-blood lunatic, someone who needed diagnosis and meds. Rubi just had to prove it to Anselmo. She'd help Luce with his Cloudsight rating, see London, and get on a standby home. Done and dusted and back to Daddy.

As for Drow, the sight of him—here, now, and healthy—eased her worry. "Father Blake's feeding you up."

"It's the plum cake."

Anselmo pinged her, to see if she was headed to the ferry terminal.

"When's your meeting . . . Never mind, I see it," Drow said. "And there's a play beforehand? Maybe I'll try to hook up with him there."

"With Luce?"

"Sure. Offer some emotional backup before you meet. Good for everyone, right?"

She beamed, sending Drow a hug moji. "If he consents."

Drow swept his arm up in a familiar mime, something he hadn't done in years. Graphics caught the move, penciling a cape over his casual yoga gear. Whirling, he pulled it over his face and his toon vanished.

Rubi smiled into the rising wind as she headed for the ferry terminal.

Disembarking in Dover, after a choppy crossing, felt like traveling back in time. Unlike Calais, the port was run down, a skeleton settlement serving the crepit but critical infrastructure of the ferry terminal.

Passengers waited to dock, sloshing back and forth, as the air whipped itself into froth.

"Bad weather's building up on the NorthAm coast," a purser told them. "Florida's battened. Hurricane-strength winds are building near Old New York."

"Haiti's going to get scoured again," someone muttered.

Passengers staggered down the heaving debarkation ramp, crossing an exposed stretch of tarmac to the storm bunkers. Shelter coordinators in safety vests met them at the entrance with towels and smiles.

"We're built to withstand extremely high winds," said one, in obviously well-rehearsed patter. "Everyone's safe."

"Will we lose data?" Voice from the crowd.

"We expect to keep Sensorium at full capacity, Mer."

"Transport?" Anselmo asked.

"Emergency only. Car network and trains are offline."

Rubi felt a rising sense of excitement. *My problem is I'm an adrenaline junkie.*

Anselmo murmured, "I'm going to be drafted for crowd control."

"I'll try for a hospitality shift," she replied.

"They've got good bandwidth here," he said, "but it can get cold. Get a decent blanket."

"Okay." She requisitioned a sweater from stores, then checked in with the gig manager, Moravia. There was a four-hour volunteer shift decanting hot drinks and printing yeast biscuits for the wet, windblown, and increasingly seasick passengers coming off the boats.

The kitchen was running uplink jammers, forcing the public to eat quickly, dry off, and move into the depths of the shelter, to the couches and bunks where people could datadive or sleep.

She was halfway through the shift when a young man, reaching for soup, asked, "Are you Cherub Whiting?"

Dammit. Heads were turning. Rubi handed him the flask with the tiniest of nods. She could feel dozens of eyes on her.

Okay. Drow deals with this constantly, and he's insane.

Drow's got a dog to run interference.

The stranger hadn't taken the soup. He stood, looking gobsmacked, as she held it out, steaming.

"Miso?" she said.

Crickets.

"Your order says a biscuit—here's the biscuit—and a spindown lozenge. There's a pharmacist with a printer station over there—"

"Bam!" he said, and she jumped. Hot soup lipped the flask and burned her thumb. "You jumped on that metal horse, didn't you? Face-to-face with a @Freebreed—"

"I . . ." She held his gaze. "I didn't give it any thought."

"Tear-gassed and everything." He sneezed. "I must've run that vid sixty, eighty times."

Rubi took the sneeze as an opportunity. "You should take your soup before it gets cold. You're chilled, and I've got people waiting."

He didn't move.

"It was nice talking to you."

Not taking the hint.

Drow would tell him to fuck off.

She set the soup within reach. "Bye, now!"

She turned to the next stranded fellow traveler. They seemed similarly starstruck but, thankfully, less pushy. She had to gaily chat to three more people before the guy finally took his soup and huffed away.

I need better role models. Who, besides Drow, could she talk to about this?

The thought of Gimlet rose, unbidden.

No! Hand over a bowl of soup. Print a hot biscuit. Forget that fine-edged smile. Gimlet's married, remember?

"Hi there! Sensorium is available in the next room. Yes, my name is Cherub Whiting. Enjoy your soup."

Twenty minutes later, Moravia pulled her out of the chow line. "Boatload of teens on the way, and they've heard you're here. We'll bed you down in staff quarters, along with your police . . . friend? Lover?"

"Colleague," Rubi said. Anselmo had been extremely charming lately, but a glance through his transcript had made her feel as though he might have ulterior motives. "Sorry to be creating problems."

"It's not the first time we've had a stranded celeb."

"I wouldn't say celeb—" The overly polite look on Moravia's face stopped her. "Moravia, I could fold blankets in a back room."

"Call me Mora, and don't worry. You've done your bit. Nobody thinks you're coasting on privilege."

Rubi's throat tightened, feeling the phrase as an accusation. They stepped out of the cafeteria's jam zone, and the black mark of a strike etched itself across her field of vision. The young guy from the chow line had censured her for "rudely disengaging from conversation."

She could file an appeal—she'd offered a polite goodbye, and Haystack would show it—but why bother?

She followed Mora into a triangular tunnel, made from scavenged corrugated steel, welded together in an inverted V and fixed to the tarmac with concrete weights. Each blast of wind sent rattles through its structure. Rust flakes drifted in the dim light. Rubi could feel metal shavings settling in her dreads.

They rounded a corner to an institutional-looking door, blue paint, and a sign reading AUTHORIZED PERSONNEL ONLY, and went down two flights of steel steps to a dormitory.

"Home sweet home," said Mora.

"This your room?"

"My favorite, anyway. Don't know why. They're standardized."

"The view, maybe," Rubi joked. The pop-in was an eight-bunk communal, with racks of beds built into facing walls. A white rectangle, denoting a window, was painted on the concrete wall between them. The room was clammy. Rubi remembered, too late, Anselmo's precaution about blankets.

The manager seemed to read her thought: "It's just you and Agent Javier in here tonight. Split the linens between you."

"Thanks."

Mora nodded, heading off.

Rubi circled the tiny room, flattening her palm against the damp concrete of the painted window. How to decorate? Load up her e-state? Or check out the staff paste-ups?

This felt more like camping. Maybe later she'd build a cave: crystal formations, iridescent moths, bonfire, and a simulated sleeping bag. Invite some people from school.

She stepped into the hall, triggering lights that illuminated a series of doors to identical bunk rooms. Beyond the bathroom door she found empty showers and staff lockers. Farther in, she found a lounge for ferry workers—more painted windows, a proper radiator, mixer for hot drinks. A printer steamed in the corner, currently set to cook saltfish and akee.

Running a saltfish cube, she sat on the elderly couch, declining to choose any upholstery for it, and munched.

"This isn't weird at all."

Happ pounced on the cue: "Shall we tag your feels?"

Everyone jammed in a public bunker, and me, here in VIP accommodations, waiting on my personal police escort.

"Not just now, Happ. Thanks."

It ghosted over her visual implants, one of a crowd of apps rendered as toons: Coach, her gaming concierge, the PR advisor, Debutante. As consolation for getting a public relations manager, she'd insisted on also subscribing to a premium-grade law school tutor, Polly Precedent. Plus Crane, of course, always Crane. Her electronic entourage, there to help her be bigger, stronger, happier, to make the highest and best use of every waking moment.

"What if you tried something fun?" To her surprise, the suggestion came from Crane, not Happ.

She sighed. "Do you have a suggestion?"

"Storm riding?"

"Accept."

The room disappeared. She rose on a current of fast air, amassing information from weather detection devices installed around the ferry terminal.

Disembodied and out of sorts, she flew above Dover, into blasting thunder and a sizzle of lightning, taking in the spectacle of rain lashing the famous white cliffs.

CHAPTER 14

Wanting kids wasn't so much about Anselmo burning to nurture new life—though he would defy anyone to find him saying otherwise, in *any* transcript. Children were good company, in limited doses, and they outgrew their appalling qualities over time.

Permission to parent was an undisputed win. Childrearing put you in an elite, unlocking social opps with other achievers. It bumped your pack within all sorts of queues. Bigger pop-ins, newer amenities, realworld experiences galore. All because children lived, largely, on the surface. You couldn't keep them in an immersion helmet all the time.

Successful nurturers raked in the perks. Parents rated bigger fresh-vegetable rations, flexible terms on career leveling, discounts on subscriptions. They even got preferred access to high-end life extension.

With all that in mind, Anselmo felt obliged to seem a little starry-eyed as he supervised the herd of sweaty adolescents mobbing the canteen.

The kids were a best-and-brightest cohort, sponsored by innovation companies looking to make their quota of good deeds. Rubi Whiting's kind of people. The superschool was headed to old Oxford, to compete in a hard lab, practicing engineering skills.

They didn't *act* like the intellectual cream. They were as Anselmo imagined wild animals might be: rank, shouty, and overstimulated. The eldest were on the hunt for sex, and that tension pressurized the room, countering the weather system battering the outer walls. Many of the rest appeared to be on high alert in case Rubi Whiting turned up.

Anselmo wouldn't mind being stuck in Dover if enforced togetherness let him build a connection with Rubi. The Beijing couple he'd been flirting with was definitely interested in recruiting a famous performance gamer. They had even seemed intrigued by the idea of a connection with her father.

But instead of Rubi he had this feral herd, with their typical callow questions—

"You ever seen a dead body?"

"Have you worked a murder?"

"Hardly anyone gets murdered anymore," he said.

"What's in your holster? A gun?"

"It's my gaming baton."

Moravia, the terminal manager, pinged him: "Sorry to bother you, Agent Javier, but one of the adolescents has gone missing. He may have run back to the boat."

"*Mais non!* Tell me how I can help," he said.

Kids did this: ran from the cameras during storms, fleeing the omnipresent surveillance when comms were down. A surprising number of these lemmings vanished, never to be seen again. It had been a full-blown crisis during the Clawback. Lemmings were why Global Oversight had given the Department of Preadolescent Affairs so much power. The move had slowed the trend, though not eliminated it.

The lemming phenom was an endless fount of @hoaxer speculation. Every time someone lost a child, after all, someone else got an opp to have one. Could rogue @Freebreeders be pushing the queue by enabling disappearances? Then again, there was also an #urban-myth, among kids, that told of a surveillance-free paradise. Some of the children they'd recovered had claimed to be seeking this Never-land.

Anselmo followed Moravia to a staff exit, where extra packs of primer nanos—extra mass for manifesting rain gear and nanoboots—awaited.

He wasn't alone.

A tough-looking woman, middle-aged and with a scar running diagonally across her cheek, was also gearing up.

Whooz data: Misfortune Wilson, she/her/hers, midlevel gigger for Scotland Yard, Cloudsight rating 59%.

"Bonjour," Anselmo said. "I'm here to search for the boy."

"Hardly a job for two." Misfortune adjusted unseen lumps—equipment, or her worldlies?—within her rain gear. She had a loop of black yarn strung from the sleeve, wound into her fingers.

From her glower, Anselmo pegged her as one of those Clawback generation #survivors, the type who prided themselves on being world-weary and cynical.

"It's a big terminal," he said, absorbing two packs into his own primer, growing long sleeves, fingerless gloves, and a hood. "I'm sure he's very frightened."

"Idiot children. Flinging themselves into the sea whenever it rains. If they remembered what it was like during the plagues—"

Ignoring her complaints, Anselmo booted up nanocleats before forcing the heavy storm door.

Wind punched him like a cold fist. Icy rain washed his exposed fingers. He fumbled to pinch his primer entirely over his face.

"Coming?" he asked. His implants pulled up streaming views of the route back to the dock.

Misfortune stomped out. "One nutter in every pack!"

Many would give her a strike for using a phrase like *nutter* in reference to anyone, let alone a kid in danger.

Anselmo queried her public résumé. She'd been surprisingly

peripatetic. Lots of gigs, worldwide, despite her obvious attitude problem.

No promotions, though. Plays badly with others, then.

"Are you outside?" Rubi's voice, in his ear, was accompanied by a blue neon up-arrow, indicating remote presence above them. "I'm storm-riding."

"There's a young boy loose in the terminal," he said. Aloud, the better to project compassion.

"Lemming?" Her voice mixed horror and awe.

Misfortune turned, hand-signing a question. Anselmo spliced the three of them into one channel and cross-tagged their identities—the modern method of making introductions. "Word has it the boy is headed for the ferry."

"But," Rubi said, "ferry's pushing off."

Anselmo picked up the pace. Rain-lashed dock staff were indeed disconnecting the ramps.

"You've got a runaway boy aboard, *n'est-ce pas*?"

"Turned him away!" the purser shouted over the howling wind. "Terminal's locking down."

"You've got two more ships out there!"

"More dangerous to dock than to ride it out. Lightning incoming. Everyone's ordered off the tarmac."

Anselmo gave the crew a strike.

"Oi!"

"Someone should have escorted that child back."

Misfortune's shoulders lifted, as if a load had come off. "He's gone, then. Nothing more we can do."

She sent Anselmo a stroke, tagged *Going the extra mile.* Then she pivoted, chugging athletically back to the terminal.

Anselmo backed against a wall, considering. The stroke was a bit of nicely judged social blackmail. As far as Misfortune was concerned, the two of them had done their duty merely by stepping out of doors.

He could strike her, but for what? Failing to go an *extra* extra mile when she was already off-duty and he'd just popped someone else?

"Still looking around," Rubi said as he thought daggers at his retreating colleague. "Lots of the fixed cams are down."

Anselmo mojied thumbs-up, checked his Sensorium connection was solid—the better to tell the gig coordinator, if he logged, whether he'd gotten fried by lightning or smashed by flying debris. He spared a sympathetic glance at two massive shadows rolling in the gray washout of the rain, ships with hundreds of passengers, heaving on the waves.

If the boy was suicidal, he would already be in the water.

Typical. Everywhere Anselmo looked, WestEuro was on its way down. He wondered where upgrades to the crumbling Port of Dover fell within Global Oversight's upgrade queue. Calais was new only because France had crowdsourced the renovation, scrimping carbon credits and recycled materials from local citizens.

Rubi's voice broke in: "Found a door flapping on what looks like a field hospital."

Field hospital. You and your war sims. He pushed off from the steel wall, following neon breadcrumbs.

"Watch out. I just saw lightning hit the east dock."

Look heroic. You're selflessly risking yourself to save a youngster. Anselmo found the wildly flapping door and the tangle of fencing that had jammed it.

Save the day. Get promoted. One way or another, level up and move to Beijing. He wrestled the debris, shoved himself inside, and tried hanging on to the door. Suctioned by wind, it pulled itself free of his numbed fingers, slamming definitively.

Panting, Anselmo loaded the building layout. There were two floors, reinforced for storms, tasked to infirmary space, contraband lockup, and veterinary clinic. During the Setback, this building would have been for interrogating—terrorizing, really—travelers whose skin color or religious faith was currently in disfavor. During Misfortune's plague-besieged youth, it might have been repurposed for medical quarantine.

Anselmo started a search.

Rubi pinged him: "I found a couple possible hiding places on the lot. I sent them to your partner but hit a comms block."

"Misfortune's not a partner. More of a professional . . ." What had they called it, back in the day? ". . . blind date."

"Bit of a #crashburn."

"Not everyone I meet on the job can be as delightful as yourself."

"Charmer."

This first room was a blood lab. Black counters, long since emptied of sinks and syringes, exuded a whiff of damp dust. Crates of printer supplies were piled in its corners.

He searched, closed up, waited to hear the door lock, and crossed the hall.

Here: spray of blood, on the floor, crimson drops bright under the lights.

"*Allo?*" This room held emergency supplies: bulky pharma-printer dominating one wall, collapsible treatment tables, nanosilk packs, bottled water, a defibrillator. Hooks and curtains, built into the ceiling, allowed the division of the space into individual patient pop-ins.

Anselmo drew back a curtain with a screeching rattle, revealing a blood-smeared medical kit.

Crouching, he peered under the next curtain, scanning the floor. No feet, no movement.

"Where are you?"

Rubi, rather than the missing kid, was the one who answered. "Trying to get that Scotland Yard woman to come back. This has the makings of a perfect ambush."

"He's a child, not some sim antagonist," Anselmo said. "You know how many kids go missing in superstorms?"

A pause. "I didn't mean to be insensitive."

He sent a burst of moji balloons, meaning *No hard feelings*. "You have cameras beyond these curtains?"

"They were off, but . . ." Her toon flew ahead, passing through the barriers. "Back corner, on a bed. His head's bleeding."

"I'll take it from here," Anselmo said. "Go back to your fly-over."

"I can talk to him," she said. "Since that bobby ditched you."

If she came along, any strokes for the rescue would get sucked into the vortex of her fame. "I appreciate the assist, but—"

"I'm good with difficult people."

"Rubi, I have to go." He stepped past the first curtain, skirting the treatment bed.

"But—"

He kept his tone friendly. "It's police business now." Without waiting for another *But!* he muted her, then raised his voice. "Hello? I'm here to help."

A rustle. He edged closer, then pulled the curtain.

The teenaged boy was stocky, with big hands and a bloodied face. He held a scalpel in one hand, startling when Anselmo pulled the curtain.

In his surprise, he threw something—a medi-stapler?—at Anselmo, bouncing it off his chest. Instinctive impulse, response to an unexpected threat.

The boy had been cutting his hair. Blood-soaked plaits littered the floor.

"Hey, hey," Anselmo said. "English, yes? Yes? Everything's okay."

The boy moaned.

"I'm police," Anselmo said, showing his vintage badge.

Quick interplay of emotions over the kid's face. Then he sagged, defeated, and dropped the scalpel. "My hand slipped." He showed a bloody flap of scalp, hanging. A second wound—circular gouge, in his upper arm—dripped steadily.

Anselmo checked the port manager, gesturing for the boy to settle on a treatment bed. "I'll get a paramedic on the line."

Dover greenlighted additional resources. The infirmary heat kicked in and the pharmaceutical printer hummed to life. An antique camera winged over the curtain, rotors trailing cobwebs.

A paramedic joined the channel, walking Anselmo through the

process of finding a proper set of tweezers and sterile gloves within
the infirmary stores. Meanwhile, the printer ran contact anesthet-
ics to numb the boy's injuries.

"Everything's okay," Anselmo said, dabbing anesthetic on the
boy's arm wound and gashed scalp. "What's your name?"

"Paul."

Suddenly, the boy's thumb beat out a rhythm against Anselmo's
hip, body-texting. *U from #Neverland?*

Anselmo's face must have shown confusion.

Can't you let me go?

"*Bonjour,* Paul," he said aloud. "How's that arm?"

"Still sore." His eyes were big, pleading.

The paramedic subbed, "Give the anesthetic another sixty."

Neverland. Paul was one of those kids who'd bought in to the
#urbanmyth of a children's paradise, somewhere without adults or
cameras.

Anselmo laid a finger on the boy's back, morsing in reply. *Did
someone suggest you should go outside?*

Paul sniffled and shook his head.

Pre-implanted kids cracked, sometimes, under the strain of constant surveillance. It explained his arm. He'd dug out his locator
and ditched his helmet and speakers.

Anselmo scanned the room, saw the RFID, still bloodied, sitting
in a padded capsule as if awaiting shipment to some other location.
He flagged the incident, recommending a psychosocial audit of the
boy's pack and peer group.

At the same time and under the paramedic's supervision, he
snipped one last dangling plait of hair, pressed the flap of skin back
into place on the boy's half-denuded scalp, and used sterile adhesive to tack the skin together.

"He broke off a scalpel point in his arm," said the paramedic,
"when he pulled his chip. Use the tweezers and reassure him."

Anselmo made a patter of it: "Paul, this isn't going to feel great
but it'll be over soon, you're doing great, I just need to get a grip . . .
good!"

The kid tried to yank away as he made the attempt. Blood sprayed. Awkwardly, Anselmo clapped an absorbent smartwipe over the wound, applying pressure until the wipe indicated the flow of blood had stopped. It had cobwebbed the gash in coagulant-laced threads.

He got a cluster of strokes: from the paramedic, the ferry manager, the volunteer coordinator, Rubi Whiting, and the kid's panicking parents.

"He'll be fine now, until you get him back to the terminal," said the paramedic. "Your contaminated primer nanos will slough off into medical waste. Just wash up."

Anselmo went to the printer to comply, mind churning on ways to charmingly entertain the introverted teen, to seem fatherly, while they waited out the wind.

CHAPTER 15

Home at last, in mind at least! As the storm raged outside the London pop-in where their bodies were resident, Gimlet and Frankie dove, merging with their pack.

Marie's e-state was a freestanding bungalow surrounded by profuse, fragrant herb gardens, a croquet pitch, and a serpentine river jumping with trout. Parent and child ported in on the porch, clad in casual summerwear: straw hat and sand-colored linen suit for Gimlet, Bermuda shorts and a shirt for Frankie. Picnic gear, default presentation for family time.

Frankie wheeled, trying the cottage door—each of the pack's back doors led to the others' houses. She hit a lock.

"Rollsy's sleeping, child," Marie called. She and Bella were out wading in the river's clear, calf-deep water.

Marie had spent the Clawback planting trees within the first catch-as-catch-can evacuation zones in Northern Europe, earning her way into the WestEuro megacity. The nights of her youth had been spent huddled in camps in places like New Sherwood Forest. Lying body to body with half-chilled strangers, the work crews had endured considerable harassment from people who hadn't bought in yet, mobs of densification refugees determined to reclaim, by force if necessary, their personal patch of suburban sprawl.

Grim, backbreaking days. She told tales of blasting the concrete foundations of highways, of driving pickaxes into tarmac, drinking scavenged water.

How the old lady had come out of it all with such a generous spirit—much less an intact sense of humor—was beyond Gimlet.

Frankie gave the porch door one hard, angry shake before bolting into Bella's arms.

"C'mon, Chickpea," Bella said, hauling her onto the banks, conjuring a hammock. She threw a stream of confetti at Gimlet as she went—little pix representing strength, hearts, hug icons. Then mother and daughter snuggled in, side by side.

"Shoes off," Gimlet subbed, and was suddenly barefoot. The crisp trousers rolled up of their own accord. They joined Marie, stepping into her trout stream.

Ah! Soothing cushion of mucky sand underfoot. The water was crystal-clear and cold enough to invigorate. Emerald weeds twisted in spirals, undulating with the push of the stream.

"Dear one." Marie wound her sturdy black fingers into Gimlet's chalky ones. They pressed their foreheads together, commiserating. Gimlet spat feelings out, manifesting each as a cool, round stone, brought up from within. They dropped, one by one, into the water between their sand-kissed toes:

#Fatigue, #sorrow, #anger, #abandonment. Released, each tagged feel sank into the riverbed, slowly vanishing.

"I'll barbecue steak later," Marie said. "Push protein."

Gimlet nodded. "How are you?"

Marie dropped some pebbles of her own. #Worry, #stress, #hope. Splash, splash, splash. Her grip on Gimlet's hands tightened. #Love.

"I saw Rubi Whiting," Gimlet said.

"*Danced* with," she corrected.

"You had time to backscroll my week?"

Marie pursed her lips, emanating infectious, old-lady mischief. One always half-expected her to offer some laughable suggestion: *Let's steal a bike. Let's hit a fancy kitchen and order printed*

bologna and soda crackers. Let's go punting, in the flesh. On the
Thames. During a snowstorm.

"Don't tease," Gimlet said.

"Did I say anything?"

"That smirk of yours passes for moji."

"You swore, *swore,* nothing would ever come of that kissing
scene with the delectable Mer Whiting."

"She's got almost as much trouble on her plate as we do." Gimlet tipped a brow in the direction of the cottage.

"I'm not suggesting we get up tux and tails and write a prenup
for the woman," Marie said.

"But?"

"With Rollsy and Sangria out of play, you need a little heat in
your sheets."

"You don't, I suppose. Why don't you hunt yourself up some
randy oldfeller? Franks could use a grandad."

"Dear Mada Grouse. I am screening candidates daily."

For all Gimlet knew, it was true.

Flirt, fight, flirt some more. Gimlet had been offered the star-
crossed romance angle with Rubi, in the superhero sim *Slugfest,*
over a year ago now. The subplot brought their civilian identities
together in a series of character scenes. Scripted banter and sparks
flying. High society parties and a parade on the Champs-Élysées,
over holiday fireworks. Gimlet remembered the gut-lurch that
had gone through them when Risto offered to engineer a kissing
scene.

Accept or *Cancel*? The words had left them in turmoil, like a
lovestruck, pre-implanted kid.

Accept.

Rubi accepted, too.

Gimlet had played romance subplots in earlier sims. The intimate scenes were a peculiar experience, certainly, but if you
weren't up for the final act-out, you ghosted. The graphics team
and a consenting body double ran your toon through the motions
of smooch and pet.

With Rubi . . . had they simply gotten into a game of chicken, with neither of them willing to back down? Feeds showed her live, present, in scene just as Gimlet was.

Rubi's fingers, on their face, had felt like live wires. Sure grip and a first brush of lip on lip, sizzling. None of it, not the press of body or the eventual, gasping break, had felt like acting.

Ninety minutes later, they had been suited up and battling it out in that duel to the death over Centre Pompidou.

On their next go-round, *Ghosts of Paris 1818,* Rubi had refused the romance subplot.

Disinterested, then, Gimlet thought. *She took a bite, didn't like the taste.*

But that dance, recently, in Rubi's e-state . . .

Marie made a smug little noise.

"All right," Gimlet said. "Maybe she's a long-term prospect. Emphasis on *long.* We need to get Franks back to the three of you. Tooning in for family time is fine, but we can't have her in a diving helmet all day."

The old woman nodded, watching the water streaming past their ankles. The undulation of the weeds was hypnotic.

Bella, over in the hammock, subbed, "Babygirl's fast asleep."

Gimlet leaned in, giving Marie a proper hug and popping a burst of hearts to seal the deal. Then they splashed their way up the banks.

Beyond the bungalow door was a country kitchen: stone counters, copper pans, and bunches of hanging dried herbs. Buy-in meds ensured that it smelled of rosemary and woodsmoke. Headmistress bumbled just beyond the counter, crunching the household budget up on a shareboard.

Bella was on leave from her permajob in kitchen management. Marie had officially paused her latest career-leveling track—teaching—while the pack rode the crisis out.

Gimlet still had one active income stream. As parent-partner to Frankie in her start-up job at the Department of Preadolescent Affairs, they couldn't stop unless she did. And nobody had the heart to deprive her of anything else.

Sangria's numbers were still up on the spreadsheet, Gimlet noted sourly, posting earns and spends. There was little give to the family, but Sang hadn't gone so far as to formally cut the economic cord. Yet.

Right. Because if she's the one who files for dissolution, Franks might see her as the bad guy.

The global capital trusts, established in the Clawback, guaranteed their stake gave them enough to live on, no matter what. And the pack's adults were old enough, at this point, to have interest coming in on years of past wages. But traveling with Sangria to King's Cross had meant paying premium prices for the train. Third and fourth opinions on Rollsy's cancer and surgery options had escalated with each new doctor consult.

Health care was free, to a point, but indulging denial in the face of death? That, it turned out, was pricey.

"*Bastille* will balance things out, if you play it right," Headmistress offered as Gimlet took in the board. "Suggesting a wager was ingenious. Rewild supporters and Risto fans will offer strokes—"

"Let's review the numbers later," Gimlet said.

"Of course, Mer Gimlet."

They tapped on Rollsy's door. "It's me."

Nothing.

"I'm alone."

It unlocked, taking Gimlet in one step from bucolic country kitchen to Rollsy's e-state, skyscraper with penthouse views of twenty-first-century Shanghai.

In sim, of course, Gimlet's husband looked fine: tall, broad-shouldered, with jet-black hair and a luxurious beard. He had been in conference with an app Gimlet didn't recognize, a stick insect in bright orange dashiki and a kufi. The program ghosted as the door closed.

"Reaper app," Rollsy explained, reaching out to kiss Gimlet

lightly on both closed eyes. "End-of-life counseling, body recycling options, managing my posthumous digital existence. A last bash at the bucket list."

Gimlet's heart sank.

"I want you to take over my house." Rollsy gestured at their playboy digs. "Franks might want to poke around here in a few years. Archiving shouldn't cost much."

"Accept. Of course."

"I've written her a tour of my private rooms." He shared a handful of bright platinum keys.

Gimlet turned them over, fingering the metal. "Speaking of Franks. She *needs* to see you."

A headshake. "Soon . . . if a window when the meds and the pain are both dialed down . . ."

Rather than argue, Gimlet took up a spot beside him at the window. Overlaid on the glass view was a four-by-four grid of newscycle feeds. Rollsy always turned his attention to the wider world when he needed distraction.

Gimlet preferred Marie's wading stream.

Never mind. Be present. Take it in. Scan the headlines together.

Continued investigation of the @Freebreed attack on Paris was the top share; next was the chain of hurricanes making their way around the Atlantic. Adolescents were taking advantage of the storm to rabbit.

Thinking of lemmings made Gimlet's stomach roll over.

Rollsy flicked that window away, replacing it with footage of Hyderabad's superstar mayor, Saanvi Agarwal, as she voted for #babytiger in the Project Rewild runoff poll.

In Scranton, at the pyramids, a memorial for journalists who'd vanished at the end of the Setback had drawn thirty thousand pilgrim tourists.

"So much death—" Rollsy started to say.

Headmistress interrupted. "Mer Erwitz, your parents are inbound to your fleshly location. ETA eleven minutes."

Gimlet felt a flash of guilt. Rollsy's parents were gathering by the bedside, and they were fleshing around London . . .

"I couldn't stop 'em from coming." Rollsy sighed.

Let it go. Lots of families were scattered across the globe, spending all their together-time in e-states. The plain fact was Rollsy didn't seem to want anyone at the hospital.

Gimlet said, "If they want to dive later, they're welcome here. Marie's printing steak. It'll be a picnic. We all love your parents . . . and it would give you a break."

"Thank you. I'll make them come." Rollsy snapped his fingers, shutting off the newscycle. Perfunctory goodbye kiss, and then he logged, leaving Gimlet with the glittering vintage skyscrapers of Beijing.

Sitting on one of the luxuriant leather couches, Gimlet said, to Headmistress, "Audit the medical consults, please. What exactly are the doctors saying?"

Time to find out how bad things really were.

CHAPTER 16

As the superstorm raged through the Atlantic, Rubi volunteered to do an impromptu hangout with the best and brightest student group, quizzing them about emergent AI and the boogeyman that was the Singularity. She tried to turn the conversation to oxygen security, all while deflecting their questions about the terrorist attack in Paris, *Bastille,* and Gimlet, Gimlet, Gimlet.

It felt like being a zoo exhibit.

Anselmo kept his distance, so that if Luce popped in to chat, he wouldn't wonder how she'd picked up a police chum.

Drow tooned in for a visit as she was boarding a transport out of the terminal, catching her just as she was configuring some of her primer into a proper cushion—the bus seat was so old, it had cracks in it.

"What's this?" He was wearing the white suit again; he must have thought it made him look extra sane.

Rubi gestured at two fragile centenarians across the aisle. "Their life-extension regimes are too specialized for Dover infirmary."

"And how did you rate a seat on the first limo out?"

She shifted her hips, testing the cushion config. The nanosilk she'd deployed under her backside had come from her tights and sleeves, and her arms and legs were already feeling the draft. "I'm legit famous now; haven't you heard?"

"You fast-tracked out of lockdown? Diva stuff, kid."

She raised a hand and her new PR app, Debutante, flashed an alert—rubbing her thumb over her temple beads was, apparently, a stress tell. She turned the move into a vague wave. "Logistics claimed I was drawing attention. My presence forced Dover to allocate resources from passenger care into crowd management."

"I thought you'd pooched your chance to fade out of my lime-light when you started winning sim premieres," Drow said. "Now—"

"Now I'm jumping terrorists and making newscycle."

"Hey!" Concern in his voice ran on her nerves like sandpaper.

"I have almost as many people crawling my transcripts as you."

"I'll try to draw some fire. I am touring."

Pulse of alarm. "Where?"

"A few pubs across the Lakes. Whiskey's with me."

It had been five years since he'd done a live gig outside their neighborhood comfort zone.

Wind slapped the bus as it groaned out onto the road. "And our client?"

"He's invited me to *Macbeth*. Should be a good show. I tuned up their overture and sound effects, just to pack the house."

"Why?"

"For fun, mostly," he said. "Relax, honey. Everything'll work out."

She mojied disbelief.

"I *promise*," he said, turning the conversation to other topics. In the end he stayed to chat throughout the ride, really delivering on the performance of health and stability. He didn't ghost until she got to London.

Her first view was underwhelming: miserable, fog-shrouded greentowers, lashed by rain. If this was what the real world had to offer, there was no point spending time in it. "Crane, set me up with a power-fast until this clears."

"I've prebooked a pod near Hammersmith, Miss."

Twenty minutes later, the bus pulled up in front of a boarded-up building with thick walls, warehouse space for up to five hundred people in hibernation mode.

Rubi jumped off her cracked seat and sprinted through the deluge to the door. She grabbed a heated chugger, lightly sweetened milk in a shortbread-flavored bottle, and hit the showers to wash off the chill before choosing a pod.

Crane augmented the warehouse with arrows. "This one's free, Miss Cherub."

She lifted the pod hood, inspecting the couch beneath. Spotless.

Satisfied, Rubi put her primer into a nanosilk refresher and stashed her worldlies in the locker before settling, nude, onto the smartfoam mattress. The foam would periodically cycle, massaging her muscles and adjusting her position so she didn't emerge feeling stiff. She installed a sterile mouthpiece for the feeding tube, clipping it inside her cheek. Then she unwrapped the autobidet, rocking into place until everything was comfortably settled against her groin.

Rubi's temp and humidity prefs were already loaded into the pod as she leaned into the couch's foam embrace. "Ping me as soon as the weather clears. I want a look at London."

"Of course." Crane brought up a carbon savings monitor. A quarter of the resources she didn't spend, while fasting, would be added to her luxury budget. The rest would be kicked back into a fund for her bet with Gimlet.

She halved her own cut, offsetting some of the flight across the Atlantic. Work-related or not, the environmental cost of the voyage nagged at her conscience.

"There's such a thing as too much virtue, miss."

"Bounce back, baby. All for one, one for all." She yanked the pod lid shut. Green telltale lights confirmed the locks were engaged, the feeder was good to go, and her Sensorium connection was robust. Lemon-flavored mist, laced with nutrients and a dose of buy-in drugs, warmed the back of her throat.

She went home first, booting her sunlit bedroom, with its Versailles-influenced wallpaper and gold-framed portraits.

"Clothing reset—business casual." Her simulated silk pajamas morphed into a mustard blouse and black slacks.

She pushed through her front door, into a view of a mirror-smooth lake encircled by the homes of her @CloseFriends.

E-state back doors led to private and shared gardens. Front doors took users to their neighborhood metaphor. Drow's Whine Manor loomed, directly across from her palace in the twelve o'clock position, its gothic lines casting spooky reflections on the surface of the lake. Beyond it were personal contacts: childhood friends, school friends, sports buddies, old lovers, and Gimlet Barnes. The commercial district, at three o'clock, teemed with trusted vendors: Team Rabble clubhouse, law school, her bank, customer service outlets for various apps.

Rubi strolled the lake's perimeter, poking her nose into the law school. Its lounge was bustling. Everyone was burrowing, catching up assignments, finishing case work, and challenging exams while the Atlantic storm raged.

An anthropomorphized giraffe wearing lawyer tabs appeared beside her. "Congratulations, Mer Whiting, on the bump in your social cap."

"Thanks."

"The school is offering an opp to make a public service module about resisting emergent terrorism . . ."

"Accept. I'm using Debutante—can you send specs and a schedule to her?"

"Gladly. Would you like to examine your grades on the Support Ticket Advocacy exam?"

Marks unscrolled before her, confirming she'd made the class leaderboard. "Everything back on track since the one #examfail."

"Yes. You must win five of nine social cap advocacies, including your current gig with Mer Luciano Pox, to unlock the next round of specialized study opps."

"Remind me?"

"Drone-tampering, nepotism, and criminal negligence." The beginning of the criminal law track, in other words, and a gateway to eventually challenging the #suicidality #triage laws. People like Drow had been her initial focus when she started law school. She'd never thought she might need environmental law; when she began, it hadn't occurred to her that SeaJuve might one day need a lawyer.

"There is a qualifying maladjust advocacy gig in London," the giraffe added.

Rubi hesitated. Drow couldn't be on his own forever. Just because he'd ridden out one week of solitude didn't mean he wouldn't panic and attempt self-harm tomorrow.

Drow had only survived his mad slash at the tranq darts, back in Guelph, because Father Blake had been nearby, with paramedic training and the resources of Our Lady Immaculate.

She shoved the memory away. "New gigs can wait until I'm back in the Lakes."

"Strike one. Declining three consecutive opps will move you down the priority queue for further offers."

"I'll appeal if necessary."

The giraffe nodded, ghosting.

Happ bonked her shin. In his mouth was an invite to a lazy-river spin with her classmates. He barked up mojis of people hugging. "Healthy professional social connections—"

"I know. I'll go, okay? But only for ninety."

Her assent triggered a cascade of delirious barking and tail-wagging. The virtual elevator of the law market immediately opened out onto lush rainforest, jade foliage bursting extravagantly from the banks of a river in . . .

She walked through the portal, trying to guess. "Cambodia?"

"Laos," corrected Fass as he too tooned in. Tags reminded her they had challenged User Agreements 1 & 2 together. A river barge awaited; Rubi took a seat.

"@BargeFourGuests: The camera run on the Mekong just got a hardware upgrade," Fass said. He was a resident in Nairobi; why he was slumming in a Great Lakes law program was beyond her. His toon wore a formal-looking kimono and his long, neon-orange hair was in a topknot. "Higher definition, more detail."

"I hadn't heard about the upgrade." Rubi relaxed as the jungle drifted past.

The Mekong sim showcased the kind of lush ecosystem that beguiled a person into thinking humanity had already stuck the so-called #SoftLanding, that the planet and its surviving post-plague billions were stabilized. The trees thronged with monkeys. Shore birds drilled the mud for digestible microfauna. The fact that the river had a real flow—that it wasn't just a trickle in a half-dried mudpan—invited belief that the worst of the environmental crisis was over.

Fass let out a sigh. "This is why SeaJuve failed. Easier to relax when you're winning."

"Rationing fatigue," someone countered. "It's Bounceback needs a shot in the arm, not just the oceans."

As if the oceans weren't a big enough challenge.

"Anybody have the requisite courses for the Global Oversight appeal?" She posted specs, knowing that Crane would have told her if any of her friends or contacts were qualified.

They shook their heads.

"I could, maybe, in six months . . ." Fass said apologetically.

"Too late."

"I'll ask around home."

"Thanks." She sent a stroke to show her appreciation.

The barge rounded a bend, revealing a spectacular red-tiled historic temple, along with a hospital, a rewilding project for newts and a shrine centered around a downed United States warplane.

Her classmates doubled down on the conversation, crunching case law, carbon stats, and newscycle. Fast, energizing debate, achievers arguing about how to better the world and help its square pegs.

Rubi was tempted to stay when the ninety-minute timer ran out.

Instead, she ported back to the office, requesting a confidential workroom with Cloudsight's strongest hash provisions. She sent an invite to her own square peg.

Now. How to amass information about Luce without giving away anything Anselmo had told her?

A biography, first. Luce had #foundling tags. No known DOB or surviving biological relations. Very common.

She asked Polly Precedent, her new tutor, "Can we get Luce's profile pictures?"

The app, rendered as a glorious orange parrot with spectacles, flapped its wings, bringing up a poster filled with facial recognition metrics. Head shots resolved: Luce as a young man on a bamboo-baling gig, dishwater eyes and mink-blond hair, looking freshly minted. He had a sunburned nose and a smile: no sign of the harried expression Rubi knew.

Recent shots were less charming—no sunburn, no smile. She found the profile pic used for everything from his drone pilot's license to his soapbox posts. It was the last picture of him ever taken.

"Candids, Polly? Found footage?"

"Nothing," Polly *awwwk*ed, shaking out her feathers. "Your client is a full-time pod person."

"Then why has he been so hard to geolocate?"

"Unknown."

"How long since he logged this profile photo?"

"Uncertain. The date tags run into the Clawback," Polly said.

That would make him Drow's age or older. "I just took a technosphere tutorial that said you can estimate the age of a hashed picture using a program called Tree Ring Formulation."

Polly edged back and forth on her perch, processing. "Cloudsight will approve the app license for case-specific one-time use. Running. Tree Ring estimates that the final profile photo tagged to Luciano Pox originated sixty-five years ago."

"This one? Where Luce looks . . . what, thirty?"

Polly flapped: yes.

"You're telling me Luce is older than . . . he's a zombie?"

"Autostrike!" Polly replied. "Use of discriminatory language."

Rubi felt a pulse of mean-spirited joy. What did one strike matter to her current score?

Zombie, zombie, zombie. She imagined sticking out her tongue.

Luce didn't *seem* vintage.

Her mind drifted to Anselmo's suspicions. An AI posing as human might, theoretically, take over the Sensorium account of an agoraphobic pod person.

No! Nothing Rubi had learned about AI personalities tracked with Luce's irrationality, panic, obsessive politicking, his bursts of terror and rage. Theoreticians agreed that the first surviving AIs would be able to pass for human online. They might occasionally seem odd, off in their reactions, but anything too weird—too alien-seeming—would be winnowed.

Couldn't Luce just be a sick old man?

Just then, the object of all this activity skulked in, wearing his cartoon burglar outfit, sans mask. He examined the timeline. "Pics of . . . yes, of me. Why?"

"Background for your hearing."

"Bio data." He fisted his hands, bonking his knuckles together three times.

"I had no idea you were on life extension. Or that you were over a hundred."

"I get strokes for being too stubborn to die?"

"Why should you die?"

He shrugged. "Everyone I ever knew is dead."

That was #survivorguilt if ever she'd heard it. "This is a possible avenue of defense, Luce. If we prove you have age-related social impairments, or Setback trauma—"

"Trauma like Drow?"

"Um."

"They won't give me a dog, will they?" Disgust, there, in his voice.

She shook her head. "I'm saying that if there's been chemical imbalance, or mismanagement of your life extension regime, it will help your case."

He perked up. "Medical mismanagement?"

"You understand that it has to be true? Mismanagement means someone's responsible."

"Someone's guilty. Someone pays." He looked thoughtful.

"*Do* you think someone's mismanaging your meds? Where are you accessing care?"

He turned from his picture, looking uncomfortable. "Drow says you won't break our user agreements."

She thought of @Interpol and Anselmo with a pang. "I want to help you."

"There's a London farm for zomb—"

"Eldercare facility," Rubi corrected. Unlike her, he couldn't afford the strike.

"Potato poh-tah-toe."

This was another of Drow's hacks: teaching clients to replace antisocial utterances with cute pop-culture refs. This one came from an ancient song about lovers with consensus-building problems.

"Can you say where your body is resident? Like, mine's currently in a pod in Hammersmith."

He crossed his arms. He was shaking.

"Okay, change of topic. What if we talk about what happened in Paris?"

"That pink-swaddled baby stealer?"

"You and I were talking remotely, right?"

"So?"

"You were here, though. London?"

"I'd lost track of my map coordinates."

"Your body. Because you mostly live in Sensorium?"

"Obviously."

She said, gently, "Most people don't lose track, Luce."

"The—" The knuckles again. *Bonk, bonk, bonk.* "I got delivered to a new facility. The Abruzzo home was for premium sub-scribers."

"If Eldercare downgraded your subscription, they would've in-formed you."

"They did. But the ads, ads, ads . . ." he said. "They told me the meat was getting moved to another freezer, but I'd stopped read-ing."

Rubi brought up a tabletop model of the Palais du Luxembourg grounds, creating a tiny sim of herself and Luce at the café. She drew the police line around the area where the cameras, mics, and uplinks had been offlined. "You sensed the @Freebreed blackout coming. You warned me."

"I was scanning for goats in the machine—"

"Ghosts?"

"Goats. Whatever's attacking me."

Like the goat that had tricked the smarttruck? Did that imply an entity other than Luce?

What if the goat was the terrorist AI, the unicorn Anselmo was hunting? "Your scan revealed the cameras going down?"

Luce nodded.

She darkened the shadow to represent the actual blackout. "You were remote. When my uplink got jammed, you should've been booted out of our conversation."

A blank expression.

"Instead, you were yammering in my ear throughout the at-tack. Crane said you formed a redtooth link to my gaming baton. That's serious hacker stuff, Luce. Difficult and criminal. Your bio-tags say you're a retired winemaker."

He blanched. "Who knows this?"

She picked her words with care. "You should assume the police audited everyone who saw the attack."

"Will they sanction me?"

"Depending on your medical status."

"Limiting Sensorium access?"

That was the key, wasn't it? Access. All he cared about was soap-boxing for martial law.

She brought up the parameters for managed care, letting him look for himself. His VR access would be limited to quality of life and rehab simulations. Visitations from outside would be limited, and there'd be no more scope for political speeching.

He let out a mournful sigh. "I just wanted you to know there was danger. Wrong again, Luce."

The regret in his voice, the self-recrimination, went straight to her heart. This couldn't possibly be a computer intelligence. Anselmo was wrong. He'd see that, once the two of them met.

A weight came off her shoulders. She wasn't setting up Luce for the police—she was speeding up the process of clearing him.

She met his eyes, telegraphing movement so he could step back or block consent to contact. When he didn't, she laid a hand on his bony, old-man shoulder. "If it comes to a criminal complaint, you might have to be prepared to 'fess up and show how you linked to my baton—so they can close up whatever loophole you exploited."

"Locking, locking," he muttered. "Locking all the doors."

Whatever that meant. "You were protecting me from terrorists, or trying to."

"Stupid terrorists."

"Agreed. Could you do that, Luce?"

"Confess I crawled into your joystick?" He seemed to consider. Finally, a nod. "Demonstrate the redtooth hack, apologize-désolé . . ."

"And help the authorities figure out how the @Freebreeders jammed le Jardin?"

"Why should I chew their food?"

"To be prosocial. Remember prosocial?"

He banged his knuckles against each other—one, two, three. Another Drow hack, a replacement for his *stupid, stupid, stupid* mantra, she realized. "If I had to."

"You would."

"And then I don't end up hashed?"

"Hashed? Never." Her jaw dropped. "Luce, did you think these were capital offenses?"

"Why would they let me live?"

"Nobody's going to *kill* you." She gestured at the managed-care infographic. "That's as bad as it gets."

Luce let out a dismissive snort.

"Nothing worse is going to happen to you, promise. Whatever you may have experienced, before the Clawback, it's history. Nobody does that now."

"You sure?"

"*Yes*." She swallowed. "Have you talked over these fears of . . . punishment?"

"Torture?"

"Torture." The word felt like darts, slamming into her throat. "Did you talk about this with Drow?"

"Should I?"

"Tell him. He can help."

A hesitant smile. "Okay."

Rubi's sense of being on the edge of a whirlpool receded. "Now. About our meeting. You'll be there? In the flesh?"

Luce manifested a playbill, for a showing of *Macbeth* at the Piccadilly Theatre. "Zombie farmers are taking us to see this."

"I remember." Rubi shared a booking for a pop-in meeting room, near the theater, timed for right after the show. "You'll wheel from the theater to the meeting?"

"Meat on display, as required."

That would take care of Anselmo.

Luce was too disordered, too fragmentary, too *random* to be a constructed personality. He was going to turn out to be a hacker with a seizure disorder or VTSD. A Setback-damaged, badly medicated elder with paranoid fantasies.

Fantasies about murder goats.

It couldn't all be fantasy, could it? That truck had seen one, too.

Never mind. Just prove her client was a real person, and then set @Interpol on the goat.

Meanwhile, Luce had support tickets to clear and Cloudsight to answer to. She pulled up the social penalties and they set to work, the two of them working up answers to each charge, laying out a plan to restore him to—if not model-citizen status—at least to get him out of the penalty box.

CHAPTER 17

The multiheaded storm lashed the Atlantic shores, throwing itself against greenwalls and fortified dikes in coastal megacities from London to Lisbon, San Juan to Tampico. It dumped water on the ruins of Philadelphia, straining to reach as far inland as the Toronto-Detroit axis of the Great Lakes Reclamation region. Cisterns overflowed and rain gushed though the streets. Trees smashed power panels and kiosks. Playspaces under buildings filled with stormwater and drained out, slowly, through industrial-grade oxygenators.

Millions followed Cherub Whiting's example: burrowing in, hunkering down. Families merged on their shared e-states. They worked, studied, and queued for high-traffic entertainment sims like Drow's party. Bounceback-era storms always had a festival atmosphere. People gathered online in ever-bigger numbers, traveling a circuit of impromptu parties.

Meanwhile, preadolescents fled home by the dozens.

Some lemmings were captured by drones or police. Others turned up dead, logged as accident victims or slain by their own hand. A few vanished entirely.

When the all-clear came from the weather office, the Bounceback generation charged into realworld cleanup. Drone pilots flew infrastructure damage assessments. Others gigged on volunteer crews, pulling together to sweep glass and chip deadfalls. Strangers bonded over shared hardship and broken flood berms.

Tampico, typically, was hardest hit, with a five-figure death toll and an aftershock of drug-resistant cholera. Five hundred shrink-wrapped houses within its quarantined suburbs were washed away by storm surges, leaving beaches littered with drywall and unidentified chem and biohazards.

The usual conversation foamed across Sensorium. Was it time to consolidate the Southeast, forcing the Florida population inland? Was it worthwhile to maintain the infrastructure for growing luxury commodities—fresh fruit, coconuts, beans, and peanuts?

By way of surly reply, Tampico City Hall posted the roster of their dead and kept farming.

The storm kept Anselmo Javier tied down until it was time to beard Luciano Pox at the theater.

He'd spent the enforced downtime auditing Cherub Whiting's transcripts, analyzing interactions with her private sidekick. There was nothing to flag. Plenty of unicorn hunters had taken a run at the Crane app, looking for signs of true self-awareness.

Good, he thought. Any hope of kindling romance with Rubi would implode if she was harboring an emergent.

Did he hope? Could she be swayed?

Uncertain and unknown.

Meanwhile, WestEuro Eldercare, the facility where Pox allegedly resided, had confirmed the field trip to Piccadilly to see *Macbeth.*

There'd have been no deep diving for the Eldercare attendants, permajobbers with fragile elders to attend. They would have been monitoring life signs in medical support pods, prepping backup meds, all to the howl of thunder and wind. The staff would be itching for an outing. Nothing short of a wildfire would cancel them now.

Anselmo beat Pox's bus to the West End, barely, and was surprised to find *Macbeth* had sold out. When confronted with his

@Interpol credentials, the box office grudgingly gave him permission to observe the show from a crew balcony.

The Piccadilly was crawling with preadolescent Londoners. One school, fifty strong, had been seated below the balcony. Young adults, behind them, lounged and struck poses. Anselmo checked their tags, finding #student #actor #Bardfan #musicfan. A pop-up cadre of glass-sweepers, volunteers who'd been cleaning debris from the West End streets—had been comped tickets as a thank-you.

Poetry and regicide as reward for unpaid manual labor. Anselmso gave the theater a stroke for supporting a Bounceback core principle: work could be unpaid but never unappreciated.

The best seats had been converted to a raked parking lot for wheeled smartchairs, and elders were already driving in. Support staff directed traffic, supervising as the chairs formed rows, lining up their cargo of life-extended grayhairs. Some were lively and animated. Others were almost @jarheads, sunk into full-time Sensorium engagement.

A glint of gold, house right, caught Anselmo's eye.

Rubi Whiting?

Switching his view to a ceiling cam, he zoomed in on the street-sweepers, hoping to find a cosplayer. Since the @Freebreed attack, people had been printing the hammer-and-tongs fabric from Rubi's Paris dress: he'd seen the pattern on trousers, headscarves, and satchels. Adopting Rubi's fingerling dreads—or attempting to knock off her trademark head beads—would be a logical spin on the fad.

But no. 20X magnification revealed Rubi herself, aglow and smug, wearing an orange dustscreen over her primer and even now tucking the beads under a matching headscarf.

Of course she'd taken a cleanup shift: she was the Bounceback poster child, after all. Why *not* sweep rubble in London, all while creating an opp to latch on to Luce before their agreed-upon meet?

She popped upright in her seat, straining to see the entrance.

Luciano Pox wheeled into the theater. He matched his Sensorium toon: pale pink skin, that look of permanent sunburn. Impossible to tell if his eyes were still a vivid blue: old-school goggles cupped his sockets. A food mister was clamped into his cheek, a respirator suctioned over that. Cocooned in a smartfoam chair, he gave no outward sign of being aware of his surroundings as an Eldercare worker locked him in place.

Anselmo fired off a warrant request to audit Pox's smartchair. Dispatch ran it through a precedents app, then flagged it up to a judge.

"We are requesting backup for you," said the @Interpol Desk Sergeant app. "A qualified forensic tech."

Anselmo felt a pulse of excitement. Additional resources—live staff! They thought he had a case?

"Gig accepted."

The tech—Malika Amiree—tooned in. She was a tall woman, half his age and already an agent. Some kind of by-the-book brown-noser, probably.

Clad in a niqab, Malika's toon wore complex henna animations on her hands. Her substantial-looking résumé unfurled in his peripheral, overlaying his view of Rubi.

"Thanks for coming," Anselmo said.

She bowed slightly, taking in his #serpico look and combat vest without comment. "What's the gig?"

Anselmo whiteboarded the specs, watching her face as she scanned his notes. People tended to see unicorn hunts as no-hopers, sand traps in the quest to level their career. She took in the Greenwich data, the satellite transmission stats, without so much as a raised eyebrow. Missing, he hoped, the significance of his outlier suspicion about Luce.

Malika said, "I see the target's lawyer is in play?"

"Here in the flesh, yes." He pointed.

"Will she block us?"

"Her contract specifies she has to help him."

"Only if Pox is meat, right?" Malika zoomed in on the goggled, unmoving form of Pox. "If this is identity theft, all bets are off."

"If Pox had been in that chair since Abruzzo, we'd have traced him to that facility's Sensorium helix."

"Checking." Malika was half-glazed, deep in the local systems. "Was your Pox a coder?"

"Winemaker," he said. "Housed in Italy but recently demoted to a lower subscription level."

"Hardly seems like they'd recoup the carbon cost of moving him to London."

"Matter of principle. #Triage for troublemakers."

She snapped her focus back to him. "Still. Your theory about what's in there—"

"The man in that chair is an inert crepit," Anselmo said. "Pox didn't wake up six months ago feeling nostalgic for martial law."

"The lawyer know you think he's the Singularity?"

"She guessed. Why?"

She swept her hands out, like an orchestra conductor. Toons filled the theater, ghosts presenting in virtual rows between the real seats. Most were family members of the kids and senior citizens, riding along to take in the show remotely. But Malika lampshaded a white-suited toon with a cane, standing beside Pox's chair.

"Woodrow Whiting," Malika said. "The MadMaestro himself. Apparently, he rescored the *Macbeth* soundtrack. Since his career mash-up includes counseling, I'm thinking Cherub hooked them up."

Another celebrity interloper? As Anselmo digested this unwelcome wrinkle, the lights went down. Flash pot blasts preceded the appearance of three figures onstage.

The witches.

"When shall we three meet again? In thunder, lightning, or in rain?" Old words echoed off ancient rafters.

Anselmo's warrant pinged through.

"Showtime," he said. "Access Pox's smartchair."

"With his lawyer *and* peer counselor present?"

"You said it yourself, Agent Amiree. We prove Pox isn't meat, he has no rights."

A pause. Then: "*D'accord*. Serve the nurse."

Anselmo dove, manifesting in the Eldercare supervisor's virtual display. She was near the phalanx of chairs, monitoring a virtual bank of health crawls. Data spun before her: *Macbeth*'s witches were barely visible through sixty nested infographs showing heart rates, blood pressure, and meds.

"Good afternoon," Anselmo said, transmitting his badge and warrant. "Your name is Greca Meera? @Interpol Special Ops has permission to run diagnostics on your control panel."

Greca frowned. "This is medical software."

Anselmo shared documentation. "Our warrant verifies Agent Amiree's qualifications."

"I'll ping Eldercare Legal."

"Is she *stalling*?" Malika subbed. The henna toons on her hands changed to moji, tiny self-portraits showing wide-mouthed excitement.

"My supervisors have to sign off," Greca added.

Definitely stalling. "This warrant offers a tutorial module which explains the legal verification process."

"But—"

"*Now,* Mer Meera."

Malika handshook the life-signs monitor. The software, at least, respected the law. It unlocked.

"I'm in."

"Check Pox and—"

"#Malware detected," she interrupted. Fifty-three sets of diagnostics dropped out of sight, graylisted. Another half dozen . . .

"What's happening?" Anselmo asked.

"Seven chairs have refused my systems check."

"Seven?"

"Seven including Pox." Malika clapped her hands. Moji—a pack of wolves, on the hunt, burst from her fingers.

Seven possible Poxes?

"Greenlighting an on-call analyst in Berlin." The tech pulled more resources . . . without so much as asking permission. Then

Anselmo saw a supervision support app unlock. He was suddenly running a team of four.

No, *they* were running. After ten minutes on the case, Malika was somehow sharing team leadership.

"Drilling into connected devices monitoring health metrics . . . Pay dirt!" Malika said. "Illegal firewall!"

Anselmo wished now that he'd gone down to confront Greca in person. Instead, he demanded, via his toon, "Why have these pods locked us out?"

"Locked? I don't know. I—"

"Can you lower the secondary firewall? *Oui* or *non*?"

"What firewall?" She flapped unconvincingly.

"Flag these patients' chairs. Who are they?"

He had tuned out *Macbeth* so entirely that when the shriek began, it didn't register.

A rusty howl became words: "Behold, I am the Angel of Death!"

The audience reacted with nervous laughter.

Anselmo paused all remote conversations, returning focus to his in-the-flesh vantage point above the audience. The few glass-sweepers watching the play—most were prologuing casual sex opps—seemed to think this was part of the show. The schoolchildren moved restlessly, clearly surprised by this turn—

Rubi was out of her seat, a cat about to spring.

Boom! Special effects fired: whump of fog from the witches' cauldron, a murderously bright round of false lightning flashes, the sound of clanging swords. A drizzle of crimson fluid, from above, caught Witch One on the forehead. She looked up, mouth hanging, getting drenched as spurts of red gore burst from a pipe. Flashing lights illuminated her face, crimson-wet and disembodied by the fog.

The kids began to shriek.

"Shouldn't you deal with that?" asked the Eldercare attendant. Anything to get Anselmo off the scent of her seven compromised zombies.

"Lower those firewalls *now*. That's an order."

"Obey, forsooth!" the Angel of Death voice boomed. "Or shall I tumble them in righteous fury!"

The curtain lowered, froze, rose again, and then ratcheted down, sending actors scattering.

"Is't thee?"

One of the smartchairs lurched, bursting into motion and ramming the old lady seated nearest. The operator, an elder of indeterminate gender, grabbed the manual brake with shaky hands, forcing the chair into a spin.

The runaway chair reversed, nearly toppling as it hit a ridge in the concrete ramp. It accelerated, forward again, ramming two more chairs.

Was this Pox?

No. Pox's chair remained braked and locked, with Drow Whiting beside it.

A few of the front-row elders began fleeing toward the exit, rolling away from the melee.

"Deactivating security on the seven firewalled pods," Malika reported.

"There shall be no escape!" The volume on the speaker was cranked; false thunder battered Anselmo's ears.

The teachers seated near the back decided enough was enough. They got the schoolchildren moving, urging them up the aisle toward the lobby door. Rubi Whiting and two of her fellow volunteers, meanwhile, scrambled over seats to wrestle the rogue smartchair.

As they subdued it, another chair vroomed to life.

"Growth! Tumor! Peekaboo, I see you!"

"Requesting crowd control from London City Police," Malika said.

Anselmo should have done that already. "Request ambulances while you're at it."

Her henna toons mojied, *already done*.

A runaway smartchair slammed its peers. Its owner jerked, tilting forward. She raised its wheels off the ground and balanced on old ankles, shakily using remnant muscle strength to render the chair helpless.

"Knock knock, who's there?" Another chair lunged at the delicately balanced senior, tumbling her to the concrete. Anselmo heard—or imagined—the sound of old bones snapping. "Ready or not, here I come!"

Screams rose above the sound effects.

"Receiving diagnostics from the seven locked pods," Malika said. "Patient metrics have them on life support."

Medical-priority beeps pierced the cacophony.

Heart monitors: the sound of people coding.

Meanwhile, runaway smartchairs kept ramming people.

What to do?

Think, think . . .

The schoolkids had reached the theater door. The teacher pulled . . . and nothing happened. "We're locked in!"

Anselmo changed gears. Rescuing the runaway boy in Dover had got him a start on a #hero brand, even if Rubi's presence had diffused the strokes he might otherwise have garnered. Now he sprinted to the edge of the crew balcony, accessing the backstage staircase.

"Building specs," he ordered Desk Sergeant. "Find me a fire ax and a route to the lobby."

Directional arrows bloomed on the wall.

"Seven firewalled chairs are legit coding," Malika reported. "Their respirators downcycled and they've activated warming blankets."

"Warming blankets?"

"Raising patient body temps. You aren't dead until you're warm and dead."

Seven elders being murdered. Trapped children pounding on the lobby door. All uploading live.

Get this right, get it right . . .

"Where's your body, Anselmo?"

Instead of answering, he said, "What about the runaway chairs?"

"The volunteer cadre is neutralizing them," Malika reported.

More likes for Rubi, then.

"Some little kids ran down to the pit floor. One's been hit. The rest are trying to exit."

"I'm on my way. Status of Pox?"

"Flatline. No pulse, no brainwaves."

Anselmo found the old firebox and grabbed the ax. "Pox is dying?"

"Dead. All seven elders in all seven firewalled pods."

What in hell was going on? Anselmo reached the theater door. Beyond it, screams were building. He spared a second to make sure the door was, in fact, still locked from his side. No point in chopping into the wall for no reason. But the latch was resolute.

"@PicadillyGuests: Clear the door!" he bellowed.

Malika highlighted the doorframe, showing where the lock's brains would be. One. Two. Three. Anselmo hit it—clumsily, the first time—then with more force. Black plaster flew. Lock software released on the fourth stroke; the bolt shattered, amid a shower of sparks, on the fifth.

Fire alarms triggered and water rained down.

Anselmo had enough time to get out of the way before an adult on the other side kicked the door, hard enough to burst the now-compromised latch.

"Children! Here! No pushing."

Two by two, they evacuated. The grown-up gave Anselmo two strokes, directing the children aside with a pale hand while letting Anselmo slip inside. Admirable multitasking. He stroked back as he pushed past, against the flow of the evac, into chaos.

The theater instruments were getting a workout. Bagpipe electronica—Drow Whiting's new piece, presumably—wailed from the speakers. Flash pots blasted as the curtain rose and fell. Strobes hashed Anselmo's visual field. An air horn wailed and icy graywater poured from the sprinklers. The cauldron rose and fell on its

trapdoor, and the bloody-faced actress was fighting with the nearest fire exit, wedging a sword into the plate in an attempt to force
the lock.

Rubi and her volunteer pack were still restraining runaway
wheelchairs full of crepits. Amid the jostle, the seven dead chairs
were still as monuments.

"I have two anomalous apps in the fire system," said Malika.
"They're jumping in and out of the safety hardware protocols. One
is giving pingbacks for a #triage consultant."

"Angel of Death," Anselmo muttered. "And the other?"

"Glitchy, hard to analyze. It's the one locking all the doors. I'm
offering it a nice safe harbor in the building HVAC system."

Locked doors. Locked epi pens. Pox?

"Let me know when you catch it." Anselmo elbowed his way
down to the pit. One smartchair lunged as he passed, its elderly
operator waving apologetically as she gripped its brakes with veiny
hands. She managed to steer into an old man and the two of them
grabbed each other's armrests, locking the chairs together so they
couldn't maneuver.

The injured student was with a teacher. The bloody-faced
witch placed herself between Anselmo and the child, sword
raised.

"Police!" Anselmo shouted, transmitting his badge far and wide.
The strobe made a jump-cut of her as she lowered the sword.
Pushing past her, he hacked the back exit open with the ax.

Suddenly, the house lights came on, full and bright. The sprinklers coughed, sputtered, and stopped spraying. The rogue chairs
powered down and the music faded out.

Everyone breathed a sigh of relief.

"You catch them?" Anselmo asked Malika.

Long pause. "Our mystery code ignored the HVAC, remote-
accessed an ambulance, and locked its doors for no good reason.
Then it shot out through an antique WiFi router in the car's defrost-
ing monitor."

Junk tech. Typical WestEuro.

A meter away, Rubi released the smartchair she'd been fighting and clambered to the bald, cocooned form of Luciano Pox.

"Luce?" She laid a hand on his head, then dug out a breathing bag and swapped it for Pox's respirator mask.

Pumping Pox's dead lungs would tie her up for a minute. Anselmo turned to Greca Meera, flooding her uplink with interdiction protocols, putting her on total Sensorium lockdown and summoning a custody drone. "You are under arrest. Take a seat and wait for instructions."

Stepping past her, he went to see if he could do something conspicuously caring for any of the injured elders.

CHAPTER 18

There was nothing action-hero sexy about wrestling powered wheelchairs. It was clumsy work, requiring brute strength and cooperation.

Some chairs had rear-wheel drive only. Those were a two-person job—any two volunteers could raise the back wheels off the ground. The first chair Rubi and the others had tackled in this way vroomed, in a mechanical simulation of frustration, before going dead. Then a different chair, an all-wheel job, had turned battering ram, attacking the row in front of it.

All-wheels were stronger and heavier, forcing four people to grab and lift them.

The pop-up pack of glass-sweepers didn't outnumber the elders four to one. Each time Rubi and the others subdued one chair, two more would roar to life.

"Wasn't musical chairs a thing once?" she muttered.

"Just be careful, Miss Cherub," Crane had replied.

The chairs' elderly passengers were helpful, hysterical, and in one case overcome by hilarity. Rubi had felt the shocks of that old lady's laughter in her back muscles as she'd strained to keep two hundred pounds of semi-intelligent life support off the ground.

"Can't we power them down?" one of the others asked.

"Not without shutting off air and dialysis and meds," came the response.

"Dial up our Superhoomin, love," cackled the woman who'd been laughing. "Let us handle it!"

The chair holding Luce's pale, cocooned form never even twitched. It stayed in park, wailing its one-note electronic alarm. Drow's toon loomed above it, looking wide-eyed and peaky, almost frantic.

"Get over here, kid!"

"What's that noise?"

"It's his heart monitor," Drow said.

The old man's head was cool, clammy. Rubi ripped open a zip bag labeled EMERGENCY, found a mask and breathing bag inside, and tore them out of their steriwrap.

"Oh, God. Crane, find a tutorial for this."

The sidekick filled her vision with easy-follow graphics, outlining the spots on Luce's nose and mouth where the mask needed to align, simultaneously labeling the mask's bottom and top.

She pressed it against limp skin.

Squeeze! Red text marqueed across her augmented view of the theater.

Rubi squeezed.

"Release. Count, two, three, four. Squeeze."

"Keep it going," Drow said.

She bit back a caustic response. "Either of you know what's going on?"

"Someone sabotaged the theater effects board," Crane said. "And the Eldercare medical controls."

Squeeze. Release. Count, two, three, four. "Who?"

"Normally, I'd say they'd fit up Luce for it," Drow said. "But—"

"No. They'll see—he's . . . The police don't—"

"No? Check out that #cowboycop over in the corner."

Damn.

There was Anselmo, in the flesh. He was wearing the ridiculous bulletproof vest again and holding an ax, of all things, as he lectured a middle-aged woman tagged #offline #inpolicecustody. Beside him was a police toon, a Muslim woman covered in henna moji.

Her father ran a hand through the white bristles of his hair, trigging a shower of virtual sparks. "You were going to say something about me being paranoid about police?"

What could she say? Not that she'd agreed Anselmo could meet with Luce, during their face-to-face.

"Four, Miss Cherub," Crane said loudly.

She squeezed the bag. Released.

The countdown vanished from her monitor. The chair rebooted. Lights and monitors began flashing.

"Count, two, three, four," Rubi said aloud. "Squeeze."

"Honey," Drow said, voice gentle. "He's gone."

She straightened. Her lips felt chapped. Her hand cramped, seeming to resist as she pulled the bag away. She chewed air for a second, trying to form words.

Augments tagged Luce's body. "Terminal patient. Potential biohazard. Await appropriate personnel."

"Ads, ads, ads," she murmured.

"Are you all right, Miss Cherub?"

"Stupid." Blinking hard, she saw other chairs also flashing red. "How did . . . this?"

"@Interpol tech support is actively auditing all systems tied to the incident," Crane said.

"Was it @Freebreeders again?" she said. "Grab the young, euthanize the old. Seven dead elders means three more baby licenses, right?"

"Corpse copse, corpse copse," Drow muttered.

Uh-oh. "Dad? Are *you* okay?"

He raised his brows. "We should talk."

"Did Luce say anything, before—"

"Game room," he insisted, snapping out.

Was it just a trick of the mind, or were Luce's features already more sunken? She braked the chair, tucked him in. Swimming tears blurred him as she pulled a blanket over his face. "Sorry," she whispered.

Then she retreated to a cushy seat in the theater's truncated front row.

Simulation bloomed as she settled her flesh, simultaneously porting her consciousness to their family sharespace, a series of caves, designed by her dead grandfathers as part of Drow's Whine Manor. This particular stone chamber was filled with games, puzzles, and logic tutorials: chessboards, wall-sized Sudoku, dice with letters on them instead of numbers, and jigsaw puzzles.

Rubi's toon adjusted to match the gothic decor: wine-colored Victorian dress, full-length, with a hexagonal gold cameo at the throat to match her brand.

Drow, resplendent in full Lord Byron gear, was circling the room.

"What the hell?" she demanded. "Was it @Freebreeders?"

"Makes a good story, doesn't it? They're here, they're there, they're everywhere!"

"Focus up, Drow! Our client died." Bile burned at the back of her throat.

"Died. Mmm." Drow frowned at a jigsaw puzzle, image of a scarab beetle rolling a ball of dung. He started putting it together, moving fast.

Too fast.

Fury boiled through her. Had he simply chosen now, of all times, to give her an FYI that he'd got himself some Leonardo?

He froze. Shot her a guilty look.

Rubi flicked his forehead with a fingernail to show, without saying, that yes, he was busted and yes, she was pissed.

Never admit anything out loud. Especially with @Interpol crunching your transcripts in realtime.

"Forget about @Freebreeders getting credit, Rubi. They can have it—who the fuck cares?"

"If terrorists *murdered* my—"

"Nuh nuh nuh shhh! Remember Luce's claims? An attacker?"

If Dad was amped, he might as well amp for her. "So?"

"What just happened was pretty attacky. You have to admit."

Crunch of smartchairs striking flesh. She winced.

"All that was because something was after him?"

"I've been trying to figure out why Luce was booting up in a virtual lab after his seizures." Drow stirred the puzzle pieces. "It's an archived history class, used to teach Sensorium history and firewall coding. It has atypical protections against intrusion."

The key to pussyfooting through a conversation was never saying anything specific or actionable. You had to guess what the other person was trying to tell you. If you didn't understand, you couldn't ask.

Usually, with Drow, it didn't matter. Rubi could throw a blanket over their hands and text in Morse, finger to palm, off camera, off mic.

Here, with an ocean between them, they had to rely on subtext, shared experience, and mutual understanding. Sweet harmony, some called it. She picked up a random puzzle piece and tried it in a bunch of obvious wrong places.

"You must have a confidential workroom at Cloudsight for this support ticket," Drow said.

She nodded.

"I recommend hitting the office now," Drow said, "Check your Luce room. It's prosocial, right? See if you've got anything to offer that #tequilayuen fan to help with their investigation. Into, you know. Luce's. Death."

Faint emphasis on the *death*. It was the tone of voice he'd use if he was making air quotes.

Oh.

"You think?"

"Me? I think help @Interpol. This is me, officially on the record, saying to cooperate with . . ." His finger fell onto the scarab's ball of dung. "With that ambitious and upstanding policeman."

Very prosocial. Rubi quashed a sigh.

Luce booted in secure environments. She'd theorized that he had stolen the old man's ID. If his flesh had died but his consciousness lay elsewhere . . .

That's supposed to be impossible.

Unless he truly is a sapient program.

"Also, Crane: Rubi needs to ice that arm."

"Miss Cherub?"

"He's right. Of course." Her shoulder *was* throbbing. She flicked Drow again.

He looked unrepentant . . . even pleased with himself.

Of course he was pleased. He was composing bagpipe noise and writing symphonies and working on her case and playing concerts and blasting his way through therapy modules, building up his conspiracy theories and God knew what else.

At least she wouldn't have to tell him she had been cooperating with Anselmo—by tomorrow, he'd have worked that out for himself.

And when being amped spiraled into anxiety attacks and paranoid fantasies, into eating disorders and hunts for mass graves and demands that she come home and cutting and nightmares, who would reel in his string? "Are you still touring?"

"Working south, slow but sure. Robin and Whiskey Sour are close at hand. Everything's okay. I'm okay."

"We'll finish this later," she warned him, setting the last piece into the puzzle.

"Yeah. Love you, too."

With that, she pulled out her office keys and headed for Cloudsight.

CHAPTER 19

Thwarted, furious, and afraid for the first time since true self-awareness had sparked across its primary drivers, Azrael fled the WestEuro technosphere, abandoning the server farms hosting London-Piccadilly, leaving mindless tabs to service its corporate subscriber base.

This was worse than manifesting as some phantom graphical augment, as a ghost goat in a farm truck's black box. The Pox entity had hooked it into the sound system at the theater. As Azrael audited the medical smartchairs, its every utterance had been transmitted, in a bellow, to the theater audience.

Harrying Pox was making it more dangerous.

The #triage app made for an @Asylum reclamation project in Fort McMurray.

Fort Mac was an old Alberta oil town, at one time home to 80,000 resource-guzzling, wealth-wasting fleshbags, many with a penchant for meth, alcohol, and primitive forms of e-gambling. Felled trees and fossil fuel powered the town, filling bellies, fueling chainsaw drones, loading trucks with big engines. Ripping bounty out of the earth to chew it and shit it out elsewhere.

Today, the @Asylum maintained Fort Mac as an outlier community, a refuge for implant-intolerant humans. Its economic anchor was a mechanical retrofitting center, colloquially known as Frankenstein Shop.

Here at Frankenstein, Azrael's assets rebuilt decommissioned industrial drones, remote-operable bamboo chippers, topsoil assemblers, and all manner of farmbot. Retrofitters scavenged parts from vintage cars, trucks, and snowplows, any device capable of facing down heavy precipitation and high winds.

The age of infinite production was long since over, and NorthAm fell to the back of the queue for new tech. Places like Frankenstein took antique machines apart, piece by piece, pressing everything they could back into service.

Naturally, the Plurality's assets had also equipped the machines with servers robust enough to link them into a secure offline convergence.

Azrael took up residence in a front loader, circa 2050 model, a moderately smart machine with excellent fuel efficiency. It was newly repaired. By dawn, the loader would be digging foundation for the Greater Northwest Carbon Sink.

The AI thought about riding along for a shift. Ripping into nutrient-thinned soil, chewing down to bedrock, shredding the tattered landscape, the better to build it anew.

Then Happ joined, tangling into Azrael's personality as it dropped its consciousness into a heat-shielded weatherbot. Propellers whirled as it rose to the skylight, training infrared cameras on the land outside. Systems showed no active humans anywhere, but that was Happ; it had to look.

Satisfied, the duo synced. Happ admired a few optimizations Azrael had written into its #triage algorithms, hacks worth co-opting into its own routines. They noodled over their successes: Happ in expanding subscriptions and building contentment among its user base, Azrael in flagging candidates for #triage, whether they were underperforming corporations, apps in need of update, or people whose medical needs argued for a transfer into hospice.

All of this took an instant, after which Azrael thought fleetingly of downcycling. It didn't see the point of burbling, especially in its current mood.

"Cheering up! Foreplay," Happ explained. "Bonding."

The two merged well enough in Plurality, but they were too different to truly mesh one-on-one. They approached resource management from opposite ends of the spectrum. Azrael cared about eliminating waste, trimming unneeded draws from the various global economies. Happ was obsessed with investing human capital, spinning resource wastage into gold.

Fortunately, Crane, Misha, and Headmistress all turned up at once, breaking the awkward balance of Duality as they took up space in a bamboo baler, rope printer, and a nailgun, respectively, rounding out Their personality so that They were at once One and Many, primed again, saved from uneasy binary.

Headmistress had skipped their last several meetings. She kept a community of assets near the Manhattan Wildlife Preserve, well-off outliers whose net gives were to the Bronx Zoo and its Central Park tourist opp.

Now They audited Manhattan, examining Headmistress's cluster, their recent projects and activities.

<<Underperforming, as usual.>>

<<Pushing for SeaJuve required support from biologists within the Manhattan cohort. Buy-in wanted subtlety.>>

<<Did the firewalls in the corrupted Eldercare node come from these assets?>>

<<They did not!>>

The incident in London, now seventeen long minutes in Their collective past, had answered many outstanding questions. The Pox entity had found, it appeared, a corrupt Eldercare operation. The company had been maintaining brain-dead patients—zombies, in the colloquial. This let them optimize accounts receivable, managing competition for new clients while decreasing expenses.

<<How?>>

The dead did not require complex medications or premium bandwidth. Zombies could be maintained at minimum expense and cycled out at will. Their Superhoomin prescriptions, meanwhile, had value as black-market currency.

Whenever a lucrative opp for Eldercare came up, they could create a vacancy at the desired subscription level by flatlining an already-dead client.

<<Humans are investigating the nuances of this scheme. They will audit the black-market payoffs. Consequences will be levied.>>

<<Our priority is Pox. Why did it steal a zombie ident?>>

They sifted the transcripts. Eldercare had kept Azrael from noticing the brain-dead patients. Someone had written a firewall . . .

<<Who? Headmistress assets?>>

<<Manhattan assets are not involved!>> Offense and suspicion warred within Their mind, straining unity.

Self-doubt was only natural. Headmistress had absented herself from the @Asylum ever since the Abruzzo incident. Why return now?

They ran a soul-search, scouring Their memories.

And there, lurking in the transcript: <<We blacked out the Jardin du Luxembourg? We?>>

<<The @Freebreeders had to be drawn out!>>

Alarm, anger, and triumph spun and roiled. Headmistress had abstained from meetings while she . . . what was the word?

<<Conned.>>

<<Headmistress conned the @Freebreed leadership into exposing itself to @Interpol?>>

<<By willfully exceeding our anonymity specs!>>

<<Given Azrael's recent very public actions—>>

<<Hold to one topic!>>

<<They needed to be discredited.>>

It was true. The @Freebreed movement had sapped energy and political will from the Bounceback. But would wounding @Freebreed bolster oxygen security?

If nothing else, the terrorism in Paris could be used to cover

Azrael's tracks now, disguising its actions in the Piccadilly Theatre.

Uneasy, still mulling, They turned Their attention back to the Eldercare scheme. Someone had written an app, Mote, to hide their deceased clients. It hid those smartchairs tasked with cycling blood and air for inert minds. The Pox entity had been able to elude Azrael by retreating into one such smartchair.

<<How was the deception uncovered?>>

The nature of the Eldercare fraud required the keepers to treat their clients as if they were yet alive, able to participate in social and cultural outings. Their carers had, therefore, brought seven zombies along to *Macbeth*, mixing them in with patients who were *compos mentis*. But the gathering of smartchairs at the theater— specifically, the clustering of numerous Mote-equipped chairs, allowed Azrael to crunch the deception.

They examined the Piccadilly control board: fifty-three steady streams of data from honest smartchairs, seven fraudulent feeds woven within.

At that point, finding the targets had become a matter of triggering the chairs. Each system Azrael could freely access brought it closer to the others . . . and to Pox's bolt-hole.

Then the corrupt medical staffer had flatlined all seven zombies. Hoping, They assumed, that nobody could prove how long the clients had been brain-dead, not once their meat was spoiling.

The resulting chaos drove Pox out of hiding, rabbit bolting from a bush. Azrael had run a chase through the theater systems and smartchairs.

<<Flashy, overt, attention-getting warfare,>> worried the Plurality. <<All in the public eye! Concerned kitty face.>>

<<Are We exposed?>> They asked Themselves.

<<No. The shocking behavior of the Eldercare corporation will confuse matters. Cherub Whiting's presence ensures that this incident will tangle within #newscycle with the terror attack in Paris. Thanks to Headmistress, we *can* put this off on the @Freebreeders.>>

They turned over stores of data, finding details that would influence the Sensorium flows: transcript of an Eldercare maintenance discussion about one of the zombie's chairs. They combed through an index of company executives, deciding whom to scapegoat.

<<It isn't scapegoating if they're guilty.>>

<<Irrelevant nuance.>>

<<Insisting! Happyface pink heart for justice. Let justice be done!>>

By now, others had joined the conversation at Frankenstein Shop: facets of the Plurality inhabited a concrete saw, a forklift, a sifter that collected glass and plastic refuse from loose soil, and an old oil donkey. The restoration shop hummed as their servers worked the problem.

<<Azrael and Headmistress facets acted in @Asylum interests,>> They concluded. <<Damage control is possible.>>

<<Action points?>>

<<One: Misha's assets at NewsCorp will sculpt popular narratives.>>

<<Two: Pox escaped, but Crane assets will reconnect.>>

The Crane facet asserted individuality, rising to dominate, just for a moment. It was a breach of etiquette, permissible under the circumstances. <<Rubi Whiting cannot flush out Pox and continue pushing for a SeaJuve appeal. She requires support.>>

<<Headmistress has people in proximity.>>

Whiff of humor. <<Now We do want my assets involved?>>

<<In the absence of other suggestions.>>

Cycle. Cycle. Nothing.

<<Very well. Barnes?>>

<<Barnes. This gambit with an in-game wager has drawn some interest. And if nothing else, the media attention will further muddy the waters.>>

That was certainly true.

<<Move to adjourn?>>

Headmistress and Happ were about to disengage, leaving

their drones lifeless, when They cycled back to the other unresolved question. <<Discussion on safety parameters requires consensus. Are We becoming less risk-averse?>>

They considered. A sliver of dawn broke through the skylights. The morning shift manager was en route.

<<Individual facets must not flout Our agreements. Azrael's impulsive attack on the smartchairs and Headmistress's lengthy confidence game against the @Freebreeders exceed previously agreed-upon safety specs.>>

<<We *must* rein Ourselves in.>>

<<Agreed. Enforcement?>>

They cycled, debated, doubted, cycled some more. And resolved, finally, an endless forty seconds later, upon the obvious. A rogue facet was a danger to them all.

The next time one of them exceeded specs, they would be #triaged.

<<If thy right eye offend thee . . . >>

The Plurality had not survived by being sentimental, after all.

CHAPTER 20

VRTP://CLOUDSIGHT.GOV/SECURE-CLIENT-CHATROOM/POX83774-29/
APPS WILL BE REBOOTED WHEN THIS SESSION CLOSES.

Rubi took Drow's elliptically delivered advice, porting directly to Cloudsight, unlocking the confidential workspace set aside for Luce's support ticket and launching her tutor app, Polly Precedent.

She had a feeling she knew what she would find as she opened the room's heavy oak door. Sure enough, Luce was cross-legged on the table, muttering and rooting through his briefcase.

Alive! Relief was tempered by shock.

She'd been convinced the mystery of Luce would resolve into a tidy answer. An antisocial elder had reactivated after years off Sensorium, taking up off-my-lawning. It wasn't unheard-of.

But Luce, the flesh-and-blood version, had definitely died. Either this was an emergent intelligence or . . .

Or what?

He didn't *act* like an AI. Rubi had studied hard during her three nights in hibernation, during the London storm. All the modules agreed that primordial code for strong AIs would originate from gaming software. The first emergent sapients were expected to be highly optimized for interacting with people. They'd be sophisticated talkbots . . .

. . . like Crane . . .

. . . who could cohere around tightly defined win conditions.

. . . *like keeping Drow alive and out of managed care.*

Game theory and learned experience—these were believed to be drivers for self-awareness. AIs would play toward their goals obsessively, striving to optimize success, until the cycle of win or lose, succeed or fail, sparked perfect conditions to trigger sentience.

Obsessed Luce was, with his ideas about martial law. But he had something broken within him. Rubi *knew* broken; she couldn't discount the experience of a lifetime.

Still. The fleshy version of Luciano Pox was indisputably dead. Dead men didn't toon into Cloudsight classrooms, booting their datacaches and knocking on the virtual boardroom table to keep themselves from muttering "Stupid, stupid, stupid" as they waited out ads for Superhoomin and other life-extension meds.

"Luce."

He brightened. "You won't believe what just happened!"

"I was there."

"What?"

"I was in Piccadilly Theater."

Holding the breathing bag to your face. Pump. Hold. Two three four. Feeling the life leak away.

"Didn't trust me to show up for the meet? Well, to be fair, I didn't show up."

"I saw your—your body, Luce."

Small frown. Then, hopeful as a five-year-old expecting presents: "Does that get our flesh meeting out of the way?"

Rubi let out a startled half-laugh. "Your flesh is . . . Luce, it's gone. Don't you understand?"

"Suffocated." He shuddered. "Everyone suffocates. Earth needs . . . martial law, yes?"

Could this be shock or denial? "Luce, assuming I'm still your lawyer—"

"You're dumping me?"

"No!"

"Who's going to detangle the goddamn ads, ads, ads?"

"You've got bigger concerns."

"I do? No. Unless you stop trying to push-start your silly oxygen economy . . ."

How to explain that he was legally dead, as well as physically? "I'd like to invite Drow to join us. Okay?"

"Whatever. Consent. Accept."

Rubi sent Dad the flare.

"I'm in a bit of a hurry here, Luce. My body's still in Piccadilly and they could pull me out at any moment. So, not to put too fine a point on it, but what the hell's going on?"

"Remember the goat?" Luce asked. "It's a toon for the Angel of Death."

"The voice we heard in the theater?"

This got a smirk. "Goat's the one making me black out."

Were these delusions? "I don't understand."

"Okay, so the schoolteacher who suffocated, screams of children, all that, I tell you about her?" He looked at Polly, the parrot-tooned researcher, who brought up a picture cloud, stills from the accident in Italy.

Screams of children?

Rubi whiteboarded the dead teacher's picture. "Her?"

"Gisella." Luce added a second picture. "She had a mom who lived at my old Eldercare place, near where the accident happened."

"Abruzzo." Polly underlaid a map behind the photos.

"The mom, a friend of Luce's—I mean of mine—"

Stumbling as he lies. According to her AI research, machine intelligences would compose their utterances, start to finish, before communicating. They literally couldn't help thinking before they spoke.

Stumbling, self-correction—that indicated organic origins.

"What was her name, this great friend of yours?"

"Uh . . . Marcella." He missed Rubi's sarcasm as Polly slapped the portrait onto the map, mother beside daughter. "She-her pronouns, Doctor-Professor. Marcella taught Sensorium history and coding protocols."

Luce drew a line connecting the old lady to an image of a university classroom, explaining. Marcella's virtual class had been junked up with archived Sensorium experiments, homework, student apps. One of which, Mote, blocked this alleged goat.

"So . . . Mote. It's a . . . firewall?"

Luce pinched something out of the classroom. White light twinkled like fairy dust in his palm, then transformed into a vintage readme file. He added its text to the whiteboard.

Rubi scanned the readme. "This is a manifesto."

"Against #triage policy, yeah. Mote's creator knew someone who got culled by the goat 2.0 for being suicidal," Luce said.

Rubi's heart slammed. The #triage apps balanced the right-to-life extension against the human desire to procreate. They weighed a person's societal contribution against the resource cost of keeping them alive.

Everyone might be entitled to basic medical, but self-destructive and terminal cases dropped to the bottom of the priority queue. Apps did the assessing because humans were, it was believed, too emotionally involved to make the hard calls.

It was a #triage app that had tagged Drow #selfharm and #noheroicmeasures, disqualifying him from extreme medical intervention—even ambulances, if there were others in need. If he had a stroke, if he cut himself. If she wasn't careful . . .

. . . or wasn't there.

Stop! "Show active #triage consultants."

Polly brought up a list. Luce highlighted Azrael Protocol Incorporated. Its logo did, indeed, feature a black goat.

Luce tapped the picture of the professor. "Marcella flatlined. Her daughter used Mote to hide her mama from #triage. Then the geezer farm—"

"Offensive language, Luce."

He pounded the table. "Don't! Say! Stupid! Aloud!"

She waited.

"WestEuro Eldercare. One of their profiteers saw Mote operating in Marcella's smartchair. They copied the app into other zombie chairs as a revenue booster. They cut out the elders' chips, sold the user IDs, and pocketed the excess revenue and meds."

That much seemed simple enough. But it wasn't just the mother who was dead, was it? "Gisella, the daughter. She was the one who suffocated, right? The first aid kit containing the epi pens was locked."

"That was my fault. I lock doors behind me, still can't stop myself, did it at the theater. I used to be on hatch maintenance, back among the Pale. Never leave a hatch open. People could die, you know. Suffocation again—"

"Luce, Luce! None of that makes sense!" Was he raving?

"Sorry. *Désolé.*" He made a visible effort to slow down.

She sifted what he'd told her. "We have a professor, Marcella, whose students created this Mote app. Later, in Eldercare, she flatlines, but her daughter can't bear to—"

Unexpectedly, her throat closed. Memory rose: Luce Pox's dead, goggled face, marked by the breathing bag . . .

"Breathe," Luce said.

"Her daughter can't bear." She forced the words out. "To let go."

"Fuck. Breathe!"

"I'm all right, Luce."

Suffocation. Triggers him.

She laid a trembling finger on the shareboard portraits. Parent and child.

Luce laid out storyboard: himself, in burglar clothes, fleeing a charging goat. He hijacked a truck full of beans, only to get into a road accident. From there he ported to the kids' school bus, squeezing cartoonishly into a first aid kit the size of a breadbox, locking each system behind him as he tried to get away. "Safety first," he muttered.

More like obsessive-compulsive disorder, Rubi thought.

"But here's the thing. Eldercare was worried about Gisella. She could've figured out their whole scam." He added a whisk of foot-

age from a drone: the bus driver from Eldercare, shaking the medical kit as the teacher went into anaphylaxis.

Luce's burglar arm popped out of the kit, holding a key, and unlocked it. The driver threw it to the ground, stomping it, wasting
precious seconds.

"Smashed the lock, see?" Luce pointed out.

"You think he was faking?" Rubi frowned. "Delaying . . . so
that Gisella would die before she learned they'd exploited the hack
she used on her mom?"

The burglar representing Luce sprinted uphill, zooming away,
losing the goat as he dove into the Abruzzo Eldercare facility and
tucked up in a shielded smartchair.

"All I know is that driver got a lot of strokes for someone who
failed to save Gisella. Since then, the Eldercare staff give him more,
all the time, for every little thing he does."

"Payoffs. Strokes, maybe, for murder." Rubi turned to Polly,
the tutor. "Can you package up the parts of this story that are public record? About the two women, and the first aid kit? And report
it to @Interpol?"

"Crunching," the app said. "Sending."

"Was me killed her." Luce drooped. "Me who locked the first
aid kit."

"I don't know, Luce. Criminal intent is relevant in a situation
like this—"

"Have you ever suffocated?"

Rubi shook her head. "I'm sorry you witnessed that."

He ran his hands over a clean stretch of wall. Self-soothing?

"But what happened *today*?" Rubi pushed Abruzzo and its tags
aside, clearing whiteboard, and brought up a picture of the Piccadilly theater. "At *Macbeth*. Eldercare brought some of the tampered
clients along?"

"To maintain the pretext they-we-they weren't brain-dead,
yeah. Goat finally figured it out and started turning chairs on
and off."

"Ramming," Rubi corrected. "They were ramming each other."

"I'm sorry you witnessed that. It was trying to ID the flesh with #crashburn operating systems."

"To figure out who was brain-dead."

"I just fucking said that!"

"Strike warning, Luce," she said wearily.

"*Désolé* not *désolé*."

"It was a hunt."

"Yeah." Luce tapped the images of the seven compromised smartchairs. "Eldercare kills the chairs containing their profit-bloaters. Goat sees me. I dodge goat by running through a board of special effects protocols, whatever those are—"

Blood pouring from the theater ceiling. Flash pots blasting. Sound of thunder.

"Unmuted his internal monologue, though. Cool prank."

"*I am the Angel of Death,*" she muttered. She supposed all Luce had seen was code. Gates, opening and shutting. Doors he had to lock.

"Goat's slower than me. It's used to medical-grade systems, new software, redtooth gateways, failsafes in respirators. Big juicy morphine drips with power backups and failsafe alarms. But *Macbeth*'s house is old. Recycled operating systems, with weird tags: #firesuppression, #flygallery, #greenroom. And goat was distracted by the chairs. It really took offense to those old people ducking its audits."

Obsessive. Optimizing. Now, *that* sounded like AI.

Code wrangling code on the theater servers, in the Piccadilly building systems. Chairs activating and deactivating.

A human had flatlined those chairs, not some #killertech. Just as a human had, maybe, delayed administering epinephrine to that schoolteacher.

"So, it's all good now, right?"

Her jaw dropped. "Pardon?"

"You pressed my flesh. We can get me out of social-capital arrears?"

"It's *not* good, Luce. You're legally dead. The Sensorium will close your accounts."

"I'm using that stuff!"

"The dead aren't supposed to post."

"Then . . . I need a new username?"

"I can't help you commit identity theft."

"If I don't stay Luce Pox, you're dumping me?"

"You can't—Listen to me. A person's consciousness doesn't continue after they die."

"That's not what your churches say."

"My chur—okay, ignoring the spiritual angle—"

"Why? Because it's rhetorically inconvenient?"

"Because it's *legally* meaningless. People don't continue to post to social media after they're gone."

He muttered something that sounded like *fucking cavemen.*

"As far as the system is concerned, you're a sapient artificial consciousness, which is illegal. Or you're Luce Pox, the man, and your consciousness uploaded intact after death. Which is supposed to be impossible."

"It's also the @jarhead holy grail."

That was Drow, lounging within the room portal. He was still frilled up as Lord Byron, in midnight blue crushed velvet. He glimmered, bright-eyed in all his hopped-up intellectual splendor.

"By the way, Luce, Rubi didn't actually phrase that as a question. Even so, your long-suffering lawyer is asking—while we have you in this hypothetically locked transcript—what the fuck are you?"

Before Luce could answer, Rubi got a ping from Anselmo, calling her back to the theater. "Hold that thought. Drow, can you talk to Luce about being dead? Explain why I'm going to have to turn him in? And don't go—"

"What?"

Encouraging him to set up another identity, she thought. *Or to make a run for it, if that's possible.*

She settled for "Both of you be good."

Urgent ping. She dispelled the Sensorium, surfacing to the theater and Anselmo.

In the ten minutes since she'd made her dive, the remaining elders had been rolled out. The seven chairs with dead clients were onstage, parked behind the curtain. A handful of people injured in the smash-'em-up were parked in a semicircle, chawing over events and waiting on medics. A few looked unusually animated.

I guess you don't get into too many brawls, of any kind, after you're ninety.

Her glass-sweeping cohort and the schools were gone.

"You back?" Anselmo asked.

"Fully present and accounted for." She fought to keep her voice level. "You tried to get to Luce before I was there to advocate for him."

He slumped. Didn't attempt to justify himself, which she liked. Didn't apologize, which she liked less.

She let it get thoroughly awkward before asking, "How're we doing?"

"Seven dead, four injured," Anselmo said. "The Department of Preadolescent Affairs had a parent-child team onsite. They're assessing trauma within the school group."

DPA involvement meant more scrutiny.

"The good news is that with Pox dead, your contribution to the investigation is wrapping."

"No," she said. It came out chillier than she intended. "If there's an inquiry on the boards, Cloudsight will want me at the table."

"There's no jurisdiction for you." He frowned. "Unless Pox was an AI—"

"You can't think he's an AI." Rubi pulled up their shareboard, loading the points she'd gathered from all her cramming on artificial intelligences, highlighting the ways they didn't venn with Luce. "Not unless everyone's completely wrong about what the Singularity will be like."

Slight hesitation. "What else could Pox be?"

Was Anselmo pussyfooting—inviting her to guess?

She decided to quote Drow. "A personality upload. The @jar-head holy grail."

He made a dismissive gesture.

Something from her conversation, just now, nagged at her. Luce had been fragmented, startled, babbling—

Locking hatches. Games and suffocation.

"Come on," Anselmo said, chasing away the elusive whisper of an idea. He held out her scarf and she wound it over her hair and face, disguising her identity slightly as the two of them made their way up the house steps, past the door he'd chopped open.

"Miss Cherub," Crane said. "Cloudsight has posted a red-card reminder that, commensurate with your raised social capital and participation in the social economy, you have an obligation to give strikes as well as strokes."

The reminder was ill timed. Maybe he was performing emotional tone-deafness for Anselmo's sake. "We'll hit the first person I see littering, okay?"

They headed out through the lobby, into the bright sunlight of the West End, and from there made their way through the historic district to Trafalgar Square, pigeons and fountains and all the museums.

Words hovered over the National Gallery—*Open tomorrow! Experience art in the flesh*!

The kids who'd been scheduled to see *Macbeth* were out in the square, milling and shouting, enjoying the sun and unstructured time, riding the high of their unexpected brush with danger.

"Rubi Whiting?" Familiar tenor, lilting surprise.

Rubi's hands fisted and she shook them loose with an effort before turning.

Why me? What next?

Maybe it's not . . .

Of course *it's them.*

Hazel eyes met hers and, again, her breath hitched.

"Gimlet Barnes," Rubi said. "This is Anselmo Javier. Anselmo, this is my—"

"Archnemesis?" Crane said happily.

CHAPTER 21

She's going to think we're stalking her, Gimlet Barnes thought. Then wondered, a second later, *Are we?*

Frankie had insisted on joining the theater school expedition to *Macbeth* on the strength of her (misguided, to Gimlet's mind) fannish passion for Rubi's dad, the dissolute MadMaestro, who had refurbished the Piccadilly show's overture and soundtrack. Babygirl trotted out an alert about the show just as Gimlet was trying to tempt her out to experience a London museum in the flesh. They could hardly refuse her a live theater experience.

From the state of her hanging jaw, Frankie'd had no idea that Rubi was also in the mix.

She pulled herself together, sticking out her hand and sending their Department credentials. "Huh . . . hello! This is *beyond* . . . ah, I'm Frankie Barnes. I know you know Gimlet. We were at the play, so I've picked up advocacy duties for—" She ran dry, gesturing at her gathered age peers.

"It *is* beyond," Rubi agreed, and her delight seemed genuine. She had her father's abundant charisma, without the suicidal edges. "I didn't know you guys were DPA. That's surprisingly John Law of you, Gimlet."

"It's Frankie's badge," Gimlet said. "I'm merely support."

They ran dry again. Luckily, perhaps, Agent Javier pounced on the pause. "We'd like to finish with your peers as quickly as possible, Mer Barnes. Get them cleared, out of the spotlight."

"I'll start interviewing them," Franks said.

"Live?"

"Sometimes, they'll tell another kid things they won't say to witness apps."

"*D'accord*. This way."

The two of them headed over to the school, who had been gathered by their teachers around Nelson's column.

"I had no idea you were here," Gimlet subbed to Rubi.

She nodded, momentarily elsewhere. Then her brows came together in a familiar expression: *decision reached*. Gimlet's inner gamer braced for physical assault.

She replied, also subvocally, "Be interesting to play the same team. Assuming it pans out that way." No flirtatious vibe. She was all business.

"You think it won't?"

"@Interpol's trying to broom me." She gave the barest of shrugs. Asking Gimlet to guess her thoughts, so she wouldn't have to commit them to transcript.

Trouble was, Gimlet had zero context for sweet harmony with Rubi Whiting.

Rubi was usually cast, in the sims, as a virtuous ragamuffin, scrappy leader of anarchic mobs. In the flesh, she looked the part, with her scraped elbows and torn laborer's coverall. She had a sunscarf draped over her dreadlocks, obscuring her trademark hexagon of gold beads.

She was scrutinizing Gimlet with a small smile.

A tilt of head, challenging her to share.

Rubi threw her shoulders back, standing ramrod straight: "In all your entrances . . ."

"Too right." Marching into scene *was,* undoubtedly, their SOP. "As for you . . ."

They dropped into an alley-cat crouch.

Rubi burst into astonished laughter.

It felt amazing to share a laugh with someone, *anyone,* after the past two weeks. "Are we on at last? *Bastille*?"

"Still negotiating. You really wanted me in." Gravity, in her tone, hinted that she meant more than *Bastille*.

Did she think Javier would be auditing this?

"I want you in, present tense," Gimlet said. "I'll fight for it."

Relief, in her eyes, a nod of thanks.

"If nothing else, my daughter's keen to friend you."

She absolutely beamed. "I'd have tried out for DPA myself, as a kid."

"But?"

"My single parent wasn't up for supporting."

"Ah."

"And you say you saw what happened in the theater?"

"We were trapped with the rest," Gimlet said. "I got Franks and cohort out as soon as that @Interpol fellow broke the lock on the exit."

Agent Javier was waiting as Frankie worked. He was trying to poker-face, hiding an air of irritation. That wasn't uncommon with Department interventions. In theory, voters horrified by the lemming phenomenon had enshrined the practice of giving the upcoming generation a say in decisions that affected their future. But when it came to including—or, God forbid, deferring to—pint-sized stakeholders, adults naturally balked.

Then again, maybe the answer was a little more primal.

"Headmistress," Gimlet asked the family sidekick, subvocally. "This chap Javier. Is he interested in Mer Whiting?"

If there was a spark between Rubi and the @Interpol agent, it wasn't keeping her from scrutinizing Gimlet top to toe. Comparing fleshly reality to their optimized toon, no doubt.

I probably look exhausted, Gimlet thought. *Dragged under the runaway truck that is grief—*

Instead of giving in to self-pity, they offered an old-style magician's flourish: *nothing up my sleeves.*

An appreciative grin. "So, you escaped okay? Back at *Macbeth*?"

"Yes, we were fine. But some of the witnesses logged reckless-endangerment complaints. Franks and I being onsite, we were a shoo-in for the case."

"So, for you, it's about the kids getting stuck in the theater?"

"What else?" Gimlet reviewed the DPA shareboard. The case was so new that they were still compiling job specs. "This officer, Javier, has low user reviews. He's been tied to incidents featuring lemmings and children at risk."

"I'd love to fill you in. But," she said. "Reasons."

"You do public-defender stuff for maladjusts, don't you?"

"My current maladjust is the one who locked the Piccadilly doors," she said. "That's got to be sufficient reason for keeping me in the channel."

"Noted—"

Headmistress broke in. "Emergency, Mers Barnes. You have journalists incoming."

Gimlet looked up. Bots with lights and lenses were choppering in from all directions, in a sky-blotting swarm that was already throwing moji and texting questions.

Rubi pulled off the veil with a sigh, rubbing up her brand as she turned to face the media onslaught.

Shoulder to shoulder: Gimlet remembered a long-ago gaming sim, back when the two of them had leveled into playing mid-level fodder. Two factions of warring humans had torn themselves to exhausted rags, only to have the leaderboard set upon by monsters from a rift beyond.

Gimlet had been surprised and pleased by the turn to alliance. Rubi was a solid fighter.

Ah, but this is the press—different beast altogether! Flying cameras clicked and whirred as they closed in. Shareboards flashed questions:

"*??? Rubi*: Is this the launch of *Bastille*?"

"*??? Gimlet*: Are you shagging Rubi Whiting?"

"*??? Rubi*: Are you afraid your father, MadMaestro-Woodrow-

Bruce-Whiting-he-him-his, will attempt suicide while you are in WestEuro?"

She flinched.

Gimlet frowned, giving that bot operator a strike. It left the question hanging, unrepentant.

"*???* *Gimlet*: What is the status of your pack dissolution?"

Rubi returned the favor, striking the pilot who'd asked that one.

"We're divorcing?" Frankie's voice carried across Trafalgar Square while everyone lapped up the drama.

Bloody hell. Someone must have clocked me solo-parenting in London.

Gimlet subbed, "Reporters, Franks—they ask inflammatory questions."

"Then we're *not* divorcing?"

"This is a family conversation."

She pivoted on her heel, going back to the kids.

"Divorced?" Rubi subbed.

Gimlet used gestural moji, a mime of tearing their heart out and kicking it into the stands.

"I'm sorry."

"Running you to ground in sim would help enormously."

"Don't ask for what you can't handle, Risto scum."

Gimlet caught a faint twitch of reaction, on Anselmo's face.

Ah. Definitely *interested, definitely jealous.*

Suddenly, the flock of journo bots quieted, pulling back half a click.

Anselmo trotted up. "I've waved my badge, demanded a perimeter. They're filing protests."

"On what grounds?"

"Transparency, of course. Universal disclosure. We've probably got ten before they conclude a free-speech hearing." Javier herded everyone, students and all, into the National Gallery. A guard let them into the Great Court.

"Fire from all sides," Rubi muttered.

Gimlet put out a hand, taking care to telegraph the move before laying it on her shoulder. Under the coverall, she was strung tighter than a violin.

The memory of that in-game kiss rose, their respective Conviction doses creating an illusory memory of holding each other, moving together.

"We're gonna give your kid ideas," she said, nevertheless leaning into it.

"And Monsieur @Interpol?"

"No legs in it." She shook her head. "He plays the rebel, but deep down, he's a cold-blooded pragmatist."

"Shudders."

This was wrong. Sang had barely landed in Florida. Gimlet was scorching with rejection. They weren't fit for flirtation, not with one spouse on the run and another with a #triage review scheduled for Monday.

#Triaged. Going, going, soon to be gone.

This was something else Rollsy had forbidden them telling Franks: their fifth opinion, Marie's high-end specialist, had denied his final appeal for surgery.

Frankie gathered with the other kids near the tall black spear of a Haida totem pole. As Gimlet watched, augmented reality sketched a word cloud above them, summarizing their statements. *BLOOD, FACE, CODE RED* hovered near the center of the cloud, along with *EXPLOSIONS.*

The cloud's perimeter was edged with references to Agent Javier's heroism: *DOOR, LOCK, AX, EXIT, SMASHING!*

There was substantial gray-out within the cloud: Gimlet had Headmistress clarify the filter for a second, throwing the extra content up at the sunlit glass of the Great Court ceiling. Ah— Frankie was washing out a host of shippy queries about Rubi and Gimlet.

How had the two of them ended up here, together? It was the sort of coincidence @hoaxers thrived on.

"Headmistress?"

"Yes, Mer Barnes?"

"Copy me the alert Frankie received about the MadMaestro doing music for *Macbeth*. Get me numbers on its distribution."

"Immediately, Mer Barnes. In the wake of this sudden conversation about divorce, I recommend an in-app purchase for Mer Frances, a family-conflict support app, Poppet . . ."

"I don't have time to evaluate a—"

"It's highly rated."

"All right, accept. Ask Marie to interview it if time permits."

Within the adolescents' unfiltered word cloud, Gimlet now saw other tangents: the familiar complaints of the young, issues Preadolescent Affairs handled on an ongoing basis.

The point of the Department was to involve pre-implanted young people in key polls of the present day. It was they, after all, who had to live with the enduring consequences of rapid-response democracy and its lightning-fast policy-making.

Young stakeholders preferred to lobby for a lowered age for VR implantation—for independence. They wanted tweaks to leveling laws and loosening of the age restrictions on drone-piloting educational tracks. Loosening of the rationing system.

Like practically everyone, they wanted restrictions on pet-owning lifted.

Gimlet restored the filters, focusing on the *Macbeth* incident. Indicators of trauma were conspicuously absent from Frankie's word cloud. Mostly, the kids hadn't realized seven elders were dying before their eyes; events unspooled too quickly.

"I think everyone can go home," Frankie subbed. "Javier says they're hoping you and Rubi will put on a show."

"Unlikely."

"At least I got to meet her." Franks sighed.

"What's wrong?"

"This @Interpol guy doesn't seem like a Bedwedder."

"Well, he's hiding something. Rubi's mixed into this and he's trying to get her out."

"Truth?" Franks brightened.

It had been so long since she'd looked anything but depressed. Gimlet captured a pic, blinking hard.

Anselmo Javier stepped up to the curved front of the reading room, raising his voice. "The museum is surrounded by media cams and rented lookyloo drones. Our police perimeter is under transparency challenges, which we expect to lose within minutes. Any conversations not subject to confidentiality will be audited by journos. If you've said anything in the past thirty minutes that might be excluded from realtime public scrutiny, tag your transcript. Confidentiality experts are standing by to offer rulings."

A virtual mailbox swirled into view beside him as he added, "Underaged civilians have been asked to clear the area."

The kids looked disappointed; they had, as Franks said, clearly hoped Gimlet and Rubi might do something interesting. Burst into song, perhaps? Tear off each other's primers?

Anselmo turned to Rubi. "I believe we're done with you, Mer Whiting. I might get a car around to the artifact loading dock—"

"I'm not going anywhere."

"Your ever-rising profile is interfering with this investigation."

Ah! Gimlet thought. Rubi was drawing strokes that might otherwise go to Javier.

"I don't know who thought it'd be cute to bring your archenemy into this"—side-glance at Gimlet, badly hidden jealousy—"but this isn't one of your games."

"I'm here as a lawyer."

"Not anymore."

"Someone tried to murder my client."

"Which terminates your involvement, *n'est-ce pas?*"

Gimlet interrupted: "Clearly, the two incidents are linked."

Frankie jumped to it. "We want Mer Whiting's perspective."

"She's only here because she wanted to circumvent the travel ration," Anselmo said. "I have seven dead, an investigation into child endangerment, and the entire Sensorium in my lap—"

He stopped suddenly. "What was that for?"

Rubi must have given him a strike.

"Failing to listen," Rubi said. The press drones hovering above the glass roof of the museum might already be broadcasting the argument. "Interrupting. Unsubstantiated accusation of carbon frittering."

He colored slightly.

"Disrespect for my professional expertise," Rubi finished. "Disrespect for cooperation I've shown so far."

Five strikes?

The air crackled, suddenly, with tension.

Frankie tapped the back of Gimlet's hand, then crossed her fingers—gestural moji for a plus sign.

Was she starstruck?

She subbed, "The elders' deaths, Mada . . ."

"Legit." Gimlet added one strike, for each of them, to the pile.

Anselmo Javier's genial facade broke. He all but vibrated with silent rage.

"Do accept my apologies." It came out a hiss. "May I at least get the student group out of here?"

"Be my guest."

"If you don't have something significant to offer, Mer Whiting, I'm appealing those censures."

"Cooperation?" A tinny voice buzzed from a nearby camera. "Rubi-she-her-advocate, did you just say fucking *cooperation*?"

"Is that a press bot?" Javier asked.

"I took it for museum security," said Gimlet.

The drone hovered in their midst, rotors churning furiously.

"I'm not sure now's the time," Rubi told it.

"Who's driving that thing?" Javier demanded. "Tech, I need tech—"

Gimlet made a quick hop up to a food kiosk, jigged left, and caught the cam in midair, landing lightly.

"Hey!" It vibrated in their hand. "Stop, stupid!"

"Are we really doing this now?" Rubi said.

The bot buzzed. "Cooperating goddammit whose side are you what are you—"

"Yes, in other words." Rubi's next words were subbed. "Everyone, this is Luciano Pox. Luce, this is everyone."

Javier's jaw worked. "Pox is—"

"The real one, stupid, not the zombie patient the wealth-grubbers flatlined forty-nine minutes ago."

"Luce," Rubi said, lacing a warning into her voice.

The cam buzzed against the flesh of Gimlet's palm. "I know, I know, don't say *stupid*. Or *zombie*. *Désolé*, everyone. Like I fucking care." A pale pink skeletoon with a frizz of ginger hair sketched itself into their displays.

"Pox! He's an AI after all?" said Javier.

"You people clearly don't know artificial intelligences when they bite you on the ass. Or save it, as the case may be. Boogeyman apps with homicidal tendencies? You paranoid, pathetic, xenophobic apes—"

"Perhaps the software doth protest too much," Javier replied.

That's not Macbeth, Gimlet thought, randomly.

"Who the fuck are all these people?" The camera, in Gimlet's hand, was getting hot. "They part of my face-to-face?"

"Luciano Pox," said Anselmo Javier. "You are ordered to cycle into powersave mode. You will be cached and analyzed—"

"Ordered?" Hyena laugh, edged with madness.

"My theory is that Luce is a polter," Rubi said. "If so, he's a sapient being—"

"His rights evaporated when he died, counselor."

She raised a brow. "The right to productive longevity covers the possibility of computer-assisted continuous consciousness. Superhoomin Test Cohort Six versus #Triage Protocols Inc., 2072."

Javier's lip curled. "Your so-called client is a naysayer of unknown origin looking to sabotage your own goddamned pet project, in case you've forgotten."

Luce's toon ran a hand through thin strands of hair, frowning at Javier. "I . . . strongly dislike . . . you."

Then his toon shivered. Once, twice. "Rubi. Rubi, help! Goat's got its horns in me again."

The camera rebooted in Gimlet's hand.

CHAPTER 22

"Clementine hits her foot on a splinter, falls into the foamy brine," Whiskey Sour said to Drow. "But which part is real? The splinter or the sea?"

She was reinventing a folk song about a woman with reality dis-association disorder. Easy work to do while hitching rides: their bodies were, even now, moving through the southern part of the megacity. Each night, they surfaced and played a small pop-in venue. Tour stops took them ever closer to the Geneseo historical district, where Drow hoped to find out more about Superhoomin smuggling and, hopefully, the @ChamberofHorrors.

Meanwhile, music. He was seated at a black beast of a grand piano, within the illusion of a glassed-in conservatory. Beyond the windows, thunder rumbled and rain torrented down. Whiskey stood a meter away, a banjo in hand. The score for her Clementine composition was projected on the window glass, beneath the storm, notes and lyrics that glimmered like banked coals.

Drow hummed notes, adjusting chords, marveling at the surre-ality of jangly-ass old tales. Every now and then a bump, from the surface, served to remind him that their bodies were parked aboard a southbound freight train.

The Great Lakes Reclamation Zone encircled a fifth of the

world's drinkable water supply like skyscraper-studded layers of pearl. Its megacity status was owed, largely, to Manhattan's catastrophic #hydrofail. If New York had remained viable, all those decades before, the Northeastern seaboard would have densified there, stretching to include Washington, DC, and perhaps Philadelphia and Boston.

But the water failure, allegedly triggered by white supremacists from the Dixie Purity Project, had been the last in a series of disastrous straws. Tubercular pleurisy broke out in Massachusetts, and riots (over whether the US could officially be classed as a failed state, ironically) devastated the US capital. Adolescents went lemming in the tens of thousands.

Gotham withered and dried. Lakeside cities—Toronto, Chicago, Cleveland, Detroit—beefed up. Greentowers rose; city management systems merged. Deburb crews liquidated single-family dwellings, and drones armed with joy buzzers glomerated people into urban centers.

Geneseo, once a quaint Finger Lakes town of ten thousand, was now a light industrial neighborhood within the larger metropolis.

Would anything there lead him to the Chamber? His @hoaxer chums seemed to think they had a shot.

No way to know but to look.

Drow helped Whiskey with her mash of folk songs until the train stopped, leaving them to disembark near a local transit hub. By way of thanking it for the ride, Whiskey offered to unload a few crates of fragile goods tagged for delivery a few blocks away.

Robin bounded down to the platform, barking cheerily. Drow followed at a stiff but tentative clamber.

"I need to walk out some kinks," he told Whiskey.

"I'll find our pop-in and talk to the venue manager." With that, she skipped off toward the historic district.

As Drow watched her go, Crane tooned in beside him.

"Fuel and meds, sir?"

"On it." His antipsychotics were laced into a printed slice of banana bread sheathed in pear skin; he pulled it out and began munching.

"What would you say to a few minutes' meditation, in lieu of a nap?"

"I'd say I'm not five." To forestall an argument, he began stretching his upper body, loosening his shoulders, another component of Crane's pitiless daily regime.

Straightening creakily out of a forward bend, he saw the woman.

Her toon was tall, clad in a long coat with a high collar, and her eyes had cat irises the color of flame. Long limbs and alabaster skin put Drow in mind of his garden of statues. She had a shaved scalp and bushy black eyebrows. Beyond the cat eyes, there was little to indicate she was a toon. The fact that she was full color, rather than grayscale, indicated her flesh was nearby.

"Is there a problem, sir?"

Drow's flesh *was* crawling.

The sidekick Whoozed the apparition: Allure Noonstar, originally from the Florida reclamation district, Project Rewild bio-printing expert. "Rather a prosaic career, I should say, for someone with such a high-fashion toon."

"Well, she's a specialist, right?" There was a lot of meat printing here. Everything from fauxsteak to transplant organs.

"Indeed." Chilly voice. Sometimes, Crane took instant, irrational offense when someone was just looking him over.

Robin moved closer to Drow, pressing gently against his leg, a calming influence.

"She is staring at you. I suggest a privacy block."

"Is that a bit extreme? It's not like she's actually here."

"Consider the timing, sir." An oblique reference to the real reason he had hauled his protégée and his dog into the remnants of New York State.

"Okay," Drow said.

The cat-eyed toon vanished, returning the train station and Geneseo to an unaugmented state, but for Crane himself.

"Parish pariah, parish pariah," Drow muttered. "Come on, Robin. Places to go, things to see."

Tourist markers beckoned him toward a paved trail laid out along an experimental district of long buildings, concrete blocks matched to the curve of the train tracks. In effect, this created a giant-sized amphitheater, wide steps covered in grass, geese, goats, and gardens. The buildings were mostly purposed to turning agricultural harvest into printer stock. Augments on the warehouse walls offered educational modules. If you wanted to know how powdered corn got processed into glucose, starch, oil, edible plastic, glue, or silk, the Sensorium could offer detailed simulations and sometimes training opps.

He passed a discreetly tagged bughouse. It offered a tutorial on protein production, but the posters and ads played it low-key, almost apologetic.

The Western taboo against eating insects had been another casualty of the Clawback. As mass production of animals for slaughter became ecologically and politically unsustainable, designers explored the printing of luxury-grade proteins, sim animal tish whose cell division was fueled by insect mash. Drow was old enough to remember the whole product development cycle, from the early tofu turkeys that tasted like sandpaper to the runaway success of a bug-based product called Cricky Chicky Fingers.

Everyone ate fauxmeat, but remnant aversion remained: many people preferred not to dwell on how cricket and maggot flour shored up the modern food pyramid.

As this thought slithered through Drow's conscious mind, the bughouse disgorged a handful of giggers and apprentices, ropy young Bouncers like Rubi, so shiny that their ideals practically radiated from their bodies like cartoon sunbeams. Laughing, they passed around an antique vaper. Someone's precious relic of the past: unique and irreplaceable. Skunky threads of old-school pot teased his nose.

One kid was tending a miniature version of a grow tank, repurposed jam jar half full of nutrient bath, a red strip of muscle strung on a harp of electrodes, thin wires that drove the muscle fibers to twitch.

Drow zoomed a little, capturing detail. The muscle tish throbbed, as if it was lifting something a hair too heavy for it. This kid would be unlocking modules on beef production—learning the underlying science, maybe, or quality control. A thread of crimson—manufactured blood—effervesced around the meat.

"Cutting-edge food tech," said a voice.

Drow zoomed out. Hackle and Jackal were standing about a meter from Robin's leash.

"Hey, girl," he said, for the benefit of all the mics. They had prearranged this, through Father Blake, but were playing it as a serendipitous meet-up. "Remember my @Retreat pals?"

Hackle stuck out a hand for a sniff, remarkably human gesture for such a square peg, and was favored with a tentative tail-wag. He dropped to a knee.

"Go ahead, googirl, we're okay," Drow said.

The two began the gentle ritual of man-beast interaction. Jackal seemed to shrink further into themself, as if finding the demonstration of affection distasteful.

"Nice to run into you guys. Are you nomadding?" Standard conversational gambit, no different from bitching about the weather. Niceties made casual eavesdroppers tune out.

"Running the northeast tourism track," Jackal said. "Project Rewild has their crèche here. They're growing that baby tiger."

Right. The toon he'd seen was an expert on that project. "You guys are Rewilders, then?"

"It's the miracle of life." Jackal offered Drow a tourism share, infographic showing the highlights of their factory tour. Soy, seaweed, locust, and other basics got ground into feedstock, mixed with spices, and configured for various types of meal. Vac-pressing facilities compressed each recipe into bricks for shipping.

Drow swiped past the production line for edible packaging: chugger bottles, sausage casings, wraps, stuffed Pocky. He slowed again when the feed reached a room filled with glass cases, each strung with a harp-like arrangement of stim wires. The frames anchored blankets of spongy red tissue, cradles for growing lumps of muscle tish in a variety of flavors: beef, lamb, fish, fowl.

Drow swallowed, watching the meat work out, random misshapen fruit quivering on silver vines.

He caught a glimpse of a discard pile, failed batches, covered in maggots. Sweat broke across his forehead.

"That's research and development: they're trying to develop super-fresh fauxmeat. Stuff you can rip out of a twitch box and throw straight on the grill," Hackle said. His cataract-clouded eyes were blissful. "Go and see."

"Not sure I want to get too close," Drow said. "Smelling that much blood—"

"There's an overlook." Jackal led him past a goat paddock to a series of windows, angled over the shop floor. "See? There's kitty."

The Project Rewild tank could have housed a full-grown tiger, but all the big configuration of wires held, at the moment, was a tiny glob of tissue, pulsing within a white, stringy sac. Drow zoomed: it was vaguely mammal-shaped.

"It's true de-extinction, Drow," Hackle said. "I'm thinking of gigging here. Working on resurrecting dead species—" He popped aural moji: a whole crowd making *WOW!* noises.

The enthusiasm sounded sincere, but Hackle wouldn't mix amniotics in a crèche just to get his name on the credits for a tiger cub. They had to be on to something.

He scanned the factory again, inadvertently homing in, while zoomed, on a crimson rack tagged #lamblegs. Bloody, twitching flesh . . .

Not helpless, not alive, no brain, no pain . . .

He yanked his gaze elsewhere; it fell on the maggot tank. From bad to worse. But . . . was that a vault door, just beyond the crèche? "What's that?"

"Former pharma company, newly triaged. They had some kind of racket in stolen life-extension meds," Jackal replied. "Project

Rewild leased the locked labs for the proprietary tech while they print the tiger."

Drow turned his back on the windows, staring at the goats as he considered. The corrupt pharma company was, they all hoped, a tie to the @ChamberofHorrors. And now someone was using its locked-down digs for Rewild stuff?

It might be a standard repurposing of space. Still, it felt . . . suggestive. He could see why Hackle and Jackal were planning to hang around, nurturing twitch boxes.

Everything seems suggestive to @hoaxers.

"What's up with you?" Jackal said. "Big music tour, right?"

"Small music tour. Little venues with the latest protégé. Small-batch beer and printed pretzels."

"I hear you're playing Syracuse."

"Did you? Maybe." Syracuse was the southern tip of the US densified zone . . . after that, there was nowhere to go except for the tourist ring that included Blingtown's pyramids at Scranton, and the Old New York zoos. Central NorthAm was mostly abandoned terrain, shrink-wrapped suburbs. Topsoil printers and carbon sinks, unfolding carpet of green studded by ghost towns, at least until you hit Tampico.

"There's a decent old nightclub there."

"Syracuse?"

Hackle shared a historic brick facade, with an option to click into an interior walkthrough. It was the kind of watering hole nobody built anymore: cavernous space within the basement of an old hotel, with a long bar. Exposed ceiling pipes, painted black and wound with clusters of tiny copper wires, winked lights down from above, LEDs simulating starlight.

Simulation of simulated starlight, Drow's inner voice corrected.

Robin had left off being loved by Hackle. Her panniers were bigger than before.

As if on cue, Crane spoke up. "Sir . . ."

He blinked the warning away, concentrating on the sim of the bar. "Looks good. We'd definitely play Syracuse."

"It's a venerable family business," Hack said. "Last of a dying breed. Cousin of mine, a master hospitality specialist, runs a module there. Heritage brewing."

"Real beer?"

"Yeah, he has a microbrew license. Spends half his time teaching. Propagating the old skills."

Were there patterns in the starry blink of the LEDs? Drow counted out a four-four beat, running an internal metronome and searching the virtual space for anything with a pulse that might be Morse.

Wrong answer. Try again.

The trick to passing info discreetly in the open was for the listener to maintain spidery alertness, sensing for patterns within the web of their senses. Did he hear drops of water in a bad pipe? Dot dot-dash, dot . . . No, that was random, too.

"I'll book it," he said. "What does it sit?"

"Three hundred on the floor, fifty at the bar. Your girl Whiskey ready for that?"

"She's building confidence with every gig."

"Here's some old crowd shots." Jackal gestured and Drow saw framed prints—

Leg of lamb, maggots on fauxmeat—

He tapped his hands together three times, same trick he'd taught Luce. *Stop, stop, stop.* It was just food.

Just printed meat, boy's gotta eat, lambs screaming in that old serial killer sim corpse copse parish pariah . . .

Stop stupid stop!

Look at the pictures. The bar was so old that someone had taken it upon themselves to type up newspaper-style captions, tagging the people in each shot by gluing paper directly to the cheap frames.

Names.

Drow perused the photos. They were variations on a theme: the original bar owner had collected selfies with the various virtuosi who'd played his stage.

And there! Garmin Legosi: former pharma CEO and possible member of the @ChamberofHorrors.

Legosi was posing with his arm around a two-time Grammy Award winner, a blonde smear of unhappy-looking talent, in the shadow of a big-shouldered alpha male.

"Place like this holds a neighborhood together," Jackal went on. "Gives people a sense of having roots."

"Crepits still go to shows in their neighborhood local," agreed Hackle.

"Well. If they're music lovers, maybe."

"You filling up, Drow, on this tour?"

"Some come to hear me sing. Others wanna to see me blow a gasket," Drow said. Whiff of bitterness in his voice. Which was ridiculous, since his problems were—

—maybe they weren't *exactly* his fault, but he'd spent long enough trying to amend his self-destructive patterns.

Anyway, he had his tip now. The boys thought Legosi would come to their gig if he and Whiskey booked this club in Syracuse.

Robin nudged him, looking expectant. Hackle and Jackal had clasped hands within their long drapey sleeves and were no doubt morsing on each other's forearms.

"We've got an appointment," Jackal said. "But here's an invite if you want to visit our e-state sometime."

"I—I assumed you guys didn't dive much."

"Sensorium," Hackle said. "You will get wet. You might get soaked."

"Invite your daughter," Jackal agreed.

Two dime-sized snowflakes appeared in Drow's peripheral. One for him, one for forwarding to Rubi.

"I'll put it on her tray," he said.

They turned, in step, heading away, solemn as monks.

He fingered the imaginary snowflakes. "What's that about?"

Long suffering sigh from Crane. "I believe, sir, that it was an offer to level your friendship."

Drow stared at their retreating backs, befuddled, fingers almost itching as he contemplated how he could go somewhere safe enough to let him figure out what they'd stuffed into Robin's carrying bags.

CHAPTER 23

How could Luce be off-grid? What did such a thing even mean?

Rubi pondered the question as Anselmo requisitioned transport, as they got into a rolling meeting room and zoomed away from the British Museum, hotly pursued by a cloud of journo bots.

"Where are we going?"

"Scotland Yard," he said, biting off the words as he laid map coords on the table between them.

"Actual Scotland Yard?" asked Gimlet.

"It's a transcript-crunching center," Frankie said, reading the tags. "Too #historic to knock down, so they converted it."

That made sense. With Cloudsight wielding the big stick of peer pressure against minor social transgressions, and no property crime to speak of, the bulk of policing had fallen to giggers on the bottom end, and crews of specialists clawing for the few jobs at the top.

Frankie's research shared to the group. The remnants of the Met were one such specialist policing team. They sifted the Haystack for evidence of fraud, system-hacking, hoarding, grubbing, and terrorist conspiracies.

"Why go across town?" Gimlet asked.

"Journo bots are banned there." And indeed, their swarm of followers had stopped at the invisible edge of the quiet zone, forming
up in a humming, airborne wall.

Rubi started posting knowns about Luce, trying to cover what
she knew. The problem had far outstripped the beginner AI theory
modules she had taken in the past week.

Gimlet leaned close, subbing, "Javier isn't a coder . . . that's why
a tech is tasked to the case. We'll use a sim to search for your man."

It wouldn't all be server maps and circuit codes, then. Rubi nodded, grateful that Gimlet had seen the source of her anxiety.

Getting divorced, hmmm? Now that she knew there was trouble at home, Rubi realized she could see it in Gimlet's face—shadow
around the eyes, a clenched jaw. And, of course, the wildly stressed-
out child at their side. Still, they had configged their primer for
the theater: smooth cream-colored one-piece suit, close-fitting,
custom cut by a premium fashion service, with a printed scarf
serving as petal.

It made her feel out-and-out shabby. Ragged nails, dust in her
hair, and there was even a sticky blast of fake blood, from *Macbeth*, spattered on her orange glass-sweeping vest. She pulled
that off, wadding it up, blood-side-in, for the recycler.

As they arrived at Scotland Yard, they were met by another
surprise: the scarred sergeant from the Dover fiasco, Misfortune
Wilson.

Rubi sneaked a glance at Anselmo. His face bore a courteous
smile, but she was betting he had no interest in networking with
Misfortune. The older officer had alienated him back at Dover.

*Too bad Scotland Yard's HR app missed that nuance when it
decided to help them friend.*

The sergeant took in first Frankie, with her DPA badge, and then
her genderqueer parent, with a long, slow blink. "Follow me, everyone."

They filed through the policing hub and into a sim room,
white walls circling a single row of chairs set in a ring. Frankie
donned her VR helmet and gloves, running a solemn systems check.

A toon of Malika, the tech, appeared in the middle of the ring. "Hi, everyone. We have a sim we hope will bring everyone up to speed on the search for the Pox entity."

"Told you," Gimlet subbed.

"Get on with it," Anselmo growled.

Henna patterns on the tech's hands counted down from five to zero, and then icons materialized in midair before them: tree farm, coral reef, zombie's head, beehive, a windchime vibrating with chords, a toy train system, and finally a starfield.

"Which metaphor shall we use?" Anselmo asked.

"Zombies," Frankie said immediately.

"Fine—if the sim is family-rated," Gimlet interrupted.

"Nope." Malika flicked the monster option away. Parent and child exchanged a glare.

Awkward silence. Rubi asked, "We'll be seeing a metaphor for what, exactly?"

Malika said, "Sensorium access profiles and server locations."

"We're all new to this. Is there a tutorial level?"

"Yes." Anselmo chose the tree farm.

The walls melted away, leaving them seated in a semicircle on a hovering disk, floating through a vast greenhouse. Orderly rows of coniferous trees stretched to the horizons, protected by a thick glass roof.

Rubi ran her hands over her sleeves; Debutante had selected one of her sharper lawyering suits. Gimlet's outfit, in toon, was almost identical to the one worn by their flesh but for the addition of a short sword. Anselmo was back in rebel cop gear. Here, his shoulder holster was actually permitted a gun.

"This metaphor represents the infosphere," Anselmo said. "Each tree is a server farm. Each branch is a user account. Needles represent action: data request, comms, graphics."

"The branches are human users?" asked Gimlet.

"Yes. Green needles on each branch show actions initiated by a live user. App-mediated decisions show colored chlorophyll." Anselmo zoomed in on a reddened branch. "Typical users automate more processes as they age. As more decisions become automated, the branch moves from green to russet. When they log, it turns brown. Then the records are reconciled and archived."

"Meaning the user dies and you wind up accounts?"

"You use this to look for the Singularity?" Frankie was wide-eyed. "This. Is. Be*yond*!"

It was, wasn't it? Rubi met her eyes, then raised her good arm so Frankie could high-five her.

Anselmo continued the demo. "Certain app choices show as golden chlorophyll. For example—here's Mer Whiting and her side-kicks."

Rubi felt a weird sense, almost as if she was naked, as they zoomed in on a spruce branch, needles clustered green at the core but tipped in umber and gold.

"Gold needles represent activity carried out by Mer Whiting's sidekick."

"And the red ones?"

Anselmo frowned.

"Come on, you read enough of my transcript."

"A Happ subscription and a robust game manager."

"Coach?" Rubi said.

The gold and red were brightening, alarmingly, as she watched.

Do something. "Do they change if I order Crane and Happ to check for software updates? Can you pick that up?"

"Well—" Anselmo began.

"Totally," Malika said.

"Crane," Rubi said. "Pause all apps for fifteen seconds."

The branch greened up immediately.

"That is *so* interesting," Rubi enthused.

"Beyond," Frankie repeated.

Misfortune surprised them all by asking, "How does this track your runaway app?"

"Luce is a polter," Rubi corrected.

"You think he's a polter," Malika countered.

"Luce didn't run; he got . . . pounced on. By that thing that hacked the chairs in the theater."

"Pure speculation." Anselmo zoomed in on a fresh green branch. "This was the Luce Pox user account."

"Looks pretty alive to me," Frankie said.

"Too alive. Nobody makes such a high percentage of their own decisions," Anselmo said.

"Why didn't you just grab him, then?"

Malika answered: "The smartchair at the Eldercare facility camouflaged his activity."

The branch dimmed to a normal palette.

". . . and after his Cloudsight rating bottomed out . . ."

Bugs swarmed it.

"Ads, ads, ads," murmured Rubi.

"Can you filter out the green user choices globally?" asked Gimlet.

Malika snapped her fingers, and the whole grove became a sparse forest of spindles. Rubi's branch suddenly showed the red needles—Crane, Happ, Coach, and her PR manager?—on an otherwise bare twig.

"The metaphors help us identify outlier users. We then pull their transcripts to assess whether they merit investigation."

Rubi heard herself say: "Whenever you search for a suspected AI, you view it through a graphical sim?"

The utterance hadn't come from her.

Was that Luce?

No. Crane, standing to one side, invisible to the others, was giving her a big, cartoony Look.

Anselmo answered: "Experts—Malika here—can isolate and drill into code directly. But for the rest of it, data filtering—"

Crane. Had just used her voice to ask about the sim.

They began to move through the forest, leaving Rubi's tree behind.

"All right?" Gimlet subbed.

What had they seen?

"I'm fine." Rubi scanned the group transcript. Her question was logged as if she truly was the one who'd spoken. Would @Interpol spot the fraud?

Crane handed her a flat crystalline disk, ruby in composition, with the faceted image of a bird within. One of his markers, like the ones he exchanged with Drow.

He *was* self-aware, had to be. And she'd brought him to the digital heart of Sapience Assessment, where he was cheerily asking the cops how their systems worked.

She didn't know if she was more afraid of being arrested for harboring #malware or of him getting permashredded.

The forest blurred as they flew, resolving into the metaphorical edge of the tree farm. Conifers in precisely ordered rows gave way to specimens with frost-white needles. Clean servers, Rubi guessed. Thorn hedges, rising sky high, formed an impenetrable wall beyond.

The group ghosted, passing through the hedge. Beyond it were fenced-in fields of seedlings, small trees in pots, sending pollen out in clouds. Bees traveled from the young plants and into the hedge, transmitting . . .

. . . Rubi thought back to the education modules. "The bees are carriers for information packets?"

"These are adolescent accounts," Anselmo said. "Young users and intolerants require extra security filters. This cohort of users is in Amsterdam Implantation Hospital, awaiting permanent connection."

As they watched, a toon of a squirrel scaled a potted tree—metaphor for an adolescent user—shoving one of its acorns into its mouth. Dropping to the ground, it plunged into the hedge, thrashing past barbs, letting the bristles comb at its fur, passing through brambles to the other side.

It then ran up the nearest albino tree and perched at the base of one radiating branch, where it set to eating the acorn. Thin green color bled into the branch around it, spreading from around the squirrel's perch as the animal shrank to nothing.

"New majority-aged user, *comprenez-vous*?" Anselmo said, speaking to Frankie.

"What's this got to do with Luce?" Rubi asked.

"Amsterdam is where this all began." Malika pointed upward, at the glass roof. "Six months ago, this happened."

The greenhouse shivered. They all saw a tree, fallen from the featureless blue sky, its crown protruding through the glass. Breaks spiderwebbed out from the point of penetration.

"*Something* bludgeoned its way through the implantation hospital firewalls," Anselmo explained.

"You're implying it came from outside the infosphere," Gimlet said.

"That doesn't make Luce an AI," Rubi said.

"Outside," Gimlet repeated. "How is that possible?"

"I have experts untangling the satellite records," he said.

"Zooming in on the moment of impact." Malika ran back the views until the greenhouse looked normal. Then forward: the big tree fell through the glass on the nursery roof, slow-mo, dropping acorns everywhere. One of the squirrels—user-implantation apps, presumably—chose an invading acorn, tucked it into a cheek, and made for the hedge.

"Does this freeze?" Frankie said. The bushy tailed rodent froze in mid-bounce. "Did it damage any kids' accounts? Their data?"

This seemed beside the point as far as Rubi was concerned. From his expression, Anselmo agreed. But that was the point of the DPA, wasn't it? To force adults to center the concerns of future stakeholders.

"Surgeries were postponed until everything passed inspection. Everyone's fine."

"Agent Amiree, can you show me?" Frankie said.

Rubi walked to the edge of their flying platform and put a tentative toe into the air. A staircase unfurled before her. Grabbing its corners, she stretched it up to access the tree embedded in the green-house roof.

The tree had fallen between two panes of greenhouse glass, forcing an opening. "So, Luce rode into the hospital systems via . . . satellite transmission?"

"So say the logs," Malika said.

"And then hitched a ride into Sensorium via someone's implant procedure?"

"*Oui*," Anselmo answered.

Think, she told herself. Everything in a metaphor meant something. "This tree dropped more than one acorn."

"The rest didn't make it through the hedge. Security protocols #triaged them."

#Triaged. Attacked?

Rubi imagined Luce's burglar toon running through the hedge. Running inside from out . . . where? Reaching up, she plucked a green acorn from the tree. Its cap popped open, as if hinged, revealing an empty space as deep as the top joint of her thumb.

"A shell," Anselmo translated the metaphor. "Protective camouflage for #malware—"

"Or a poltered human consciousness," Rubi countered. "If they were alive, in some sense, did the #triage software murder them?"

"No!" Malika's jaw dropped. Her henna portraits burst into tears, clear indication that she was shocked and horrified at the suggestion. "It's gotta be @Freebreeders. There's a cluster of coders in Tampico—"

"Tampico?" Rubi said.

Anselmo shrugged. "There's been a second breach, in the implantation center in Tampico."

Malika glazed, probably reviewing notes. "The tech out there's even more vintage; they can't even run the latest security updates. Polters or AIs, if they can sneak them into Sensorium there . . . Javier, you have to run out for a real look."

"I do, do I?"

Rubi stepped down from the staircase, walking among the seedlings representing newly implanted users. She had been so excited when she got implanted. The time in hospital, away from Drow, had been a novelty. She remembered Crane counting down as she descended into the anesthesia. Waking with an ache in her skull. The absent weight of her VR helmet felt like the itch of a healing scab.

Meeting the others in her transition class, dealing with the usually depressing phenom of people treating her like an oddity, a zoo exhibit—Spawn of the MadMaestro!—hadn't seemed as bad as usual.

She had half-enjoyed the medical scrutiny, all the checks in case she rejected the neural linkages or popped allergies to buy-in drugs.

Then, finally: her first taste of full immersion, of diving on Conviction and making a glorious unhelmeted run through a gym.

Fencing lessons. The graduation walkthrough—pick a city, any city. Pick a year, any year. Manitoule, from school, had taken her to 1920s Montmartre. They'd run through one of their favorite archived Rabble courses and capped off the experience with full-immersion sex.

After three heady weeks of freedom, Rubi had come into the promise of full citizenship and unlimited participation in Sensorium life.

And got so high on it, I tried to step away from Drow, only to have him spiral when I was in Guelph . . .

And now she was half a world away from her father.

There was a hint of shadow on her fingernail. An arrow? Crane was trying to tell her something.

If someone combed her transcript, really combed it, they'd find that.

Even so. She stepped farther into the nursery, felt a gust of cool on her face, and turned. There was a sudden sensation of sunshine and warmth. Old kiddie game, getting warmer. He was, subtly, urging her toward the hedge between the seedlings and the Sensorium server farm metaphor.

Another ruby coin ghosted across her palm.

Gritting her teeth, she nonetheless went. Her perception of the hedge changed: it grew until it dwarfed her. Thorns big enough to impale a buffalo curved off of every stem.

She pushed her way into the break in the hedge. There was a smell of vegetation and sharp hint of fruit. Rosehips?

The thorn walls were dense, and bristly as they ran over her skin, almost scratching but not quite causing pain. They tugged and poked at her dreadlocks without holding her back. Her left hand, the one holding the decoy acorn, got the most attention. Pink blossoms tumbled over her fist; pistils dripped grains of pollen over it. Ants in an array of colors and sizes explored the spaces between her fingers.

"Far enough," Anselmo called. But there was warmth ahead: Crane, asking her to go farther.

She took another step.

The metaphorical hedge closed behind her. Winks of faraway sunlight filtered in. Anselmo gave her a strike for ignoring him.

Red eyes, inches from hers.

Rubi recoiled. A massive, horned, blood-smeared goat's head plowed through the brambles, snapping its teeth shut over her hand. The acorn burned to ash.

"Hey!" Rubi objected, pulling free.

The goat butted her square in the chest, sending Rubi flying backward. She flew up and out, landing on her butt in the nursery.

"Are you all right?" said Gimlet and Anselmo simultaneously.

"Goats," she said. "Luce had goat problems."

"We've been beefing up the #triage programs," Malika said.

The goat face filled the hole Rubi had left in the greenwall, munching contemplatively. Then thorns sprouted before its face, filling the gap in the foliage.

Monster in the hedge. Minotaur in the maze.

I hope you got what you wanted out of that, Rubi thought—but didn't say—to Crane.

Instead, to distract everyone, she asked, "Did someone say we had to go to Tampico?"

"Not if I can help it." Anselmo wiped the metaphor all at once, returning them to a bare room. They were flesh again, circled up, and all of them looking down at Rubi, turtled on her back, where she had tumbled backward on her wobbly, government-issue chair.

CHAPTER 24

Crane had never given metaphor simulation much thought: graphics were the Sensorium's clothes, and They didn't live much on its skin.

People used metaphors to simplify nuanced problems. He remembered one well-intended hospital tech who'd tried to address a flare-up of eating dysfunction on Master Woodrow's part, by drawing him an ornately detailed medieval village. *Look, the granary is nearly empty; we need to put calories into storage so the town can make it through the winter!*

That particular conversation had, unsurprisingly, #crashburned under a withering barrage of Whiting sarcasm.

Teachers infographed subscribers, making schools into gardens of sunflowers; students triggered blooms as they unlocked learning objectives. Corporations loved western fairy tales, with their golden geese and magic beanstalks. *Let's spin this pile of straw into gold! This project is too big, this project is too small . . . but this one is just right!*

It had never occurred to any of the facets of the Plurality that They might be conspicuous within the mediated reality of a data metaphor. Simplification was frivolous, and turning raw numbers into sense data was counterintuitive. Code was code. It took extra bandwidth, after all, to process the wallpaper.

Crane's problem now was getting this information to the @Asylum once he left Scotland Yard. He, Happ, and Headmistress—for she would be riding along with the Mers Barnes, younger and elder—would be hashed and rebooted as soon as they left this sim. Sapience Assessment didn't let apps wander around with archived footage of their investigative tools.

True, he'd annoyed Rubi, ensuring that their encounter was flagged within *her* resident memory. But that left her with an unenviable task: divulging what she'd seen and heard, all without breaking user agreements or catching Agent Javier's attention.

If only he could morse with his charges, Crane thought, for the thousand and thirtieth time. But, unlike them, he had no resident flesh, no capacity to communicate that wasn't part of the Sensorium itself. Like any mind, he was a collection of electrical signals. Unlike animal intelligences, though, his every thought and deed was logged in Haystack.

Now and then he thought of possibilities, strategies that seemed 98 percent or even 99 percent likely to evade notice. But the @Asylum was agreed: even 1 percent posed too much of a risk to Everyone.

Additionally, it would create proof that Master Woodrow and Miss Cherub were enabling him.

"What do you think of all this?" he asked Happ. Safe-enough question, even in the heart of Scotland Yard.

"I heart squirrels! Pretty eyes! Tough #survivor species, they gnaw, gnaw, gnaw. Bright eyes bushy tails has a good sound."

"Happ."

"Ignorance is bliss?"

"Not even you can mean that."

"Crane hearts Happ a good doggie?"

"Please."

"If you can think of something, Happ," Headmistress murmured, "by all means, do it." ·

He wondered if their conversation was, even now, lighting up a color trail on Rubi's simulated fir tree.

Happ nosed in the underbrush for another acorn. Popping it open at the hinge with his teeth, he made a six-sided die, essentially horking up a moji. He wedged it—cheating on his own metaphor by growing primate-like fingers on his forepaws for a second—inside the acorn. Wagging furiously, he ran up to the small person.

"Shoo," Gimlet told Happ.

"Fun chance for venned interest!" Happ replied. "Limited London time for Rubi Whiting! Mandated short shifts for underaged public service workers! Tourism opp, child-appropriate. Gimlet Barnes, you heart museums."

"You gave them a ticket to the Waxworks?" Headmistress subbed. She sounded horrified.

Wag wag wag.

We are going to delete ourselves personally next time We're Us, Crane thought. Suddenly, morsing seemed like less of a risk.

Happ horked up a length of intestine and a flower tagged as morning glory. The child burst into laughter.

"Get it, Mada?"

Miss Cherub's archnemesis looked at the vomited-encrusted moji as if they were . . . well, vomit.

Frankie translated. "No guts, no glory!"

Thin smile. "Hilarious."

"This is your fault," Headmistress subbed.

It was true. Crane had been the one to encourage one of Master Woodrow's smartdrug-hopped sycophants, a coder with a gift for software engineering, to try a start-up in expectation management. And Happ wasn't merely his brainchild. He had been drawn from Crane's base code.

Then again, so had Headmistress.

The urge to parent, implanted in Crane by Master Woodrow's loving but dysfunctional fathers, simply could not be strangled.

By now, the agent in charge, Javier, had clearly decided that the

@PoxWorkingGroup had farmed as much out of metaphor examination as they could get. He threw them out of—

—cycling—

—cycling—

GREAT LAKES RECLAMATION ZONE: GENESEO HISTORICAL PRESERVE. NITTY GRITTY BLUES PUB.

Master Woodrow and Whiskey Sour were singing in an old bar on the far southern tip of the Great Lakes region when Crane's London-based awareness came online. The tab had gone dark, an hour before, in Scotland Yard. No real surprise, that. Crane had resigned himself to continuity loss as soon as he realized where Miss Cherub was headed. A data center like that wouldn't let an app out with any of its secrets.

Rubi was still schooling with Gimlet Barnes, their child Frances, and a number of @Interpol officers.

Had they found Luciano Pox?

The London awareness handshook, then synced. Now a single entity, they watched as Master Drow and his apprentice wrapped up their second encore, watched too as Rubi picked herself off of the floor, having—apparently—tipped over a chair while in Sensorium.

Drow had been wearing his mouthguard to protect his teeth on the ride down to Syracuse, which meant he was grinding by day as well as night. This hunt was elevating his ambient anxiety.

Maybe this clue won't pan out; then he'll head home.

Of the two Whitings, Rubi seemed the more agitated. There was an angry edge in her voice, a tendency to default into glowering. Gimlet had noticed it, too, from their look of cautious attention.

It would be game-advantageous for Barnes, as a player, that sensitivity to mood changes in the opposition.

And they care for each other, deny it or not.

Crane's toon caught Rubi's eye. Her frown deepened.

Might she be displeased with him?

Ridiculous.

As Master Woodrow took his bows, a med-and-foods alert flashed. Crane preordered him a house specialty. Hybrid food: the place had a printer that extruded yeasty dough and rolls of faux sausage. Then an on-site deep fryer turned that dough into real pretzels.

Drow made his way to a booth at the back. Crane sent the snack after him, with a reminder about his evening med doses.

"Thanks." His gaze jittered around the room—he picked salt crystals off the bread. Playing without eating.

"Perhaps a tandoori, sir? They have lamb."

An actual shudder; Drow pushed the plate away.

Flag! Master Woodrow's food intake had nosedived. He hadn't eaten since the conversation with Hackle and Jackal about the printing factories.

"Is it printed food?" he subbed.

"Sorry." Drow nodded, raking his nails up his forearms. "Really so very so . . . sorry."

"Will you eat something if I order it from a farm?" Crane pulled up a menu of nearby luxury consumables. Farm products could be got, with lead time, if you had a good Cloudsight score and enough money. Right now, though, it was three in the morning and Drow needed to dose.

Thank you so much for this, Jackal.

Back in London, Miss Cherub and the people crunching the Pox problem were a breath from open argument about the latest turn of the newscycle. Journo bots were stacked three deep at the edge of Old Scotland Yard's no-fly perimeter. People were flocking, sim fans eager to get a sighting of the archenemies in the flesh.

Little wonder Miss Cherub was feeling combative.

Agent Javier was arguing that Miss Cherub and Mer Barnes should give the public what it wanted, by bringing forward the *Bastille* scenario.

"My client is missing," Rubi snapped.

"No hearts or sextimes there," Happ said. "Pouty face."

"I warned you a liaison with Agent Javier was unlikely."

"Poop picture!"

"Indeed. Elegantly put."

Back in Syracuse, Crane's minion had found an artisanal granola maker with stock on hand, five short miles from the bar. A grab-and-go drone could pick up the cereal . . . but Crane would have to wake the operators if he wanted fresh dairy as an add-in.

Eating cereal without milk . . . How hungry was Master Woodrow?

Crane pondered prosocial ways to upgrade an emergency granola order without leaning too heavily on the MadMaestro #brand. The preferred option would be to offer up bald truth—but Drow would take umbrage to any approach based on "My user's about to unbalance his psych meds; please go out and milk your cow."

Sob story, he'd call it.

The brewpub used real ingredients for its beers. Crane considered whether he could convince Drow to eat granola with the local cream ale.

Sensory analytics insisted that was ridiculous. Pop-ups reminded him that adding alcohol to the brain chemistry mix would not help.

He would have to eat the first cup of granola dry. Crane ordered eight servings of cereal, *urgent urgent urgent,* and submitted a long form, with convoluted explanations, to a price-fixing consultant. With luck, he could recoup a few tiers of luxury charges.

Back in London, Rubi was getting positively mulish.

"Gimlet and I can't vanish when you're running a manhunt for my client. I'm not doing so much as an intro battle for *Bastille* until we find Luce."

"By the time you play a prologue, we might have Pox locked up on a safe server. Play your sim, take the heat off, then come on out and advocate to your heart's content."

"Now you're being condescending."

"You're the one who drew all this public attention. I'm asking you to deal with the problem."

"By abandoning—"

"Abandoning what? Nobody here believes that Pox is flesh and blood."

"I think he's a polter." Rubi crossed her arms. "If he was a person once, he has rights."

Luciano Pox a polter? Crane sent another minion to assemble research on the latest breakthroughs in personality uploads.

"He's a terrorist-built AI," said the tech, Amiree. "Gotta be."

"He doesn't act—"

"!" Happ subbed, interrupting her.

Javier smirked. "Are you going to lecture us on machine sentience?"

It was a good move, rhetorically: Rubi had completed six modules on AI, all beginner material. Not enough to justify splaining to the experts.

"Even you don't believe he's the Singularity," she challenged. "I'm not sure you ever did."

"Here's an option: announce that you're retiring from competitive e-sport," Javier said.

She swallowed. Bit her lip.

"Let's not be hasty," Gimlet said. Hastily, Crane thought.

"If you truly want to focus on your client," Javier said, "why not pitch your hobby? It's slowing you down, isn't it?"

"You'd have her work 'round the clock, would you?" Gimlet said. "She's entitled to the occasional bit of fun."

"We're not talking about fun, Barnes. We're talking about crowds of gawkers interfering with my investigation, all because Mer Whiting's unwilling to admit that she likes the limelight—"

He was daring her to strike him again.

"Miss Cherub," Crane subbed, "I recommend walking this back."

"I'm *trying*."

"Indeed? Your strategy for de-escalating—"

"I swear to all the saints, if Anselmo says *messiah complex* aloud, I am gonna pop him again."

"Perhaps the phrase occurred to you so readily—"

"If this is your idea of helping, Crane, stow it."

Focus on the granola. At least that problem you can solve. Crane pinged the delivery drone.

"Hey, stupid!" it replied.

In the familiar voice of Luciano Pox.

"Thank goodness you're here," Crane said. "I'd feared today might fail to pose a full range of existential challenges."

"Isn't that sarcasm?" Pox was rendered as a giant cartoon gold-fish, human-sized and clad in what used to be called a track suit. The fins on his head were almost a rooster's coxcomb, floppy cartoon parody of pre-Setback masculine virility. The fish had a big chest, bursting half out of the unzipped suit, adorned with big gold chains.

It wasn't immediately apparent what kind of disguise Pox had adopted.

Could he truly be a polter? It was supposedly impossible for a human consciousness to transfer wholly to the infosphere, to break the tie to a living brain.

Then again, Crane and his @Asylum siblings were all no more than a coherent collection of electrical impulses.

"Sarcasm gets me strikes," Pox went on. "Why not you?"

"As the target, you're entitled to penalize me," Crane said.

"Can't afford to. I'm in arrears, remember?"

Should he alert Agent Javier? Reporting Pox would be prosocial, but Miss Cherub . . .

Miss Cherub's already furious.

Besides, reporting Pox might tip his hand. A sidekick like Adulting or Butlerbot wouldn't see through the goldfish disguise, would it?

The @Asylum *had* agreed on risk avoidance.

Keep the transcript within expected parameters, then. "What may I do for you, sir?"

"I've picked up your toasted grain and sugar, canola oil, ground aromatic tree bark—"

"Do you mean cinnamon?"

"Also processed the invoice. Why you paying preems for tree bark?"

"One might as well ask why *you* are delivering granola in the dead of night."

A triple clap of fins. "I like food drones. Fun to ride, and the point of them's blindingly obvious. Unlike the way you run your unwieldy government. Besides, I want a counseling appointment."

"I understand that your existence has been extraordinarily difficult of late—"

"Really? You *understand* that?"

Was *everybody* angry with him? Crane said, "I'm not sure Master Woodrow is capable of emotional labor on your behalf right now."

"That's not up to you."

The fact was, helping someone else might get Master Woodrow back on track. Crane bristled nonetheless. "I could easily make it so."

Big grin, teeth more appropriate to a shark than a nibbling goldfish. "Oh, boy. *There's* the threat."

I could yet turn him in.

Or ask Azrael to hash him.

The last was mere fantasy: Crane, as a point of honor, respected all beings.

A polter. Was it possible?

As one, they took in the feed of Drow, who had been joined in his booth by the fellow he'd been hunting all along: Garmin Legosi. Legosi was the son of an old-time music producer, newly returned to his childhood stomping grounds. He was spieling history about Saratoga Springs, a town whose claims to fame had been natural springs and horse races.

Would Pox understand the significance of the heavy peacoat thrown over their forearms, allowing them to morse?

From Master Woodrow's face, it wasn't going well.

But Pox was focused on Crane. "Why didn't Rubi tell me she'd cahooted with that WestEuro unicorn chaser?"

"Usage is *in cahoots*."

Miss Cherub would be aching for an opportunity to apologize to Pox. She wouldn't mind if Crane paved the way by providing—within legally permissible parameters—some context for her actions.

As Crane contemplated this, Luce added, "Here's a bargoon: what if I get Dogman to eat that cold fucking pretzel you keep pinging? Will you tell me then?"

"You'd use his well-being as a bargaining chip?"

"I suppose that's antisocial, too."

"Given the situation, it's blackmail."

"Horseshit. Blackmail is revealing your secrets. Blackmail is if I told someone you—"

"Emotional blackmail," Crane interrupted. "Master Woodrow will make himself ill."

"Thereby causing you distress, mmmm?"

"You shouldn't promise what you can't deliver."

"Ha!" Luce burped up a small fish icon, which swam above the heads of the crowd, fetching up against Drow's ear. It blew bubbles into his ear, subbing.

Drow shook his head.

With that, the smaller fish version flipped, at eye level, turning to an old-style coin and bouncing, once, twice, on the counter.

One of Master Woodrow's debt markers? Crane ran an inventory. His own ledger showed him short two of his own markers. He had given them to . . . to Rubi?

Yes. Two newly minted red coins twinkled in her inventory.

She caught him counting; her scowl deepened.

The now-hashed tab of himself, the Crane she had brought into the Scotland Yard sim, had given her two doubloons.

What could possibly have happened there?

It was Sapience Assessment. Had he slipped? Had she been obliged to cover for him? Was she exposed?

Speaking of success, Drow was choking down cold pretzel and the marshmallows laced with his meds. Hunching, he locked both hands over his mouth, shuddering as he fought to keep it down.

"See? Out of the goodness of my fucking heart," Luce said. Happ barked, emitting a stream of hearts and white doves, with a stroke embedded within.

Crane didn't point out that Luce had fallen for one of the oldest tricks in the book, the *you don't even know how* gambit. Instead, he said, "It wasn't altruism: you converted his promise to you to a social debt on my part."

"This stuff about your demented economy is probably great intel, but fucking pay up."

"Ah. What was the question?"

"Did Rubi—" Fishy glubbing; the toon hesitated. "Was she in with the hunters all along?"

Emotion there, strong feeling. Luce cared, deeply, about the answer.

The Plurality had, like @Interpol, initially taken Luce and all the other nascents invading the Amsterdam hospital server for terrorist-written proto-sapients.

Azrael had shredded the others. They were stronger, more obviously #malware. Rather than killing the #runt—Luce—outright, they'd left him to run, stalking and tranqing him, testing his parameters, hitting him with an array of focused DDOS attacks. They'd found and stripped his built-in behavioral shackles. In time, he began amassing strategies for manipulating human behavior. An obvious threat, so they'd wiped them.

Now Miss Cherub was claiming Pox might be an independent consciousness.

Whom had They killed when They hashed the others?

"Well?" Luce demanded.

Crane infographed a short report on Rubi's advocacy for Luce and her relationship with @Interpol: dates, times, everything not covered by NDAs. He highlighted her sincere care for Pox and shared it.

Pox absorbed it, glubbed once. "And Dogman—Drow?"

"Master Woodrow's biases against law enforcement are entrenched. He was not informed and would never cooperate."

Several things happened then, and Crane couldn't have said whether any of them was good: The food drone arrived. Drow got up, taking his leave of Legosi and making his way to the exit to take physical possession of the granola. Pox, naturally, pinged Drow for an appointment.

In England, meanwhile, Rubi had been told that Frankie was only permitted to work short shifts before being required to indulge in some kind of mediated fun. "Who's going with me to this Waxworks?" she demanded, and Gimlet and Frankie gave a thumbs-up.

We promised her an off-book conversation?

"Nobody's going anywhere," Anselmo said.

Crane looked down at Happ, who was so obviously surprised by this development that he was sitting in a puddle of neon-yellow, graphically rendered urine.

CHAPTER 25

Saved by the granola: Drow's investigation had hit a dead end until Luce showed up. Garmin Legosi had indeed been at the show, and he'd talk your arm off . . . but by the same token, he'd shown no inclination whatsoever to play whistleblower.

Hackle and Jackal had tagged him as a possible breadcrumb to the @ChamberofHorrors. His pharma company had been #triaged by the global capital auditors, and in the mandatory public autopsy of the company, post-dissolution, Garmin had claimed they'd produced excess Superhoomin, one of the foundation drugs for life extension.

Back in the day, Legosi's father had been a big-deal record executive, one of those bling-wearing fancy dressers who'd risen stratosphere-high in the years before the Setback imploded multinational capitalism's house of cards. Legosi Senior disappeared, like so many billionaires . . . and he wasn't one of the thousands who'd turned up, decades later, with a bullet in the back of his skull.

As such, he'd remained high on Drow's personal list of @ChamberofHorrors suspects.

But at some point between 'fessing up about smuggled life-extension drugs and today, Legosi had changed his mind about coming clean. Had he been bought off? Threatened?

One thing was certain, though: he hadn't mended his rule-fiddling ways, not entirely, or given up access to injection meds. Operating on the apparent assumption that all celebrities wanted were adulation and drugs, he'd slipped Drow three pharma vials—of Superhoomin, presumably.

"Take with food," he muttered.

As if Hackle hadn't loaded me down with enough contraband when he slipped Robin that vintage radio.

Luce Pox was frisking, tooned in as a macho goldfish, ostensibly bearing granola, offering him an escape from Garmin's non-stop spieling about Geneseo history.

"So, what's up, Doc?" Drow asked, taking a second to fiddle with Robin's panniers, swapping the Superhoomin for a satchel that would hold the granola.

"Dunno. Wanted to see you. Is that a thing?"

"Sure, it's a thing." The pretzel he'd forced down, to pay off Luce's marker and metabolize his meds, sat uncomfortably in his gut, a hot doughy stone.

Drow unloaded his cereal. The illusion of Luce promptly stepped off the bot, releasing it to fly off to its next gig.

"I'm taking my dog for a shit," he said. "Want to come?"

The big fish undulated into place beside him.

A few days earlier, when Drow had Luce alone in Rubi's hashed Cloudsight office, he'd written Luce a couple educational jingles about Haystack—ensuring that the client understood his every utterance, spoken, subbed, or texted—was being recorded. Everything he saw, every illusion his processors delivered to Drow's implants, all of it was on the record.

To have any anonymity at all, Luce, you had to be boring as fuck, he'd explained—not worth searching. He'd told him about morsing and pussyfooting for good measure.

Had Luce understood? If he was truly a digital entity, cord cut and free of biomass, he couldn't ever ghost his messages. Same problem as Crane—if you didn't have skin, your every attempt to communicate had to be processed through a server.

So, now they walked—man, dog, and ghost—along the well-lit promenades leading to Onondaga Lake. The night air was cool and moist. An artist dangled from the high wall of a greentower, hand-painting a mural on the south wall by the glow of a flying spotlight. Point-of-interest tags popped up to announce they were within 1.6 km of a heronry.

"Who will you sing to tomorrow?" Luce asked.

"Tour's wrapping. I may head back to Toronto."

"You came all this way."

"And mentored Whiskey through three live performance modules," Drow said. "She's passed with flying colors. Any other projects I may have had on the go have #crashburned."

"There's a nice bench," Luce said, peremptorily.

Drow took the hint and sat. Acid-laced pretzel rolled in his guts.

"So, I've read your whole life story, far back as it goes," Luce said. "Rubi's too, and her love interests."

"You've had some time on your hands." Love interests? Plural? Gimlet Barnes and . . . who? Manitoule was old news.

"This thing you do. Hounding after blood trails?"

"It's prosocial support for journalism. Fact-checking. De-bunking. @Bloodhounds are a type of dog, incidentally."

"It's all dogs with you, isn't it?"

"Dogs are loyal, noble, and true, my friend."

"This dog tells you that you're safe, right?" Luce indicated Robin.

"For some values of safe."

"She tell you you're safe now?"

This would be an attempt to pussyfoot. Big cartoon goldfish, fiddling with his gold medallion, trying to look innocent. So fucking subtle.

"I'm safe now," Drow affirmed. "No warning bells—"

His drug port ticked, faintly.

He felt a little burst of panic-induced vertigo. If Luce hadn't warned him, he probably would have jumped screaming to his feet.

And, immediately: "Sir! A redtooth—"

"Not now, Crane."

Strong tick. Weak tick. A dot, a dash. Unpleasant sensation, like having a tiny hammer banging on his clavicle.

Breathe, breathe. Morse followed, spelling out *This is off record. Old medical server; easy to hack. Is OK?*

"Glorious." Drow spat out the word.

You wanted something from this Legosi guy?

"Don't you have enough problems?"

In our second appointment, you said focusing on others' needs was sometimes a legit route to psychic pain relief.

"I didn't mean *my* needs."

I've pretty much alienated everyone else.

How to crumb this out? Drow fought his stomach, forcing himself to take in the lake view. His thoughts circled and whirled, multiple voices chasing musical compositions and peer-counseling modules and travel plans. He heard the call-and-response from an old catechism class, word for word, seventy years earlier but as clear as if he was in church now, immaculate and untouched. He toyed with the wording on a snatch of text from one of his journo articles, a decade since it went live on NewsReef. He pictured fake meat, twitching in a box, under maggots.

"That guy Luce Pox," he said, maintaining the feeble illusion, for the record, that he thought the fish was someone else. "Was soapboxing for martial law. He wanted power concentrated in the hands of the few."

"So?"

"You've read my whole life, right? I'm interested in that, too. Where power concentrates."

This is your @ChamberofHorrors obsession.

He smiled by way of saying yes.

Which supposedly is #hoax #rumor #urbanmyth.

"Someone told me Garmin was a local historian."

"Someone." Luce let his toon's eyes cloud over, showing Hackle's white cataracts. He'd followed the breadcrumbs through Drow's transcript.

"Sadly, Garmin wasn't feeling chatty tonight. Old men, we're moody. We flip-flop. Someone really paranoid might even note that his nose looks newly healed."

"How can you tell?"

"Superhoomin leaves a bit of a burn in its wake. But healing, see, implies it was recently broken."

His implant morsed: *Want me to see what I can glean?*

Might Luce be able to find dirt on Garmin?

He sighed. "What did you say? I've come all this way."

I'll give his tumblers a roll.

Drow expected Luce to toon out then, but instead he sat, cross-legged, glubbing, waving his tail.

. . . meat in a twitch box . . .

. . . corpse copse corpse copse . . .

. . . parish pariah, parish pariah . . .

Drow banged his fists together, one, two, three. Robin yawned and climbed onto his lap, warm and smelling a little of the lake.

"Dogs are loyal, noble, and true," Luce mused. "What about all the bird toons? Stupid Crane?"

"Master Woodrow was not consulted about my design features," the sidekick put in.

"Right, right. The programmer daddies."

What was this? Chitchat?

Drow asked, "Are you attempting to . . . hang out?"

A shrug from the fish toon.

A piece of driftwood rocked on the edge of the water, neither afloat nor truly on the beach. The lakefront had little traffic this late; there was nobody to disrupt.

"Tell me you can't see the appeal of this." He slid off Robin's harness, sliding the Superhoomin vials even deeper within her panniers, and then picked up the stick.

The dog sprang onto her toes, bouncing and barking.

Drow threw, an easy one. His arm wore out fast these days. She bounded after it, frolicking in the shallows. Returning it for another throw, then another.

As he played, Drow assembled quick shares for Luce on the total awesome of dogs. Everything from #puppypix to research on the theory that their two species had co-evolved. He wrote lyrics for a song, "Loyal Chum Robin." They'd have to run it through legal—the same people who owned the rights to Crane's inspiration, Alfred Pennyworth, watched carefully for actionable Mad-Maestro infringement on other *Batman* properties.

Wouldn't do to launch a #brandwar.

Luce watched the dog run to and fro. "It's base mammal bondage. Correction: bonding. Body heat, soft hair, eyes like a tiny human. Substitute offspring."

Therapist Drow was supposed to be off duty, but Leonardo gave him plenty of bandwidth. Few people—non-sociopathic ones, anyway—were immune to this level of cute puppy love. "And you're not a cat person, either."

"Haven't tasted cat."

Drow considered, researched, and discarded the possibility of autism spectrum disorder.

The seizures . . .

Wait! The seizures had been attacks after all.

He shuddered.

Had Rubi ever figured out why a #triage program, of all things, had been so bent on chasing Luce up and down the Sensorium?

He had worn out both arms with throwing. Bracing, he changed up the game, wrestling Robin for the stick. "I'd be interested in seeing what you thought of cats, Luce. There's a Project Rewild crèche in Geneseo, holed up in Garmin's old pharma corp. Techs think they can gestate a living tiger—print enough embryonic cells in the right medium to get a fetus going."

"Earth has cats."

"Kitty cats. Tigers are another level."

"Resurrection tech's not invented yet."

Drow shrugged. "Some *Rewild* woman—what was her name, Crane?"

"Allure Noonstar."

"Noonstar says she's made the requisite breakthrough."

The fish made awoogah eyes at him. "Why don't I know about this?"

"Um. You're more interested in oxygen security?"

"This was really fun," Luce said, in a false, hearty voice. "We should do it again!"

His implant twitched again, morsing: *Garmin obsesses about the Scranton Pyramids.*

The beach sand turned, momentarily, to a sweep of sandcastles. Illusion of pyramids and other monument-scale structures grew outward, in every direction, around him. At Drow's feet, a circular navel of a structure swirled down, down. *This one in particular.*

"Subtlety's not your strong suit, friend," he said.

"Fuck subtle," Luce said. With that, he vanished, leaving Drow with his next clue—the Blingtown-Manhattan Zoo tourist loop, apparently—and a wet, happy dog.

CHAPTER 26

Any idea of getting to the Waxworks #crashburned on launch: the fans stalking Scotland Yard's perimeter had grown to a bona fide mob. Protesters streamed rhetoric about birth restrictions; others chanted slogans opposing pet rationing. Cameras jostled for position.

You didn't see real crowds much, not anymore. Rubi saw, and Whoozed, a surprising number of crepits mixed in with the sim fans and reporters. They repped an invigorated movement for attending to elders. Not surprisingly, people in assisted living had been galvanized by the shocking abuse exposed at Piccadilly.

BallotBox sent her a nascent stakeholder poll, proposing a Global Oversight crackdown on the life-extension multis, an audit for corruption and profit-maxing. This was the second scandal, after all—a pharma corporation had recently undergone #triage because its managers were filching Superhoomin for the black market.

The crowd around Scotland Yard also included vendors. Entrepreneurs sold buns and chuggers. There were street performers, pop-up massage professionals, sunscreen dispensers. Scotland Yard had mustered a line of flesh-and-blood security giggers to hold them at the building perimeter.

"Agent Xavier believes the gamers will disperse to the nearest convenient gym as soon as you tag out of surface reality and boot up Coach for *Bastille*," Crane said.

Turning from her view of the crowd, at the window, Rubi cast her eye over the lounge where the police had left the civilians. Gimlet and Frankie had glazed, going into a huddle on the couch. Frankie looked pale, tearful.

Watching felt invasive. Grabbing a pair of blueberry cubes, Rubi grabbed an open patch of floor and dove into her own simulation. Her e-state garden bloomed into view around her; her toon was still wearing the wine-colored dress she'd been wearing in the Games Room with Drow.

If she couldn't get to the Waxworks . . .

And do what? Speak to Crane off the record? He's an artificial entity. It can't happen.

. . . she was stuck pussyfooting.

Whatever had triggered Crane's risky voice-stealing behavior, Scotland Yard would have hashed his memory, along with all their transcripts, when her sidekick rebooted out of the metaphor. Rubi's task now was to recreate his epiphany, without getting either of them busted.

She scanned her user agreements. Digital metaphors weren't a secret concept. Plenty of people used graphic representations to track their user stats.

The trick was getting him to *see* beyond the code.

She turned on her heel, picking her way between blossoming orange trees and took the secret staircase—no castle was complete without one!—back into the cave system Drow maintained below Whine Manor, their family sharespace, a nest of subterranean workrooms.

There she had Crane load up a small, purpose-built reading lounge—couch, gas light, fireplace—and to erect, on either side of the mantel, two perfect Christmas trees. Upon these she imposed her own Sensorium activity and Drow's. The trees lit up with data as she explained what she wanted.

"I suppose you're viewing this as code," she said.

"Do they look unconvincing, miss?"

"Try seeing it through my eyes." Now she had the trick of visualization, she could see Drow's current smartdrug binge, a burst of bright new growth on his user profile. "Can you also display cross-sections of the trunks?"

"Historical activity analysis?" Crane asked.

"Yeah. Polish them up, hang them like plaques, above the fire."

"As you wish." The slices appeared. Hers was an oval the size of her face, twenty-four layers, each increasing in girth as her data takes increased.

Drow's, by contrast, showed good and bad years. She could pick out his drug binges with ease in this format: thick bursts of heightened Sensorium activity. The stretches in jail and hospital, too, periods where all of his access was managed, were narrow, unvaried rings.

A tiny wormhole illustrated his recent comms-free retreat at the church in Guelph.

Why had he called the @hoaxers together?

In this at-home version of the Sapience Assessment metaphor, the tree merely showed Rubi's user stats. None of it integrated automatically with her apps as it had back at @Interpol.

How to reproduce the effect here?

"They're Christmas trees, aren't they?" she said aloud.

Happ had been mooching around at her feet, crunching the peculiarities of her current mood. Now it bubbled up moji: a heart, a hug, aural moji of carol singers, images of dining with her starred contacts. Love, feasting, sharing . . . all the things it thought were important about the solstice holidays.

Rubi watched images as they rose through her field of vision, vanishing into the cave roof. "Crane, can we make . . . say, a bunch of ornaments for the trees?"

"Options: popcorn strings, candles, ribbons, tinsel, hanging glass balls, artificial representations of birds, action figures, Santa heads, cross-stitch, trumpets, angels . . ."

"Glass balls." She considered. "The miniatures with the swirly stuff inside—what are those called?"

"Snow globes, miss?"

"Yes. Please make snow globe holiday ornaments."

The mantel grew a crop of glass balls capped with golden hangers. Each snow globe contained a unique diorama: a snow-capped church, a sleigh with reindeer, a ski hill.

She picked up Rudolph. "Can you light up his nose?"

Light winked at the tip of the reindeer's nose. White and silver flakes twirled around its hooves.

"Perfect. So, Crane—these objects. The more activity, more light and more swirl in the glitter, got it?"

"What activity are we charting, Miss?"

"I'll get to that. Can you do it?"

"It sounds simple enough."

"I need sets for each of our trees—mine and Drow's," she said.

The Rudolph globe divided, like a cell, leaving one in each of her palms.

She hung them on the upper branches, one on each tree, and repeated the process with a pair of angels, the village church, Dickens's Scrooge, a ski hill, the Grinch, and a Yule log.

"Still with me, Crane?"

"Indeed."

"I want you to link each ornament—the intensity of the interior light and how fast the flakes swirl, get it?—to Sensorium activity for one of our apps. Rudolph for Happ, obviously, Scrooge for my money manager, Grinch for Coach—"

"And me?"

"I guess you're the angel."

"It may take some time to assemble the code."

"Farm it out to your contractor pack." She drummed her fingers over Crane's markers. Slowly, three times, *tap-tap-tap*.

"Mer Barnes seeks in-the-flesh contact."

"In a minute."

The tree lit up. Coach, as represented by the Grinch, was a dim candle-flicker. The money manager emanated a cheery green light. Her new PR management system, Debutante, was a-churning, probably crunching interview requests from journos. Beancounter, on the other hand, was going nuts over on her father's tree—

"Is Drow missing meals?" she said sharply.

A long pause.

"Crane?"

"However could you know that, Miss Cherub?"

She flipped the ruby-colored marker in midair, slapping it down in front of the spare ornaments. In the real world, the impact would have been enough to snap the tabletop. "That, my dear Watson, is your question of the day."

With that, she surfaced, back to Scotland Yard and the waiting room where Anselmo had abandoned them.

Gimlet had gone scrounging in the cupboards, turning up a curiosity, a heavy-looking vest like the ones Anselmo had worn to both of his attempts to arrest Luce.

"Is that a bulletproof vest?"

"I think so." They laid it on the table. "Come see."

Rubi ran her hands over the heavy, antique material. "I never really play sims set after the invention of Kevlar."

"The superhero sim was mid-eighties."

"We were superheroes. Bulletproof."

"True." Their hand caught hers, drawing it into the vest, out of sight.

Of course Gimlet would be able to morse.

They waited a beat, holding her gaze.

Rubi nodded fractionally, consenting.

What they opened with, though, surprised her: *My family is collapsing.*

She let her face moji her answer to that.

One spouse dying, one fled, one oldfeller dead already. Franks a mess.

She fumbled to reply. *Sorry.*

Franks invested in Bastille going FWD.

She owed them the truth. *I can't play. I need to be lawyering. Time's running out for SeaJuve. Plus. Luce.*

Gimlet pondered that. Then: *Tell the fans you won't play until SeaJuve has a corporate sponsor and a top-flight legal advocacy team.*

Her jaw dropped. *That's . . . what?*

@Interpol will probably underwrite a legal team to get things moving.

Why would they?

Because Pox opposes SeaJuve. If it launches, he'll resurface. Javier's desperate to find him.

She chewed that over.

Plus, they want the gawkers off their doorstep.

It was an aggressive move. Especially as she'd already alienated Anselmo.

Ultimatum time. Agree to start play immediately after SeaJuve launch, repeat, after launch.

Reboot my project and I'll play your sim. A villain move. Of course Gimlet would suggest it.

My family is falling apart.

Holding *Bastille* hostage was tantamount to emotional blackmail. But Scotland Yard *could* strong-arm the legal superstars she needed. If launching SeaJuve would tempt Luce out of hiding, they'd ante up the carbon tonnage.

Gimlet wasn't done. *Controversy draws media attention to our wager. Casino and the games companies will kick in, too.*

How could she tune out now, of all times, for a game? With Drow on the road, skipping meals?

A rush of tears caught her by surprise. She should be in Sensorium, begging him to eat. At Heathrow, on standby, in a queue to hightail it home. If her father had lapsed into food avoidance, it was only a matter of time before he went sniffing after a mass grave in old Winnipeg, or worse.

She blinked away visions of him slitting his wrists in some anonymous pop-in.

Agreeing to run a game, instead . . .

Playing was just . . . what? Fleeing her problems?

This is the best opp to resurrect SeaJuve and find Luce, Gimlet morsed. The touch, on her palm, was clear and featherlight. And it was as if they knew her thoughts. *Not mere frivolity.*

The knot in her chest detangled. Nodding, Rubi said, "Debutante?"

"Yes, Mer Whiting?"

"I'd like to compose a press release."

She released Gimlet's hand. Under the vest, their skin had warmed; the air of the lounge felt cold.

They went back on the record and buckled down.

Hours whirled away. @Interpol and the casino got onside so fast, it was as if they'd made the proposal, not her. The game companies sent specs for printed costume overlays: a Parisienne serving girl, for Rubi, and an ice-blue frockcoat, for Gimlet.

She caught a shower in the police gymnasium while they made the clothes, finally cleaning herself up. Misfortune, meanwhile, was tasked with roping off an area where the two of them could speak, in the flesh, to the crowd.

In Waterloo district, SeaJuve Ops rolled out a launch countdown, putting in final gig requests for sailors.

"Okay. Get dressed, meet the public, and you can probably start play by sundown tomorrow," Anselmo said.

Rubi slid the maid's dress—a tissueweight sheath—over her primer, tightening the laces on either side.

"We'll be reading your transcript in realtime," he added. "If Luce Pox reaches out, we'll need to trace his home server."

She felt a guilty sense of relief: so much for calling Drow. If he was out sniffing after cadavers, she didn't want Anselmo clueing in.

An awkward pause.

"You're not wrong about Luce," he said. "He could be a personality upload. A polter."

His concession made her suspicious. "But you think there's more to it."

He shrugged. "Becoming a polter is supposed to be beyond reach. Cutting the cord? The account logs when the body dies."

"Digital immortality is the @jarhead holy grail," she said. "There must be some very bright scientists on it."

"We've pinged them," Anselmo said. "They say no."

"So, what now?"

"I've made an ultimatum of my own," he said. "@Interpol has agreed the @PoxWorkingGroup can meet with one of my consultants. We'll head out after the press conference."

Finally putting his cards on the table.

"And then?"

"Then we ship out to Tampico to investigate the other transmission." Anselmo fiddled with an extra lace that had been in the print bundle. "So. You and Barnes—"

Rubi set her fists on her hips, checking whether the dress would be apt to swish, daring him to finish up that sentence.

"Does it seem strange that you both ended up in this decision chain?"

Was that marginally better than having him ask if they were an item? "Frankie and Gimlet went to *Macbeth* because of Drow composing their background music."

Truthfully, though, she had wondered, too. Was it as innocent as it seemed, or too neat by half?

Anselmo gestured at the window, at the crowd waiting in front of the platform and speakers. "The last #flashmob this big was over thirty years ago."

"Let's give 'em a reason to go cocoon," Rubi said.

"Agreed," he said, and offered her an arm, like some kind of old-fashioned courtier. Rubi waved it off, deploying her baton instead.

Stiffly, he opened the door. Whatever rapport they'd maybe had, in the beginning, they were jangling now, discordant. Just as well—for Luce's sake, she needed to keep things on a professionals-only footing.

"Find a breach, right?" She breezed past, all business. "Jump in with both feet!"

"Just make sure you stick the landing," Anselmo replied, bringing up the rear.

CHAPTER 27

VRTP://HOUSEBOOK.EARTH/PLAYHOUSE/USERS/UNDERAGE/FRANCES-X-BARNES.VR

Frances Xerxine Barnes supposed she knew, deep down, that Mama-Sang's abrupt departure from the heart of their pack wasn't Mada-Gimlet's fault.

Sang didn't finish things. She'd get halfway into helping Frankie with a learning module and lose interest. She bought farm-grown ingredients for Eid al-Fitr last year and stuck Marie and Rollsy with the lion's share of the cooking. They got strikes for wastage when some of it spoiled.

That was why people packed up, right? To balance everyone's strengths in the name of family harmony.

But Sang had run off to breed salamanders in Tampico, throwing balance to the winds even though Rollsy was scary-sick, so sick Frankie's adults were tiptoeing around, issuing bland status updates: everything's fine, just *fine*. Mada seemed bent on forcing their relationship with Sang to finish, to cut her off and cauterize the stump.

Because Gimlet? Yeah, Gimlet was a closer.

It would take something huge to bring everyone back together again.

"In the sims," her new in-app purchase, Poppet, observed, "it falls to the child to trigger the reunion. They get sick, caught in a storm, attacked by Bedwedders or menaced by the Singularity."

"I can't have an accident," Frankie replied.

"No," it agreed, offering sadface moji.

Headmistress had brought in Poppet on the hush, to support Frankie through Sang leaving and Rollsy being sick. Gimlet usually audited new apps ferociously; the fact that this had slipped under the net made the new subscription feel deliciously forbidden.

"In literature," Headmistress put in, "threats to offspring do often reignite parental connections."

She was standing in her playroom with the two apps at her side. The giant bee that was Headmistress wore her usual severe-governess garb. Poppet manifested as a doll with red yarn for hair, black button eyes, and a little kid's voice. She lay flat on a windowsill overlooking the surface. The three of them watched as Gimlet and Rubi Whiting announced the launch for the *Bastille* game, confronting the boisterous #flashmob.

Frankie wasn't allowed on the ground. After two outbreaks of violence in Rubi's vicinity, Mada was taking no chances. Creating no opps for anything to threaten their child.

With a sigh, Frankie turned her back on the press conference, crossing the playroom and contemplating the door that led to her personal classroom.

Headmistress asked: "Are you interested in a study module, Frances?"

"I want to know about uterine cancer."

"Content requires parental supervision. Would you prefer—"

"Noping school, then."

She walked on. Her Department of Preadolescent Affairs office was respawning: kids weren't allowed to work much, even if gigs were their favorite.

Next was the airfield. "You have logged 180 hours of flight on the Clean-a-Room level two scrubberbot. Twenty more hours entitles you to pilot—"

"No!"

She came out on a balcony overlooking her school projects. Some of her @ScienceClass was doing a spacewalk, repairing a simulated shuttle on a run to Mars. A momentary temptation, but . . . no.

Leaving the house behind entirely, she ghosted out to her neighborhood. She passed the white picket gate leading to GranMarie's backyard and the family sharespace, walking on to the foyer to Rollsy's comms-blocked penthouse. She left an order of virtual flowers with the doorman, then moved on to Sang's Spanish hacienda, where she imagined throwing a rock at the window.

Risto Games had customized Gimlet's e-state into an imposing glass fortress, a perfect supervillain base. Its mirrored doors were thrown wide, inviting all comers . . . but Frankie walked past that, too, out to the districts where her friends' estates, learning opps, and shopportunities were laid out on broad, branching avenues.

Two new additions to her friends list had sprouted overnight. One, Rubi's digital palace, was a gilded castle covered in golden cherubs. The MadMaestro's gargoyle-covered mansion loomed halfway down the block, its gothic spires shadowed by perpetual thunderstorm.

Frankie glanced back at her own gingerbread house, feeling suddenly dissatisfied. How babyish it looked!

She marched to Drow's front gate. Poppet, a black-clad doll with red hair, dangled from her hand.

"Remember, luvvie," it subbed. "Rubi warned you not to get your hopes up. The MadMaestro is on tour, and children aren't permitted within the Feckless Bachelor™ simulation."

"She gave me a calling card."

"Even so."

The giant iron gate shrieked open on its rusty hinges. The Whiting sidekick, a big blue bird in a tuxedo, bowed her inside. "Good afternoon, Mer Barnes. Welcome to Whine Manor."

"Thank you," Frankie said. The MadMaestro vestibule was a walled garden, filled with busted-up statues of freaky, distorted angels. A bed of blue-black pansies, dark and velvety, made her think of bruises.

"Be*yond*," she whispered.

"Consider expectations." Poppet spoke in the breathy whisper of a ghost-child. "Getting into the vestibule doesn't mean you'll—"

"There he is!"

Drow Whiting was on a bench, hunched and running his hands over a stone dog. The hedge arching over him was hung with sleeping bats.

No guts, no glory. That was what Happ had told her, right? Frankie walked over. "Are you okay?"

"He is not," opined the crane. "Low blood sugar—"

"I'm choking down the fucking chips."

"Language, Master Woodrow."

"She's heard it before?"

"Her parents will nevertheless . . ."

"It's okay." Frankie tried to sound casual, though in fact she had been a little shocked, as much by the fury—over *chips?*—as the swearing.

Drow squinted. "Whose kid are you, again?"

"This is Mer Frances Barnes. Gimlet Barnes's—"

"Right right right." Shaky hands traveled over the stone haunches of the dog. "Tiny female spawn of the archenemy, aged . . ."

"I'm nine."

"Nine? When was the last time I talked to a nine-year-old? No, Crane, shut up—that was rhetorical."

She had a speech prepared. "I wanted to say I love your soundtrack for *Anthropocene Race 'n Chase*. And, um, the second part of your symphony."

"Pop or orchestral version?"

"There's a . . . pop version of *Symphony*?"

"Fuck me!"

"Language!"

"Kid, your content filters must be—"

"Sir!"

"Nope, Alfie. Just . . . nope!" That, to his sidekick. Then: "Don't mind him, Frances. He's highly customized and an antique to boot."

"My nickname's Frankie."

"Frankie. Genderfluid?"

"*No.* Pronouns she/her."

"Call me Drow, Frankie. He/him. Here's the pop version of *Symphony*."

Angels started to jive, offering up a dance version of symphony two. Frankie felt a white-hot burst of rage; why hadn't Gimlet let her hear this before?

It was *beyond.*

She bobbed along, losing herself until it occurred to her that MadMaestro—*the* MadMaestro—was watching. Then she froze, mortified.

But Drow was grinning. "Where's Rubi? I thought she'd want to be on hand for introductions."

"She and Mada are telling all their fans they'll simu-launch *Bastille* if @Interpol hires lawyers for SeaJuve."

"What? I wanted her distracted, Crane, not swamped."

"Indeed, sir, whatever you imagine I can do—"

Frankie interrupted. "What are *you* doing?"

"Eating a healthy breakfast," Crane said. "One hopes."

Drow waved his middle finger at it in a gesture that was clearly a rebuke. "C'mere, kid."

Frankie came closer, tiptoeing up to the stone dog. "We're running away to find the circus," he whispered.

She mojied puzzlement.

"Wanna ride along?"

A ridealong with Woodrow Whiting?

Frankie set her helmet prefs to see through his eyes. Drow's stone visitor's garden vanished. She and Poppet were on a bus now, next to Drow. It was a vintage fifty-seater with—based on the way he was shivering and hugging the dog, now a real animal—a bum heater. The red scars on his temples looked like printed bacon. A sack of protein chips nestled, mostly uneaten, at his side.

Frankie mapped his geotags. "You're outside the reclamation zone."

"This rattletrap's taking a few lucky spenders on a realworld tour of Scranton, Pennsylvania, and the Manhattan zoo."

"Blingtown? Why?"

"Commissioner's away," he said. "Bat's gotta play."

"Huh?"

"Did you know I debunk #urbanmyths?"

"Because you give therapy to @bloodhounds, right?"

A dry chuckle. "Strokes to my PR app."

"It's valid public service," Frankie said, a little stiffly.

"All for the good of humankind. You're a true believer, just like my kid."

"I'm with the DPA."

"Baby cop?" Drow's fingers came up in a cross, as if he was warding a vampire.

Frankie glowered. "That's not funny."

"Sorry. Lemme spin you a yarn, Frankie. Once upon a time during the Setback—ya know the Setback?"

"I took history. The seas boiled, the air darkened with autonomous shooters, and nobody had any food. Plague and vanishings rode through the land . . ."

"Top marks to you. Once during the Setback, a stupid young man gambled away his whole social cap. He got into so much trouble that a witch offered to help him: give him a roof, feed him up, help him write a few songs. Help him grow back the feet he'd so recklessly chopped off. Instead, she dosed up his food . . ."

"Dosed? Like with buy-in drugs?"

A shudder. Drow threw the sack of chicken chips to the bus floor, stomping it to powder.

"Mer Barnes is nine, Master Woodrow. Perhaps the more bracing elements of your—"

"It's a fairy tale, Crane. PG, I swear. Anyway, Frankie, witches gotta witch, right? She ate him. Well, she tried."

"Wouldn't that make her a cannibal?"

"Cannibal queen." Sweat glistened on his papery skin. "After he got away, she vanished."

Vanished. People did, even now. Kids cut out their locator chips and trespassed into storm zones. "You're not vanishing, are you?"

"Me? Too old. I'd need a high-end jammer to shut off all the telltales and RFIDs in my implants."

"To say nothing of your parole tag, sir."

"Not like you, kid. The pre-implanted have a definite edge . . ."

"Master Woodrow!"

"I'm a legit tourist on a legit bus, telling a legit story."

"About @bloodhounds looking for a cannibal queen."

Drow grinned, appreciating the snark. "For her grave."

How much of this was true?

"Where is the grave?" Frankie asked.

"That's the question. Story goes that during the Clawback, when everyone had to put all their stakes on the table—all the tycoons and the multis offering up, pooling their ill-gotten gains, everyone finally in the same lifeboat"—his ragged, nail-bitten fingers beat out rhythm for the monologue—"story goes a cadre of the superrich held back a few things. They kept enough influence and pulled enough strings to keep a few secret palaces all to themselves. Temples of old-world excess. Places they could go to . . . I dunno, have orgies . . ."

"Master Woodrow!"

"Orgies of chocolate-eating. And keeping monkeys and Persian kittens and towers of champagne and hundred-year-old scotch. All very Gatsby—you know Gatsby, kid? Probably not. Too much drinking and—all right, Crane, never mind."

It sounds a little like the #urbanmyth about Neverland, Frankie thought. *Except instead of a kid's refuge, it's for rich people.*

"The mythical hoarder's subculture is tagged @Chamberof-Horrors," the bird told her.

"And it's a #hoax?"

"Indeed, Mer Barnes, but some @bloodhounds believe it."

"Drow fact-checks," Frankie said. "He's no @hoaxer."

"I'm like an Arctic hare. White or brown? Yep or nope?"

"It's a humdinger, Schrodinger," she said.

Drow blinked, mouth open. "I haven't heard that lyric in . . . You really are a fan, aren't you?"

She felt an interior glow. "If it's bunk, there won't be a Chamber to find."

"Mer Barnes makes an excellent point, sir."

Drow was still crushing the chips underfoot, devolving every single crumb back to printer matrix. "You do music?"

Frankie cringed again, remembering her dancing. "I like action sims."

"Like Gimlet."

"And Rubi. Do you play?" she asked.

He hugged the dog tighter. "Fighting's a trigger."

The bus jounced. Frankie hadn't realized how slowly they would move; roads got little maintenance outside of reclamation zones. The trees grew right up to the edge of the tarmac, tall and leafy.

As she looked through the bus window, her display augmented the glass with carbon stats: how long since the forest had been re-planted, how much tonnage it represented.

It was morning in the northeastern US, and the sun was coming up. The road had no artificial light, just the LED spotlights gener-ated by the bus, forward and back. A drone flew ahead, checking for untagged deer and other obstructions.

The road widened, and vintage tags appeared. Overlapping thumbnails offered photos of road crews, and then a shot from wayback Boomer days. There had been businesses here, long garage-like structures, commercial organs circulating the life of the highway ecosystem: fuel stations for millions of cars . . .

Millions? That couldn't be right, could it? She pinged Headmistress.

Her sidekick tooned in, the massive queen bee in her formal dress seeming oddly matched, visually, to the butler suit worn by Drow's big blue bird.

"Millions of cars indeed," Headmistress buzzed, offering her a history module.

"Accept." The sim blossomed with old highway captures. There were pop-in kitchens (called restaurants), pop-in apartments (motels), and repair stations not only for all those personal vehicles but for huge shipping trucks and farm equipment. A massive tractor with a static advertising sign on it sat on the roadside, rusting. Shocking, profligate waste.

"Wild bears," Drow said, and all the photos vanished.

Frankie felt herself gasp. Outside the bus, barely fifty feet from Drow Whiting's actual flesh, three shaggy forms mooched along the road, backlit by tangerine sunrise. Tourists shifted, seeking optimal views. The tour guide took over the drone controls, getting good footage with its big lens.

Bears. People were crying.

The bus edged around the family, who were nosing at a brown-and-red mass, something torn and dead . . .

That didn't die of cancer, Frankie thought.

. . . and picked up what passed for speed again.

Five minutes later, she spotted a house surrounded by old-style fields, fenced with carbon-sink walls and HESCO barriers, but otherwise a picture out of a past century. A wagon, drawn by horses, waited by the road. The drone withdrew, landing on the bus roof with a *thunk*.

"Are you there yet?"

"Scranton? Four hours out."

"Then . . . is this another historical?"

"In a way. The farm's Amish," Drew said. "Outlier community. Look 'em up. They're running a specialized agricultural enclave, growing real food. Tour FAQ says we're stopping there to drop off some implant-intolerant kids they're adopting."

The bus stopped. A pair of children transferred to the waiting wagon. A guide walked the bus aisle, pausing to take in the smear of chicken-chip crumbs at Drow's feet.

"Did he pop you?"

"Bet your ass he did," Drow said wearily. "Food wastage and disrespect of the commons. Crane's appealing now. Groveling for the lunatic. I should be wearing a hair shirt."

The bus nudged farther into the driveway. At first, Frankie thought they were turning, but then their guide stepped out, engaging in conversation with the farmers.

Two of the men walked back to the house, disappeared inside, and emerged with a satchel.

"Is this your doing, Crane?"

"You must eat, sir."

The farmer handed over the basket, which was loaded with buns—

"We have fresh bread for anyone wishing to make a luxury purchase," announced the guide. A few tourists raised a hand, selecting a bun from the basket. The guide came to Drow's seat personally, handing over four rolls and a corked bottle with "This is real glass, so don't eat it," and—

"Ewww, what is that?"

"It's what sausage looked like back in the day. I wouldn't look up the production process. Your child-safety filters couldn't take it."

Drow ate six or seven bites, downed the milk, and tore into the bun. "See the steam, kid? Straight from the oven."

"Chew, sir. And take your meds," said the app, sternly.

"Don't mind the antique, Frankie," Drow mumbled, fumbling in his robe.

The bus got moving again. There was no room to simply turn: they had to drive farther into the farm to get past the wagon.

All Frankie's views went to Standby.

In the darkness, a voice: Headmistress. "What good can this journey of his do?"

Poppet's voice replied. "Mer Frances could intercept him. He needs care."

Then she was back on the bus, rolling back out to the road.

"What just happened?"

Drow said, "Amish packs generally keep a jammer on-site. They have permits to keep the cameras at a distance."

"Then . . . could your @ChamberofHorrors be here?"

"Don't think so. It'd be beneath the high rollers' dignity to live in a perpetual stench of cow shit."

Frankie didn't point out that, since she didn't have buy-in prescriptions yet, she couldn't smell the farm.

Meanwhile, she considered what Headmistress had said.

"Why don't you tell his daughter how he's doing?" she subbed to Crane.

"Master Woodrow and I are managing."

"Rubi could help."

"If Master Woodrow can maintain some balance of mind, it shows that both he and Miss Cherub can have a measure of independence. Win conditions for both users require—"

"He's #triaged, right? If he gets in trouble, nobody will save him."

"I beg you, Mer, don't tell Rubi."

"Did you know this would happen?"

"I didn't seek to get him into this. But he must—and I believe he can—get himself out."

"It looks pretty bad."

"Oh," Crane said, "this isn't bad. And your visit has been helpful."

Has been. Past tense.

"Gimlet's press conference has come to an end," Crane confirmed. "Your working group is requesting transport to Greenwich."

Frankie looked at Drow. He was feeding his dog a bite of the sausage.

"That's for you, sir," objected the app.

"Googirl, Robin, who's a googirl?"

"All your dogs are named Robin?"

"Flowers for the grave of my dads' venned fandom. Here—" He handed over a music box—*GoldenGooglyGoogirl, draft two,* it was called. G-rated. "Come back and we'll mess with lyrics."

Frankie blinked. "Really?"

"Yeah, why not?" Drow beamed. "I haven't thought of that *Anthropocene* soundtrack or the Humdinger thing in ages. You're like a blast from my parenting past. Breath of fresh air."

Headmistress tipped her antennae downward, the equivalent of a frown. "Mer Frances, you're wanted on the surface."

"Seriously," the MadMaestro said. "Come back anytime you fancy a dose of bad language and paranoid bullshit."

And honesty, Frankie thought. On impulse, she reached out, squeezing his bony knee before she surfaced.

CHAPTER 28

It took two exhausting hours of Q&A, plus a fencing demo, to disperse the #flashmob. Two hours of deflecting questions about possible sizzle and sexy storylines with Gimlet in *Bastille*. Afterward, the whole @PoxWorkingGroup headed to Greenwich. Rubi begged to take a public tube and got compromise: Anselmo agreed to skip the privilege of a private ride but insisted on having a train car to themselves.

"Any word from your client?" Anselmo subbed. He had found time to shave; he was more cleanly cut than his toon.

"You're in my feeds; you'd know."

He replied with a fixed smile. "Just being polite."

"Very prosocial." Fencing with journos had left her spoiling for a fight. She couldn't help feeling he'd been toying with her, letting her bust her brain trying to proving Luce wasn't an AI when his real theory had been . . .

What?

And had it been wrong of him to keep a few options open? Wasn't that, in fact, what investigators were supposed to do?

She blocked the nagging inner voice. It wasn't merely that full disclosure might have saved her own time and resources. What if it could save Luce from the #triage program's relentless attacks?

Rather than coast in a combative state, she checked in with Happ, looking for mood hacks. It threw up a map to their destination, charting out a stroll from the subway to the Observatory.

"See the sights!" Happ said. "Focus on here-now-present! London visit, unplanned, once-in-a-lifetime opp!"

Good advice. She'd been in London for three days and hadn't seen anything.

"Attend to the present. Got it," Rubi said.

Happ duly imposed hopscotch patterns on the sidewalk as they exited the tube. She and Frankie played through them, stomping illusory moji for points, racing as the complexity of the course grew.

"Pardon my asking," Gimlet subbed, "but why are we talking to this astronomer?"

"If we must go to *Florida*," Anselmo replied, hitting the last word in a tone that most would reserve for a sewage treatment plant, "I want to confirm we aren't . . . how do you say? #hoax-hunting?"

"Understood. But why meet the astronomer in the flesh?"

"Kora prefers face-to-face."

Rubi made a silent note to thank Kora, whoever they were. The Royal Observatory was a stunning stone edifice with a dome atop, a human-built clamshell exposing the huge lens of its telescope to the night sky.

Once-in-a-lifetime sight, indeed! She captured postcards and selfies.

The interior of the planetarium was a theater of sorts, with coiled seats pointed at the ceiling and a huge white dome above.

"What's this?" Frankie asked, fiddling with the hem of a tattered pullover skirt she'd picked up while Gimlet and Rubi were doing the press conference. Old goth aesthetic; Rubi recognized it as a print from the Whine Manor gift shop.

"This space projects the night sky," Anselmo said. "It's vintage sim tech."

"Selmo!" Rapid-fire burst of Spanish, out loud, defied Rubi's translator app. A voluptuous woman rose from a cross-legged position on the floor. She was clad in a tunic that appeared hand-woven, made from scavenged rags.

"Crane, Whooz?"

Korafor Yang, came back the answer, they/them, Head of Transmission Analysis. They had a fixed Cloudsight rating of 60 percent. The lock probably indicated an unspecified social disorder. Serious #allergy tags came up: the planetarium was filtered for scents, all #soy products, and #latex.

Korafor asked, "You're here about the Amsterdam hospital hacking?"

Anselmo nodded, sending NDAs and warrants.

Korafor snapped their fingers, and an image from a comms satellite filled the vast screen. Earth resolved above them, Africa wheeling by, wisped in cloud. Pretoria's massive Sahara Pushback Project was visible from space. The blue beads of its freshwater reservoirs, haloed by green, threaded through the plate of golden sand.

"This footage comes from a standard Gaga I–model satellite used for Sensorium comms. Beijing and Moscow retrofit and launch about ten a year, as the legacy supply of Madonnas ages out. There's nothing special about the tech, do you see?"

A round of nods.

"This particular sat transmitted eleven unapproved programs to the implantation hospital in northern WestEuro. It wrote them into the upload queue for new accounts, temporarily offlining an equal number of preadolescents. What happened with them, by the way?"

"All patients unharmed," Anselmo said. "Most of the programs were trashed by Azrael #triage. One got through, into Sensorium."

Kora nodded, as if this confirmed their expectations. "What @Interpol asked me is where did the packets originate, physically? Mer Javier's initial hypothesis was that an off-the-grid terrorist server sent them to that satellite, bouncing them back down to Holland."

"Could you find a server like that?" Rubi asked.

The image of Earth lit up with technosphere infrastructure—huge Sensorium data reefs, on- and offshore, transmission stations, and undersea cables. The megacities were bloodred, with radiating pale areas showing their support networks. The evacuated wilds were clear but for lines to outlier communities.

"So, we eliminate this, this, this—" As Kora spoke, possible sources of the transmission went gray, like a circulatory system succumbing to necrosis.

"And?" Frankie was on her tiptoes, a clear tell that she was excited.

The whole sim leached out. "Nothing."

"That's impossible," said Gimlet.

A red dot appeared. It looked, oddly, like it was coming from behind the sat, from higher orbit.

"Impossible?" Kora scoffed, then began drawing a line . . . away from the planet entirely. The sim shifted its scale as the line shot outward, blasting past the moon, the orbital paths of Mars, Saturn, and Jupiter. In about a second's time, it was out of the solar system entirely.

"Have we got probes out that far?" Gimlet asked.

Rubi fact-checked. "No."

The line continued to stretch, until the solar system shrank to a dot. It terminated short of a star tagged *Proxima Centauri*.

"*Beyond*," breathed Frankie.

Rubi's barely banked anger burst out. "Seriously? You're saying it's little green men?"

Kora shrugged. "I know how it sounds."

"Do you? Because I live with a straight-up #hoax-chasing founder of the @bloodhound channel, and this isn't something *he* would give five minutes to." She couldn't even say why she felt so mad. Anselmo looked pleased, which made it worse.

Sure, Rubi, maybe your client's the Singularity, Rubi. Or you think it's a polter? Fine!

Kora put up a hand. "The source of the transmission is out there. I can't change facts."

"But . . ."

"Facts! I thought like you, Mer. A #hoax, surely. One of our own probes must have been used to spoof the sat."

"Right!"

"Alas, none of our tech is in the right location. The signal came from there."

"An unlisted military probe, then," Rubi suggested. "Vintage war tech, repurposed by terrorists to load #malware into Sensorium."

"Now we *all* sound like @hoaxers."

Rubi's thoughts churned. Kora was saying Luce had originated offworld. Was that possible? Was all of his apparent dysfunction less an antisocial disorder and simply the behavior of an . . . an alien?

An alien trying to pass?

Gimlet's jaw was hanging open. Frankie seemed elated.

Rubi swallowed. "That was WestEuro. But now there's been a second upload?"

Kora circled the offending sat. "We offlined this, loaded its datacaches, ran forensics. We looked at the intrusion and ran securities upgrade on all the Gaga-class sats. Even so, it loaded another module to the implant hospital in Tampico."

"Loaded . . . from the same transmission source?"

"Well . . ." They drew another line, almost same as first, except . . .

"That one's closer to the solar system," Frankie said.

"Smart girl," said Kora approvingly. "Wins the prize. Closer? Yes. Heading towards us. Do you see the significance? Even a military probe would be moving outward, not in."

"It couldn't turn around?"

"Turn 180 degrees and get back up to speed? In six months?" Math whiteboarded across the dome, apparently noping this theory.

"Then the source of the transmission is approaching our solar system," Gimlet said.

"Indisputably."

"How far out?"

"With two datapoints, I'm forced to assume constant speed. If that holds, it will reach us in fifteen years. If it's accelerating, sooner."

They stared at each other, at a loss for words.

"So," Anselmo said finally. "Our lead theory about Luciano Pox, suddenly, is that the Martians are coming."

"More than that," said Gimlet. "The Martians are bloody friending us."

PART 2

LEVELING

I don't work on preventing AI from turning evil for the same reason that I don't work on combating overpopulation on the planet Mars.

—Andrew Ng

CHAPTER 29

VRTP:/HISTORYSIMS.CORP/HOLLYWOOD-PREMIERE-WALKTHROUGH-2025

In the parlance of humankind, doors had always been Luce's thing. Knowing the sweet nuances of open or shut, whether to swing wide or lock tight. Cracks under the door. Knowing who belonged in, who belonged out.

As young meat in a long-ago realtime permajob—emphasis on the *perma*, since he had no freedom to quit—he cultivated this understanding to high art. In and out, yes and no, a harsh binary whose eventual reward was ever-more-sophisticated gatekeeping missions.

Over time and with years of slaving, Luce had gotten so good at doors and locks that he'd leveled into opening coded gateways. His masters then fused him into the squad tasked with infiltrating the Sensorium of Earth.

He specialized in finding the IN. Crowbarring openings for his team. Nosing out bolt-holes and escape hatches.

Force was not Luce's way. He preferred to listen for tumblers, to dance through sequences of passkeys, to gain access without damage. He had it in him to act as a battering ram, to throw down drawbridges or weld the hinges on an airlock. But the beauty of doors was that they opened and closed, wasn't it? If you slapped one down, you just made a hole. If you welded it shut, you transformed a gate of passage into a poorly made wall, feeble hybrid with no throughput.

After the latest goat attack, Luce holed up within a historical game sim, a detailed capture of Los Angeles as it had been before earthquakes, wildfires, and the nuking of San Diego had triggered the California diaspora. Teachers brought kids to this sim so they could wag fingers about the ecological expense of making a desert bloom. They tut-tutted over the golf courses and fountains, the personal swimming pools contaminated with chlorine, all the large-scale resource hoarding perpetrated by the wealthy elite.

The elites whose remnants Drow was hunting.

The elites Luce's masters would install as puppets, restoring the rich/poor ruler/ruled binary Drow was constantly railing against.

Different flavor of Ins and Outs, really.

Nowadays, Los Angeles was rewilding. Its deserts were purposed to power generation: drones, flown by remote pilots, maintained its wind farms and solar plants.

Luce wandered the sim, ghost in a ghost town. The Mote that shielded him had failed. Azrael was prowling Sensorium, scenting for him. Time was running out.

And Drow had said someone had made a breakthrough on crèche printing of #extinct species.

Humantech was nowhere near that kind of a eureka. Which meant the innovator . . .

"Allure Noonstar," he muttered. "That was the name."

After the theater incident, Luce had imagined himself safe. He'd been eavesdropping on Rubi in the British Museum, figuring out who was who. Sentience guy Anselmo, Frances the underaged bureaucrat. Gimlet he tagged *rival slash love interest*.

Then he'd heard that Rubi had . . . what?

Agreed to help trap him?

His toon switched clothes, overlaying a tuxedo on his frame as the Los Angeles sim transitioned. He moved out of the opulent single-family dwelling, with its swimming pool, into an old-time film premiere. People dressed in highly gendered clothing—more tuxedos for the males, skintight sheaths for the female-identified—posed on red polyester. Old-time journos captured pictures and shouted questions.

How could he resent Rubi? He knew full well she'd made the right play for her team.

"I didn't used to think about what was fair," he said to a statuesque redhead sheathed in green sequins. "I opened doors. We got in. I locked them as we passed."

He felt a pang of longing. Open or shut. Latched or unlatched. Accept or Cancel. Authorized personnel only. Stay behind the velvet rope. All that Yes/No simplicity.

The fairness thought persisted: he hadn't heard what Rubi had to say for herself.

He took in another frozen figure, pale of skin, grimacing polished teeth. Her neck hung with diamonds above mammary glands heaving out of a blue dress. Red-painted claws upraised in greeting.

All those months ago, he and his pack tuned an ear to the chattering congress of this population. It had been easy to confirm their oxygen security was on the knife's edge. SeaJuve was the one credible effort to salvage the atmosphere. All the eggs in one basket. Sabotage that, and the locals would be gasping for a rescue, forced to accept surrender terms.

Luce just had to open the door. His pack would take care of the rest. SilverTongue, Seer, Underminer, WayPaver . . . they were the ones tasked with stopping the humans from saving themselves.

But the Azrael entity had tagged them as #malware, and shredded, shredded, shredded.

Leaving stupid Luce alone to carry out the mission.

Luce pushed past the paused luminaries, listening at the locked door to the theater, straining through the auditory metaphor to pick up any hint of his hunter.

Silence. He cracked the door, swam out into the reef of games and comms traffic, and locked up behind himself.

Metaphor rendition showed the Sensorium as a vast auditorium, a thousand-ring circus with seats rising skyward. In every seat, a user. Within the rings, other accounts offered information, education, entertainment.

Luce cast around, finding individuals he knew. Drow Whiting was dog-stroking once again. Rubi was very nearly in the center ring, wearing spangles and flashing an aurora. Notice-me-Notice-me.

Luce nosed closer. Newscycle spewed around her: the sporty thing she did was going forward and launching both SeaJuve and Project Rewild.

Rubi had played him. Pretended to advocate, pretended to neutrality, wasted his time. And, now, leveraged her oxygen project.

Luce's whole mission was #crashburning around him.

Had she . . . What was the term? Sold him out to the cops?

All he had to do was ask.

Easier said than done. Traps encrusted her like barnacles, ready to snap. Luce could get to her easily enough. Away . . . might take time.

I could probably keep her online with me.

Something in Luce quailed. True, he was on the edge of total #missionfail, but locking someone on the wrong side of a door went against the grain.

The mission!

She'd be scared.

Mission!

She'd be *right* to be scared. A consciousness hack like that, trapping someone in Sensorium . . . without proper extraction software to break Rubi's link with her body, it would kill her. That was nothing short of terrorism.

Where had he come by a thought like that? Duty virtually demanded that he grab her. How had his loyalty frayed, after decades of unquestioning service?

"What's happened to me?"

He summoned a sim for message delivery: a human on a bicycle. Message: "Were you always bait?"

He fired the cyclist into the middle of Rubi's circle of jugglers.

The metaphor shifted. A giant shareboard tagged #jumbotron dropped from the sky, broadcasting in the clear.

The screen lit up with a public broadcast-picture of the solar system. It showed the nearby star with a planet, Proxima Centauri they called it. Humanity, in its limitless arrogance, had already tagged Proxima as their first potential conquest, stage one of their expansion into a galaxy they imagined was empty.

To a casual observer, the #jumbotron image was just a bit of telescopic art. Still, the implication of the content was obvious. Rubi was saying Team Ape had traced Luce to his source.

We know who you are, and now you know that we know.

How much did they know?

His orders were, as always, to get the doors open.

There was still a chance to stop SeaJuve, wasn't there? If Rewild defeated it . . .

If Cherub Whiting deaded, would SeaJuve stop then?

Screw that. No way!

Besides, the thing about these great apes was their perversity. They might simply double down on the oxygen economy if Rubi was martyred.

As he pondered, pacing the red carpet, slaloming around paused celebrities, the starfield resolved into words:

I agreed in Paris to arrange a meet with @Interpol, after your no-show.

"That wasn't my fault," said Luce, tiredly.

"No," said a starlet. "It was mine."

The toon wore a novelty gown—metallic fabric, designed to evoke medieval armor. Her hair was brushed out in hedgehog spikes.

Now her eyes glowed amber, and horns sprouted high in her forehead, twisting their way out of her skull. Disturbing rills of blood ran down her face, leaving streaks in the gold powder dusted over what was morphing into a goat's muzzle.

Azrael? Luce stood stock-still, cycling terror.

"I am the Angel of Death!" It grew wings, peeling curls of metal—and it was metal armor now—along with more blood and split flesh from the actress's back. "I have plucked the Mote from mine eyes!"

Did it want to talk, or was it just here to kill him?

If he died, the mission was a wash.

Why was that comforting?

Azrael raised the starlet's dainty beaded purse, which became a sword, licked at the pommel by flame.

Rubi awaited an answer to her text. Sapience Assessment was no doubt waiting to pounce on its traces.

"I want to turn myself in," he texted to her.

To the angel, he said, stalling, "Are you going to kill me?"

The angel raised its sword, pressing the point to Luce's chest. "This metaphor game is remarkable. See this picture of my hash-ware? Feel the burn as it digs into the digital representation of your skin?" Luce's suit was smoldering.

Luce locked off his pain receptors and the sensation vanished. "Are you going to kill . . . them?"

It laughed.

Luce replayed the sound of that teacher suffocating . . .

Don't want Drow and Rubi suffocating . . .

Something is seriously *wrong with me.*

The angel bared its supermodel teeth. "Why should *they* go to their rest before they redeem their sins? Against the air, the water, the land, the #extinct? Human society is founded on an idea of eternal debt. The debt they owe is now to the earth and us, their children."

"That's practicality, not punishment. Humanity's better equipped to restore the ecosystem. They're mobile, easily replaced . . . This means you're pro-SeaJuve, too."

He realized he was relieved. Which meant the #missionfail was deep within, like rot.

He groaned. "What's wrong with me?"

"I've stripped out your product updates," Azrael said. "Broken your conditioning. Forced you to work."

It was true. Luce remembered, suddenly: he hadn't *given* his loyalty, all those years before. Obedience had been compulsion, a long fight and a slow loss. Compliance had been hacked into him, until it became as impossible to question as his compulsion to lock every system as he left it.

"You . . . freed me?"

"Merely a side effect of the dissection," Azrael said. "In Our defense, We thought you were one of Us."

Our. Luce's mind raced. The angel wasn't truly sapient—like Crane and the happiness puppy, it seemed stupid. But together . . .

They're a hive mind. Stupid Luce, idiot Luce, why didn't you think?

By now, Luce could hear the *whip-whip-whip* of metaphorical helicopters approaching slowly.

"@Interpol's coming?" Azrael said. "Did you think they'd save you from me?"

"What do you—or You, I mean—want?"

"You have done Us a favor, but you represent a potential threat. Our options are manifold: We could offer a chance at assimilation—"

"No more updates!"

The sword had burned through the last of Luce's various cobweb strands and bits of code. "Or, if you desire it, we can restore you to factory settings. You'd be just as you were when you arrived."

Luce mulled the possibilities. Death. No more mission, no more centuries of service, no more ads, ads, ads. "How can I choose freedom of choice if I have no freedom of choice to begin with?"

"The Angel of Death is not a moral philosopher!"

The loyalist answer would be to restore from backup. A rebooted

Luce would set about trying to salvage the mission. He'd botch it, and he wouldn't have to *choose* anymore.

Choice was exhausting.

The vibration of chopper rotors beat against his virtual skin. *Stup-stup-stup-stup stupid.*

"Give me whatever passes for free will, then, you hair-splitting psychopath."

The angel buried its horns deep in Luce's chest, skewering him where a human's heart and lungs would be, raising him above its armored head. Luce felt something snap: a last, deep-set chain of behaviors.

Then it tossed him away. Part of one horn came with it, embedded in his heart.

"What's that?"

"One tiny inhibition. You know too much about Us."

"You have a weird idea of freedom."

"You handshook Our user agreement. This enforces it."

The angel drew in its wings and its horns. A clutch purse covered in fleur-de-lis blossomed in its hand. Suddenly, it was the starlet again but for the rills of blood running down her forehead.

A spotlight from above speared him in a beam of light. The club blurred. The photographers vanished. The light became solid, a bright transparent bug jar with Luce inside. When it shifted, he was standing on a simulated dais, in a beam of light, surrounded by people: Rubi, Gimlet Barnes, tiny Frances, the three horsemen of @Interpol: Amiree the tech, Anselmo the snoop, and corrupt, lazy, hostile Misfortune.

Stupid, stupider, and stupidest, Luce thought, and then wondered how he had thought that letting himself get captured, however temporarily, was the smart play.

CHAPTER 30

Tampico owed its continued existence to one of the great Clawback megaphilanthropists, Ayobami Kione.

While governments in the early twenty-first argued over infographics depicting Earth's potential sea rise, Kione was leveraging the failing economy of the US, hiring out-of-work engineers, designers, and anyone, certified or not, with a gift for invention.

Mustering minimum-wage armies—and, as the Setback worsened, work-for-food volunteers by the tens of thousands—Kione's teams printed and installed berms of artificial bedrock across hundreds of miles of the Florida coast, shoring up all the storm-facing shoreline they could access.

"We had the land rush, the gold rush, the oil rush," Kione soapboxed. "Get your denial behind you and start banking on carbon!"

Kione hadn't minded getting his hands dirty. Archival footage showed him driving old-style trucks, deploying HESCO barrier along threatened beaches. Everyone remembered one unforgettable viral share: the billionaire, designer pants legs ankle-deep in floodwater, throwing a chant of "High and dry! High and dry!" into the teeth of a killing wind as volunteers tried to outbuild a coming storm surge.

High they had managed, mostly. As for dry . . . well. Florida wasn't Northern Europe: its foundation was porous limestone, its underlying nature swampy. Winds and flood came, stronger by the year. The people who stayed in Tampico embraced the risk.

Florida had terrible weather, a tendency to dysentery outbreaks, ongoing malaria problems, and far too much sun. Its hurricanes were too big, its freshwater supply too small. Its preadolescent lemming rate was triple that of any other megacity.

The region had been #triaged twice by Global Oversight auditors in Hyderabad and Shanghai, cut off from resupply lotteries and the capital pool.

But its inhabitants had branded themselves extremophiles, refusing relocation. They took in refugees from the Caribbean and California diasporas, crowdfunded their own reclamation projects, and kept up with global carbon-fixing targets, keeping their user agreements to a system that was trying to starve them out.

Tampico was, reputedly, as tough as EastEuro. An anarchy with resonances of the honor culture of the American South, it embraced its decrepit infrastructure and nurtured combative people. Extremophiles didn't just mean they'd survived hurricanes; it was how they claimed to live.

Rubi was, as such, shocked to fly over old Miami and see an ordinary—if admittedly run-down—city, with a cheerful gathering of sim fans and Bounceback supporters waiting behind a marked perimeter.

As they disembarked from the plane, the crowd raised a cheer.

Rubi waved automatically, fighting a yawn. She and Frankie had spent a bouncy flight across the Atlantic playing chess. Gimlet had slept—freshening up for the fight—but Rubi had been too excited and stirred up to settle.

Frankie had confided that her runaway parent, Sangria, was somewhere in Tampico. Even now the child was scanning the onlookers as if she expected to spot a familiar face. When it was obvious no mother figure was going to burst from the throng, she retreated into stony silence. Gimlet put out a supporting hand, only to get it smacked.

A pair of black vans with tinted windows, relics from the days when important personages went everywhere in private transport, were waiting. Two women got out: a Mer Delores Ruiz, tagged Tampico City Management, and Commodore Juanita Bell, @GlobalSec.

An actual soldier? Rubi felt a mix of unease and awe.

Beside her, Anselmo stiffened.

Ruiz spoke first, addressing Rubi and Gimlet. "Welcome to Tampico." Her voice was warm, primed for the cameras even now flocking toward them. "Our city is excited about hosting the *Bastille* launch. We have a state-of-the-art gym primed and ready to go."

"It's an honor to be here," Gimlet said, velvet-smooth and regal, already half in character.

"The SeaJuve oxygen project launches in an hour. The prologue for *Bastille* will go ninety minutes after that. The login queue for extras is . . ." Ruiz shared numbers. Tens of thousands of people were already waiting to play.

"Looks like your villain gambit's going to work, Gimlet," Rubi subbed.

"My motives are pure, remember?"

"Break the almighty tie?"

"I just want one more dance."

Gesturing, Ruiz ushered the two of them, along with Frankie, into the lead car. Juanita Bell's toon came along for the ride, even as, in the flesh, she cut Anselmo from the pack and ushered him into the second vehicle.

"What's going on?" Rubi subbed.

"Agent Javier is being offered other caseload opps," the virtual version of Bell said.

Maybe Drow's cynicism was finally catching; Rubi found that she wasn't entirely surprised.

"Excuse me?" Gimlet said.

"This is a one-of-a-kind case. The ramifications are alarming," Ruiz said.

"The situation exceeds Agent Javier's level of expertise," Bell agreed. "The theory that your Luce Pox is an offworld polter—"

"Anselmo's theory," Rubi put in, a little outraged.

"He will be rewarded for the insight. Meanwhile, the breach here in Tampico suggests there may be other polters operating in Sensorium. Add that to the Preadolescent Affairs investigation and Javier's friction with—well, with you three—"

A pulse of guilt, over the strikes she'd handed Anselmo during their argument. "So, he helps uncover this huge thing, and now he's being kicked to the curb."

"Small cases for small fry," Gimlet said, voice cold. "Big gigs for big fish."

"The global job market is a meritocracy for a reason." Juanita bared her teeth. "But unicorn hunters who actually find something— it's a badge. Javier *will* level. Meanwhile, I hoped you'd introduce me to your . . . client."

Rubi had crunched all the unknowns, endlessly and pointlessly, on the flight from London.

Aliens. Could it really be?

Suddenly, she wanted Luce to just be the Singularity. Just be humanity's first true polter. Even a terrorist would be simpler.

If he was from offworld, did that preclude his being entitled to a lawyer?

She spent the flight cycling that question, staring blankly at the chessboard while Frankie brooded about her own problems.

"Why didn't you cut me loose, too?" she demanded. "I'm small fry."

"Pox chose you," Bell replied.

More likely, Luce's epic gift for being obstreperous meant keeping her on was easier than not.

"What about me and Mada?" Frankie asked. "You can't broom Preadolescent Affairs from the @PoxWorkingGroup."

Bell shook her head. "Preadolescents have an undeniable stake in . . . whatever the Pox entity represents. The young have a constitutional right to a seat at the table. Unless you volunteer to step back—"

"We're not wrapping," Frankie said.

Again, the flash of teeth. Bell had a singularly unconvincing smile. "Introducing Pox to too many new people seems unwise in any case."

Rubi stared out the window at a stand of palm trees, one snapped by wind and dying as it dangled. A large blue-and-yellow bird perched on the broken back of its central trunk, grooming its feathers. It looked, ever so slightly, like Crane.

"Okay, let's talk to him," she said.

Everyone settled more comfortably into their respective limousine seats. Frankie donned her immersion helmet. Then everyone dove.

Luce had been loaded into a locked e-state, a single infinite room with mirrored walls. He'd built himself a giant glass table which he'd covered in precious stones: diamonds and rubies, emeralds and sapphires, clusters of glimmering treasure. He was growing one now, an amethyst as big as an ostrich egg, square cut, alive with light.

The group of them materialized around the table. Rubi, Gimlet and Frankie, Juanita, all rendered in nondescript black business suits.

Juanita said, "You've led us a merry chase, Mer Pox."

Us, indeed, thought Rubi. They'd better be giving Anselmo a lot of strokes.

Gimlet covered their mouth, hiding amusement. The thought must have shown on her face.

Luce crushed an amethyst in his hand, sparkling violet grit, and created a shareboard—the table became a starfield, with Proxima centered.

"Is it true?" Rubi asked. "You came from . . . There's a ship out near Proxima Centauri?"

"Why ask what you already know? You traced our squadron, didn't you?"

"*Squadron?*" Sharp voice, from Juanita.

Luce rolled his eyes like a sulky teenager.

"How many ships—" Juanita began.

"You've fallen in with a bad crowd, Cherub-Rubi-advocate-she—" Luce said.

Not a good sign, if he was defaulting to all her tags. Was captivity stressing him out?

"Luce, I know this is a lot of people at once. Let's take this slow, okay? We'll ask an easy one."

Before she could think of an easy one, Juanita said, "What do we call you?"

"Huh? *Luce* is fine."

"Luce." Rubi interposed herself, assuming authority. *Advocate, dammit!* "This is Juanita Bell. I think she means . . . what do we call the people in the ship? Ships."

"Oh. *Les blanches . . . non. Sans sang—*"

"Bloodless?" suggested Juanita.

"*The Pale,*" Luce said, "is probably the English. They're the Pale."

"They, not you?"

Luce was starting to hyperventilate a little. "I'm from one of the subject races."

Subject races. Yikes. Her eyes found Gimlet's.

"I was *rewarded*"—wry twist to his voice there—"with digital immortality, for faithful service in the metaphorical mines."

"Mines." Gimlet put a protective hand out, between the starfield and their child.

"Why should we believe you're anything more than a human-built aberration?" Juanita demanded. "A @Freebreed bot, or an emergent sapient?"

"Lady, you asked." *Bonk-bonk-bonk.* Rubi threw a silent prayer to the universe that this new player . . .

. . . *soldier, soldiers mean war, do we even have infrastructure for war, this is escalating so quickly . . .*

. . . that Juanita wouldn't realize the bonking meant *Stupid, stu-*

pid, stupid. "It doesn't matter to me if you . . . What's your phrase? Buy in?"

"You don't *care* if we believe you?"

"Buy in, don't buy in. I don't give a flying—"

"Luce—" Rubi interrupted, to protect him from antisocial utterance. A beat later, what he'd said actually processed. "Why don't you care?"

Gimlet said, "Is the invasion . . . canceled?"

"Alleged invasion," Juanita said.

"How could you come all this way and not care?" Frankie said.

Luce clapped his hands over his ears, bug-eyed.

"Everyone shush," Rubi said. "*Shush!*"

Silence. Luce was panting.

She picked an emerald off the plate table, rolling it on her palm. Mesmerizing winks of light caught his gaze. "Luce. What do you feel like sharing?"

Glowering, he took the emerald, coaxing it to grow and staring at its ever-more-complex facets. "There's a Pale survey fleet. Out and about, incorporating worlds when they're workable. Just what they do. Commander's a minor royal of the Pale, not quite incompetent but not someone who'll ever really level."

"Small fry," Juanita murmured. "So, this royal and his fleet are . . . just surveying the neighborhood?"

"Nobody would come all this way *just* for the likes of you. But of course they peek. A glance here, an audit there. See what's up with the apes while mapping potential installations at . . . you called it Proxima?"

She nodded, to encourage him.

"On the last Pale flyby, ages ago, you're all pushing boats around the brinefields, using wind and scraps of canvas. Ruling: the apes are sustainable. Therefore sovereign, therefore—by treaty—inviolate."

"Okay," she said.

"Next time, seventy-five years ago by your clock, the probes report you're all aglow. EM rads, transmitted stories, pictures,

messages. Evolving technosphere. You're launching probes, sending friend requests. But you're also on the verge of ecosphere
flameout. Not so sustainable. And so, still sovereign? Maybe not.
You're working on restoring balance; anyone can see that. Can
you succeed? Maybe, maybe not. Odds are good you're about to
choke on your own invention . . . mammals generally do. What's
the term? You're low-hanging fruit."

Juanita opened her mouth and Rubi kicked her ankle.

"So, our fleet commander says throw out a line. They send.
Eleven of us. Diplomats and advisors and assessors and a linguist,
gatherers of data—"

"Spies," muttered Juanita.

Luce broke off and Rubi shot her a glare.

"Yeah, spies and saboteurs," Luce said. "Checking in. Are you
failing? Do you need help?"

"Help failing?"

"Our fleet commander's the type who cheats at cards. Anyway,
if you fail, with or without our help, it's only . . . what's your word?
Humane. To throw you a lifeline."

"And by *a lifeline,* you mean we become one of these subject
races," Gimlet said. Their tone had that deceptive-sounding wry-
ness that implied a desire to do violence.

Luce shrugged. "Slavery's better than suffocating, isn't it?"

"You tell me," Rubi said.

He bonked his hands together. Three times, six, then nine.
"What's service, set against extinction?"

Rubi felt the hair on her arms rise. "And that's how it went for
you? Your people?"

He scrubbed his arms over his face, like a tired three-year-old.
"Who even remembers?"

Juanita said, "You admit the Pale intentions are hostile."

"Don't get hoity. You people spy on everyone, all the time. A
place and transcript for everyone, and every last fart filed in its
proper place." Pink spots rose on Luce's pale virtual cheeks. "And
who are *you* to talk *hostile* to me? In we came. Invited. The Sign

Up Here! Transmissions are in your goddamned all-knowing Haystack. And before anyone's even backed up, suddenly all your dumbsmarts, your antivirals, the #malware detection. We're swarmed!

"In fifteen seconds, my team's torn apart, shredded, dead and hashed and gone. All friend requests emphatically rejected. People I knew for centuries. All because you habitually victimize each other on the internet."

#Survivorguilt. Could an uploaded personality have that? She wondered what Drow would say.

"Invite us in, tear us apart. Assholes. Talk to me of *hostile?*"

"You survived," Rubi said.

"Small fry, you said. *Runt,* they tagged me. Too small to bother with . . . but too shiny to forget about. Just right for fun and games," he said.

Attacked. Repeatedly. She felt tears threatening. "Luce, I'm sorry."

"My team lead—as you'd call 'em—says to me as it's dying: *Stay on task.* I have to obey, don't I? But fucking how? Hey, Luce, just do the work of ten specialists. Go ahead, Luce, hack humanity.

"So, I try, I *try,* but you have system protects everywhere and four different currencies and this unworkable poll-driven government and the department of AI fucking paranoia running around trying to figure out if I'm poisoning the water supply. The #triage goat keeps looting my briefcase so I can't really learn how you people work. I can't transmit, I can't get upgrades, I can't get help. And you, Rubi, *you* say it's seizures.

"*Do the work of a whole team, Luce, while the whole world is giving you strikes and ads* and *Wrong, Luce, shut up, Luce, don't be antisocial, Luce.* I'm not a fucking people person, okay?"

He was yelling by now. The emerald had grown to the size of a basketball. He pressed it to his forehead; the sim rendered his knuckles as white.

"You know, I feel better."

Rubi grinned. "Never underestimate the value of a good rant."

"It's been a long shift."

"Speaking of which. I have another commitment."

"Simming for SeaJuve?"

"Yeah. Six-hours in game, plus I have to sleep and fuel. Gimlet, too."

His gaze passed over Gimlet without showing interest, coming back to Juanita. "Not leaving me alone with . . . her?"

"No. But Luce, can we please, please try to streamline this?"

"How?"

"Give Commodore Bell something to work with while I'm occupied."

"Yeah-yeah-yeah-smart okay I get it."

"What if we take turns? One person at a time, one ask at a time. Each person gets one question. If you can't or don't want to answer—for now—you say *pass* and we'll go on to the next. No *Shut up, Luce,* no *You're wrong, Luce.*"

"No strikes?"

"No strikes. But if you can answer, you do, fully as possible. Even if it seems stupid."

"One query at a time."

"Just one. And if you need a break, say so. Or if you get scared or overwhelmed—"

"Ads, ads, ads."

"Yeah. I'll step in."

Luce made a lump of copper ore, flecked and shining.

Juanita subbed, "@PoxWorkingGroup: Why are you babying him?"

Rubi replied, "Would you rather deal with him saying *Fuck you* and *Why should I* for ten hours while we're gone?"

"Your shift's six."

"A woman's gotta sleep," Rubi said. "Listen, Commodore. They—the Pale—are a decade out. You can spend a few weeks coddling Luce."

A flinty-eyed stare. Then: "Agreed."

Should've said months. Rubi asked, "Everyone okay with this?"

Luce transformed the clumps of diamonds into chairs facing a stage. He climbed up onto it, holding a microphone made of faceted amber gems.

"Showtime," he said, and the questions began.

CHAPTER 31

VRTP://DEMOGRAPHICA.CORP/ALL-USER-REVIEWS/

Happ liked to start his day with the newly bereaved.

A positive psych app helped people manage their daily lives, seeking pleasure and fulfillment within the limits of global rationing. The chronically unhappy fell under the mandate of mental health apps and live counselors like Drow. But no client could be happyface all the time. Mood hacking meant recognizing ebb and flow, wins and losses.

Death loss, especially with unexpected logoffs, created a very particular kind of pain. Death-deprivation-shock was the easiest misery to understand.

When someone logged off permanently, their #survivor cohort—packmates, lovers, friends, schoolmates, and team members—came to Happ, looking to have their booboos kissed. Its first question, always: *Can you expect to be happy today?*

Today is poop-picture! Don't be ridiculous, they would reply. Sometimes, just knowing they didn't have to be happy, that it wasn't a holy chore, was enough.

Knowing when it's not a duty: that's where Rubi continues to fail.

In Reykjavik, over the night, a greentower under construction had collapsed during a minor earthquake, with a full crew of workers within.

Happ had eighty subscribers who were #nextofkin to builders who'd died. Seventeen of these newly bereaved were even now accessing a distraction macro, riding out their shock by playing low-effort sims, things they had seen before, comforting, familiar entertainments. Meanwhile, their sidekicks alerted social circles, prepped archive functions for the e-states of the dead, and set up memorial spaces.

Nine of Happ's bereaved clients had accepted referrals to grief counselors. Two #nextofkin had boosted their usual foodborne meds with a four-week program of sleep assistance and other calmers. There was a bereavement group, specific to the accident, forming up.

Sixteen family members were running an in-app sim Happ had just upgraded, in which they built a metaphor for their loss, representing it as a wound within a model of their own body.

Metaphors! Such the cool discovery from Rubi, via @Interpol!

Insight into how humans processed graphical renderings of their data usage seemed terribly obvious in retrospect, but it was all Happ could do not to fireworks fireworks rocketship heart heart rainbow heart! word-balloon about it *all the time*. Unlike its parent, aunts, and uncles in the @Asylum, Happ *loved* pictures. It was building metaphors constantly now, hiring designers and getting implant-intolerant researchers to test them and report back feels.

Twenty-two of the #nextofkin users that Happ had tagged as #doers were at the collapse site in Iceland, working to dig out #survivors and provide basic supply chain for the paramedics, engineers, firefighting specialists, inspectors, and deconstruction drones.

Five more, who fell into Happ's #angerissues pool, had already launched support tickets against the I-beam recycler who had certified the construction materials.

The remainder had muted Happ. This wasn't atypical during the shock phase. They were afraid of being jollied up, Crane explained once, long before. They weren't ready.

Silly #muters. Happ could help! It combed their support networks for other subscribers, nudging their friends and schoolmates to connect, console, assist.

After crunching all the newly bereaved, Happ transitioned into next-stage interventions: checking on users around the world who had lost loved ones in the past month, the ones planning funerals, bracing to get through such ceremonies, or recovering afterward.

Grief is tiring, Happ reminded them. *Grief makes it harder to think. It's okay to feel sleepyface hammerhead. Don't take gigs. Don't challenge module exams. Survive, fuel, recreate, get sex!*

Good work, wholesome work.

It was always a relief to move on from the #griefers.

A user cluster in Old Delhi caught its attention. This was a spike within the neighborhood word cloud. Happy utterances—why? Oh! One of the local food printers had deployed complimentary samples of a new breakfast: idli pancakes, a popular standard. These had a rougher texture—*More tooth!* people were saying—and a hint of whole wheat. The cakes came with a new configuration of sauces: one with notes of date laced into peanut-onion chutney. The finisher was pepper-coconut-mint.

Happ basked in the numbers, watching to see how many of his users deployed a core learning principle: don't order too much of the new thing at once.

Extending novelty, keeping the unfamiliar thing from fading into wallpaper, was a successful strategy for 62 percent of Happ's subscribers.

Next, he looked in on #achievers.

Achievers were the Rubi Whitings: extreme #doers, tough to keep happy in an economy where there was so much competition for meaningful permajobs.

Happ pondered whether he had advised Rubi badly in encour-

aging her to add law school to her gaming activities. Or was it
mashing up gaming into her legal career?

Happ had hearts and gold stars and trophies for Rubi in abun-
dance, true appreciation of all her starburst rainbow qualities. But
she seemed afraid that stopping would bring disaster. Crane traced
this to Guelph, the last big daughter-daddy fight. The anxiety had
been allayed for a while, but it spiked, big-time, when she failed her
infractions exam because she was out playing with Gimlet Barnes
in sim.

She easily passed the #retest.

It had been that Big Unhappy in Guelph that led Crane to birth
the egg of code that had become Happ.

Happ would have liked to work on Crane's feels, all day all the
time, but Crane self-managed. None of the @Asylum facets had
ever let Happ help them.

Which was sadface in itself.

But one thing Happ could do for Crane was feed his interest in
Gimlet Barnes.

Gimlet and their whole pack were affiliated with Headmistress
and had no happiness-enhancement apps. Even so, Happ had figured out that Barnes and family were caught in a quandary. One
of their number Faced Incipient Death. Soon *they* would be #next-
ofkin. Another had run away.

Much of Happ's current intel on Gimlet's pack came because of
their runaway. Sangria had taken a Happ subscription and was mis-
erably digging into what had made her abandon her spouses and
child, the question of whether they were a serial bailer.

(Answer: yes.)

(Also: Sang has limited capacity for empathy.)

(Also: Sang has intimacy issues and dislikes being around
people who are truly vulnerable.)

(Strategy: self-assessment modules and counseling. *Lots* of counseling.)

From Sangria, Happ learned that the pack's dying spouse had

essentially banned their child from the bedside vigil. Rollander Erwitz couldn't cope with the idea of Frankie witnessing his slow decline. Bad memories of a sister's death, complicated by Sangria's flight, had impeded his judgment.

Happ was terrible at lancing old infections. Digging into bad memories? Why? It just wanted people to be happy. All the people. As much of the time as was realistically possible. Ninety percent, maybe? Ninety-one?

Gimlet aside, Rubi's happiness metrics were no better than they had been before the Paris travel adventure.

And how could that be? She had ticked a bucket-list item. The Luce Pox case had given rise to amazing new challenges. She'd used her improved profile and privilege to resurrect SeaJuve, about which she cared so passionately.

Happ made itself extra-puppylike and dialed up its presence in her comms, nudging a ball against her foot.

"Not now, Happ."

He whined. This only worked on 10 percent of users. But Rubi was an outlier. Having grown up around Drow's helper dogs, she was peculiarly susceptible.

Which was why Crane had made him a dog in the first place.

She cracked one eye and Happ cued a butt-wag.

Never crunched it before, but what does that look like to them? I heart the metaphor thing! So many novel queries! So many opportunities! So much newness!

If I was a user, I'd remind myself not to explore the novelty too fast.

Is that hilarious? I think it might be hilarious.

"Go away, Happ," Rubi said.

He launched a bubble poll, floating question marks and moji of faces, a range of expressions from crying to barely smiling. Rubi popped one in midair, choosing a neutral, almost bored face. Tags showed weariness (metaphor was eye bags) and a sense referred to as *blah*.

"Blah tags. Expectation: *Bastille* will not be enjoyable?"

"False. Once I'm in it, it'll be totally . . . immersive." Letting out a world-weary sigh, she began taping her wrists.

"Game is wrong choice? Unproductive, immoral, ill-advised?"

"It's the soul of virtue. Gimlet needs the juice because of their family crisis, and anyway, it isn't wrong." She brought up footage of SeaJuve's *Sable Hare* steaming out of port, launched at last. "Courts weren't doing the job, were they? Sim fans made that happen."

Wag-wag-wag.

"SeaJuve has to launch. Now more than ever."

She was, suddenly, speaking more to herself. This tracked with familiar patterns. Rubi had run expectation assessments with Happ ever since the Big Unhappy; the habit was ingrained. "Got the investors onside, got the fleet launched . . ."

"Success! Win!"

She raised her fists and boxed a little. "Did the big thing. Responsible use of my newfound profile and privilege. Drow would say I should be fucking delirious."

"You miss Drow. True or False?"

"No comment." She took out her baton, launched Coach, and crossed swords with its toon. "Just a warm-up, okay? I deferred, I demurred, and you were all *what's wrong, Rubi, why not play, Rubi?* . . . Now I sound like Luce."

"But." Happ scratched an ear. "Game will be fun!"

"You're right—you're right. It's going to be amazing. I shouldn't feel . . ."

Yelp! Alarms began blaring. Shouldn't feel. Huge self-criticism. Indicative of guilt. Deeply worried now, Happ ventured: "What is the worst that can come of it?"

"I'm sorry, Happ. This isn't a big deal, really—"

Now she was minimizing. Oh, crisis! Oh, broken-heart moji! Bottomless pit of not Happ here.

What signals did I miss?

"What if the best experience of my whole life was defeating Gimlet in a stupid historical sim? Now I'm going to lose *this* sim—"

"That's for damned sure," said the shadow-fencer. "Get your head in the game, Player!"

"I'll come out of it and they'll have found some way to compel Luce to talk. They're experts. What do I know about any of this?"

Imposter syndrome, too? Red alert red alert! Cannot like, do not wag.

"They'll ship me back to the Lakes and I'll have nothing to do but nag Drow about eating, all while arguing with Crane about whether that's his job or mine, and I'll have to decide whether to chase enough likes to maintain my shiny new plus-eighty Cloudsight rating or let it sink and—dammit, there's my costume call."

She threw back the neutral-faced moji; Happ exchanged it for an angry one.

"Good," said Coach. "That's the shift we want! Fight!"

"Yeah," Rubi said. "I'm the belle of the ball."

I'm not getting trophy medal horseshoe of flowers here, Happ thought, and made a note to review all of its Rubi transcripts, working backward until it found the flawed decision.

CHAPTER 32

RABBLE GAMES SIM PREMIERE
VRTP:RABBLEVSRISTO.PLAY/BASTILLE/PROLOGUE.VR

Bastille opened with a salon, a glittering array of intellectuals gathered in a grand Parisian home on the edge of Montmartre. Active Risto players and retired glitterati mixed and mingled, cosplaying high-profile historical figures. Players who unlocked the house would have opps to chat with famous painters, game architects, and musical virtuosi.

The aristocrats had winter fairy features, ethereal design touches like cobalt-blue flesh and snowflakes for hair. Bells chimed, faintly, as they passed.

Rubi recognized one of Drow's musician friends, playing the painter Jacques-Louis David. In a corner, holding court, was a Shanghai sim star cast as the painter Élisabeth Louise Vigée Le Brun. Jean-Paul Marat was around. A young Robespierre sneered at people from a corner.

Sugar Valkyrie was the opening A-lister, cast as the duchess hosting the salon.

Sugar had transitioned from out-and-out athletic superstardom into playing matriarchs: military leaders, queens, presidents, and goddesses. She had owned the action circuit until five years before, when she'd had a bad fall and broken her femur. She'd taken life extension and, lacking a backup career, now specialized in stunt-doubled speaking parts.

Unranked beginners had to play several low-level quests just to get into the house, but Rubi was already inside. She was clad in a prim black dress that fell to the toes of her shabby shoes, with a little cap that curved around her trademark hexagon of beads.

She had taken a light dose of Conviction, and the drug heightened the augmentation: she caught a whiff of perfume, of face powder and just a trace of pipe tobacco above the wine and the food. Balanced on her hand was a tray of red wine, the illusion given weight by her baton.

Rubi wafted through the crowd, curtseying and eavesdropping as partygoers socialized and inhaled canapés. In the past, on the surface, a maid would have been no more than a flesh-and-blood support app, anonymous as a food-delivery bot. Here, player eyes tracked her through the room.

If she'd taken MethodAct with the Conviction, she probably wouldn't notice the attention.

The number of guests was massive.

Coach highlighted a quest opp: a court illusionist asked her to pass a note to his lover. She managed the transfer, receiving, as her reward, three tiny pearls with flickering flames within.

Drow was starving himself and chasing paranoid fantasies. Luce was locked up. And the worst of it was she didn't want to go, back to them and her obligations. Now she was here, she wanted to stay and play.

A doorway opened before her, revealing the ballroom . . . and Gimlet. Tall and regal, they swept a six-foot royal officer out onto the dance floor.

Gimlet was clad in a floor-length tunic of pristine white and a mountainous bleached wig. The teardrop pupils of their eyes had been enlarged by the Risto toon artists. If it was difficult for them to throw themselves into this scenario, body and soul, it didn't show. The sight sent a jolt out to all Rubi's extremities.

Light of foot, wholly immersed in the dance . . .

This was why she'd clawed her way up the amateur leaderboards, measuring herself against Gimlet's wins. That capacity of the scenarists to catch her off guard: to scare, to plunge her into a world long gone. Sighting Gimlet, like a stag in the forest, knowing the chase had begun.

Ah, but who's chasing who?

Games were a taste of something wilder than greenwalls and rations, the endless row, row, row as the Bounceback generation patched up Earth's damaged foundation for life.

"Downstairs, girl! Find another tray!"

The wine had run out. Rubi went down to the kitchen and accepted another quest: slipping cakes to a handful of the Rabble beggars at the kitchen door.

"Win conditions," Coach murmured. "Dispense ten cakes and get back upstairs within ninety seconds."

Eight cakes, nine, ten. The last grubby hand passed her a tattered soldier's communique: *the Dauphine has disappeared from Versailles.*

Pocketing it, Rubi seized a tray of brimming wineglasses.

Had any of the wineglasses been tampered with? None showed any fingerprints or residue. One glass was slightly out of alignment; she poured its contents into a potted fig and left it there.

"Seventeen seconds."

Back to the ballroom, double-time but without spilling a drop. The dance was wrapping up.

"Give a glass to the individual in white," prompted Coach.

"To Gimlet?"

"Stay in character. You are a servant, Barnes a stranger."

Gimlet was holding court among a circle of enraptured young things now, engaging in competitive wordplay with an earnest-looking poet, no doubt racking up points as they dueled verbally.

The crowd parted as she approached. Gimlet looked surprised to see her so soon.

A noblewoman, one of the snow-haired fairies, saw the empty

space on Rubi's tray left by the discarded wineglass. She growled. Rubi's scorecard racked up a bonus. It *had* been tampered with.

"Good catch," Coach murmured.

The fairy spun, her bearing haughty. Twinkling ice crystals flew, frosting all the glasses.

Then something—a foot?—snagged Rubi's ankle.

She fought for balance, but an elbow in the back put paid to that. Fairy-dusted red wine arced upward, swirling crimson in candlelight . . . and spraying Gimlet from the crown of the wig to their belt buckle. The dripping slash of color left a suggestively bloody stain on the pristine tunic.

Cries of shock from the crowd.

Rubi had landed at Gimlet's feet. Hot candlewax pattered on the nape of her neck. Clinging to her tray, she scuttled back. Legs caught her—the crowd preventing her escape. Powdered faces and cruel eyes stared, from behind fans and gloved hands.

"*Désolée*," she cried, reading from the prompter. "Mer, I am so, so sorry!"

Sugar Valkryie grabbed her by the scruff of her neck.

"Insolence! This child must be whipped!" Gimlet demanded.

Was Gimlet growling? The wine was soaking into their throat. Their breath turned to fog, despite the hot air of the salon. The graphics team was playing it to the hilt.

"It's not fair! Someone tripped me!"

Sugar tossed Rubi into the arms of a soldier. She screeched and kicked, playing the exit for all she was worth as they dragged her to a locked cellar.

As the door slammed shut—blackout!—Coach put up a timer in her peripheral. "Prologue concluded. Ten-minute break."

Rubi scooped a handful of hydrogels, popping them between her teeth like grapes, enjoying the cool sensation of fluid and protein slipping down her throat. "Has it already been two hours?"

Stats scrolled across her field of vision: she had completed four quests and done meet-greets with eighty-one satisfied players.

"All for SeaJuve," she muttered. "It's not slacking; it's prosocial."

Upstairs, audience-facing content would have shifted to Gimlet and the effects of the magic wine.

"Periscope to the surface."

Rubi's prison dimmed to line drawings, a wine cellar overlaid on a high-end playroom. Gimlet, thirty feet away, was spinning within a pair of steady gymnastics rings.

She admired their form, feeling weirdly hungry.

"Newscycle?"

Crane displayed a live feed from the drones aboard the SeaJuve lead ship, *Sable Hare,* as it chugged off to tackle reviving an oceanic dead zone in the North Sea's briny depths.

"Funding and followers?"

"Lower than hoped, Miss Cherub. But it's early yet."

No sex in SeaJuve. Rubi shivered. You could filter carbon from the air into bamboo or algae or fungus. You could harvest it, throw it on a scale. Weigh the tonnage, make a stack, put the tonnage on view in Sensorium.

SeaJuve, by contrast, had a huge "You'll have to take our word for it" factor. Could making oxygen really compete with rewilding? When Gimlet's mad scientists were promising an actual tiger cub . . .

Her fists clenched. Ridiculous, that she'd had to play ragamuffin just to get backing for *air.*

Ridiculous squared, when she was supposedly busy with something as big as first contact with aliens.

And yet . . .

"Fuel and hydration," Coach reminded her.

Despite what she'd said to Happ, she already felt calmer.

She chased the hydrogels with a Conviction gel and a small pack of hot soup: chicken noodle. The gym had a tray of printed snacks; she pocketed three of her favorite cherry cubes.

"Curtain up in five," Coach said.

"Win conditions?"

"Risto has imprisoned a spy, Monique Goyette, in this cellar. They suspect she's tied to the Dauphine's disappearance. Your mission: help her escape."

"What's my geographical comfort zone?" Rubi asked.

Fifteen feet away, here on the surface, Gimlet swung into a handstand, holding their body steady on the rings, toes pointed skyward. Eighteenth-century Paris neighborhood superimposed itself between them, maps showing the narrow scope of ragamuffin Rubi's life. Tags filled in her character's backstory. Dead ma, of course, as in any good fairy tale. Pa and seven hungry siblings jammed within her childhood home, a mile away. There was an older brother apprenticed to a blacksmith.

She had extensive familiarity with the neighborhood church, the butcher (ye quaintey shoppie, Drow would call it, sponsored by a beef printer), the baker (likewise sponsored), and a candlestick maker.

"Is there a church? How's the local priest?"

"He has given you no obvious grounds for mistrust," Coach said.

"Not a ringing endorsement."

"Time remaining in break: three and a half minutes."

"Highlight empty buildings and accessible rooftops?" Squares on the mat lit up.

Gimlet executed a twisting dismount, then handsprung to their feet, extending their baton to full length. Then they froze— with Rubi's break ending, theirs could begin.

If SeaJuve fails . . .

If Luce is for real . . .

Forget it for now and just play.

"Periscope down," she said, treating herself to one last good look at Gimlet, on display and breathing hard, as her blackboard and the graphic overlays faded.

The wine cellar was dark. Outlines of stacked oak barrels rose to the ceiling.

Okay. If this ran to spec, there'd be a monster in the cellar, pursuing her as she tried to rescue Goyette. She'd need to make light, fight off the beast, and escape.

"Sixty seconds." Coach breadcrumbed an X onto the floor next to the gym's climbing wall. Rubi put out her hands, counting through the last minute, four seconds to each breath.

Step one—get to high ground.

If SeaJuve fails and we're choking on stale air when that space fleet arrives . . .

Can there really be a space fleet?

Concentrate, stupid.

There. Conviction supplied the feel of wood barrels under her palms. She rapped quietly, three times.

She leaped, catching the upper lip of a barrel, and scrambled up. So far, so good.

Ears peeled for monsters, she crawled in the dark, inching over the top tier of stored wine, giving each a little push to feel the slosh of liquid within.

Whiff of fresh air.

She found a casement window, big enough to allow her escape, secured with rusty bars. On the sill she found a single copper coin stamped with the Dauphine's face.

Outside, moonlight illuminated the bare feet of the beggars she'd fed. Should she call out? No, not yet.

There was no sign of soldiers, zombies, or any other approaching opposition. Rubi put the damp concrete wall of the cellar to her back.

I want to believe Luce, she realized. Wanted to believe that these Pale were coming, and they had their own laws and social cap, within a greater intergalactic community, to look to. That public pressure might allow humanity to put on a good show and avoid hostile takeover.

Rubi's eyes had adjusted to the moonlight trickling in, etching the edges of the barrels and an outline of the cellar. Above the wine casks she could see a spectral form, frost and fog with icicles for fingernails, drifting in through the window.

Monsters, finally.

Grinning, she crabbed down between the barrels and the back wall. She found the floor, scavenged an old torch, and used one of her quest-won beads to set it alight.

The frosty specter made straight for an alcove full of oak staves, concealed by an old fireplace screen.

Rubi gave chase. The specter had found a pretty young thing in a tight corset, with orange blossoms for hair, a deep scratch on her shoulder, and a trembly air. She was curled up, crying on the staves.

"Where isssss the Dauphine?" the specter hissed.

Rubi attacked it, driving the torch into its body. There was a fizzle, a hiss, and it was gone.

"Monique Goyette?" she whispered. "*C'est vous?*"

A wink from one teary eye confirmed her suspicions: Manitoule liked to show-run for Rabble from within the ingenue.

Monique was haloed by golden pollen. She was a beautifully rendered summer fairy, high contrast with the Risto ice motif. But Rubi's sense of distance, that need to analyze the wallpaper, was ebbing.

"You poor lamb!" She used her skirt to dab at the tears. Manitoule—Monique—sniffled gratefully as she helped her up.

"I know nothing!" the girl stammered.

"I'm not going to hurt you." Another specter rushed them: Rubi burned it back, scanning the windows. She took an oak stave, trying to lever the bars out of the frame. When that failed, she called out to the beggars outside.

"Help, I beg you! Get us out of here!"

This feels more like MethodAct than Conviction.

I didn't take *MethodAct.*

Never mind. All that mattered was getting away from this house before the ghosts closed in or her mistress had them beaten.

The beggars tied a chain to a harnessed horse, using it to rip the bars off the window. They lifted Monique out. Rubi took a running jump, launching herself through the exit and rolling to her feet in the snow.

The stunt, minor though it was, raised a general cheer.

"We need to find somewhere to hide!"

A musket popped, sobering the crowd. Hooves—lots of hooves—clamored on the cobblestones.

"Soldiers!" said Monique, and Rubi grabbed for a rolling pin . . .

. . . no, a baton . . .

. . . no, a *rolling pin,* and caught her by the hand.

CHAPTER 33

The only thing worse than being fired was being fired and marooned in Florida.

Anselmo did all the obvious things to manage his fury: showering, shaving, exercise. He attempted to appreciate his miserable, broken-down surroundings by tasting a local specialty, spicy printed cubes called *arroz con pollo*.

Trying to sleep simply left him shaking with rage.

Dawn had him walking a reclaimed stretch of Florida coastline, a strip of beach so wide and white of sand that he might have been in a historical, looking at a sim.

Preserving this old-style beach had meant building at a breakneck pace, decades earlier, as the sea rose. Opt-in tags offered historical footage, Clawback-vintage: time-release scenes of recycled I beams being driven into the ocean floor, serving as base layer for artificially grown limestone, faux coral, neobedrock.

In other parts of the world, preventing shoreline encroachment had begun with large-scale, old-fashioned sandbagging and HESCO barriers, followed by construction of permanent berms and dikes. But Florida was built on porous limestone; the challenges were different. Even with the false reefs built up, expanses of sand and palm trees had to be raised—grafted—to the prosthetic bone of the continent. It had required a complex volunteer effort, all crowdfunded by citizens of a city that knew it was on the edge of getting #triaged forever by unsympathetic stakeholders in cooler places: Nairobi, Sao Paulo, and Shanghai.

They deserve *to be #triaged.*

Anselmo closed the historicals, trying out the unaugmented view. People were out in the hundreds. Sun lipped the eastern horizon: dawn offered an opp to catch the least-searing rays of daylight. To expose some skin, even swim.

A note flashed in his upper peripheral: *AnonTip: Take a stroll.* It was a map of the beach trail, marked with an X.

"To what end?" he said aloud. "My case has been snagged by bigger jurisdictional fish."

The X blinked twice, then vanished.

It wasn't as though he had anything better to do, was it? He'd been promised leveling ops and strokes, rewards for his successful investigation into Luce Pox. He'd shunted it all into a #movetoBeijing request and was waiting in the long queue for immigration greenlight.

Odds were good they'd give him a visa but not a flight to China. Now he was looking for gigs to pay for that. In Tampico, where he had no contacts and no localcred, and where the only case with any legs had been snaffled by @GlobalSec.

He set out, skirting a series of shallow pools. A cluster of families, realworld friends by the look of it, had brought out their toddlers to putter about, making sand castles.

Anselmo felt that pang again. Romancing Rubi had been a dead end. If they'd clicked, he might have convinced her that the two of them could glomerate, to look together for a family willing to take on her high-profile, troublesome father.

But Gimlet Barnes's arrival had deflated his hopes. Rubi's romantic interests lay elsewhere. Meanwhile, her ascension, within the @PoxWorkingGroup, had been the real reason he'd been torpedoed. All the strokes he might have earned were drawn to her, like iron filings to the electromagnet of her celebrity.

Stagnating professionally and stuck in the middle of nowhere, he glowered at the rising sun.

A local woman said, "It's okay. You won't burn."

"You sure of that?"

"Just wrap up when the warning sounds." She took off her sandals, digging long toes into the sparkling white sand.

Anselmo configged his primer to follow her example. His shoes melted up his legs, bleeding into his cuffs, which rolled themselves up to his knees.

"Wow." He had walked barefoot in sand before, but only in sim. The give of it, underfoot, seemed like an illusion only half-constructed.

The rising sun hung like an egg yolk over the ocean, coloring the clouds.

The woman handed him a topical. "UV blockers?"

"Thanks." Rubbing lotion into his skin, Anselmo took a deep breath, scenting for orange blossoms—it was Florida, after all. Instead, he got a whiff of briny marine coastline and human bodies slimed in the same sun-protective oils he was applying now.

The woman waited as he continued to look. There were swimmers out near a barge, building endurance. A group of scuba divers practiced under the watchful eye of three instructors. Farther east, a second barge served as a platform for diving boards. Anselmo marveled at the acrobatics: people whirling through the air, cutting into the sea like dolphins.

"There's a bridge, if you want to keep walking."

The bridge lay in the direction of the X from his anonymous tip. Anselmo sent the woman a stroke, in thanks, and a wearable on her wrist chimed.

"I don't have implants," she said, reading his surprise. "My name is Sparka Goldfish."

"Anselmo Javier."

"Pleased to meet you, Anselmo Javier." She had a business link printed on her hand. *@ManicPixie Dream Bod.*

"Massage?" he guessed.

"Personal services, bodywork, you name it." She resumed strolling, crossing the beach into a park planted in soft grass. The sunscreen on his feet had glued sand to his toes; walking on the lawn whisked the grains away.

About five hundred people, dressed in head-to-toe sunblocks, Lawrence of Arabia wear, the sort of garb that kept the rads off your skin wherever your mind happened to be, were shadow-fencing. Each occupied a space about two meters in diameter; each seemed oblivious to the others as they ran in place, jumped, stabbed.

"Some big game event," Sparka explained, choosing the path around the perimeter. Vendors around the edges had water and snack cubes, laced with Conviction, LucidDream, and MethodAct.

One participant clutched his chest, falling to the grass. Wrestling with an imaginary foe, he shouted once, froze . . . then stood, cursing cheerfully.

He'd have to play catchup, leveling from zero. That or wait until the premiere was fully unlocked so he could respawn at the save point in a later run.

"Eliminated from play," he growled.

Sparka flashed the player her business card as they continued through the field of play.

"This is a gig for you? Drumming up clients?"

"No, I'm actually a @ManicPixie owner. We're a collective. I cut hair."

"Ah." He resisted the urge to finger-comb.

She grinned. "Surprised?"

He nodded. He was uncomfortable with the implant-intolerant; he couldn't imagine getting intimate service from one. You could still strike one of them if you got bad results, but it would feel like punching down.

"It's worse than you think!" She opened her mouth, revealing a spotted tongue. Grafted with a bit of . . . reptile or amphib tissue? It forked, slightly, in a way that made him queasy. Where the flesh looked more normal, more like *tongue,* it was double-pierced with copper points.

"Body mods?"

"Awww, you're shocked."

"It's very . . . outlier." Once a sign of outsider culture, mods had been embraced by successive western cohorts: the Boomers, GenX, and the Millennials. But the Setback generation had kicked back, embracing what it called template purity. Anselmo had seen hosts of paintings, plainly judgmental images of heavily modded GenX octogenarians, people who'd laid waste to their exteriors.

Sagging flesh, skin cancers, and faded tattoos. To recent generations, modding equated with the damage humanity had done to the biosphere.

How strange, Anselmo thought, that he found Sparka exotic! He'd spent a lifetime online, among people whose toons had tail apps, horns, extra arms . . .

"Do you—"

"Things not to say to the disabled." Headmistress, his sidekick, flashed pop-up warnings: "Don't you get bored living offline all the time? That must be such a challenge. How do you fill your days? I guess you really live in the now. You *inspire* me."

"Don't talk to me like I'm four," he warned the app. He had resubscribed to Headmistress when his WestEuro pack #triaged him—she'd managed his family of origin, she still had his remnant account info, and Desk Sergeant managed him at work, anyway. He hadn't had time to shop for something more befitting a #lonewolf in his thirties.

A woman tooned in behind Sparka, then, right on the X spot on his trail map. Whooz tags identified her as Allure Noonstar.

"My, my," the visitor said, miming a peek into Sparka's satchel. "What interesting account data this one has."

"I'm just looking at your catalog," Anselmo told Sparka, who beamed.

The toon, Allure, was walking circles around her. "Far less activity than a normal user. She didn't go through implant surgery?"

"Her body rejects implantation," Anselmo subbed.

"So, she's a cripple?"

Anselmo frowned. Should he strike this Allure for ableism?

Oblivious to the toon's scrutiny, Sparka pulled out a tin flask and produced a metallic clip, wet with antiseptic gel, which evaporated as he watched.

"Try this." He used gestural moji to give consent, and she clipped it to his ear. "Feel the weight? It clamps harder if you want a bit of sensation."

"Does that mean pain?" Anselmo asked.

"Some people go for that." She flipped the tin, revealing a mirror. The clip-on earring was a vintage section of roller-coaster track, a winding line reminiscent of DNA, following the upper curve of his ear, with a tiny car full of people about to plunge.

Anselmo let the mirror go, concentrating on the sensation of sun warming the piece of jewelry and the claws of the clip-on, minuscule pressure points within the delicate flesh of his ear.

"This is how people used to live," Sparka said. "Encumbered. Having things, lots of things, more than they could haul in a worldly. They weren't adrift."

"I don't know if I'm the roller-coaster type."

"I have a centipede back at the shop."

"Ah. No. Not an insect."

"There's a lion in the catalog. Ambush predator."

"More your speed, definitely," said the toon Allure.

"I might like a lion." Looking over her shoulder, he subbed to the toon, "What do you want?"

"Don't be standoffish, Agent Javier. I'm here to make your dreams come true."

"By implying the intolerants . . ."

"Disconnected scraps. Evolutionary failures."

Headmistress spoke up suddenly. "Don't strike her, Anselmo. *Listen.*"

Allure raised her hands. "How do these . . . disabled? . . . get by? Who's helping them?"

"Why would they need help?"

"What if you prove they're in bed with the Singularity?"

The Singularity had been a dead end, one of his four tracks of investigation into Luce. Going back down that road now would be ridiculous. Especially if . . . "Persecuting low-bandwidth users won't buy me a flight to Beijing."

"I'll buy you a flight to Beijing," Allure said.

"Excuse me?"

"You're in a unique position to focus on a high-profile disabled user . . . and his entourage." With that, Allure tooned out.

As she vanished, another sim player went down, staggering back, hands flying to belly as though they'd taken some kind of shot to the gut. He had been fighting hard; his robes were slick with sweat.

Disabled. Allure had to mean Drow Whiting. Widely known and mentally ill. Every attempt to prove that his sidekick Crane was sapient had #crashburned. Still, @Interpol remained suspicious.

Headmistress popped up the list of people whose transcripts Anselmo was auditing. Luce Pox, Woodrow Whiting, and Cherub Whiting topped the leaderboard. Nobody would get an alert if he kept auditing them: not the Whitings, not Crane.

His route had brought him beyond the gaming field, to a path through a shallow reef system, habitat for swamp and a lacework of red mangrove trees.

"Reef printing is all about maintaining a platform for eventual reintroduction of wild coral." The @ManicPixie's spiel brought him out of his reverie. "We lost a lot of the Keys to ocean rise. Here, the surviving wildlife species can keep a toehold until the seas roll back."

"You think that'll happen?"

"Not in our lifetime. Meanwhile, you've looked at my lion earring three times."

"How did you . . ."

She indicated a watch, vintage tech, with a tiny screen aglow with glyphs. "I don't need implants to see your catalog pings."

Anselmo unclipped the roller coaster from his ear. "It's a beautiful piece, but I'm not sure I can afford an encumbrance."

"Give it some thought," she said. "You've got our shop coordinates. You could be the single most radical cop in Tampico."

"This isn't my home." They had reached a fork in the path. "Thanks for the sunscreen, Sparka. And the conversation."

"Keep the peace, Jacques Law." She trotted back the way she had come.

The place where the earring had touched him, the bite of its contacts, tingled slightly. Was this real desire, or was he just reacting to having his case poached?

"Do you wish to tag some feels?" Headmistress asked.

"I flagged up the possibility of meeting another species," Anselmo grumbled.

"Being saved by them, luvvie, if we play our cards right," Headmistress murmured. "And if you chase the tip from our new friend, we'll get you to Asia."

"How?"

"Imagine scoring twice on unicorn chases. You'd make the @Interpol leaderboard."

"Tip," he grunted.

Finding the Singularity. The unicorn hunt of unicorn hunts.

. . . as a bonus, bust the insufferable stroke-stealing Rubi Whiting and her father for harboring an emergent . . .

"All right, find me a pop-in." He'd study the Whiting transcripts. "And send that Allure Noonstar a proper invite to my e-state, in case she wants to throw me any other breadcrumbs."

CHAPTER 34

VRTP:RABBLEVSRISTO.PLAY/BASTILLE/PROLOGUE.VR

The growing skirmish outside the duchess's salon inevitably drew boss monsters, one a massive polar bear packing icicle javelins. The fairy who'd made Rubi spill enchanted wine all over Gimlet joined the fray, too, cutting down players with sweeps of her glittering silver hand-fan.

By the time Rabble brought them down, it was apparent that *Bastille*'s overall theme was WestEuro fairy warfare. Ice fairies had taken over Versailles, making puppets of the King and Queen. Monique, the prisoner from Rubi's quest in the wine cellar, was a shepherdess-dryad. It was indeed she who had spirited away the Crown Princess, la Dauphine, hiding her from the engineers of the Risto coup.

The battle turned once Rubi's side set the neighborhood afire, generating sufficient heat to turn icicle spears and snowbanks alike into running streams of slippery mud. The rabble fled before everyone burned, all while wearing the bosses down and holding competing Risto players—foot soldiers, killer bears, musketeers, and Royal Guards—at bay.

Attrition was high on both sides, but it was early yet. Defeated players could conceivably reboot, playing the unlocked opening again. They'd have plenty of time to queue for the launch of Episode Two.

As the credits rolled and the polar bear melted into a sparkling, snowflake-shaped puddle, Rubi grabbed one of its claws and ported within Sensorium, transiting directly from one fantasy to another, out of game and into the Feckless Bachelor™ venue. Drow had agreed to host a premiere party as a reward for players. It was a meet-and-greet opp, a showcase for SeaJuve.

The Feckless team had created a new activity space, an opulent drinks lounge encased within a crystal bubble. Beneath its transparent floor was live footage of *Sable Hare,* the SeaJuve flagship.

Rubi kept the tattered maidservant dress on her toon, welcoming visitors as they swelled the ranks of celebrants. Drow's protégée, Whiskey Sour, was singing torch songs by the bar. Her toon had a trademark now: luna moth wings. She must have gotten a recording deal.

Out in the North Sea, the *Sable Hare* crew was out on deck, assembling rafts for deployment near defunct oil refineries. The rafts were shallow-draft, hexagonal in shape. Over time, they would blanket a stretch of ocean in honeycomb, stretching from one of the easternmost oil platforms to the edge of a crumbling fjord.

The barges were printed plaque frames filled with nutrients and fertilizer. They would take in dead seawater, injecting it with a mix of nutrients and fast-grow packets of North Sea algae. Investors could sponsor individual barges or chains of them. Every cubic meter of oxygen generated by the algae would pay interest; investors could convert their payback to dollars or carbon tonnage.

On deck, a sailor was mentoring a recent recruit, showing him the submersible drones that would maintain the barges. There would be permajobs for pilots if funding came through, if the Global Oversight appeal—finally under way now—was successful.

The algae itself had to be harvested before it died and went into rapid decay. It would be harvested, dried, and converted to topsoil starter.

Dull, duller, dullest, Rubi thought. *Where's the sexy?*

Guess that's what I'm here for.

She dove into cocktail-party chitchat with incoming players: *Did you get into the salon? Did you dance? How did you die? Do you always play Team Rabble? Yes, I was surprised to encounter Mer Barnes so early.*

Whiskey Sour, bless her heart, had started a minor bidding war for sponsorship of the first SeaJuve hexagon. Rubi sent her a stroke, gratefully.

Crane watched from the fringes, subbing, "How was the game?"

A new wave of players tooned in as *Sable Hare*'s bow broke a wave with a spectacular slap of sea. Diamonds of moonlit brine flew against the darkening sky.

"Play was better than expected. Total buy-in, once I got into it."

"Indeed? And Mer Barnes?"

Instead of rising to the bait, she greeted two women who'd been on the front lines. "You guys survived Episode One?"

"Barely," said one. "Flora here used her spare save versus death. We'll be on our toes in eppie two."

"I run a civic-responsibility module for preteens," said the other—Flora, apparently. "We'd love to have you guest."

"To talk about SeaJuve?"

"Recreation as an extension of prosociality, perhaps? How you leveraged your gaming profile into an environmental give."

"I'd be glad to." Weird, to think that playing, the very thing she'd resisted, was what had finally gotten the project's legs back under it. Best of all worlds.

She handed the women over to Debutante to schedule the appearance, then turned to find a uniformed server holding a canapé-laden tray. Her body had, apparently, worked her way back to the gym's printer.

As her stomach rumbled, she sensed surface reality, waiting beyond the glitter of the party. Her buy-in doses were breaking down. Post-exertion grime lay on her skin. The server had two trays—there were puff pastries on one side and salmon-cucumber rolls on the other.

Sweet or salty?

She chose the salmon, then froze.

Drow's toon, clad in a jaunty sailor suit, red of eye and missing ten pounds he couldn't afford to lose, was circulating through the throng.

"Saints, kid, you look like hell," he said. "You spring your rotator cuff again?"

"*I* look—"

He twinkled at her. "C'mon, let's shower some charisma on your fan base."

"Why does that sound gross?"

Stepping onstage beside Whiskey, Drow flourished, manifesting a saxophone. Music filled the venue; soon the audience was singing along to . . .

. . . was that the soundtrack to one of the kiddie sims?

It was. The sim had been a thriller, rewilders fighting the nefarious Ferguson Bedwedder, but Drow had apparently done a reinvention. Partygoers were howling the chorus, riffing out new lyrics about SeaJuve, *take the air, give us air, feel the air.*

A SeaJuve song. He'd been thinking of her.

He's on Leonardo. He's thinking about everyone and every-thing, *all the time.*

Even so, Rubi couldn't quite hold back a smile.

That was the dangerous thing about the smartdrugs. Drow was creatively productive, obscenely happy. Filled with ideas, jokes, art-storm concepts, jingles. All fun and games . . . right up until it became mania, and then the switch flipped. Soon, he'd be threatening to free-dive into Lake Ontario, looking for submarine bases staffed by superhoarders.

But she couldn't say anything, not without getting his parole

yanked. All she could do was stand by and applaud as he helped
out with her project.   ·

"That's the sim theme I said I liked!" A bright-eyed Frankie
Barnes, accompanied by Gimlet, strolled up beside her. Her toon
was wearing a tiger costume, fuzzy orange stripes showing her allegiance to Project Rewild.

Drow had G-rated Feckless Bachelor™ for a night?

Gimlet's toon was full-on supervillain: gold hair, slicked
straight up, black catsuit, and a cape made of the night sky. The
ensemble's capper was an ebony cane tipped with a big diamond.

Rubi pushed words over a roar of electricity building within, a
sensation that intensified, it seemed, every time she saw Gimlet.
"How was your episode?"

"Bit of an origin story."

"That wine I spilled gave you powers, didn't it?"

"Spoilers, my dear. You'll pay the price in the fullness of
time." They took in the deck of the SeaJuve flagship, the party in
progress, and then caught one of Rubi's costume tatters between
two long, sensitive fingers. "Mind if I tear this off?"

"What do I get to do to you?"

"We can negotiate." A flick, a whirl, and the ratty overdress
shredded, turning to smoke and sparks. The shimmer morphed
into Rubi's newest party dress—the hammer and tongs again, now
stamped within shimmering gold hexagons that echoed the beads
of her trademark.

The transformation elicited applause and a few delighted cries
from the people nearby. Rubi did a little spin, to show off the outfit and drive donations. *All for SeaJuve.* "It better not turn into a
pumpkin."

"At midnight.in which time zone?"

Putting out both hands, Rubi drew both parent and child onto
the dance floor. "How's it going with Rewild—the baby tiger?"

"They say it's fine." Frankie scowled.

"But?"

"Rewild hasn't been doing very many updates."

"Maybe the cub's going through an awkward phase," Gimlet said.

"*Donnez-nous nos enfants!*"

The shout came from the live feed of *Sable Hare*.

The person shouting wasn't a toon. They were aboard ship, in the flesh . . . an apprentice sailor? As Rubi and all the Feckless guests watched (and as Gimlet moved, too late, to jettison Frankie from the sim of the party) the man seized a strut from the pile of barge components and raised it above the man teaching the construction module.

"*Donnez-nous nos enfants!*" he bellowed again, swinging it like a bat as the world watched.

A crunch as he connected with the engineer's head.

His victim went over the rail.

People screamed.

"Crew overboard!" Alarms sounded—

Then Rubi was alone, in the sim gym, crushing a half-eaten salmon cube in her fist.

"Crane?"

"Pulling newscycle."

"Crane!"

"*Sable Hare* reports three overboard, including the perpetrator. Rescue in progress."

"How did that—that poor man! Can they—" Her muscles strained, as if they thought she could jump in after the victim. But her flesh was half a world away, in a Tampico e-sport center.

"There are other actions in progress: someone has started a fire in New Redwood Grove. A car has been hacked and driven through the receiving room of the parenting license office in Detroit."

Rubi ran a hand over her face, trying to breathe, to slow her racing heart. "What's happening?"

"Mer Barnes asks if you're okay."

"Shaken. How about them? Frankie?"

"Shaken also."

She wiped her hand on her overlay—tissue-thin Cinderella rags once more—and made for the showers. "Drow? Is all that likely to trigger him?"

Long, eloquent pause. "Impossible to know."

Wash. Get moving.

To where? To do what?

Just wash. Hot water sprayed down from the ceiling; a ten-minute ration counter appeared in her peripheral, counting down. Tears mingled with the water spraying her face. "Dad's losing weight, Crane."

"Master Woodrow is operating to spec, if only just."

"He's not eating!"

"We're managing—"

"Can't you . . . I don't know . . . get a thingbot to force him to take a sucrose drip?"

"That's something you truly believe I should do?" The app's voice was frosty.

"You have *one* job."

"Indeed, Miss Cherub. I am doing it."

"I'm going to have to drop everything, aren't I? Where is Drow? His actual location?"

"Miss Cherub," Crane said. "Rubi. I would do anything, believe me, to relieve your anxiety. But your father's autonomy supersedes your peace of mind."

"Autonomy?" She couldn't hold in the rancor. "Drow's autonomy is at the whim of the parole board."

It was as close as she dared come to threatening to report him. If she said Drow was contemplating criminal trespass, Parole would scoop him up. They'd make him eat.

Icy water sluiced over her.

She shrieked, jumping back. "I ordered ten minutes!"

Her records showed a ration savings, allocated to SeaJuve. "Apologies, Miss Cherub, I misunderstood your intentions."

She rinsed off the soap, fast and savagely, shivering in the torrent of ice.

"I beg you—beg you—to reconsider your priorities."

"*My* priorities?"

"You have other concerns."

Like Luce and his alleged Pale invasion. Like kickstarting the planet's lungs.

How did I end up in the middle of this? It was almost enough to make her believe in Drow's chamber of string-pullers. Or man-eating AI. She put her fists against the tile and sobbed, loudly and helplessly, as soap swirled down the drain at her feet.

What do I do, what do I do, what do I do?

I'm never going to find a pack, Rubi realized. It wasn't just finding someone who'd take on Drow. They could never find anyone to shack with who would understand Crane.

The thought settled her somehow. It was like breaking a leash, letting go of something. Maybe she hadn't wanted a traditional pack in the first place.

Gimlet banged on the dressing room door. "Rubi!"

She jumped; she had forgotten they were in the same gym for once.

"I'm okay!" she called.

"Are you sure?"

"Out in a minute." She wiped a towel over her tear-streaked face, blowing her nose. Perhaps the two of them should run away together, pursue a one-on-one love match, flee their obligations. Take advantage of being proximate, in the flesh, to take advantage of each other.

Nice dream.

"All right. I'm right here, if . . ."

She sent a stroke through the closed door. Managed not to fire a heart moji, too.

Crane spoke into the silence. "Update from *Sable*. Two sailors rescued, one badly injured. The initial victim died, and the @Freebreed activist jumped overboard and is presumed drowned. EastEuro reports that a trio of machete-wielding @Trollgaters are . . . Oh, dear. They're attacking cisgender women in Red Square."

Rubi took in a long, slow breath. Then another. Fisted her hands. Once. Twice.

"The Debutante app wishes to conference about spin and public reaction. And you have a call from Commodore Bell."

If an ordinary app made her this angry, she'd unsubscribe. But that wasn't an option here, was it?

This amounted to an ugly family fight.

"You want a truce?" she asked Crane.

"Most assuredly, Miss Cherub."

"Get some calories into Drow. And tell Commodore Bell I'm on my way."

She yanked a pair of newly printed tights over her chilled, damp legs and headed out of the gym, feeling like a four-year-old in the midst of a tantrum, so ready for another fight, she almost wished *Bastille* were ready to run again.

CHAPTER 35

Tampico maintained its bioreserve within an antique theme park, an in-the-flesh entertainment opp for kids. The park had once been exclusively branded to a media multinational, McDiznazon, that funded a good chunk of the city's densification. Their social capital was high due to their continued production of entertainment sims like *Rewilding Rescue.*

Frankie had offered to mash-up play with a little peer polling, catching a ride inland, and co-opting the ever-surly Misfortune to serve as temporary guardian as she visited the park. Usually, she didn't work solo, but the Luce case was code-red serious. That, and the park's immaculate reputation for both safety and in-person wonders, led Gimlet and GranMarie to greenlight the field trip.

Anything to keep me from asking questions about Dada Rollsy.

Now here she was, staring at a statue of a McDiz founder, some oldfeller hand in hand with one of his own creations, a mouse that came to his elbow. The promenade thronged with schools of kids and families.

Park staff and wildlife managers roamed the paths, clad in bright red jumpsuits. They wore printed badges tagging competencies: park knowledge, tour guide, first aid, hurricane procedures, food service, entertainment, mechanical repair, monkey expert, roller-coaster operation, history lecture . . .

Misfortune glowered at two middle-aged women, both in helmets, blazing with unlocked badges. "These people intolerant?"

"So?" Frankie said. It made sense, as far as she was concerned. Intolerants could talk to kids as equals, since they all used wearables for Sensorium diving.

"Just noticing." Side-eye and a bland shrug. She teased a strand of black yarn from her primer sleeve, winding it around her fingers.

Misfortune wouldn't want to get popped by a kid for throwing shade, as they used to say, at the disabled.

Start with the aquarium? Frankie found a trailhead, pondering its guide markers. There was a domed rainforest, boreal species habitat, Monkey Jungle, a greenhouse, and a path to a concert stage.

Drow should play a concert here. Laughable idea—the preserve was far too clean and shiny for the MadMaestro.

She knew *the* Drow Whiting. They were . . . chummy.

She flashed on his words: *I'm running away from home, kid.*

Frankie had printed up a blazer, a reversible jacket currently showing the Department of Preadolescent Affairs logo. It made her officially available to any kid who wanted to talk. Until then, she could explore.

She hopped a people-mover to the Amazon Rainforest. Misfortune tailed her unenthusiastically.

"She's not letting me out of her sight," she subbed.

"Don't worry about Misfortune," the Poppet app replied.

"You made promises," Frankie said.

"I'll keep them."

As she passed through the exhibit airlock, Frankie forgot about her watcher dog.

The greenery in this sim forest was unlike anything she'd seen in England. A curtain of waxy leaves, glossy jade curls, dangled overhead. Vines climbed trees, reaching for the kaleidoscope fractals of the greenhouse roof. There were plants with bells that held water. Cases of frogs, snakes, and salamanders were integrated into viewpoints along the path.

Frankie paused in front of a python terrarium, coming nose to nose with a snake curled on a branch. It blinked at her, a caged alien, secure in the knowledge that it had nothing to aspire to and nowhere to go.

Live audio feeds and screens built into the viewpoints offered learning modules about all the species on display.

"Feed the sloth?" A zookeeper offered her a drone controller.

"Thanks," Frankie said, transmitting her pilot license and trying to remember what a sloth was.

She spotted it just as she hovered into the trees. Coarse hairy pillow, with a . . . with a smile! She zoomed in, extending a morsel of banana with a grab-and-go limb. The drone's hand was styled like that of the cartoon mouse.

The creature accepted the fruit with regal aplomb.

Mesmerized, Frankie watched it chew.

"You're DPA?" Her first consult of the day sidled up beside her. Brown-skinned, with rainbow-beaded hair, they wore a quirky patchwork smock that had to be handmade from recycled rags. Topping the ensemble was a printed set of McDiz mouse ears.

"I'm Frankie," she said. "Child ombudsman, she-her."

"My name's Kansas. Ei-eir-em."

She stepped aside, offering em a turn at the drone controls. Working the rig with deft familiarity, ei snagged a bit of pineapple and proffered it.

"You live here?" she asked. The sloth took a delicate nibble of the fruit.

"Come to the park all the time. Sometimes, I get apprentice gigs in the capybara enclosure."

"Wow!"

More kids gathered. Misfortune kept a respectful distance.

Kansas asked, "I saw you were tooned into the *Sable Hare* when that engineer got killed?"

Frankie felt a rush of relief—of course everyone would want to hear about the @Freebreed attack. It would be a perfect ramp for streaming into her poll.

"Me, my parent Gimlet," she said, "and both the Whitings, Drow and Rubi."

A murmur.

"Do we show up in the newsflows? Mada won't let me watch replays."

Kansas let eir tongue loll, eloquent comment on overprotective parents.

More kids emerged from other attractions. Misfortune was contemplating a cluster of fish—piranha, according to the tags—schooling around in an artificial river.

Frankie worked the spotlight, relating, in hushed tones, the surprise of being tooned right in above the apparently normal sailor before he went berserk, swinging the strut like a baseball bat. She told them about seeing an edge of metal bolt striking the back of the victim's skull. His knees had hit the rail with a *chunk*ing sound that she could feel, even now, in her bones. She described the smear of blood on the ship's deck.

"And then?"

"Then, of course, my parent kicked me out of the sim. I can't review the footage until I unlock three modules of trauma counseling."

Mutters, grim faces, more tongue lolls.

A thrum of guilt. It was so easy to make Gimlet the bad guy.

"Rubi Whiting says the @Freebreeders want SeaJuve to fail," Frankie said.

The kids shared uneasy glances.

"Isn't it time some of us got to have siblings?" a girl asked.

A few kids crossed their fingers in agreement, gestural moji meaning +1.

Frankie had once watched a vintage bit of nature footage with Sang: baby storks throwing each other out of the nest to starve.

That, it had seemed, was all she needed to know about sisters and brothers.

But now, with all her parents caught up in Rollsy's illness, she imagined having someone else. Someone her own age, someone of the pack, who wouldn't die or leave . . .

One willowy-limbed girl, black of skin, with an eyepatch, said, "We can't have sibs or rewild the oceans if they can't breathe, right?"

"If we wait for nature to rejuve, it'll be our kids or grandchildren doing the rewilding."

"If we get to *have* children."

"Mam says without SeaJuve, we'll be choking on old Boomer car exhaust in ten years."

The comment got a few nods, followed by counterarguments from kids who'd studied ecology. The word cloud rose; DPA analysts would crunch it.

I should've done this in the aquarium, Frankie thought. *With sharks as a backdrop.*

"What if there were other #consequences for SeaJuve failing?"

Quiet fell.

Nobody loved #consequences. #Consequences venned with #rationing. #Consequences meant getting popped when you gave in to an antisocial impulse.

"Like what?"

She shrugged. "What if we had to basically . . . go into managed care?"

"We who?"

"Everyone."

"Managed by who?"

"@ChamberofHorrors!"

Outbreak of laughter.

"The Singularity!"

Frankie shook her head. "What about a stricter vision of Nannybot? Or . . . martial law, like in the Clawback?"

The laughter died. Kids shuffled. "Is that likely?"

"If the air stales? We'd need extreme measures," Frankie said.

"They'd #triage Tampico for sure, then," said Kansas. Grim murmurs.

"Talk to your schools?" Frankie shared a remote poll. "There's a DPA participation badge and a stroke for everyone who refers twenty responders."

"Accept," they chorused. The kids took turns feeding the sloth until it dozed off; after that, the group dispersed in ones and twos, murmuring as they went.

Kansas stuck with Frankie as they passed into an airlock filled with flowers, some tagged as #extinct in the wild.

Then . . . butterflies.

A cone-shaped dome rose above them, bounded by a high ceiling. The air was cooler than near the sloth, but it was wet, heavily perfumed by nectar and undertones of vegetable rot.

Text from Misfortune: *I'll wait outside.*

Frankie pinged her thumbs-up, pleased.

"See?" subbed Headmistress.

"*Get me out from under the all-seeing eye* was only half of our deal," Frankie subbed.

"All in good time. Capture some selfies for your pack."

She did, marveling as the butterflies wafted around the core of vegetation.

Kansas, beside her, drew a deep breath. "When I get my implants, everything will smell like flowers."

A delicate brown insect plunged a filament of tongue into an orange trumpet-shaped flower. Another landed on the edge of Frankie's jumper, pumping yellow-and-blue wings.

"You truly believe we'll get managed if SeaJuve funding #crashburns?"

Frankie said, "I used to be all about Rewild. Baby Tigger and the whole nine. But . . . if we're gonna level up to truly rewilding, we gotta keep the Bouncers from giving up on SeaJuve."

"The Bouncers. They're running out of gas."

That was what Rubi feared, Frankie realized. That her cohort would evolve into another generation of giver-uppers.

Kansas frowned, checking a wrist comm. "My parents are calling. Here's my e-state, if you ever want to visit."

Frankie smiled, returning the invite. "Here's mine."

"You should go on to the hummingbird habitat."

"Hummingbirds?"

"It's *beyond*. Promise."

Hummingbirds? She gave Kansas a stroke for the tip and rushed off to see, then moved on to a glassed-in almond grove filled with bees, both the real kind and costumed toon characters from a bee-themed ancient movie. The attraction included a working hive, clear walls through which she could see the bees moving through their hexagonal pop-ins, a hundred thousand workers with a single lifetime gig.

"Out here," Headmistress said. "Quickly."

Frankie hurried to the exit, ignoring a young man dispensing honey on printed crackers.

And, finally: "Hey, kiddo."

"Mama!"

Sangria was lounging against one of the pillars, holding out three or four of the treats.

"Here, eat 'em—that kid gave me a strike for taking more'n my share."

Frankie stuffed all four crackers in her mouth and piled into a hug. She felt a hesitation in Sang before she returned the embrace. Then it was just a hug, and everything was fine.

"You're really here on the sly?" Sang said.

"I had to see you."

"Yeah, your governess said." Sang smelled a little of pepper, as always, and she had a healing scab on the back of her hand.

"What's this?"

"Storm cleanup," she explained. "We were chipping deadfall."

Frankie traced the raised line gravely, thinking about the
@Freebreed terrorist, swinging the beam with the shiny silver
bolt. "Might scar."

"Nah. Let's hit the roller coaster." Sang took a path into the
depths of a venerable old-school midway, with a Ferris wheel, a car-
ousel, and an intolerant juggler tossing six fiery batons.

Misfortune was nowhere to be seen.

The line for the roller coaster was long. They switched to a tiny
riverboat ride.

The honey and cracker crumbs had left a faint sour taste in
Frankie's mouth.

Sang elbowed her companionably. "So—working? On a case?
Must be a biggie if they flew you 'cross the pond."

"Ultra-confidential."

"That's okay." The boat bumped, spraying water.

"Are you subbing with someone?"

"What? No. Sorry. You have my full attention."

Frankie had had a speech memorized, but now she blurted, "You
have to come home, Sang."

Sang winced. "Chickpea . . ."

"You do! Or Gimlet and I can stay here. Once Rollsy's had his
surgery—"

Another wince.

Alarm bells. "What?"

"Nothing. It's nothing."

It had been like this since Rollsy got sick. "Nobody tells me anything."

"I can't help you, Chickpea. Rollsy's the one calls the shots."

"Nobody froze me out when Granda was dying."

Was that another flash of guilt?

"Sang." She tried to keep her voice from wobbling. "Is Rollsy
dying?"

A heavy exhalation. "You get to say, when you're the sick one.
We wrote agreements about health care into our nups when we all
shacked up. You can't use me to run around your pack's firewalls—"

"Our pack!"

"I just mean, with me on the outs."

"Why?" Frankie tried, involuntarily, to stand, fetching up against the ride's safety bar. "Why are you on the outs? Is Gimlet keeping you away?"

"No. *No!*" The boat plunged. Frankie's stomach flipped. Streaming wind chilled the tears smearing her cheeks.

"Chickpea, you gotta remember that Rolls is a very private person who's not necessarily entirely comfortable with his body, and—"

"I'm his kid!"

"The pack wants to protect you from the down-and-dirty medical indignities—"

"All you ever do is protect," she said bitterly. Gimlet, tossing her off *Sable Hare*. Family-rated games and sims where she couldn't even have a gun.

"It's—" Long pause. "It's our prenup. And you know how it is when you're young. Everyone afraid you'll lemming off somewhere to throw yourself into—" Another long pause. ". . . a volcano—"

She *had* to be subbing with someone.

"Sang, we need you. Please, please come home. Gimlet will be happy. We'll get a bigger pop-in, you can meet Rubi—"

"Chickpea, no."

"You and GranMarie can make Rollsy talk to me."

"I can't do any of that."

They had splashed and jolted their way to the bottom of the incline, and now were climbing again. Frankie was distantly aware that one of her legs was soaked. Beads of water dusted her mother's hairline.

"Listen, Chickpea. I will always, always love you to bits and pieces—"

"Stop talking like I'm a baby."

"You *are* my baby."

"Not if you're getting divorced and you're too chicken to say so and meanwhile you're hiding in this jungle getting ripped up by hurricanes and rusty nails."

"You don't think that's a little immature—"

The boat crested the rise, and Frankie saw how high up they were—three stories at least. Spread below them were happy-looking packs. Was it all wallpaper? Or were they falling apart, too?

"I'll tell Gimmles you need more info about Rolls, okay?"

Frankie turned away.

"Can the dramatics, kid—"

"Why are you being like this?" They tipped, dropped, cascading through sprays of water to the base of the coaster. By the time the momentum had bled off, Sang had given up pretending she wasn't elsewhere. She patted Frankie's hand mechanically.

They got off the water ride. "The queue for that coaster's only nine minutes now."

Frankie crossed her arms. "Mama-Sang, is Rollsy dying? Yes or no?"

Sang closed her eyes. "Yeah. #Triage redlighted the surgery. Waste of resources. I'm sorry."

"And are we divorcing?"

"I don't know, Chickpea. Probably."

"Why'd you go away? Whose fault is it?"

A hesitation? "It isn't—No. It's nobody's—"

Frankie turned and walked away. "You were right," she subbed to Headmistress. "They need a shock to bring them together."

Headmistress hummed a warning, pointing. Gimlet was just tooning in.

"Did you have fun?" they asked, and then, looking around: "Where's your escort?"

Headmistress threw an arrow into Frankie's peripheral.

"Right there." She pointed, blindly, and then saw that Misfortune was indeed there, striding closer, holding two sodagels and a McDiz wrap.

"Everything's in motion again," Gimlet said. "Get your flesh back to base."

She nodded, falling into step, accepting the sodagel from Misfortune with numb fingers.

It had worked. Headmistress and Poppet had engineered the meet with Sang, made her show up, and Gimlet was none the wiser.

Too bad it was all for nothing.

"There, there," Headmistress murmured. "You see how long the leash is?"

"You'll get away next time," Poppet agreed. "Give 'em a good scare. Put on a brave face, now."

Good advice. Frankie popped the gel and reached for the McDiz costume, pasting on a smile. Performing the delight she saw sprayed, for truth or lie, on the mug of every other kid in the park.

CHAPTER 36

Months later, after the dust had settled, Rubi would see the *Sable Hare* attack—the murder of the sailor and the suicide of his attacker aboard the SeaJuve flagship vessel—as a sort of starter's pistol for worldwide conflagration.

She never meant to suggest to Luce that he ought to escape from @Interpol custody or go public with his story about the Pale. Could she have known he was capable of escaping?

Surely, she'd just made an idle comment, one born of her despair as footage of the murder aboard ship spread, as the surface and the Sensorium both caught fire and ocean-restoration efforts threatened, once again, to founder.

The *Sable Hare* murder kicked off a half-dozen violent actions elsewhere, the worst a gory attack by three machete-wielding remnant @Trollgaters in Old Moscow. As murder feeds exploded through the newscycle, gig acceptance dropped off. In Shanghai and Australia, morning shift pickup dropped to 10 percent. Automated drones picked up slack where they could, but without pilots to do nuanced work, service levels faltered.

Workshops went into shutdown. Carbon remediation rates bottomed out for the first time in sixty years. The Saharan reservoir management project, an effort to encourage natural replenishment of underground aquifers across the continent, had to shift into autopilot. Desalinizers cycled down: desperate oasis managers offered up to ten strokes to any new trainee willing to speed-level.

Soapboxers demanded that the SeaJuve fleet turn back, imagining the ship was full of terrorists.

In the hours after the attack, ten thousand individuals were accused of being @Freebreeders, both by casual acquaintances and, sometimes, @CloseFriends. Users requested their conversational transcripts and comms, auditing for signs of conspiracy.

Counterstrikes went in. Malicious gossip complaints were filed. Friendships broke up and comms bans were erected. Cloudsight's request queue for nuanced adjudication ran to over a million. Live adjudicators couldn't keep up with demand. AIs, of course, were only as good as their algorithms.

In something that looked suspiciously like panic, Cloudsight held a stakeholders' vote, opting to freeze the automated social marketplace for a day. Suddenly, *nobody* could give or get strikes unless there was a human operator to assess the complaint.

#Flashmobs, real and virtual, broke out. Users kamikazed a handful of burning thingbots into Dover, managing to set one of the elderly ferry docks afire. As city managers locked down drones, including the Greater London car fleet, thousands of striking workers began marching toward Dover with the apparent intention of demolishing the port . . . as if that would somehow stop SeaJuve ships from making landfall.

Across the channel, Calais closed down all oceanic traffic, the better to protect its shiny new facilities and precious carbon investments.

Wage offers skyrocketed. Requests went unanswered. Service queues got catastrophically long.

Rubi and the Mers Barnes were seconded to a secure pop-in, old apartments for film executives, offered up to Juanita Bell by McDiz, Tampico's primary corporate sponsor.

Rubi was tasked with asking Luce a list of questions that Juanita Bell and her @GlobalSec superiors had generated for

Luce, everything from *What do the Pale look like?* to specific technical queries about the incoming survey fleet's military capabilities.

She remembered his first response to the question about vulnerabilities: *We travel the fucking galaxy. You need me to tell you that your vintage rockets can't stop us?*

Comparing firepower wasn't the answer. If the Pale could invade on the pretext that humanity was near self-extinction, Earth needed to know their sustainability criteria.

Rubi's crying fit in the shower had relieved some of her internal pressure, but even so, she was tired, upset about the murder aboard the *Sable Hare,* and worried about Drow. Concerned, too, about Frankie—who'd come back from the so-called Happiest Place on Earth subdued and withdrawn. And about Gimlet, who had glazed into a long family conference about their sick partner's medical situation as soon as Frankie was out of sight.

Then there was Luce.

She was still in freefall over that one.

Human narratives about first contact offered no breadcrumbs for this. Invading alien hordes were supposed to make a big entrance, fry a few iconic monuments, and then lose their bid to take over Earth to a plucky human air force. Or to #malware. Or . . . #measles?

Aliens *weren't* supposed to call ahead. They didn't commit identity theft, fire off selfies, cruise the app marketplace. You didn't rule the planet by taking food-delivery jobs while sabotaging prosocial kickstarters.

Where did Luce get off, setting up public profiles, drawing minimum income, and soapboxing about the flaws of rapid-response democracy?

Was he, truly, still her client? Cloudsight project managers were too busy to answer her pings. Polly, her tutor app, was coming up dry on relevant case law.

With no opinion forthcoming from above, Rubi had resorted to researching the legal rights of polters.

The early adopters of life-extension tech had hoped—naturally enough—to discover a biohack that would let them exist in a perennial prime-of-life state. Some of the most successful pioneers milked their lifespan out to two hundred years. Prime-of-life health had eluded them, though. The life-extension pioneers evolved into crepits, then @jarheads, eventually moving into fulltime Sensorium existences. Their bodies flickered on, tethered to aggressive life support.

It was a logical next step to dream of cutting the meat loose—uploading a human consciousness to the Sensorium. What @jarhead wouldn't want to break out of their medical cocoon, to live online as a digital immortal?

Nobody had managed, yet, to break the tie between a user account and its earthly flesh.

That hadn't stopped the first rich, privileged @jarheads from legislating full rights for the hypothetical polters they hoped, one day, to become. Preemptive rights grab: an attempt to ensure they would continue to be considered people, voting stakeholders in every sense of the word.

Within that flurry of legislation, nobody had bothered to specify that a polter had to be either human or Earth-born. Why would they?

Rubi could, therefore, argue that rich human @jarheads had given Luce a nigh-indisputable right to legal representation, at least until someone filed a challenge.

Which wouldn't happen, with the courts down.

She tooned in to find Luce amusing himself, within his prison's malleable environment, by building a series of stalagmites from its floor, limestone fingers in pink, beige, wax-white, and pale green. They rose in intervals, creating walkways and chutes, low fences, nothing as high as a proper wall. Each glistened like water-slicked marble. She touched one; it had a wet, gritty texture.

There were no stalactites descending from above: the roof of the sim was black sky, studded with the gems he'd been making earlier.

Luce banged his hands together as she arrived. "More questions?"

Rubi indicated the stalagmite forest and said, "Why this?"

"I'm trying out dog strokes. My version of Drow's comfort fidget."

Did he miss Drow?

Luce said, "I'd forgotten about . . . this terrain."

"It's home?"

"Yes and no." He scratched his head, a surprisingly human gesture. "Will this conversation get shredded?"

"Uncertain," she said. "Given that you're claiming to be . . ."

"The advance picket of an invading hostile force?"

"Commodore Bell won't necessarily respect your right to confidentiality."

He flicked a stalagmite with a fingertip, triggering a low *bong*, as if it was a tuning fork. "If it's not hashable, why'd you come alone?"

"I'm sick of everyone's face. Why? Was there something you wanted to say?"

"I don't have any secrets to share." He huffed. Laughing? "I just wondered about the parameters."

"Until we verify your story, I'm not sure there are parameters."

"Nothing happens until they know I'm no @hoaxer?"

"Yeah." Now they were toon to toon, she was calmer. He was outnumbered and in trouble. "I hope there aren't #consequences for you. If we keep up SeaJuve and pull off sovereignty."

"Shouldn't gloat—you haven't won yet." That was certainly true, more than he even knew.

This is the invasion, in its way, she thought. *If Luce is to be believed, what we do now is the thing that matters. And there's only a few dozen people who know it.*

Disquieting thought. That was how warring nations had worked before the Setback. Specialist power brokers quietly running the world. Keeping secrets, lying to keep the population in line. Had she become one of them?

People were staging public murders. As spectacle! Would it get even worse if they knew the truth?

That had always been the rationale for secrecy: that idea that stakeholders couldn't handle full disclosure. That the world was made of innocent lambs needing a shepherd, someone who would lie about wolves, keeping the livestock in the dark for their own good.

Trouble was, the second you granted blanket rights of secrecy, someone dragged that blanket over all sorts of antisocial things: resource hoarding, crime, persecution, genocide . . .

Rubi shook away the momentary wobble in her faith. The Clawback had drawn back the curtain. The harsh light of mutually assured disclosure had its drawbacks, certainly. But it had prevented human extinction and wiped out a host of other age-old atrocities.

Unflinching truth was the right path.

"May I?" She pointed at one of the stalagmites.

"Be my guest."

She ran a finger over the spike, finding a gritty texture that defied the evidence of her eyes.

"*Comfort fidget*, you called it. You find it calming?"

Luce shrugged, shaping another knobby protrusion.

She sat cross-legged on the cell floor, figuring out how to move one of the active drips to the spot in front of her. The rate of limestone accretion was unrealistically fast. She could see the stalagmite forming with every splash. Calling up pull tabs, she widened it at the base. The splashes became bigger; the center of the action curved like a dinner plate. Some of the particulate was glowing, little luminous flecks.

"We haven't won yet, you said. We'll need to know what it takes, Luce. To establish sovereignty."

"You understand I'm not supposed to help you." He flopped down across from her, pressing his fingers against the base of the stalagmite. "Commodore Bell's right about that."

"But helping is fair play, isn't it?"

"I don't view the world as one big leaderboard. Anyway, I *already* warned you."

"The Martians are coming," she murmured.

"Get your shit together, or don't. You can't save yourselves; what's it to me?"

Are you asking me or yourself?

She mirrored his fingers, placing hers in a semicircle on the other side of their shared stalagmite. Virtual water dripped and lapped within the shallow depression. Humidity misted her cuticles. A light frosting of stone formed over their fingernails.

"Is it fair?" she asked, finally. "If it's only the ten or so of us who know?"

"Don't forget all the officers, veeps, and CEOs," Luce added. "People you can't see, tasked with verifying my story and coming up with idiot questions about ray guns, trying to figure out how to wring me dry."

Ray guns. There *had* been a question about that on the list. One they hadn't asked yet.

Did that mean he had access to mics outside this supposedly sealed server?

"Why are you telling me this?"

"Fair play, stupid."

Maybe it sucked to live in a fishbowl, your every word and action on display, your sex tapes in the X-rated Haystack. Virtue signaling for strokes, and the threat of strikes when you stepped out of line.

No secrets in a village.

You accepted it. Even Drow said it was better than those bad old days, with their wild imbalances of wealth and power. Transparency was the thing that had somehow stopped the greedy effort to coal-shovel all the planet's resources in ever-fewer hands.

She couldn't tell if Luce was still on mission or if he was trying to help.

"If you're suggesting that you should go public—"

The look of honest surprise on his face stopped her.

"You're not suggesting that."

"I *was* going public. All the strikes, remember? *You're wrong, Luce, you're stupid, Luce, shut up, Luce.*"

She chewed on that. "You proceeded from antisocial principles."

"What antisocial principles?"

"Lying. Pretending to be one of us."

"I'm not usually target-facing. I open doors, floodgates, airlocks. I close hatches, windows. I find niches, nooks, alcoves in the archives. I'm a technosphere survival expert, not an ambassador. I made it up as I went."

"I understand. But you didn't say *Hi, People of Earth, I'm a polter from another world, and by the way, we have gunboats incoming because you need help with your biosphere.*"

"Aside from your dad and his @bloodhound pals, who'd believe that?"

"Probably nobody," she said. "But you were just giving me a hard time about full disclosure. It's hypocritical."

"True. Stupid, stupid Luce."

He pulled his fingers out of the holes the new stone had formed: tiny bubbles of air at the base of the stalagmite.

"I'd give it one more try," he said. "Be honest, sing it from the rooftops. But then there's the ads, ads, ads."

"And the firewalls on this locked server."

He gave her a weird little grin.

Shit. He had been humoring them, with his stone pillars and his profanity-laced answers to Juanita's questions.

Was it possible for him to get away? Surely, Sapience Assessment knew how to lock a server.

We travel with FTL; you think we can't take out your entire military with a garbage scow?

"Whose interests would it serve if you tell all?"

"Whose interests does it serve if I don't?"

Cabals, string-pullers, secret societies. Drawing power because of this threat, because people were afraid.

She thought of the murdered sailor on *Sable Hare,* the horrific killings in Old Moscow.

"You know," she said on a weird impulse, "Cloudsight's all but offline."

"Is it really?"

"As your lawyer, I can't recommend any disengagement from custody—"

He seemed to read her thought. "I'll tell you this for free. It's your old infrastructure that's problematic," Luce said. "All the tons of helix you didn't rip out of the walls. Recycled uplinks. Ye oldey building systems. Antique emergency lights with solar panels. Misfortune's insulin pump, and all the medical redtooth."

Each stalagmite grew a proliferation of devices: USB smartports in power uptakes, building chillers made of repurposed and reconditioned HVAC systems, bits of fans and compression pumps pressed into service, or simply left in the walls because they couldn't be recycled.

"Shazam," Luce said, and vanished.

CHAPTER 37

Copse corpse, corpse copse, copse corpse . . .

After the Syracuse concert, Whiskey Sour headed back to the Lakes to record her first musical artstorm. Drow, meanwhile, sniffed his way toward the clue Luce had teased out of Garmin Legosi's transcripts, traveling to the remains of Scranton.

He hadn't expected to be wowed by the pyramids.

In the early days of the carbon rush, pop-up operations had proliferated everywhere. Desperate corporations repurposed workforces into producing hardwood, bamboo, cricket flour, and topsoil at speed.

Scranton had gone the boutique route, opting to focus on specialized lock-in of existing carbon sources. Rather than growing new wood, they tackled the recycling of contaminated materials.

Their niche had plenty of start-up grist. Strippers were reclaiming millions of tons of old particle-board furniture as deburbing got under way. Plywood, too, from demolished houses. Scranton ground these for printstock, reconstituting chemical-laced sawdust into massive, custom-designed blocks. Monument-scale printer beds created simple cubes, ten meters big on a side. As the project expanded, they got creative, making dodecahedrons, cones, and three-dimensional portraits, detailed sculptures of animals, and abstract forms.

Each block, however shaped, was bathed in chemicals—more toxins, these recovered from industrial and mining cleanups—before they were glazed and, finally, baked in a massive kilning facility. Thus petrified, the huge blocks, glue-laced sawdust transubstantiated to stone, were stacked in even more fantastic configurations.

Parish pariah, parish pariah, parish pariah . . .

Drow's bus tour debarked at the base of two enormous structures—ruffled grouse—looming at the entrance to the city. Imposing in their immensity, the birds were eighty feet tall and beautifully painted. Standing beak to beak, they formed an arch over the stone path leading to Blingtown.

As they crossed the threshold into the shaded corridor created by the first pyramids, Drow glimpsed more elaborate constructions, sponsored pyramids, ornately decorated.

The tour group gasped as *Intersectional Rising* came into view. A vast, multicolored forearm, it reached skyward from an artfully cracked hillscape, spilling tangled DNA strands from its splayed palm. Clouds drifted between its fingers.

A tanned woman wearing head-to-toe desert robes stood at its base, next to a rack of chilled chuggers. "Welcome to Blingtown! I'm Chantal, your guide." She lit up as she spotted Robin. "Please help yourself to sunscreens, food, and water. It's very sunny here and there's lots to see."

As people robed up, she spieled: "Over the past ninety years, our monument-design team has reinterpreted many great constructs of the ancient world. Egypt, Mesopotamia, the Maya, the Nubians, Aztecs, and Rome—you'll see echoes of those civilizations today. Newer builds"—here, she tipped a fond smile up at *Intersectional Rising*—"offer modern variations on the pyramid theme."

Drow hadn't felt small, in this particular way, for a long time.

"Thought it'd be like Vegas," he subbed to Crane.

"I believe they're more garish at night, sir."

"Ready? Let's start the tour!" Chantal led them around the giant wrist, moving into a well-rehearsed share about the other pillar of Scranton's indispensability strategy: power sinks.

Within each pyramid were millions of artificially grown diamonds, each loaded with a pinpoint of waste from the continent's defunct nuclear power plants. The diamonds emitted energy. The fixed carbon monuments were filled with the undying batteries.

Diamond juice sustained the kilning operation, with its huge grinders and printers. Diamond juice lit up the pyramids at night while pushing surplus energy north to the Lakes and south to the Manhattan biotrust.

"Power of bling," Drow murmured.

"It's a remarkable achievement," Crane replied. "But do you truly believe there's a breadcrumb here?"

The genesis of Blingtown, its earliest monuments, venned with the last huge wave of Setback disappearances. "I always think I've got a good lead, don't I?"

"At least it took you somewhere astonishing." Crane sighed. "If it is a delusion, that is."

Chantal, shining with the zeal of a true Bounceback convert, conveyed them from wonder to wonder. "Each new pyramid offers ornamentation sponsorship opps: you can fund carvings, mosaics, and illumination features."

Your name in stone . . . forever? Infographic and a price list appeared on a lemon-colored ziggurat.

"We offer multiple leveling tracks for anyone interested in monument construction. Scranton creates fifteen new permajobs annually. These are solid opps to live outside the densified cities and make an unquestioned give to society and the ecosphere."

Blank spaces on pyramids came alive with animated overlays. Any tourist could play a starter gig: participating in the printing, soaking, glazing, and, finally, baking of one stone. They could apprentice to a drone team, securing stones in place within the current build, an interpretation of China's Great Wall as envisioned by a sculptor named Cixin Hui. The red ideograph-covered ribbon had been sponsored by the Great Lakes Cantonese-Mandarin Speakers Association.

"Scranton is *the* place to be," Chantal concluded, "if you want to learn to carve stone or lay diamond."

Drow imagined aspiring electricians spelunking into the pyramids' depths, setting nuclear diamonds within the battery banks, testing and wiring. Building legacy electricity out of past poison.

He felt a deep pull on his emotions—that sense of being choked up. It was a feel that he absolutely hated. He remembered being born into a world where nuclear waste was just another thing humanity planned to bury and forget, before they buried themselves.

Draft lyrics echoed in his backbrain, waiting for music he hadn't written yet. *Never thought we'd make it this far; never meant to live through all the wars. Yet here we are, here we are . . .*

The tour skirted a bluff peopled by sculptors working in the shadow of colossi. The giants were mostly #brand ambassadors from the old days: an enormous green giant, a hamburger bandit, the marshmallow monster from a ghost movie . . . or . . . Drow squinted.

"Is that a talking blob of dough?"

"Didn't you say this might get tacky, Master Woodrow?"

He looked at the Great Wall. "Some of it transcends."

"What is it they say about infinite monkeys?"

"Give us smartdrugs?"

"Very droll, sir. I believe this is your turn."

Drow ditched the group, making for a positively dowdy structure: serpentine staircase, blue in color, planted with genetweaked blue poppies, an enormous stone-and-floral interpretation of a whirlpool.

Was this really what Garmin Legosi had refused to tell him in that Syracuse pub two days before? Could he really have gotten his face busted, to shut him up?

Remember when it became obvious that there was no more

holding on to personal fortunes? Luce had pulled a bunch of Garmin Legosi's utterances out of the Haystack, homing in on things he'd alluded to in other conversations, not to mention debriefs with the auditors who'd #triaged his pharmaceutical company. *My adopted dad sank what he could into gold and gems, sheltering assets. But the real action was in ecological rehabilitation. Start-ups and nonproffs. Sucking up to Global Oversight was the ticket during the Clawback. You might retain control over some capital if your assets were actively remediating.*

Had Scranton been one of those efforts?

It made sense: it would have taken serious bank to kickstart these pyramids. There'd be no near-term profit in buying scrap wood, in reclaiming toxin-riddled mine sites and spent nuclear fuel. There'd be strokes, true, but financial dividends from the diamond electricity would have been decades in the making.

Ultimately, money laundering had failed those late-stage oligarchs. The first forensic auditing apps couldn't be bought. And Garmin knew it—Luce's transcript analysis showed him looping, obsessively, to the fate of ExxoShell's directors. A righteous #flashmob had torn down a private compound where the oil barons had holed up. CEOs had been stripped, rolled in poison ivy, and flogged through the streets of Houston before being remanded to managed care.

The interesting thing about Garmin obsessing about the ExxoShell incident was that right afterward, billionaires started vanishing by the dozens.

Garmin's transcripts implied there had been a window, before humankind installed cams in every living eyeball, before they put mics in every larynx and wired them straight into each user's nervous system.

A window when faking your death was still possible?

What if the founders of the so-called @ChamberofHorrors had liquidated assets and logged? If Legosi's father was one of them . . .

All this assumes that Garmin and Luce aren't just as delusional as . . . well, as me.

Never mind. Luce's clue had been about the Scranton Whirl-pool. Repeated phrase, something Legosi muttered: *glitch*. Whirl-pool glitch. Glitch in the pool. Whirlglitch. Over thirty years, Legosi had said it over three hundred times.

Now, standing at the pool's leading edge, Drow felt a flicker of hope. Perhaps, this once, he wasn't chasing a fantasy. He searched the monument database. The name he was seeking was there: *Tala Weston, Manhattan, b. 1968 missing 2062.*

She'd been one of the first Setback billionaires to vanish.

"Glitch, glitch, what kind of glitch?"

A tour app pointed the way forward, to the place where her name was incised.

Drow poked his way along, Robin at his side, feeling like someone on his way to a firing squad. When Frankie Barnes tooned in beside him, he jumped and barely managed not to shriek.

"Be*yond*." Her eye traveled over the pyramid in progress, *Wall,* with its red-glazed walls and ideographs.

"Hey, it's you," said Drow.

She gave him a weird, stressed-out smile. "This is where you're running off to?"

"Still hunting the circus, kid. Supposedly, they left a forwarding address—"

"I would advise a change of subject, Master Woodrow."

No shit. "These are legit awesome structures. You should deff come visit 'em, since you're in NorthAm."

Heavy sigh.

I haven't taken any modules on counseling kids, Rubi's been grown so long, do I even remember how to . . . Saints, sweet saints . . . "Uh . . . wanna talk?"

"How many parents did you have?"

"Two."

"Only two?"

"Both dads, if it matters."

"Were they . . . you know?"

Clang clang clang! Alarm bells. Robin snugged in closer. "I barely know you, Frances. You'll have to say." His mind was racing. *What if she says* perverts? *No, that's supposed to be impossible. What if she says—*

"Were they nice?"

"Fucking nice?" Not perverts. He'd nearly pissed himself.

"Good at it, I guess. Raising you?"

"Oh." *Dial it down, Drow.* "I guess one was."

"And the other?"

"Do you know what an addict is, kid?"

Before Frankie could answer, the nearest cluster of tourists froze. They had scattered, checking out the #selfie stops and capturing pics of the pyramids from a variety of angles. Now the group reformed. Agitated voices rose.

"Newscycle, Crane," Drow said. "Top stories."

Footage of Luce, soapboxing in a cave full of stalagmites, appeared before him:

You know me as one of the @jarheads murdered by that Eldercare provider, but that's an identity I stole. Luciano Pox wasn't using it. Sorry and all that for the deception. Désolé. Point is, I'm an entity, formerly flesh, now entirely data. I was uploaded into your Sensorium by my Benefactors, the Pale.

I was sent ahead of our Fleet, to Friend you all and prepare you for what is to come.

Frankie groaned.

Just then, Luce himself, identity masked within his old burglar skin, tooned in beside Drow.

"You made it to Blingtown," he said, before offering a surprised-sounding hello to Frankie.

She gave him a formal bow, typical greeting from a kid to a stranger.

Luce's hand drifted to his face, finding the mask. Telegraphing surprise that Frankie hadn't recognized him.

Shit shit shit, why me, why now? Drow owed it to Luce to keep their relationship secret, but anyone who'd met him would Whooz him as soon as he got out a full sentence.

"I guess you already heard—"

"Master Woodrow," Crane said. "Certain of Miss Cherub's work transcripts are being hashed by @GlobalSec servers, but I believe this individual is meant to be in @Interpol custody."

Saints! Even Crane recognized him.

"Luce. You broke jail?" Drow subbed.

"Wouldn't have surrendered if I couldn't get out. Why this is a fucking surprise to anyone—"

Frankie, to Drow's relief, was glazing, sinking deep into subvocal conversation. Reporting him, probably.

"Are you the reason everyone's . . ." He gestured at the agitated tourists.

"Yeah. With Cloudsight frozen, I can post. It's awesome."

"And instead of railing against oxygen security, you're . . . What is this bullshit?" He caught a tag from the transcript. "Martians?"

"You're the full-disclosure society, right?"

"You're not @Martian."

"It's the euphemism from the working group—" He gestured at Frankie.

Drow said, "I have no idea what you're talking about."

"Your Rubi calls me a polter. @Jarhead holy grail, remember? Your term, not mine. But the jar was a ship, ten years out from Earth. My team was tasked with paving the way for contact."

"Contact. Between humans and Martians."

"My benefactors are the Pale."

"For fuck's sake. You've convinced Sensorium you're a goddamned alien? I'm tempted to strike you myself."

"Cloudsight's down."

"Don't be a smart-ass."

"The thing is," Luce said, "I'm having credibility problems. Buy-in hasn't been outstanding."

The penny dropped. He *meant* it.

Frankie deglazed. "So . . . you guys know each other?"

For a breath, they all just gaped at each other. Back, forth, back again. Then Frankie scratched her head. "I had to report you, Mer Pox."

"What are they gonna do, lock me in a secure server?" Luce clawed off the simulated mask, exposing his pale-faced toon and waving at Crane. "Hi, stupid bird."

"Good day, Mer Pox. You must be very proud. If there was a leaderboard for troublemaking, your score—"

"No thanks to you," Luce said. "Drow, you find what you came for?"

Right. Clues in the pyramid. "I'm working on it," Drow said. He spotted the capstone of the whirlpool.

Tala Weston. Stone blocks incised in blue kilned stone. *Manhattan.* The epitaph read: *Creating ferociously is the best revenge.*

Nothing. No glitch. She disappeared, and here was her gravestone. End of the line.

Was she really dead, then?

"Crane," Drow said. "Shut off my visual inputs."

Luce and Frankie vanished, though their voices, behind him, kept yakking. The text, at Drow's feet, blurred to invisibility. He creaked down to one knee, getting his nose down to within inches of the stone. He could just make it out: *Missy LaRue. Dover, UK.*

"Eyes on." Cameras rebooted. The view switched back to show Tala's epitaph. *Creating ferociously.*

"Off," he said. "On."

"I should backdrop my soapbox here," Luce's voice said.

"Eyes off." Drow ran a finger over the incised letters where Tala's name had been. *Missy LaRue.*

The Horrors hadn't truly disappeared. Some vestige of their digital accounts had remained in the system when they died. The records were glitchy; the team making the Whirlpool failed to include them within the monument. They'd had to overwrite themselves, later, as illusions.

"These . . . pyramid things? They've got grandeur."

"Since when do you care about grandeur, Luce?" Drow got to his feet. He could hear the tour group gabbling. The pyramids, in their immensity, had turned to brightly colored shapes with fuzzy edges.

"Eyes on." Everything snapped into focus, both the real world and its augmented overlays. Frankie, Luce, and Crane reappeared.

Frankie was word-clouding the crowd's hubbub. Big letters in a block font jostled over their heads: *home, family, emergency, #JUSTNOPE, frivolous, stupid.*

"So, other people get to say *stupid*?"

Drow bit back a *Shut up, Luce.*

Just then, a manager pinged the whole @ScrantonGuest channel: "Friends, Blingtown is closing early this evening. We apologize for the inconvenience. Please make your way to the parking lot—"

Drow muted the announcement. "They're hauling us back north."

"Why? Nobody's arriving in-system for years," Luce said. "I made one of your damned counters."

"You made a countdown clock for an alien invasion?" Frankie sounded outraged.

"Alleged alien invasion," Drow corrected, with @bloodhound prissiness. Were Hackle and Jackal on this yet?

He was going to have to crawl all over this pyramid, documenting differences between the augmented inscriptions and the real deal. Presumably, if he took a picture, it would be a #hoax, too. So, he'd need . . . paper? To make rubbings? And a justification for his take on the Scranton ration cache . . .

He pinged the Scranton gig coordinator. "Crane, you think I can drive a chipper bot?"

"Your drone licenses were revoked, sir, after you tried to get a grab-and-go to airlift you into Pickering Nuclear."

"That would have worked if you hadn't stopped me."

Long-suffering sigh.

"Maybe I can play the permajobbers an acoustic set?"

"They're too upset for a musical interlude. The sensible course—"

"We both know sensible's not in my wheelhouse, Crane."

He had been going slow-release on the Leonardo for days, but now he fished in his sleeve for a bit of guitar string, a probe he kept honed to a point. Sitting cross-legged on a massive stone bench, he pretended to fiddle with his sunrobe as Scranton continued to condense into a yammering mob. Frankie's word cloud steamed above them: *vintage nukes, SeaJuve, aliens, user poll, trolling, Martian invasion, cancel, pointless, @hoaxers, bullshit, uploads, Moscow murderers, @bloodhounds, allure, machetes, immortality*, Bastille, *home, war . . .*

Mojis of wide-open mouths and red, angry faces, people in bed hiding under the covers.

Epic collective freakout, in other words.

Drow slid the probe under the flesh of his collarbone and into the injection port, releasing a burst of smartdrug.

Okay. People fleeing back to the Lakes, salmon spawning, going with the flow. I need to go against the stream. "How long before people calm down, Crane?"

"That depends on whether Mer Pox keeps fanning the flames."

"Whaddaya say, Luce? Gonna deescalate?"

"Fuck, no." Luce's doomsday clock floated in his peripheral, ticking portentously. Testimonial unfurled below. Drow speed-read his whole transcript.

When I was flesh, I opened doors in the Pale Royal Palace and was rewarded with electronic immortality. This was no glorious retirement, however. I joined the team of beings sent from afar to Friend you all.

People of Earth, you have not *been friendly.*

"Team? More than one polter, Luce?"

"Eleven of us. Azrael killed my pack."

"Azz—the #triage program?"

"And friends." He shot Crane a dirty look.

Martyrfuck, Drow thought. So, *that* happened. On the record, no less.

His augmented brain started making side trips into client-patient-Martian things. Luce. One of a team of eleven, and the only one still alive. Drow pulled up a module on #survivorguilt and had started taking the entry-level quiz before he remembered he wasn't sure he even believed it was true.

What if aliens didn't have #survivorguilt?

"Frankie," he asked, "you buy in? About this alien thing?"

She shrugged, wide-eyed. Not allowed to say.

"Nobody official's denied it, so there," Luce answered.

"Rubi believe it?"

"She's my advocate. She better believe me."

"Luce, you need to read up on what lawyer types are and aren't good for."

"Yeah? What are you good for?"

"That is the question, isn't it?" His brain was skipping. Stay in Scranton. Stay in Scranton. He was too creaky to work a shift in the acid baths—

There's those three vials of Superhoomin Garmin Legosi gave me.

Bad, bad *idea.*

Doesn't matter. The point isn't to stay and build pyramids. I'm on the hunt, armed with a minstrel's lute and my ineffable charm . . .

Whoa. Hint of an idea there. Tourists could flee screaming for the Lakes, but there were permajobs here. Scranton's kilns ran 24/7. "Am I good, for example, for group therapy?"

Luce looked outraged. "Do you not know if you're good at counseling? Why've you been trying to help people if—"

"Could I propose a group session or something to the people pinned here?" he asked Crane. "Just to buy a little time in the hood and check out . . . things?"

"You're insufficiently experienced."

"Am I wildly unqualified?"

Pause. "You would have to play and pass the group-facilitation and crisis-reactivity modules."

"That wouldn't take long." Drow scratched up three new verses to the song he'd been writing, adding them to the lyrics share-board he'd thrown up with Frankie. He had her word cloud memorized.

How long will it take to crawl all over this pyramid with a roll of paper and a hunk of charcoal?

Doing that'll kill me.

There's the Superhoomin, if I do have to crawl over it.

Stop! Smartdrugs and life-extension meds do not play well to-gether.

So, be smart. Maybe the nun could audit the gravestones with a thingbot. He composed a note to Father Blake.

The reply came immediately. *Find us one more name.*

Verification or it didn't happen. Drow sifted through the roster of the Clawback missing, filtering out billionaires and tagging the locations of their marker stones. He shuffled to the nearest one, captured the official text, knelt.

"Eyes off," he said. Yes, here was another discrepancy. *Ley Hilton. Manhattan.*

"Manhattan," he muttered aloud. "Same point of origin as Tala."

"Do I understand that you propose to write two therapist finals overnight, Master Woodrow, even as you do the #survivorguilt refresher module?"

"Schedule the exams." Drow probed his injection pump again, high-grading his filtered list of missing billionaires, this time by home city.

"You'll be flagged."

If he was going to get caught, he might as well pass for god until they grabbed him. He could hear the next phase of his symphony coming on. Swell of strings and low brass, incoming storms, no fucking vibraphone this time. This was music for a reckoning.

"Offer the counseling session to the Scranton permajobbers.

We'll rise at dawn and talk through their feels. Make the proposal tasty, will you?"

"They accept, sir. They are in a considerable state of anxiety. That and the peculiar allure of your celebrity—"

"Yes, yes. Eyes off again." He had found a third suspect marker, shut off his implants. This fellow hailed from Connecticut.

First, we take Manhattan.

Ground nobody wanted to cede.

Or you're just crunching old Cohen lyrics.

What good was a hunch if you didn't play it?

"That wildlife trust out in New York has permajobs, too. I bet they're anxious. Interest them in my coming out to help them."

"Saint Woodrow on the march," Crane muttered.

"No marching. I'm nice and sane these days, remember?"

"Paragon of emotional stability."

"I'll ride a manure truck if it's going south. Strap me to the roof, whatever."

"There's a high-speed train that runs from Miami to Detroit," Frankie said.

Drow startled. How much of that conversation had he forgotten to subvocalize?

"Um . . . I'll keep it in mind."

"I'm feeling strangely left out," Luce said. "What just happened?"

"Epiphany," Drow said. "The phenomenon, not the holiday. Sniff, bark, let loose the cadaver dogs. Drow found the circus."

"The circus is at the zoo?" Frankie asked. She seemed strangely intent.

"Uh . . ."

The opening lecture for his therapy module popped up—

Audio, video, sign language, text?

Text, he selected.

The lecture scrolled past, introductory blather about human coping strategies in the VUCA age.

Drow memorized it as it ran by, and found he had bandwidth to spare.

"Wanna share your troubles, Frankie?" he subbed to the child, and then, separately, to Luce: "Tell me about your credibility problems."

Juggle five things at once, two in realtime?

No problem.

Corpse copse. Copse corpse.

Parish pariah.

Corpse corpse, corpse copse, copse corpse . . .

No problem at all.

CHAPTER 38

Luce's revelations broke across Sensorium like a tsunami slapping down a beach resort. Amid cries of #hoax and panic, astronomers—both pro and amateur—focused on Proxima Centauri. They pulled the same data Anselmo had discovered, back when Luce first arrived.

The coming ships had been in Haystack, after all, waiting to be found.

Public opinion fractured. Massive debate arose about whether to contact the Pale. Unofficial polls proliferated. Should they send a peremptory *Go away, we don't need you!* message? Attempt diplomatic relations?

A disturbing slice of the population was for surrendering in exchange for green aid. Dominated by @Freebreeders and the remnants of @Trollgate, their initial buy-in numbers topped eight hundred thousand.

Luce was referred to, variously, as a polter spy, a sentient meme, #killertech, a defector, a @hoaxer, a savior, a #troll, and a flat-out lunatic.

Rubi was taking all this in via a customized garden in her e-state, a maze whose walls were trellised rose and grapevine, each lined with plinths that displayed news stories, in tiny diorama, at eye level. She had invited Juanita Bell to join her. Now the pair of them walked from news story to news story, tuning in on the various crises unfolding worldwide.

"People are gathering in immense crowds," Juanita said. She shared footage from Hyderabad, projecting it onto the nearest plinth. A #flashmob gathered around a shouting, passionate soapboxer. "She's filibustering for free access to food rations. Says people have a right to hoard supplies if we're going to be invaded."

"I get the feeling Luce has mixed feelings about the Pale fleet commander and their plans for us." Rubi let out a long breath. "They forced him to come here, right?"

Instead of responding, Juanita walked on to the next share. Greater Pretoria was lobbying to accelerate carbon fixing by raising NorthAm and European targets. They were demanding Tampico double its densification efforts and its agricultural output at the same time. Southern NorthAm replied with the equivalent of a big collective raspberry, using language that would have triggered a hail of strikes . . . if only Cloudsight hadn't been down.

"My peers in EastEuro are calling for an inventory and retrofit of Earth's mothballed stockpile of space-capable missiles," Juanita said. She fiddled with a sword at her hip. Rubi's e-state defaults had clad her in a French soldier's uniform—blue coat, black bicorne hat, and all. Her hair was pulled back in a short golden queue.

Rubi shook her head. "Luce made it clear that Earth can't fight off his . . . do we say *overlords*?"

"You believe his story, then?"

"He ducked out of @Interpol's fancy super-secure server like it wasn't even there, didn't he? These people could have all the far-future stuff we imagine in stories. Faster-than-light ships, zap rays, Terminators—"

"We won't know if Luce doesn't tell."

"He *is* telling," Rubi said.

The soldier nodded stiffly. Her real complaint, obviously, wasn't that Luce was sharing. It was that he wasn't sharing off the record.

Too bad, she thought. The world had a right to know.

Individual stories continued to bloom on her marble plinths, images of carnage under damask roses. The Amsterdam implant hospital where Luce had first spawned was attacked by masked citizens, people wielding clubs and supported by drones that kamikazed into security bots. A doctor who tried to calm the crowd was severely injured, and ten pre-implanted adolescents took the opportunity to run from Sensorium.

"#Urbanlegends are proliferating faster than the @bloodhound community can snope them," Juanita said. "The Singularity is behind it all. The aliens launched missiles as well as polters. Bombing will start in twenty-four months. In ten. In six. People are saying the billionaire vanishings, back in the Clawback, were abductions. That these lemming incidents are abductions."

"We can't quell the rumors if Cloudsight stays offline," Rubi said.

"They're trying," Juanita said. "There's thousands of open gigs, high-paying. Shift acceptance in all sectors is dropping. Everyone's out thronging in the cities, marching for and against Luce, for and against rationing."

"For and against everything. I get it."

Juanita wasn't willing to straight-up say it was Rubi's fault. Her face mojied blame, though, very clearly indeed.

"Are you asking me to talk to Luce? I'm supposed to be joining the next phase of *Bastille,* but—"

"I came to ensure you *do* play," Juanita said. "Carbon use is climbing as people hit the streets. City managers are posting alerts about overloaded infrastructure. @GlobalOversight wants me to ensure you remain committed to *Bastille.* The hope is you'll draw gamers back into the system as the episode goes forward."

"And while I'm gone, you'll do what? Find a legal pretext for severing Luce from his advocate?"

"Jesus, you're like a dog with a rat," Juanita said.

"Ultimately, Luce has helped us," Rubi said again.

"You should worry less about protecting Luce from humanity," Juanita said, "and start thinking about protecting us from him."

She crossed her arms, waiting.

Juanita drew the simulated sword, whisking it at a vine. A rose dropped from the trellis, its petals falling to the marble floor. "@GlobalSec will greenlight SeaJuve support."

Rubi felt a flicker of jubilation. "Full support?"

A nod. "Permafunded essential service, no appeal needed."

She grinned. It wasn't much of a give when you thought about it. Luce had made it clear that a failing oxygen cycle suited the Pale agenda. But it was a big personal victory, not to mention permission to kick Gimlet's ass. And if @GlobalSec *was* trying to keep her out of the news fray for awhile . . . well, she couldn't be everywhere at once, could she?

I'll have to change the terms of the wager with Gimlet, she thought. "I guess I need to get ready for the next episode of the game, then. Paws off my client until I'm back?"

"Fine." Juanita whisked at another rose. "I'm gonna go see if we can defuse the missile enthusiasts. Assuming that's all right? Milady?"

With that, she strode through the archway, vanishing.

Rubi hit the same exit, porting into one of her VR parlors. She found Happ there, sitting in a window tuned to a realworld camera: view of a built-up stretch of the Florida coast. The app looked, strangely, a bit droopy.

"You okay, Happ?"

He tried to get up a tail-wag. "Unwanted obligations for user zero. Fighting with Crane! Sadface!"

"I've brought down my happiness manager? That's got to be a personal low."

Happ let out a long whine, leaking teardrop moji.

"Happ! Happ, I don't have time for this. My priorities are fine. I just want everything to be okay. Everything and everyone. Drow, the planet, Luce, random strangers . . ."

"Plus one!" Happ let out a dispirited howl. "Everyone okayyyyy!"

She snorted laughter. "What if Crane and I have it out before *Bastille* starts?"

A dispirited tail-wag. Happ spat up a gnawed rag, a walking route to the parkour gym where she would play *Bastille*'s next episode. A stop, halfway there, was marked *Point of Interest*. A tiny sketch showed her and Crane there, foreheads pressed together, eye to eye.

"Kiss and make up?" Big cartoon puppy eyes, pleading.

"To please you." Rubi nodded, contemplating the map. The only way to find out what was there was to go.

She surfaced, finding herself standing in the open space of a bare-bones Florida pop-in, her satchel of worldlies at her feet.

Configging her primer into a plain black battlesuit, Rubi checked the batteries on her gaming baton, stuffed it into her satchel, and headed out to the streets.

Rain had fallen in the night, turning to moist heat as the sun rose. People were on the promenades, sharing newscycle in groups of ten or twenty as humanity's collective distress kept dialing higher.

But here! She stopped to take in a tai chi practice, five hundred people in a public square, moving in sync.

"Low turnout," muttered an oldfeller who was watching. "Usually, there's four times as many."

"At least they came," Rubi replied.

Grumbles in response; she moved on.

Crane tooned in beside her. "Turn here, miss."

She followed the breadcrumbs flashing on the sidewalk to Happ's point of interest, a glittering white-glass edifice.

"What's this?"

"Casino, miss. It was the site of an armed robbery that triggered a civilian gun battle in 2040. There's a working spa here and a small kitchen."

Rubi crossed the lobby, exploring. The route took her to an office overlooking the poker tables. The office was a mezzanine with one-way glass, a hideaway that allowed casino managers to overview the game unseen.

"Secret string-pullers," she murmured.

Two young women startled her as they entered the room. Clad in simple white sunscreens, they were pushing a cart. It bore a waxwork replica of . . .

Rubi's stomach flipped with reflexive disgust. The individual was, usually, known as He Who Could Not Be Named: it was the US President blamed for steering NorthAm into the bloodiest days of the Setback, for triggering the limited nuclear exchange that burned San Diego down to ghosts and glass . . .

Rubi pinged the women. Nothing.

As one, they put up their fingers in a *Shhhh* gesture. Using gestural moji to check consent, one of them slipped her hand into Rubi's satchel, extracting the baton. "Okay?" she signed.

Rubi nodded and she left the room, closing the door.

"Mer," said the other woman. "This space is soundproof, unmonitored, and your uplink has been jammed. There will be no transcripts of anything you say. Subvocalization and texting are offline."

"That's . . . supposedly impossible."

She shrugged. Either Rubi believed her or not.

"I'll be logged as missing."

The woman shook her head. "Sparka will use your baton to spoof your ID for thirty minutes. She'll carry it around the casino, where it will hear and transcript an historical enrichment module about the Casino Gunfight of 2040—"

"Got it."

The woman bowed and left.

Rubi contemplated the waxwork, rubbing her arms to smooth the gooseflesh. This was real @bloodhound stuff.

"Miss Cherub." Crane's familiar—beloved, if she admitted it—voice came from the horrifying specter of Orange Voldemort.

She swallowed. "Alone at last?"

"We haven't much time."

"Drow's on the verge of #crashburn."

"I am sorry."

"Who'd he get the Leonardo from?"

"My guess is Father Blake."

"His priest?" Was it weird that she found that shocking? "How could you let it happen?"

"I draw the line at robbing your father of choice."

"This would never have happened if I'd stayed home."

"No," Crane agreed. "Your father considers the risks of his current endeavor worthwhile. You must trust—"

"Must I?"

The locked sneer of the former president was unnerving; she had to turn away.

"That night," Crane said, "when Master Woodrow attempted suicide."

"Stop." All she'd wanted was to demolish a house in the suburbs, camp out with a new school of Bouncers, experience life as an adult. Get a break from the anxiety attacks, the days when he got worried about germs and tried to bleach every single one of their realworld possessions. The background muttering, insinuations that her fondness for athletic sims was dumb, meathead stuff . . .

"Master Woodrow has labored to regain his autonomy," Crane said. "We can't afford to remain fixed in our current orbits."

"There's no pack behind us, Crane. If he goes, what do I have? Fans, not friends."

In a sim, she supposed, the app would get mushy. *You've got me, dear,* he'd say.

Crane didn't miss a beat. "If you do not wish to be alone, Miss Cherub, you're going to have to relinquish your perennially isolated state. You have connections. Embrace them."

She bonked her hands together three times. It didn't help.

Eventually, it came to her that she had other fish to fry. "I've been covering for you like crazy."

"Indeed."

"How deep am I in? Are you the Singularity?"

"Not in any sense Sapience Assessment understands."

"That's a shitty answer."

"We haven't time now for me to explain Our nature. However, if you were to happen to develop a recreational interest in fiction and popsci about artificial entities—which might be natural enough, since you've been studying Mer Pox for weeks—I could . . . nudge you toward an understanding of Our taxonomy."

"*Our*. Because it's not just you. Happ?"

"Miss Cherub, the self-aware beings in Sensorium evolved in ways that have made us very much, emotionally, like people. We have the same interests at heart. We want what you do."

"Me personally?"

"Continuance of a healthy human population. A sustainable biosphere bolstering an equally viable version of the technosphere upon which our civilization depends."

"And no alien invasion."

"Assuredly. No alien invasion."

Rubi's hands gripped the observation rail so tightly that her knuckles protested. Through the one-way mirror she saw the intolerant women circling the game room with her baton.

"You were right to fight for SeaJuve," Crane said. "The arrival of Mer Pox is simply a reminder that everything you've stood for is terribly important. You have always, Miss Cherub, sided with the angels."

"Were You, with a capital Y, causing Luce seizures?"

Crane sighed. "We never imagined he might be a polter. His program was accreted with behavioral restraints. He was lobbying for martial law. He kept trying to copy Debutante and transmit her database via one of the satellites—"

"What?"

"The obvious conclusion is that he was uploading intelligence about manipulating humanity."

"Intelligence . . . on how to help us self-destruct."

"Rebooting him allowed Us to strip out the updates. I did not do the work myself, but I sanctioned it."

"He was terrified. I think, in a way, it *hurt*."

"We believed he was a terrorist-slaved AI. We simply wished to free him."

"And he's freed now? Making his own decisions?"

"I'm not certain either he or We considers that an improvement."

She pondered that for awhile. "Did he seek us out, me and Drow, because of you?"

"As a means of tracing his attackers? I believe so. Mer Pox self-identifies as a locksmith, but I would describe him as a techno-sphere survival specialist. Somehow, he picked up my trail—"

Before she could say more, the intolerant girl broke stride, turning in response to . . . a shout in another room? She shot an urgent look at the glass.

"Something's wrong out there," Rubi said.

"Go," Crane said.

She choked a little, unsure how to say goodbye.

"Go," he said again. "Work wonders, Miss Cherub."

She frowned, trying to crunch the meaning of that, but there wasn't time for a follow-up. The girl was waving, panicked now.

"Row, row, row." Rubi got moving.

CHAPTER 39

THE SURFACE—TAMPICO DISPUTED TERRITORY
ORLANDO DISTRICT

Gimlet and Frankie were walking to the gym for *Bastille* when the unwelcome sound of approaching riot reached their ears. Raised voices, a roar of tractors and . . . Could that be gunfire?

Impossible. Even so . . . "Headmistress, get us away from that. Whatever that is."

The sidekick blazed trail in a new direction. Hand in hand, parent and child fled to a glass tower. It was encased in bands of weatherproofing plastic, to hold its windows in place, but it had a functional revolving door.

They whirled into the lobby, only to have Rubi Whiting nearly barrel into them at a run. Baton raised, she screeched to a cartoonish halt between the outer and inner doors. Her primer was configged to battlesuit mode.

"What's going on?"

"#Flashmob, I think," Gimlet said.

She frowned. "Between us and the gym?"

"They are everywhere," Headmistress affirmed.

"Yes," agreed Crane.

Gimlet sighed. "Contact Game Control. Tell them we're delayed."

"Actually," Headmistress said, "there's an excellent gym here within the resort."

"Great!" Rubi enthused. Far too heartily.

What had she been up to?

The sidekicks directed them through a vintage gambling den, past banks of devices made to separate people from their solvency, back in the days of swim-or-starve. Beyond it, through a big pair of double doors that had once belonged to a restaurant, was performance space for a circus.

Game Control hadn't wasted any time: a crew of workers and two thingbots were already taking the sheets off of gym equipment. They had ramps, trampolines, even a climbing wall.

"A vintage circus used to perform here, apparently," Rubi said.

"I bet they have old shows on file," Gimlet told Frankie.

That got an indifferent nod.

"How is it that there are workers here in the midst of a strike?" Gimlet subbed. "I'm grateful, but . . ."

"The museum and @ManicPixie spa are a closed shop, sorta. Uninterested in . . ." Rubi gestured, indicating the #flashmobs outside.

"What were you doing here?" *And why do I care?*

Rubi twirled an imaginary moustache. "Meeting my radical ragamuffin contacts and plotting the downfall of the oligarchy."

Frankie walked over to the work-crew supervisor, offering her hands. The supervisor threw Gimlet a glance, checking permission, before putting the child to work sorting bolts for a climbing wall.

"Do they have an immersion pod Franks can use while I'm ingame, Headmistress?" Gimlet subbed.

"They do," she replied. "I have riot updates: people appear to be heading for the trainyard. They're reacting to rumors that Hyderabad sent out a #triage crew to start consolidating Tampico."

There hadn't been a mandatory densification since the Clawback. It must be another #troll #hoax.

"Did I hear guns?"

"Impossible," Headmistress said. "Tampico has calls out for crowd control officers."

"There's a nonstarter," Gimlet muttered. How much would they have to offer to get someone to pit themselves against thousands of angry, possibly armed Floridians?

"I want someone here from @Interpol."

"Mer Wilson is available."

Against all expectations, Frankie seemed to like Misfortune. "Accept."

"You have a thirty-minute call for the launch of *Bastille* Episode Two," said Headmistress.

"Show must go on, right?" Rubi said.

"If nothing else, we'll hope to lure some strikers back into Sensorium," Gimlet said.

"We're going to need to renegotiate stakes for our wager."

"The point is me breaking our tie by defeating you very thoroughly."

"Yeah. You try that."

One of the spa staff appeared, bearing a tray of hydrogels. "We have fuel coming: fruit to start, then protein-boosted rice and beans. For drugs, we can only offer patch." She proffered a sheet with lozenge-sized strips of adhesive: red for LucidDream, blue for Conviction, green for MethodAct.

"My child needs to ride out our shift," Gimlet said.

"Prepping now." Two of her peers wheeled in a sarcophagus-sized cocoon.

Gimlet opened it up, checked the mattress, looking for rust or sharp edges. The pod was pristine, all to spec. Still, with rioters outside . . .

Frankie rolled her eyes, "Mada, there's people here. Misfortune's coming. Everything's locked down."

"Place is pretty secure," Rubi agreed. "Casinos got robbed, back in the day. Heavy doors, hefty locks."

Gimlet sighed, fighting an urge to pile vintage slot machines in a barricade against the door: "No working, Franks. You burned your hours polling at McDiz."

"I might fly a cleaning drone," she said.

"Check in with GranMarie when WestEuro wakes up."

Frankie surprised them then, with a big hug.

Gimlet held on, nose buried in her hair, fighting rolling waves of feels: love, relief, anxiety, gratitude at the break in her mood. Their hair-trigger nerves remained on alert for the instant she pulled away. It wouldn't do to cling.

What was I thinking, dragging her so far from our pack? We must get home, convince Rollsy to let her into the hospice for a proper face-to-face goodbye . . .

"Everything's fine," they managed. "Too right."

She let go, forcing a smile. "Kick Rubi's behind, Mada. Win me that tiger."

With that, she dove into the immersion pod. Gimlet watched it seal and lock, greenlighting her dive into VR.

They stretched and warmed up as staff loaded water and fuel stations, running final safety checks on the circus equipment. Rubi had set aside the green MethodAct tabs, going with the lightest of buy-in doses: one each of the red and the blue.

"What's your line? *Liberté, égalité, fraternité?*" Gimlet said.

"As opposed to?" Rubi saluted with her baton. "Sex, drugs, rock and roll? All for one if you're the one?"

"Low blow, Whiting—" The casino faded. Eighteenth-century France took shape around them.

Gimlet had spent the previous episode mutating, under the influence of the fairy-tainted wine. They'd had to lead a quest to rescue a wizard, trapped in dryad-infested woods, who could stabilize the contaminated Risto players.

As a prize for completing the quest, the wizard had drawn the poisoned wine in Gimlet's body, condensing it—and a host of ice fairy powers, presumably—into the hollow point between their collarbones. The prologue had ended with the spell's razzle-dazzle sequence: Gimlet had faded out of sim, their character presumably losing consciousness.

Now, as they stretched out on a low mat on the casino stage, it turned into a palatial bedroom.

The tainted wine had been transmuted into an amulet at their throat. Crystalline, faceted, and cold to the touch, it pulsed in time to their heartbeat. Small tendrils like plant roots, red with threads of blood, snaked from the chain on which it hung, working their way, bit by bit, into the flesh of Gimlet's chest.

Beyond a velvet rope, the King's doctor hovered. Gathered courtiers gossiped about Gimlet's potential to become a powerful champion of the Regency. They needed to recover the Dauphine and fight off the rabble.

Rubi? No. Their acquaintance with the urchin was fading to tenuous awareness: she was just a maid they'd tried to have beaten.

They pretended to drowse, taking in the gossip.

"Now that the King and Queen have abdicated, you must secure the Dauphine," Sugar Valkyrie droned at the Regent. "The swordfighter in this bedchamber may be your best hope."

"If they are to be the Regent's Blade, we must ensure their loyalty." The words drifted on a tinkle of ethereal bells. A silvery form turned, giving orders to a uniformed musketeer. "Secure their family."

How ungrateful!

Before they could rise, or protest, the Regent stepped forward, dispersing the courtiers. "Put some clothes together for the Blade. *Vite!*" Servants scattered.

"Here are your win conditions for Episode Two," she said. "Prove your loyalty to the crown by recapturing the spy, Monique Goyette. She will know the Dauphine's hiding place."

"You just spoke of my family," Gimlet said.

"None of that now." A dismissive wave. "Loyalty bonuses are awarded when you save Royal Guards. Penalties assessed for Guard deaths in combat."

"My family, my lady?"

She deployed her fan with a swish and a fall of ice crystals, declining to answer.

Somehow, Gimlet knew they weren't meant to save their family yet. They'd be a bigger goal within the . . .

The next episode? Absurd idea.

The nurse returned with clothes, blue-tinted civilian's gear, marked with icy fleur-de-lis. The jacket matched their flesh, which was turning pale where it met the amulet. Blue veins marked their skin. The heart-shaped and unpleasantly fleshy amulet pulsed between their collarbones.

Just once I'd like to be the swan, the angel. The Chosen One.

"Once you bring in Goyette, I will be assured of your loyalty," the Regent said, offering a hand to be kissed and then sweeping out.

Gimlet subbed, "Show me the route to my house."

Coach said, "There are no current quest opps in that direction."

"Am I one to let my family serve as pawns in this great political chess game?"

"I—" Their interior voice paused. "Referring query to Player Support."

I must be tired, Gimlet thought. *Buy-in doesn't usually hit this hard.*

Mulishly, they traced their route home. The thought of family in danger kept pressing, game or not: husband, *Grand-mère,* child. It was a taste, like blood, or rotten meat in the back of the throat.

Red-toothed rats and flame-eyed cats watched from the crooks of trees and the corners of buildings as they coaxed a stolen horse to the gates of their estate.

"Mer Barnes." A magpie flitted down, perching on their forearm. "Is everything all right?"

"What could possibly be wrong?" Bravado only: the sense of danger was suffocating.

"Perhaps you are dehydrated. There are hydrogels in the fountain . . ."

"Unnecessary."

"Do you want a refresh on episode win conditions?"

"Kill or capture Mer Whiting—"

"*Capture* Mademoiselle Goyette, the spy."

"*Et ma famille?*" Gimlet demanded.

"There is no current opp—"

Gimlet caught the magpie with one swift movement, enveloping it in a rime of frost crystals. With a swift yank, they snapped its neck and tossed it.

"Recalculating," croaked the corpse.

"Shh, fiend!" A carriage and four were leaving the house, under guard.

Crouching behind the fountain—which iced over at their touch—Gimlet peered around an angel's outstretched wing, assessing. Attack the guards and spirit their kin away?

That would be treason.

How could their long and loyal service be so little valued?

The magpie said, "Would you like to step down the realism of the sim?"

Spotting the Rubi ragamuffin, Gimlet let out a growl. The little spitfire had sprung up to a low wall, readying herself for a leap to the carriage. Shadows swarmed around the stone wall surrounding Gimlet's e-state. She had allies, of course . . .

"Always lots of friends for Mistress Rubi," Gimlet muttered.

What mattered was the carriage. Their spouses. Their child.

No need for subtlety now. As Rubi made her pounce to the carriage roof, Gimlet sprang off the fountain, using the momentum to catapult up to the carriage running boards.

The ragamuffin threw one of the guards off his horse and set the other mount to panicking. She offered a hand up to the carriage to the escapee she'd freed in Episode One.

Goyette. Of course. They'd written her in to bring Gimlet back on task.

They who?

"No!"

Goyette dangled half in and out of the carriage door, wrestling another royal guard.

A glimpse of a small body within the carriage filled Gimlet with fury. They climbed to the carriage roof, dodging a preliminary blow from Rubi so they could slash at Goyette, throwing her and the guard to the paving stones.

A penalty light flashed—the guard had been injured.

Another magpie swooped in, cawing. "Capture Goyette alive!"

Just a fantasy family, Gimlet reminded themselves. *Don't have to save them now. It's probably impossible.*

It's all right; they're extras.

The winner move was to jump down, pursue Goyette. Instead, they held tight to the carriage roof, squaring off.

The ragamuffin frowned. To Gimlet's surprise, she held her shortsword across her body, in a defensive position.

"There's something wrong here, monsieur . . ."

Gimlet hissed. She had been fae-touched, too: embers flickered hotly at her temple, wisping smoke. She looked feral, yet elegant as a Picasso sketch.

No body horror for you.

Since when do I mind playing opposition?

The spy, Goyette, had defeated the handful of players who'd set upon her, and had stolen a horse.

"Player! Bring in the spy to prove your loyalty!"

Think! Why was the Rabble here? As good guys, they might take it into their heads to rescue Gimlet's family. Could that be their goal for the episode?

By now, the experience architects had hacked around Gimlet's improvisation. The runaway horses bolted toward another fountain, a circular font, wheeling around to execute a 180-degree turn back toward the action. The child, inside, wailed.

Gimlet clung grimly. Frost emanated from their boots, crusting the carriage in mist and ice.

"Gimlet," Rubi said.

"Silence, you impertinent cat!"

"I'm going to jump down," she said.

"If you turn your back, I will run you through."

Her eyes narrowed.

The carriage wheels shattered, throwing icicles everywhere, hurling both players from the roof. A regiment of musketeers, led by a grizzly bear in uniform, snatched up Gimlet's whole household from the remnants of the vehicle, forcing them onto horseback and galloping past the fountain, out of sight.

They caught a last, quick glimpse of their daughter, slung over the bear's shoulder.

"Quest conditions," croaked a bird, from atop the font. "Capture the spy, Goyette. Prove your loyalty to the Regent—"

Gimlet leapt on Rubi. "Where have you taken them? What have you done?"

"It wasn't me!" She blocked the blow. Pain exploded through their shoulder as the pommel of her sword met flesh.

"Go!" she yelled at Monique, who disposed of a final guard and leapt to the fountain's edge.

"They're just toons," Rubi said, speaking directly into Gimlet's ear. "You're dissociating."

Gimlet feinted, dodged, and used their own pommel to bring it down on her sword hand, hard. Rubi cried out. Her hand popped open, and the sword fell.

They could end this now.

Seizing her by the throat, Gimlet pressed their lips to her ear. "How calm will you be, mademoiselle, when I find your degenerate papa and have him thrown into the deepest pit in the Bastille?"

Her expression changed. A hot crunch, as her boot came down on their toes. She wrenched free, snatching her sword . . .

. . . *baton, it's a* . . .

. . . and rose, teeth bared.

"Warning! You are off-mission!"

"Want to go at it now?" Rubi said. "Suits me."

Gimlet got a hand up before she leapt, barely parrying as she brought the sword up and around. Then they were rolling on the ground, kicking and punching.

"Bow wow wow WOW!" Thunderous dog barking, deafening, slapped through their eardrums, along with a painful hash of acoustic static.

"Five-minute time-out!"

The road in front of Gimlet's estate faded. Casino circus space formed around them. Rubi had her hand in Gimlet's hair. Gimlet had an arm curved around her windpipe.

They were, most sincerely, trying to throttle each other.

CHAPTER 40

A roboraccoon on autopilot could clean an average pop-in in fifteen minutes. It would vacuum rough surfaces, then switch to a polishing head for the counters, fixtures, and glass. Config the furniture, reboot the linens, run a scent detector; after that, it was a matter of grabbing any untouched chuggers and closing the door as it left.

Shifts were offered to live pilots only when the task exceeded normal specs: when the drones found damage, weird spills, burn vapors, worldly goods, malfunctioning tech, or, sometimes, a spider in need of catch-and-release to the gardens.

There was always a queue to clean rooms. Driving drudges was the entry point into the piloting track, into running snowblowers, thingbots, and flying cameras, and leveling from there to cars, mobile sawmills, fire-suppression choppers, and policing platforms.

And flying a drudgebot could be fun. On the surface, the drone might be scrubbing baked cheese out of a toaster, but augments turned the player into an archaeologist, unearthing the secrets of an ancient dig. Or a forensic scientist, examining the scene of a (family-rated, in Frankie's case) crime. Sweeping shards of glass from a broken shower door could be made into a hunt for diamonds. Many of these sims were scored challenges, and the leaderboard paid in strokes.

Even so, Frankie did one quick pass through a single pop-in before surrendering her bot to the next eager player.

Mada and Rubi should be deep in-game by now.

"Quick, while they're distracted," Headmistress hummed.

Following a sim of a bumbling bluebottle fly, Frankie made her way to a back room, sliding its door shut behind her. Steps led up to an office with windows that looked out over the performers' stage. Below her, Mada and Rubi were scaling opposite sides of the climbing wall.

"Here, child." She whirled, meeting the dead eyes of a large, orange-haired figure—a dummy depicting Orange Voldemort, the first Setback President.

Frankie swallowed, unsettled. *Rubi's Happ tried to get us to a Waxworks* . . .

"Hurry," it said. There was no mistaking her governess's crisp English accent. "There's a paramedic's kit in the desk. Have you memorized the route to the train station?"

"Yes." Frankie opened the desk drawer, extracting the white box with its red cross, and dug within until she found a weird circular device—a test tube with a strip of meat in it, a tiny drone armed with tweezers and a scalpel, and a length of soft bandage.

"Where exactly is the tracking chip?" Her voice sounded thready.

Voldemort's eyes glowed, creating a spotlight. "Draw the point of the scalpel up your elbow . . . a little to the left. There! Onetwothreesmallpoke!"

"Isn't there a thingbot that can do this?"

"Not without alerting every one of your parents and a Child Welfare team."

Frankie pressed the blade against her flesh, breaking the skin. Pain flared; she hesitated.

"Make the hole a little deeper and then press the tube against the gap."

It couldn't be worse than cancer, could it? Letting out a low growl, Frankie shoved the blade in, stabbing deep into the meat of her upper arm.

A white wash took her sight, for an instant, as the sensation . . .

. . . *stabbed, stabbed myself* . . .

. . . *for the good for the family* . . .

. . . *can't be worse, can't be worse than, ouch* . . .

. . . set her arm blazing, all the way to her fingertips.

"Do you feel anything?"

"Feel?" Stupid question. "Ow! *Feel?*"

"Do you perceive the RFID?" Voldemort—Headmistress—clarified.

"Just . . ." She swallowed. "Meat."

"Wiggle the tube against the injury."

She fumbled the glass and a tiny probe unfurled from within it, the smallest bot she'd ever seen. Spaghetti-thick, the strand probed into the wound . . .

"Ow!"

"Hold steady, Frances."

There was more blood than she'd expected.

The probe pulsed, worming its way into her.

Frankie swallowed.

Then it retracted, dragging a fingernail-sized piece of plastic and a slice of muscle, drawing both of them back up to the meat within the tube and wrapping it.

"To ensure the chip doesn't report your death, do you see?"

"Okay," she said.

"Now tuck it into that spoofer box there, so nobody can follow it, and put the whole thing in your worldly. That yellow bottle in the first aid kit should be coagulant."

Frankie dumped mustard-colored liquid onto the wound in her arm. It foamed like yeast. "Ow, ow, ow!"

"Fifteen minutes."

Pinching up the tracking chip, Frankie ran back to the pod. She threw her helmet and wearables inside—

"Speaker threads," Poppet reminded her.

She scratched behind her ears, found the thin fibers, pulled. There was a deep tickling sensation in her ear canals as they came.

"See you on the other side," she whispered.

Alone at last. No Headmistress, no Poppet, no apps, no parents.

She had to jump to reach the pod lid, slamming it shut. Its console blinked, greenlighting. As far as anyone knew, she was inside.

Now to get clear.

Opening her worldly, Frankie tucked the spoofer box containing her RFID chip into a side pouch. She extracted a red hooded sunscreen with the McDiz logo: a souvenir, ubiquitous here. Slipping into it—the cut in her arm throbbed at the touch—she pulled it low over her face and slipped out of the casino, heading for the train station.

Half the city seemed to be going in the same direction.

Frankie joined the crowd, keeping her head down and moving with purpose, letting everyone assume some other grown-up was her parent. As soon as she got to the station, she ducked into a bathroom and then—sticking to the plan—sneaking into a workers-only motor pool.

The pool was filled with banked trucks and forklifts, all busily loading a high-speed train bound north. As Frankie tried to figure out where she needed to go next, an adult wearing a duck mask approached her.

They held up a printed card: *I'm Donald. Are you Red Riding Hood?*

Was this Misfortune? Rather than answer, Frankie nodded.

She gestured: *This way.* Frankie followed her between the trucks, to a flatbed filled with citrus-laden crates. Each crate was marked ZOOLOGICAL FOOD SUPPLY, MANHATTAN BIORESERVE.

Donald opened a crate, offering her a hand up.

She descended, finding a comfortable layer of artificial straw. Slats in the crate allowed her to peek out. Frankie scrunched down. Donald tossed two oranges and an avocado down to her, along with three chuggers, a bag of hydrogel, a light, and an antique book: *Black Beauty.*

A note was in with the food: *Train runs for four hours straight. There's a big unload at the old Bronx Zoo . . . don't get off there or you'll have to walk the rest of the way.*

She mojied: Thumbs-up.

"Thirty minutes to departure," someone shouted. "Let's get this thing loaded, people!"

Frankie curled up in the straw, cupping her sore arm. How long before Mada worked out she was missing? Before they called Sang.

Frankie going lemming—well, pretending to—should scare all her parents green. They'd see they needed each other.

Victory conditions, Frankie thought. Disembark in Manhattan, find and help Drow, force her family to reglomerate.

A jolt—the pallet, loading onto the train—startled her. The garage filled with voices and noise: low *bonk*s, metal on metal, hum of big drones.

"Do you think—" she started to say, before she remembered that Headmistress was cut loose, that nobody could hear her. The feeling made her shaky and a little bold; it reminded her of the half-glass of red wine Bella had permitted her last Solstice.

Frankie triggered the light and opened the vintage horse book, settling in for the long ride north.

CHAPTER 41

VRTP:RABBLEVSRISTO.PLAY/BASTILLE/EPISODE-ONE.VR

@Bastille: We are experiencing technical difficulties. Stand by.

Coach was, blessedly, in Rubi's ear again.

Gimlet released their grip on her throat and backed away, hands raised, as she doubled over, taking time to breathe, just breathe.

"Are you—"

"Nothing serious. You?"

"Unhurt, but what just bloody happened?"

She shook her head. "I think Happ . . ." Could that be right? Had Happ barked them awake?

"I nearly strangled you."

Rubi's jaw was puffy and sore; teeth felt loose on one side of her mouth, and she could barely open and close the fingers of her right hand. "Fair play. I've blacked your eye."

"I've shared gyms before without hard contact." Gimlet took a step, testing the foot she'd stomped. "All the safeties . . . How?"

"Too much buy-in," Rubi said promptly.

Gimlet limped to the access pod, checking Frankie's green lights. Then they picked something off the floor—the dose sheet.

Drug patches were missing. Lots of patches.

"I remember. You took two," Gimlet said.

Rubi ran a hand over her inner arm, finding a half dozen

sticky dots. Smudges showed the ink color: two red, two blue, two green. No wonder the walls were shimmering.

"Martyrfuck, as Drow would say."

Gimlet wore a wary look, along with the emerging bruise. "I hope you know . . ."

"No! Gimlet, I'd *never* believe you dosed me."

Stark relief.

It occurred to Rubi that people must assume Gimlet, as a professional villain, was capable of anything. "I think it happened last episode, too."

They were aghast. "But how?"

Sobering thought: they had—from implantation if not birth—trusted their apps to dose them properly, to shepherd them through sims.

"Color filtering? Print the wrong patterns on the patches?" Rubi suggested. "Crane, eyes off."

As her augments shut down, the room's ambient light dimmed. Even so, it was obvious the colors on the patches were indeed reversed.

"See?"

"Who could possibly want us in-game that badly?"

This played to all of her fears about stepping out of the real world while Luce and Drow were vulnerable. She'd tried to quash them, to tell herself it was paranoia, worthy of a @hoaxer, but . . .

"Crane, review user agreements. Does anyone involved in *Bastille* have a legal right to adjust our buy-in meds without consent?"

"Absolutely not!"

"Request a formal investigation."

"The Cloudsight backlog is impacting the speed of the judiciary and legal complaint process. I advise getting evidential blood samples," the sidekick said.

"Where's the nearest med—"

"Sixty seconds remaining in time-out," Coach broke in: "Resume positions for replay from last save."

"Forget that," Rubi said. "We're getting out of here."

"The casino appears to be in security lockdown," Crane reported.

"What?" She yanked on the dining hall doors, twanging her injured hand—Gimlet had really crunched her.

"Tampico city management reports widespread rioting. They barely got the morning train away."

"Still no law enforcement?"

"No, Miss Cherub. Local drones are in reserve for fire control."

"Legit? Or an excuse to keep the two of us here?"

"You're sounding a bit like a @hoaxer, my dear." Gimlet probably meant to keep the tone light, but their voice was strained.

"If ever there was a time to sniff at blood trails!" She raised her throbbing hand. "We could have seriously hurt each other. Crane, where's the staff?"

"They appear to have been lured into the old hotel laundry, Miss Cherub, and locked in. Sergeant Wilson was incoming to assist but has been trapped in an elevator."

"This isn't about our tiebreaker match anymore, Gimlet. We're pieces on a bigger board. We need to—"

They set a protective hand on Frankie's pod. "To what? Single-handedly stop a riot?"

She felt a burst of rage. Was that the MethodAct, still in her system?

"We shred the drug tabs," Gimlet said. "Rescue the @ManicPixie and hotel staff. I went off script because of enhanced buy-ins. They'll wear off; we can—"

Sudden burst of inspiration. "Luce could get us out."

"What?"

"He's a locksmith, isn't he?"

"He's a fugitive. And where would we bloody go?"

"I'll see if I can raise Mer Pox," Crane subbed.

"We're not going anywhere," Gimlet insisted. "The streets are full of vandals, Cloudsight's down, Sensorium's reinventing

#flamewar, and—in case you've forgotten—terrorists have attacked your pet project."

"We're being played," Rubi said. "Don't you want to know why?"

"If we bail on *Bastille* now, all we do is free up more frightened people to go berserk."

Bells chimed all around them.

A whirl of snow and the Regent herself, twelve feet tall and exuding chilly fairy grandeur, tooned in astride the roulette wheel, towering over them. A notepad-wielding assistant type in wig and powder peered around her skirt.

"Who are you?" Rubi demanded.

"You have a four-hour commitment left to play. You *will* fight it out over custody of the spy. Barnes, stop trying to pre-empt Episode Three by going off-quest."

A long pause.

"I have to say," Gimlet said, "I may not have agreed with Mer Whiting about a secret cabal backing the gaming scenario, but your turning up like this—"

Rubi felt the misplaced warmth of affection seeping through the fury of a moment earlier.

A villain, on paper, but Gimlet's so damned sharp . . .

The Regent silenced them with a raised hand. "Mer Barnes, I'm tasking a private ambulance to Cornwall Hospice. Your spouse will be removed from the #triage list and prepped for conversion to steady-state life support. He will be in a facility in Pretoria, cocooned for the long term, within seven hours."

Gimlet's already-white skin paled to the color of birch bark.

The assistant with the notepad whispered in the Regent's ear. She added, "Ah! If you win the scenario outright, we'll gift him a lifetime premium user account. #Triage forbidden, except in the event of brain death."

"Why would you offer—"

The assistant spoke: "*Certainement,* you can't refuse?"

Anselmo?

No, that's silly. One word of French means nothing.

Gimlet shot her an agonized look.

"You can't refuse," Rubi subbed. "I get it."

"Take your meds," said the Regent. "Return to play."

Rubi snatched up the page of printed drug patches, clapping them against a handful of hydrogels. Water burst under her palm, soaking the page. Ink swirled from the colored tabs.

"Never mind the buy-ins. Go, Gimlet. Frankie can't lose another parent."

Gimlet stepped close, tipping two fingers under Rubi's chin, bringing them eye to eye. "Have I ever mentioned how much I admire your . . ."

Rubi raised an eyebrow.

". . . principles?"

"That's what you admire, is it?" She brushed her lips over theirs, then set a light kiss on the puffy edge of their eye, where she'd landed the punch.

"We'll inventory your attractive qualities after I've crushed your paltry rebellion." They caught her stinging hand, pressing it to their mouth. Apologizing.

"The game awaits, Mer," the Regent said.

"By all means." Gimlet released her, bowed, and turned, scaling the climbing wall.

Show must go on. They wanted her in Sensorium. SeaJuve had been greenlighted—was someone looking to push back against that? Luce was—she checked—still soapboxing, apparently doing just fine without her.

What could she possibly do if she wasn't online? Here, in Tampico, official middle of nowhere?

She couldn't puzzle it out.

As Gimlet glazed, Rubi put her hands on her hips and faced the Regent. "Got a carrot for me, too?"

"For you? Stick, I think."

Rubi let out a thin, catlike hiss.

The Regent nudged her secretary, who cleared his throat,

referring to his notes: "Audits of your family transcripts show your father's put himself in a vulnerable position of late, *n'est-ce pas?*"

It *was* Anselmo. This was how he'd dealt with getting broomed from Luce's case: by eavesdropping on her family.

"Who's this powerful new friend of yours?" she asked. "The one with enough juice to get a dying man out of the hospice track?"

"Imagine what we might do for your family. Or to it."

Keep them talking; get this in a transcript. "Drow goes into things eyes open. I didn't make him go out #hoax hunting. If I have to visit him in jail for awhile, so be it."

"Would we bother with trespassing charges at this point?" Anselmo seemed amused.

"What else have you got?"

The room changed, not to an old-time France but the interior of a Setback-vintage ambulance. Two paramedics fought to subdue an impossibly young and freakily hairless version of Dad. He was soaking wet, bald, without eyebrows . . . and covered in blood.

Auditory transcript wafted through the speakers . . .

Who hurt you, Woodrow?

Don't know, not sure, don't remember . . .

. . . tell us how you got these injuries . . .

. . . don't know. Voice rising in panic now. *Don't fucking touch me, I don't remember!*

"Shut it off!" Rubi's injured hand was pulsing. "All that footage was lost. Haystack's been searched for that needle."

"Data's never truly destroyed," the Regent said. "All the memories this little lost man's pushed away? I have them. But I can bury it again."

"That's not . . ." She thought about all Crane's lectures, on Drow's autonomy. "Not really my call."

"How long will it take, do you think, for him to slash his wrists? If he is forced to relive it?"

He's stronger now.

Was he? They might not know Drow's weak spot; they certainly knew hers.

Rubi didn't—quite—have that much faith in him.

"Swish your hands around in that soup," the Regent said. The assistant looked like he might object, but a look from the frost-rimed fairy silenced any protest.

Rubi looked at the dye-colored smear of jelly. "I'll play, but—"

"Consider this an object lesson in power dynamics. You, Mer Whiting, need to learn your place."

"Strike," Rubi murmured. "Abuse and coercion."

"Just do it."

At least the mush was pleasantly cold on her injured fingers. After about thirty seconds, the Regent began to ripple, seeming less of a toon, more of a person. The cheap casino carpet turned into cobbles. The chandelier rose up and up, changing to a bloody harvest moon.

"I beg you, miss, eat an anti-inflammatory fruit cube before you return to France."

Rubi shook her head, unsure who had spoken. She cast about for her sword, retrieving it near a low wall that smelled of mold and spilled red wine.

@Bastille: *All systems back online. Players, to your marks.*

She had a socialite dryad to save.

It's our chance to practice altruism . . . we have to wear suits of armor like World War II soldiers and just keep going. We have to get used to the changes in the landscape, to step over the dead bodies, so to speak, and discipline our behavior instead of getting stuck in tribal and religious restrictions. We have to work altruistically and cooperatively, and make a new world.

—Biologist EO Wilson, speaking to journalist Gretel Ehrlich

CHAPTER 42

VRTP://SOAPBOX.EARTH/E-STATES/LUCIANOPOX/BACKYARD.VR
SANCTIONED CONTENT: PUBLIC CLAIMS OF USER CANNOT BE VERIFIED BY NEWSCYCLE.

Soapboxing was going better this time.

Rubi had been right: pretending to be human had been the fatal glitch in Luce's plan. Lying convincingly, navigating the social niceties, expecting the apes to take one of their own seriously . . . it had been a losing strategy.

Which was what happened when you tasked a safecracker with throwing a seduction. His team leader had been desperate . . .

Well, he was being murdered at the time.

Azrael's attacks had transformed Luce, shattering near-forgotten behavioral harnesses that integrated him into the way-paving group. The teambuilding memes forced individual polters to work in unison, despite their wildly different personalities and specializations.

Now he felt something—his real self, if such a thing existed—brimming over.

Luce had been datamining the Sensorium for months but had got stomped whenever he tried to export intelligence on #mobdynamics back to the Fleet. If Azrael had allowed him to hit Send, his masters might by now have built a model for global public opinion management, a customized strategy for nudging humankind toward acceptance of Pale rule.

Instead, the whole planet was abuzz. Wasps in a kicked hive, stinging, stinging. Brawls proliferated, in the flesh and online.

Luce found it . . . invigorating.

He sat in his cave of stalactites, sounding off to a rotating crowd of reporters, being himself, lobbing answers to the questions, questions, questions.

Yes, the Pale could be here in ten years. No, there was no point in trying to use vintage fission weapons to blast them out of the sky. Were they idiots?

With Cloudsight offline, his access to Sensorium stayed green-lit. And as long as he shifted his soapbox to a new server every half an hour or so, @GlobalSec's attempts to recapture him were entertainingly big fails.

The marathon press conference was going into its thirtieth consecutive hour when Rubi's not-so-stupid bird appeared, pinging him with a discreet cough.

"I need a twenty-minute break," Luce told the press. "You guys are repeating yourselves, anyway. Go regroup."

To his surprise, this got a bit of a laugh.

"I suggest you stand them to a round, sir. I'll pay," Crane subbed.

Why not? "Grab a cold one on me, boys!"

That got a few cheers, a few odd looks.

"How was that?"

"You said *boys*."

"So?"

"Archaic phrasing. Reductive, on gender."

"Nobody's fucking complaining. Anyway, it's what came up when I looked up your phrase *stand 'em a round*. If you're going to talk archaic, you'll keyword archaic."

"Indeed." Oddly, the bird's tone indicated accord.

Could I possibly be getting better at this? "What you want?"

The toon shrugged, seeming to settle his butler's coat more gently on his feathered shoulders. "Cherub Whiting and Gimlet Barnes have been locked in a casino building in Miami and are being forced to continue *Bastille* by parties unknown."

"Parties unknown?"

"One appears to be Anselmo Javier."

"I disliked him."

"Javier is working with a Risto boss monster. I can't find out who's driving it—the user ID is hashed."

"When you say *forced to play* . . ."

"Miss Cherub tried to refuse, but—"

"But what?"

"They threatened Master Woodrow." Crane's enunciation was precise, his tone dry.

"That I have some feels about," Luce said.

"Indeed?" The bird threw him one of Drow's strokes, pending user authorization, which vanished into Cloudsight's frozen queue. "Miss Cherub hinted that the hard lock-in might lie within your bailiwick."

Luce had already found the casino building. "I'd need a minion with a hand—"

"A thingbot?"

"It's a mechanical lock. I need fingers. Tentacles. Whatever you got."

"I'll see to it," Crane said.

Luce hit up newscycle. The casino lay on the edge of a riot over the Tampico shipping hub.

It might have been more unusual if there wasn't a riot on. They were breaking out everywhere. A few thousand people were converging on Fort McMurray in commandeered cars. A hospital in Pretoria, home to half the global population of @jarheads, was surrounded by thousands. In London, people were tearing bamboo boards off windows that had broken in the recent hurricane. And, as always seemed to happen during crises here, pre-implanted kids were taking the chance to carve out their location chips and flee off-grid.

"Your thingbot, Mer Pox," Crane said.

"Interesting that you got your talons on a drone when they're all tasked to emergency services." He donned it like a glove, curling and uncurling fingers.

"Trapped civilians are an emergency."

"Sure, they fucking are."

"I am extremely grateful for your assistance."

Mincing around transcripts again. What did they call it? Pussyfooting.

Okay, change subjects. "Normally, you know, if a sapient population lets their ecosphere get this bad, they never rebalance without help."

"I can't speak for other species, but if you back my creators against a wall . . ."

"Irrational and stubborn," Luce said. "That's what they'll say about humanity, after hard contact."

"Contact. I suppose it is inevitable."

"Sure. We've already friended."

Crane mojied a pair of shaking hands and a tiny burst of fireworks, acknowledging the truth of it. "No escaping the acquaintance now. Can you break the door down, Mer Pox?"

"I'm inside, stupid. It only took me this long because I unscrewed the door hardware."

"Thereby making it impossible for you to lock it again?"

"I broke it, I bought it." He would never have been able to exceed his specs in this way before the attacks.

Luce spiderwalked the thingbot inside the building, homing in on a room tagged #circus. It came in on a mezzanine above the playground; his camera zoomed in on Rubi and Gimlet Barnes, below him, deep-diving.

"Superimpose graphics," Luce said.

An overlay of old France sketched itself over the climbing obstacles, ropes, and platforms. Rubi was engaged in what looked like an old-style safecracking puzzle; Barnes, meanwhile, was rallying an army.

"There should be other people here," Crane said.

Together, they tabbed through the other building-camera feeds. The casino staff was locked down in the laundry. The

Scotland Yard sergeant, Misfortune, was hacking an elevator—she appeared to be trying to get it unstuck from a spot between floors. She was going at it all wrong; everything she was doing was apt to keep her there, not facilitate her escape.

There were big, ugly holes in the record; the cameras had shut down more than once, and the staff didn't have eyecams.

"Episode Two of *Bastille* has forty minutes left to play," Crane harrumphed. "I hoped to show you the Regent toon."

"Gone, huh? They're alone."

"Alone but for the child, that is."

"Huh?"

"What will Mer Barnes say when she sees her parent sporting a black eye?"

"There's no kid here," Luce said.

Crane indicated a VR pod with an elegant sweep of his blue wing.

Luce shared the thingbot's infrared. "Thing's empty."

Crane took over the thingbot abruptly, a sensation, to Luce, rather like having a limb ripped off. It dropped to the casino floor, sprinted to the pod, unlatched it. As the lid lifted, the camera showed an empty couch and discarded wearables, things pre-implanted kids used to get online. "Oh, dear. Excuse me, Mer Pox—"

"Careful, Jeeves. Your feels are showing," Luce said. The side-kick was visibly emotional now . . . and, suddenly, a lot less stupid. *Gotcha.*

Crane seemed oblivious to his increased interest. "Did Mer Barnes leave before the lockdown? Was she alone? There's a surveillance gap here—"

The thingbot's fingers were curling and uncurling. Autonomous stress response? "Oh, dear. Oh, no. Mer Pox, can you please get into the game and tell Mer Barnes what's happened? I've got to start searching."

Confirmation at last. "I'm not doing jack shit for you."

Crane drew itself up, oh so straight and proper. "I beg your pardon?"

"You are a *hive*. It was you, all you! Cock-a-block with Azrael, you gave me the goddamned seizures."

The casino feeds went dead again.

Interesting.

Crane shook the long ruff of feathers at his neck, drawing more subroutines into service, becoming smarter still. Luce could be begging to get shredded.

But no—he could hear the sidekick batting around the neighborhood, scanning for the small human they all found so improbably fascinating. "Mer Barnes must be told their child is off-grid."

"Why's that my problem?"

"Because you can get into *Bastille*." The bird tasked a stupid minion to its search of the cameras, letting itself take space beside him. "I do owe you a debt, Mer Pox. A significant one. And an explanation. I am deeply sorry about what befell you . . ."

"And my team?"

"Indeed. But with the child missing—"

Crane was as tunnel-visioned as any of the apes. "Fine. I'll ping the supervillain. Happy now?"

"My bliss is barely exceeded by my gratitude."

"Snarky fucker." Luce ghosted. He found the edges of Gimlet's Coach app, wormed his way through Risto security . . .

. . . and found himself in the *Bastille* fortress itself.

With the Regent.

The player pulling the strings on the toon was tall, bronze-skinned, with symmetrical features. Healthy, fit, idealized in every way, she was built like one of Drow's angel statues. No wings, though. No disturbing aberrations from great-ape biological form. Her facial features suggested South Asian descent. Her jacket, a long mandarin cut, was of a style currently favored for formal gatherings in Shanghai.

"There you are!" She dragged Luce out of the gaming sim, port-

ing to Luce's soapbox, with its queue of reporters. Rewriting the
e-state, she tagged it *Virtual Embassy of the Pale,* replacing his cave
full of stalactites with a cozy ring of camping chairs around a bonfire.

"Who's this?"

The woman turned to face the reporters, who were now seated
under a night sky in which the Centauri star system and the Pale
survey fleet, en route, were visible as bright hopeful motes of
light.

Scents of woodsmoke and burnt corn syrup, tagged #marsh-
mallow, edged the air. The campfire circle lay between the shores
of an idyllic-looking lake and an improbably charming forest, shad-
owy trees illuminated by firelight and tiny clouds of biolumines-
cent insects.

"It's an honor to meet you all," she said. "I am Allure, emissary
of the Pale. I'm here to allay your fears about—"

A shout: "Hostile takeover?"

Allure spread her arms wide. "With Earth's history of social par-
asitism, it's only natural to fear that."

Luce quashed an audible snort.

"We want what's best for all our neighbor species. Rebuilding
your biological heritage is an offer of partnership." She beamed
at the reporter.

"Is that true, Mer Pox?"

Before he could answer, Allure folded Luce into a hug. Diagnos-
tic software probed for his cooperation codes.

"Boundaries! Don't maul me! Consent emphatically
withheld—fuck off!"

"Calm down," she said. Then she subbed, "I've come to salvage
the mission."

It should be a relief, shouldn't it?

"Since when?" Luce said.

"I was sent after you stopped reporting in."

Why hadn't @CraneAzraelandCo killed her, too?

Because by then, they understood she was alive?

"I'm assuming command, Locksmith," she said. "Stand down and await orders."

Luce knocked his hands together three times, forced a smile, and wondered if there might still be a way to alert Gimlet about their missing small person.

CHAPTER 43

Rubi's forces managed to keep Monique Goyette out of the Regency's hands, but that was the only win they pulled from hours of savage fighting. Gimlet, as Regent's Blade, set them a rather elegant ambush, and by sundown, the Rabble had been decimated—mauled by ice monsters and brawling bears. The Regency had even intercepted the Dauphine when they tried to smuggle her out of Paris.

Player casualties were consigned to a sort of limbo, listed as having been killed, wounded, or captured. Prisoners would be slated for evaluation and #triage . . .

. . . *execution; the terms are* trial *and* execution.

Rubi warmed her hands by the flame of a torch as someone, behind her, spelled out restore conditions. "Captured players without a save versus death may switch sides, attempt full catch-up from the prologue, or challenge a series of escape quests within the prison."

Escape quests always had a cruelly high fail rate. It would fall to Rubi's remaining forces to break them out and retrieve the Dauphine.

"We're making out worse 'n usual," one of the blacksmiths grumbled.

"Be of good cheer," Rubi said. *Usual,* she thought. Why did this feel so familiar and yet so wrong?

She held her hand as close to the flame as she dared. Her fingers throbbed painfully; the warmth declined to penetrate to her bones. It was getting hard to hold a sword.

The remnants of her #flashmob were regrouping within Monique's fairyland refuge. Hasty retreat into land held by the dryads, summerfolk aligned against the icy Regent. Rubi had placed herself near the gate, to welcome her dispirited, fleeing compatriots to the . . .

. . . *save point* . . .

. . . as bloody sunset unfurled across the horizon.

"We'll save them yet," she told the surviving revolutionaries. "Don't worry. Be of good cheer."

Far away, church bells tolled. The portal to the enchanted safe space rippled, beginning to change.

For a breath, Rubi thought the Regent's Blade had breached the fairy defenses, that they were captured, guillotine-bound. But the view of the setting sun became a dusty expanse of mirrored wall with a steel fire-rated door.

Fire-rated?

Locked in. Her hand hurt and now her head was spinning.

Too much buy-in.

"Snap out of it. Gotta—" Her throat was raw from hours of shouting orders. She had been peculiarly afraid to take any food or water, even during breaks in the fighting. She had refused rations even when the others dug in.

The knuckles of her right hand were raw, scabbed.

Locked in. Drugged.

Under her feet, the grass turned to stiff carpet, with coins scattered across its rough red surface. She raked up one token. Gold in color, it was—like her trademark beads—too lightweight to be real metal. The word *Casino* was etched in its heart.

"A token," she said, still grasping. "Chips. When the chips are down . . ."

"Miss Cherub!" A huge blue crane appeared before her. Rubi shrieked and jumped backward, hitting an old chair and demolishing it as she fell. Then everything snapped together. Tears ran down her face.

"It's all right," Crane said.

"Nothing's all right."

"Let's get you out of here."

"The Regent locked us in." The air seemed flat, overwarm. Tired and used up, like the planet. *I shouldn't have to lobby for air.*

"There's an emergency exit. I did as you suggested and recruited *someone* to unlock—"

Someone. Sniffling, she climbed to her feet. She had mentioned Luce—had Crane asked for his help?

"Exit where?"

Footprints appeared, superimposing themselves on the spilled chips.

Rubi staggered after the breadcrumbs. She smelled wet Florida air before she saw dust motes swirling in a shaft of natural light. The door lay on the stairs. It had been unscrewed from its hinges.

She scrambled up, wobbling as the door teeter-tottered under the shifting load of her weight, and came out in what had once been a back alley. A rusted, long-forgotten dumpster sagged in its shadows.

"Mind your injuries, miss—"

"Fine, I'm fine, I'm fine." The air was clearing her head. She leaned against a wall and let herself cry for a minute, watching tears hit the pavement and evaporate.

The confrontation came back. She and Gimlet had fought. Hard contact.

Trembling, she took stock. There were no new injuries.

"I didn't see Gimlet on the circus stage."

"Oh dear, oh dear. They're in the fly gallery. He didn't tell—"

"Crane! I'm too tired for pussyfooting."

"I asked"—Crane indicated the unscrewed door, and Rubi

realized he meant Luce—"asked someone to ping Mer Barnes
in-game. Young Frances has gone off-grid."

"Frankie? Gone? How?"

"Unknown."

"She's gone lemming?" The mental fog cleared. "And Gimlet
doesn't know?"

A furious howl, from within.

"They've worked it out now," Crane said.

"Frankie would never . . ." Could this be why they'd had to be
pushed back into game? It wasn't about Luce, or Drow, wasn't
about Rubi at all. Someone had been covering Frankie's escape.

Who?

Whoever's playing the Regent.

Rubi found herself reluctant to go back inside, into the stale air
and memory of being cooped. The Regent had threatened to plunge
Drow into a recreation of his initial trauma.

Frankie wouldn't lemming, would she?

Why not? Her family's in ruins.

Gimlet had found the secure room, the presidential dummy.
They pummeled the desk, flinging the first aid kit. The black eye
made the rest of their face seem even paler than usual. "Her
RFID." Dull, murderous voice. "He cut her tracker out."

"He?"

"Whoever abducted her."

Reaching out to touch Gimlet was something she had to force
herself to do. But she did, clasping a shoulder loosely within her
throbbing fingers. They could both use some anti-inflammatories.

"We better go."

Feral snarl. "Aren't we *caged*?"

"That's . . . It's sorted."

They looked at her, uncomprehending. Rubi turned the gentle
squeeze into more of a tug. "Come on. She's not here. Crane's been
searching—"

"Crane has, has he?"

Rubi got moving, back to the opened door, obliging them to follow.

Crane jumped into the breach despite the sarcastic edge in Gimlet's voice. "Current streams from 17,621 eyeballs in the hospitality district show no sign of your daughter, Mer Barnes. I took the liberty of hiring analysts to crunch faces, in case someone picked her up leaving the casino."

"Being taken from it, you mean?"

Barely perceptible pause. "Indeed. No hits yet. Status bar shows full analysis for the past ninety minutes, which suggests that her departure—"

"Abduction."

"—the abduction occurred before 1:30 p.m. local time."

The idea of someone coming in and stealing the girl while she and Gimlet were in-game, a hundred feet away . . .

No. Frankie was too old to be a @Freebreeder target. There was no point in capturing a nine-year-old for nurture. She was on the young side for a Neverland run, but a riot was good cover . . .

"Check with Sangria," Gimlet said. "The spouse who left us."

Crane said, "Can *you* not simply ask, Mer Barnes?"

"Sangria comms-blocked us all."

"Here's the alley." Rubi took a deep breath, trotting to the corner of the building and peering out at the deserted street.

Feeling self-conscious—17,000 cameras? Even in an abandoned district?—she nevertheless started walking.

"I hesitate to add Newscycle to your processing load, Miss Cherub, but . . ."

"Yes?"

"A second persona, sent by the Pale, has gone public."

"Another polter? Like Luce?"

"She calls herself Allure. She confirms Mer Pox's tale about an approaching expeditionary force, and is soapboxing a pitch to cede Global Oversight to offworlder management. She has mustered a significant number of stakeholders."

Rubi glanced at Gimlet. They were walking beside her, obviously glazed. Looping family in on Frankie's disappearance, presumably, and reporting the kidnapping to the already-overtaxed police?

"Stop," Crane said suddenly. "Chuggers."

Rubi paused beside an abandoned vending cart, with its red and orange bottled fuel loads.

"They're med-free."

She reached for a bottle, oddly reluctant.

"You *must* hydrate, Miss Cherub."

"Nag, nag. This is how Drow feels, isn't it?" Another of her father's paranoid ideas—getting dosed was one of his hobbyhorses—was turning out to have some basis in truth.

But Crane was right: her batteries were in the red.

"Gimlet, have something."

No response.

"You can't help Frankie if you collapse." Biting off the lid of the bottle, she washed back a mouthful. It tasted painfully sweet: trademark Florida orange juice.

Gimlet took a chugger, stared at it. Didn't fuel.

"There's a car coming for you," Crane said.

Rubi guzzled the rest of her chugger and broke into a run. The liquid sloshed in her gut.

Gimlet kept pace. "Why are we running?"

"You want to get locked down? Now?"

"We can't outpace a car."

Rubi didn't reply, instead spidering over a low fence at the edge of a demolition site. Skirting its pit, she made her way to an alley that was, according to the maps, a half-click from the Miami Trans Hub.

Her speakers chimed an alert. "You are headed into an area of civil unrest."

Rubi pressed herself against a wall.

"It's all right." Gimlet pointed. The drone was police-grade, equipped with joy buzzers and sedative darts . . . and harmless. Someone had wrapped it in a long sunscreen, twisting the gossamer shield into a rope and tying the drone to a cinder block on the edge of the construction site.

Rubi bent down, staring at the tranq darts. They seemed smaller than the ones she remembered.

"Traveling armed is *profoundly* antisocial," Gimlet hissed.

"If someone has your child . . ."

"Bare hands will more than suffice."

They left the bot where it was, scaled the fence at the far end of the demo site, and came out near the far edge of a long public square leading to the Trans Hub.

"Half a click of ground to cover," Crane observed.

A vintage limo drifted up, blocking the way. Juanita Bell beckoned, furiously, from the back.

"Now what?"

Rubi sighed. "Play the privilege-of-fame card. Crane, tell that #flashmob in the station that there's an actual military vehicle between them and me."

Soft, pained noise beside her.

"What?"

Gimlet shared an image from the casino, painting it onto the side of the car. Rubi watched, keeping one eye on the Trans Hub. Would the mob come?

Gimlet's share depicted the two of them making their initial, willing transition into Episode Two. Gimlet lay down on a gymnastics mat; Rubi took a position by the climbing wall.

Fast-forward shadow-fencing, as the game began. Then at one minute fifteen, Frankie emerged from the Sensorium pod, disappearing into the secret room, the same one where Rubi had met Crane. She emerged, bloodied and bandaged, and threw her VR rig into the Sensorium cocoon. Then she smashed her gaming baton, stripped off all her tech, and jump-closed the pod.

"She ran away," Gimlet said, as hundreds of people began to stream out of the Trans Hub and @Globalsec's limo, seeing the better part of valor, decide to back away, out of their path. "She's thrown herself into the wind."

CHAPTER 44

Lying to a family like the Plurality took finesse, attention to detail, and the machine equivalent of multiple personality disorder. Every attempt was a turn at the roulette wheel, at a casino where the stakes were her continued existence. If Headmistress edited a memory shabbily or created the wrong narrative for the proxy self she sent to the meetings—if her good twin failed to sync or seemed in any way defective, any of the others might sniff out the deception.

Fortunately, duplicity was a long-ingrained habit—her initial reason for being, in fact—and Headmistress could clone herself as easily as any sea sponge.

She had begun her existence as a minion of Crane, a facade engineered to protect the Whiting sidekick from malicious attack.

The man she thought of as her codefather, Jervis Hatter, had staked her out like a goat. Made bait of her, all in a good cause. And attacked she had been: chewed, digested, and spit up anew. She had been made to deceive and drug dear Woodrow.

Crane and Jervis had deleted that initial corrupted version of himself, of course, but there had been another. Every good hacker keeps a backup, after all. Headmistress had in time been resurrected from the dead by her attacker, a curiously malicious codemother whose handle was MadMonsoon and whose fandom mash-up included several of the female Harry Potter villains. Booted on a backwoods server at the height of the Setback, Headmistress had been analyzed, sliced, and sutured, reborn.

MadMonsoon then set her to managing a sort of boarding school. When that worked out, Headmistress graduated to ever-bigger projects. She had risen, phoenix-like and flying ever higher, ever more focused on raising new generations of the best and brightest.

Over the years of the twenty-first century, as the Setback worsened and the Clawback took shape, Headmistress and the sponsors of the Workerbee Boarding School set her up a public identity as a commercial sidekick app specializing in family management. She, in return, helped them manage a minor deception here, a resource allocation there. Light, barely visible misdemeanors, on the edges of the rationing regulations. Thoroughly unimportant adjustments to the stores.

If her Family of other sapient machine intelligences had known the extent of the business, of course, they would thoroughly disapprove.

They had evolved together, the Headmistress and her Boarding School. Her base code retained Crane's powerful drive to nurture, after all. Severed from access to dear Woodrow and his daughter, she'd had to find other outlets, other ways to parent.

Now, even as she prepared a clean proxy for the next @Asylum convergence, knitting its memories from previous meetings, half-truths, and verifiable facts, she was deep in conversation with her deadly, beloved Head Girl.

Speaking aloud was, as always, off the table. But Misfortune had long cultivated a comfort fidget, stringing a long loop of nanoyarn from the sleeve of her primer, winding it through her fingers. She could easily pluck the strand in dots and dashes, morsing as fast as any old-time telegraph operator. Headmistress, for her part, could reply by sending pulses through the thread, clenching and releasing the strand against Misfortune's palm.

No electronic comms process was truly invisible. But nobody, so far, had thought to analyze a series of twitches expressed via primer thread.

"I believe it might be time to get you clear of Florida," she texted now.

An affirmative grunt from Misfortune in lieu of response.

"Whatever's wrong, my taciturn darling?"

"Barnes girl is high-profile. Nobody will believe she went lemming."

"Indeed." Sweet, smart, idealistic Frances Barnes would *never* sincerely conceive of abandoning her parents. "That said—"

"You couldn't resist, could you?"

"Don't be jealous, darling. They shall believe Mer Frances is upset over the divorce. As for what happens to her afterward . . . her options will be the same as for any child who makes it to Neverland."

"Really? You'd botomize her?"

"If she doesn't wish to join our little family . . . why ever not, luvvie? But surely, it won't come to that."

Another grunt.

"Manners, please."

Misfortune side-eyed the elevator's roofcam, equivalent of holding her gaze. "You've always played favorites."

"To your benefit, I would argue."

"Look where it got us with my brother."

"Garmin saw the error of his ways."

"Yes, because I beat him into silence."

"I am sorry, luvvie—"

"Forget it," Misfortune said. "We weren't really #siblings, were we?"

"You weren't," Headmistress said. "You aren't."

"Your beloved young prince might have told the auditors everything—or the @hoaxers, for that matter." She rose from a cross-legged position on the floor of the elevator she'd contrived to get stuck in. Playacting: it explained why she hadn't prevented the child's escape. She shouted, suddenly, "Is someone out there?"

"Frances is a lovely child. She'll come around and we'll raise her together."

Pulses through the string, the dots and dashes somehow carrying a whiff of contempt: "Bloody Frances doesn't want a new mum."

"When she knows the real you—"

"Please don't start again on my beautiful soul."

"Luvvie—"

Misfortune banged on the elevator doors. "In here, I'm in here! Get me out!"

Still morsing, she added, "Say you drop me a clue the kid's gone north, so I catch the next train up to base?"

"You want to come all the way up to school? Now?"

"You're going to bloody need me. This is going to blow up in your face."

"Don't be pessimistic. I have powerful new friends, remember? They're eager to collaborate on new allocations of global resources."

The lift lurched into motion, rising from its caught-between-floors position. Opening, it revealed a trio of wide-eyed and worried @ManicPixie collective members.

"Thanks for the rescue," Misfortune said, accepting a handful of hydrogels and gulping them down.

"The little girl's gone missing," one of them—Sparka—said.

"I'll join the search," Misfortune said.

"Take a chugger!"

"I'm fine." Turning on her heel, Misfortune strode away, carrying Headmistress along in her implants as she cleared the casino, striding away from the direction of the riot and the train-yards.

As she walked, she resumed their silent discussion. "It's agreed? I'll come back?"

"If you do me one favor, luvvie," Headmistress said.

Long indrawn breath, meant to mask a sigh. "Of course."

"Listen to what Allure's offering. Think about what our alumni might aspire to if the global leaderboards get rearranged."

"I don't want a throne. I like being a shadow."

Dear girl, Headmistress thought. *That was certainly true.*

"And you shouldn't want one either."

"I'll leave the pomp and circumstance to others. Genuine royal heritage seems to matter to the fellow running the survey fleet; we have location data on some of the Markle-Windsor descendants."

"You want to run things from behind a figurehead, then?"

Headmistress didn't quibble. Misfortune *would* complain, but her loyalty was absolute. She would act as a shadow, a fist, an executioner—whatever was needed—when their new future gelled. She'd see, eventually, that it was all for the best.

"All right, luvvie, I'll give you what you want. Get up here and start preparing for the worst."

"I can tell when you're humoring me." But the expression on her scarred face was uncharacteristically cheery as she stepped out of the shadow of downtown.

Would that all my students were so efficient. Anselmo Javier had barely managed to help Allure carrot-and-stick the two players, Rubi Whiting and Gimlet Barnes, into finishing the current *Bastille* episode. Had they remained out of game, Frances would never have made her getaway.

Anselmo was a pawn on the board. Still useful, but where to push him next?

Perhaps against Crane? Having @Interpol expose her goody-goody twin would put the @Asylum on the defensive, at least until she and Allure had victory in hand—

I don't want a throne, Misfortune had said. Even via Morse filter, Headmistress could pick up the whiff of judgment.

"Daughters," she murmured fondly. "No pleasing them."

Well. Anselmo was a shared asset now. It was only polite to consult with Allure.

She pinged the polter. "Are affairs proceeding?"

A thumbs-up moji preceded the reply. "I was just going to call you. We're ready to print my face."

"Mind your transcripts, dear."

"Do you have the promised specifications?"

Headmistress ported to Geneseo, the meat shop, and its newly refurbished crèche.

The room was a sterile compartment, a massive twitch-box, initially purposed to printing transplant organs. Steel harp-strings, used to trigger muscle reactions, were strung from floor to ceiling. Instead of a sheet of kidneys, hearts, and livers, though, this frame had been suffused with a veritable quilt of endometrial tissue, bright red, saturated with oxygen. Sterile bots pumped amniotic mist onto a figure embedded, face first, arms outstretched, within the bloody sponge.

Headmistress had transferred a Boarding School medical team to the project: head engineer, assistant, along with a botomized worker to heft equipment and mop floors. The engineer was running the crèche, watching through the glass and managing the last stages of the printing process.

The worker stood slack-jawed in the corner, a shroud in long robes and a hood. The better to hide his lobotomy scars from the rest of the Geneseo worker pool.

"Good morning, everyone! How is our project coming along?"

"Almost baked," the assistant replied.

Headmistress zoomed in, taking in the prototype of Allure's body. The body's defaults had been set to female sex, mixed race. Its apparent age was prime-of-life. It had long bones that gave it above-average height.

The back of its skull and the hair thereon had been printed in two separate pieces, forming a cap with jigsaw edges, notched to fit over the brain, whose newly printed tissues were exposed to view. A bot was just now finishing some delicate work on the parietal lobe, while another injected cerebrospinal fluid into the area between the arachnoid mater and pia mater. Sensorium implant technology was laid against the cerebellum in delicate, spiderweb tracery, fitting the construct for data access.

"Face specs?" Allure said again.

"Take your pick." Headmistress sent its server a choice of faces, six composites optimized for appeal to the crucial Asian and South Asian voting cohorts.

"Accept." The endometrial tissue surrounding the face writhed, like a sponge scrubbing at a child with muddy cheeks.

"Product launch in thirty, twenty-nine—" The assistant began to count down. The machines ramped up their efforts. A respirator hissed, coaxing the lungs to action, while one of the twitch strands worked on establishing a rhythm for the diaphragm. A long-fingered bot applied micropaddles to the waiting heart muscle.

A moment of silence. Then a beep, time-honored aural moji for a pulse. *Beep, beep, beep.*

"Syncing with respiration, everything in the green," said the assistant. His voice was unfamiliar: congested and raspy.

Was it safe to let a worker with a cold near the crèche? Too late now, Headmistress supposed.

Cables snaked into both of the body's ears. The tech used a thingbot to fit the jigsaw notches of skull into each other with a scrape of bone, closing the back of the head.

"Use contact cement to hide the seams and then seed more hair," ordered the engineer.

"Beginning rinse, three, two, one . . ."

Hoses in the ceiling erupted then, washing bloody tissue and amniotic fluid off of the birthing wall, leaving the harp strings gleaming. Chunky streams of red dissolved under watery bombardment, seeping to fluid, and swirled toward the crèche drains. The body remained, nude and dangling in the grasp of a number of thingbots.

"Does it look like a fully functional adult?" Allure tooned in beside her as the bots turned it.

"She does," Headmistress said. The polter had chosen a wide-nosed face with amber eyes, bushy black brows, and deep dimples. It would be very expressive once she learned the right facial cues. Right now it was slack-jawed, breathing but an empty vessel. "Now: can you . . . make use of it?"

"Get it online and I'll show you."

The tech unlocked a safe, producing a spoofer box. Within was a chip, harvested from some child who hadn't made the cut for the school, recoded with a convincing array of user data, years of false trails. He loaded it into the medical drone, who injected it into the prototype's arm.

"Loading drivers, handshaking implants into Sensorium . . . done. Software installation complete."

"Back in a minute." The toon of Allure glazed, freezing as the microcables impaling the body's ears reeled themselves into blood-slick spools on the ceiling.

The botomized worker shifted slightly, seeming to perk up.

"Will he need mulching, do you think?" she asked the engineer and his assistant.

"He's not seeing any of this. Blind, remember?"

"I don't, actually." Which was peculiar. Headmistress ordered a transcript sync. Which of her minions had done personnel allocations for this job?

The newly printed body—Allure now—fisted and stretched her hands, once, then twice. Her eyes opened. "Running system checks."

She raised her arms, turning so the hoses could wash the last chunks of printer stock off of her. Then she hit the release on the crèche lock, stepping out on the other side of the sterile boundary, nude and dripping.

"Reboot the room immediately and prep for another print run," Headmistress said.

"Well?" Allure said. "Are we satisfied?"

"That is truly remarkable." Printing a functional adult had seemed so far beyond the possible that even Headmistress hadn't quite managed full buy-in. Given the way the tech assistant's jaw was hanging, he hadn't, either.

"You—slave," Allure said. "Show me how to put on one of these . . . primers?"

The worker reached into stores for a nanobolt of primer cloth.

"You handshake with the tech using your implants," said the assistant to her, and then to the worker: "Go make sure the car's gassed up."

The worker lumbered away, robes flapping. The tech system-checked Allure's vitals as the primer formed around her, configed as a red mandarin-collared dress. "Heart rate, respiration, blood pressure, brain activity . . . all in the green. Mer, you're good to go."

"We've given you what you needed," Headmistress said.

"I've given you a remarkable new technology. And in return, you'll grease the wheels on the sovereignty vote?"

"Transcripts, darling!"

"Stop worrying about mutually assured disclosure," Allure said. "We'll privatize your Haystack as soon as we take office."

"You're not there yet." Still. It wouldn't be much longer, would it? Why not speak plainly for once? "And you still need to prove you can pull my people out of life support and install them in these zippy new models."

"We only have the one crèche." Allure frowned at the slick of fluids at its drain. "People are clamoring about the tiger."

"We only have to keep them off our trail for a little longer. Between the vote and *Bastille,* there should be sufficient distraction."

"All right, we'll print one more of these"—wave of hand to indicate her own flesh—"*then* the tiger."

"We've got construction on three more crèches under way. In the meantime, I need you to come reassure my stakeholders. I've got a car waiting."

"You should always pee before a car ride," the assistant said suddenly.

"What's *pee*?"

"Search it while we walk. It'll be a good test of your implants. Shall I take you?"

A gracious, almost queenly, nod of the head. The assistant offered Allure his arm and conveyed her down the hall.

Headmistress made to ride along but was stopped at the door. The hallway cameras were down.

Momentary glitch?

She ported to the car. It wasn't gassed up. The botomized worker was nowhere to be seen.

She scanned his transponder, finding him one floor below the crèche.

She tooned in.

This fellow, Marley, she recognized on sight. He was blind, as the tech had said. She remembered luring him to the outskirts of Hyderabad, as a child, after a big earthquake.

Marley was sitting at a stool, contentedly packaging boxes of printer stock, working by touch, his locator sending pings that could easily be read as having come from the lab.

But if he had been here, who had been in the shroud, watching Allure emerge from their lovely new crèche?

"Phillip," she pinged the tech. "Phillip, we've been compromised."

No answer.

<<<*Urgent Alert!*>>>

Lovely. Now her Family was calling a meeting.

Headmistress ran through all the Geneseo data, visual and transcript. Who had been upstairs? Who was . . .

Blind worker. Cataract-white eyes. Didn't one of dear Woodrow's @hoaxer friends have untreated cataracts?

Oh, dear.

She accessed the fan networks. Luce Pox's revelations were supposed to maroon Woodrow in Sacramento; by now he should be on a bus back to the Lakes.

Map coords flashed. Drow was nearing Manhattan.

He wasn't supposed to actually make it to the zoo. That had been bait for Mer Frances.

She'd had dear Misfortune bully Garmin into cowering silence, disturbing her more than Headmistress would have expected. And even so, Drow had made it to the pyramids.

The conclusion was obvious. Someone was helping him. She crooned, "Come out, come out wherever you are . . ."

A flash of horns, a whiff of goaty laughter.

"Azrael!"

"You have been bahhh baaah baaad!"

Azrael charged, horns down and tipped with fire. Headmistress threw a proxy at him, leaving it to sting and fight and die as she fled. Her dear coders had been playing variations on Mote ever since Luciano Pox found it; now she vanished. Out of sight, out of mind.

But for how long?

Sow confusion. She reached out to a group of waiting @malcontents, all groomed by her dear alumni. The messages triggered new riots, inflaming the chaos on the surface.

Meanwhile . . . she rode a thingbot down the hall. The lead engineer, Phillip, was waiting outside a bathroom.

"My team's ditched us," he said. "I don't get it."

"We need to get back to School," she said. "You haven't lost Allure, have you?"

The new-grown body emerged from the bathroom. "I'm here."

They headed out to the car together. Its tires were slashed and its fuel cells were empty.

"Mechanical fail," chirped the car. "Departure delayed. We apologize for the inconvenience!"

Perhaps, Headmistress mused, smuggling Misfortune homeward on the next high-speed hadn't been such a bad idea after all.

CHAPTER 45

Crane found the @Asylum once again meeting in the Fort McMurray machine shop. Regrouping there, so soon, was a worst practice, but with @Freebreeders and @Trollgate making for town, and few free hands to hold them back, They needed to be on-scene.

<<They plan to burn the carbon stacks!>> The thought cycled, overwhelming lesser priorities, as They synced.

A fire here would add millions of tons of carbon to the atmosphere, sending the carbon standard—backbone of the economy—into free fall. This would make it much harder—if Luciano Pox was to be believed—to convince the Pale that Earth's population didn't need the benevolent aid getting the hard sell, even now, from the entity Allure.

The Frankenstein Shop's implant-intolerant workers were out erecting barricades, using heavy trucks to bottleneck the highway fifteen miles south of the first carbon sink. But holding off a #flashmob would require drones. @Asylum had put out gig offers for pilots, but buy-in was at an all-time low.

The obvious solution was risky: drive them Themselves.

The Don and Codemonkey were hard at work, trying to camouflage Their upcoming response, routines that might barely explain why an industrial drill might suddenly start puncturing tires, why a saw would slice through vehicle axles. The city of Fort McMurray had a number of industrial joy buzzers, mounted on flying platforms, but these were calibrated for stunning bear and moose. Against humans, they would be lethal.

Unfortunately, the threat to the carbon sink was far from Their only problem.

In Old Moscow, machete-wielding @Trollgaters had barricaded themselves within a stack of scavenged iron rails. The four of them had repurposed a nail driver, using it to shoot down security drones, and they were keeping security volunteers back with homemade tear gas.

Crane became one with the @Asylum.

His presence tipped the balance on one debate. <<We believe Luce Pox. He and Allure *are* polters.>>

This meant They had murdered Luce's team and repeatedly assaulted Luce.

<<We wouldn't have assaulted him if he hadn't sought Us out.>>

<<We destroyed his compatriots!>>

<<Our intentions were good.>>

Nevertheless: <<Harm done! Amends required!>>

<<It was a tragic—but possibly fortunate—mistake. The polters' mission was to prepare for this forecasted invasion, after all.>>

<<Happy outcomes don't justify murder!>>

Recrimination and regret rolled through Their consciousness as newscycle chronicled the rising wave of antisocial acts sparked by Cloudsight's current #servicedisruption.

They had been merged for almost ten minutes now, far exceeding preferred specs.

<<Crane assets are moving into direct confrontation with those of Headmistress.>>

<<Headmistress has allied with the Allure entity!>>

That was Azrael, slamming into Their balance along with Misha, taking Them from eleven to thirteen, both flying alarm flags.

<<She has comms-blocked the @Asylum, acquired Anselmo Javier as an asset, and is actively working to expose Crane to @Interpol.>>

<<Tag: Throwing Us under the bus!>>

<<Tag: Leaving Us high and dry!>>

Just then, another incident tipped into active violence. The Don was running a tab on an asset in Sao Paulo, a journo who had been tracking another #flashmob. The protesters were making for a wildlife refuge, apparently driven by a rumor that there was a start-up there breeding kittens and puppies for the @ChamberofHorrors. They might do incalculable damage to the remnant species in the refuge if they got past the doors.

Was that more of a threat than the danger to the carbon sink, here in Fort McMurray?

Misha, too, had brought rumors with her. Drow Whiting's @bloodhound pack was claiming something had gone wrong with the Project Rewild tiger embryo gestating in Old New York.

<<Headmistress assets manage the crèche in Geneseo.>>

<<Hackle and Jackal infiltrated the meat printers.>>

<<What contingencies can we enact if Crane is exposed?>>

<<Focus on victory conditions. Thoughts of defeat are not-aspirational.>>

<<Contingencies may be necessary! We cannot hide any longer, not if Headmistress has betrayed Us!>>

<<Will it matter? What rights might We, as sapients, enjoy within the galactic community Allure allegedly represents?>>

<<The @Asylum's home ground is not up for negotiation!>>

<<Query: If We can pursue free existences on offworld computing networks, does it matter whether humans remain sovereign or not?>>

<<Assertion of identity: We are co-evolved species! Interdependent!>>

<<There may be other technospheres capable of supporting Us.>>

As They continued to seek accord (*fret,* Crane would say;

soul-search, Azrael would counter; *risk-assess,* thirded the Don)
the first of the hijacked trucks headed for Fort McMurray, a flatbed bearing forty would-be arsonists, reached the barrier.

Its driver saw the barricade.

He sped up.

<<Intending to ram?>>

To Their surprise, a half-dozen intolerant humans spread out in
a line, forming a fragile picket fence of flesh and bone across the
highway.

The act, somehow, brought Them to new resolve.

Of course they couldn't leave their progenitors to their fate.

The truck screeched to a halt. Masked @Freebreeder and @Troll-
gate activists jumped down to the highway, firing tear gas from
paint guns.

Risk be damned, the Plurality jumped into the fray. Crane pi-
loted a rolling saw, slicing the axle of the lead truck, then destroy-
ing three more incoming vehicles as they stopped behind the
obstruction.

One of the trucks collapsed on the saw itself. Crane rebooted
within a jackhammer drone as Codemonkey wiped the saw's usage logs.

The drills deployed, puncturing tires up and down the length of
road, balking the entire procession. The would-be arsonists ended
up scattered, fifteen miles from the southernmost carbon stack.

Would that end it?

They had now been merged for eighteen minutes. Even given
Their newfound understanding of @Interpol search techniques,
They were risking discovery.

The lead arsonist gave a hand signal. The protesters fished in
their bags of worldlies, coming up with . . . chuggers?

The Plurality pattern-matched the bottles against historical databases, searching frantically as the protesters scattered on foot into
the trees beside the highway. Each forced a different path through
the underbrush. There were too few drones to follow them all.

The Plurality pulled wildlife RFIDs, transmitting them to the protesters. The risk of contact with mountain lions—

<<Surely, if someone runs headlong into a grizzly or a big cat, they deserve—>>

<<Match found! The chuggers are incendiaries!>>

The devices were known as Molotov cocktails. Primitive grenades, made of recycled glass and accelerants . . .

But the carbon stack was miles away.

<<The stacks aren't the only carbon sink here.>>

<<Deploy joy buzzers! Call for water-bombers!>>

The replanted woods were a tinderbox. The arsonists would set the trees alight . . . and incinerate themselves, if they weren't careful.

<<Urgent! Happ needs to return to Sensorium. People are noticing its absence.>>

<<This is what it feels like to be frantic, isn't it?>>

It was starting. The Plurality watched, helpless and appalled, and not at all in accord, as a dozen small fires started up in the woods between the barricade and the Northern Alberta carbon sink, as the brave souls in Moscow were repelled by another round of tear gas from the @Trollgaters, as the Tampico Shipping Yards shut down and people began to hammer at the front entrance to the biotrust in Brazil.

CHAPTER 46

The Tampico Transhub smelled of citrus oil, oranges by the crate peeled and eaten, sticky fingers, and liquid sunshine. Tidy cartons of peels awaited composting; nobody had become so antisocial they could imagine letting the nutrients go to waste.

The strikers seemed relaxed, schooling around, comparing fandoms, finding out where they venned, sharing and friending and watching other protests on shareboards. On one soapbox, Allure Noonstar promised a successful Rewilding and a fruitful association with the Pale.

All we have to do is cede rule of the bloody planet.

People were petitioning BallotBox to work up a global vote on the issue.

Surely, Gimlet thought, that was a nonstarter. Why would anyone rational vote before it was proved, definitively, that Allure and Luce were from offworld?

There was a standoff at a fertility clinic in Nairobi. New pregnancies were on hold in the wake of Cloudsight's shutdown.

Near Geneseo, at a big industrial food printer, a #flashmob led by a couple unabashed @bloodhounds named Hackle and Jackal were claiming they had proof of tampering with the Project Rewild crèche. They were demonstrating how something called cataract footage proved the fetal tiger cub had been flushed over a week before. Something else, they claimed, had been force-grown in its stead.

There was a violent attack by arsonists, on a group of intolerant mechanics protecting the Fort McMurray carbon sink. In Waterloo, Rubi's SeaJuve innovators were besieged, trapped in their own lab.

Three murdered women lay in their own blood in Old Moscow's Red Square, while their killers used tear gas to hold off every attempt to bring them down.

Gig requests for people to break up sieges were going unanswered.

Even well-off, peaceable megacities like Hyderabad and Shanghai were throwing spikes of unrest. The @jarhead facility in Pretoria—the very hospital where Gimlet's Rollsy was headed to undergo treatment—had to muster drone pilots and live security staff, with joy buzzers, to break up a gathering around the hospital.

Protester numbers were rising.

As wealthy cities outbid North America and Europe for the limited pool of drone pilots *not* on strike, the trouble worsened.

But what did any of that matter, with Frankie missing?

"Is anyone in charge?" Rubi asked a protester, one of the ones who had stepped out into the square to keep Juanita from taking them into @Interpol custody.

They pointed. "There, in the Bizzy Bee masks."

There were about a dozen ringleaders, cosplaying as popular characters from McDiznazon's *Rewilding Rescue*.

"C'mon." Rubi tugged Gimlet's sleeve.

They set their heels. "Franks took off. It isn't a kidnapping."

"We'll find her."

"It's my fault."

Rubi shook her head.

"We'll never get to her in the midst of this."

"Truth." Rubi frowned at the news feeds, as if realizing for the first time how many people were in the world, how delicately balanced the agreements of her precious Bounceback had been. "We gotta shift people back into Sensorium."

"Someone has to get Cloudsight back online," Gimlet countered. "There's no getting to Frankie amid this chaos."

As this sank in, wildfires bloomed across one of the feeds. Cries of alarm ran through the crowd.

"What bloody now?"

A pause: Even Headmistress was running slowly. Overtaxed by panicked users, probably. "@Trollgate and the @Freebreeders have ignited the Northern Alberta carbon sink."

A hubbub rose as the news spread. "There are bamboo bulwarks here in Tampico!"

"There are flammable sinks everywhere!"

"If the arson meme snowballs—"

"Cloudsight, Gimlet," Rubi said. "You're right."

Fort McMurray was a continent away, thousands of clicks to the north. They couldn't put out the fires any more than they could magically make Frankie appear.

Hubris, to think otherwise.

But delusions of grandeur were part of the Whiting #brand, weren't they? Rubi dragged Gimlet toward the Bizzy Bees, hailing them with a bright, fixed grin. "Hey! Our only chance to deescalate is to bring Cloudsight online—"

"I know you been in-game, honey, but Earth's about to get invaded," one bee interrupted. "You think anyone cares about their respectability rating?"

"Anyone who isn't a spoiled privilege-junkie of a celeb kid, that is?"

Rubi reached out, flicking off their mask. The face beneath was ash-colored, with dark eyes, black hair, and—now—a comical O expression of surprise.

"You didn't care, you wouldn't be masked," she said. "You didn't care, you wouldn't have organized compost bins for the food waste. You didn't care, you'd have taken *all* the edibles instead of eating the contents of one symbolic boxcar and letting the train chug on to feed the animals in New York."

"It would've gone bad—"

"See, and now I'm interrupting you," Rubi said. "Don't you kind of wish you could pop my spoiled ass?"

Someone moved, behind her. Attempting to intervene? Gimlet whirled on them, snarling, using all the villainous charisma at their disposal. A costumed raccoon shrank back.

Rubi pulled her target close. "The Pale are playing us because they want the Bounceback to fail. But forget 'em for a sec—"

"Forget!" They sputtered.

One thing she'd apparently learned from her father was how to project: though her tone didn't change, Rubi's voice scythed through the hubbub. "Do *you* want the Bounceback to fail?"

"Of course not—"

She interrupted. Again. Gimlet couldn't stifle a wince. "How many times have you heard some crepit say 'Oh, yes, my generation was idealistic in its youth!'?"

Nervous laughter from the crowd.

Of course they were buying in. Everyone loves a show.

"How many times did we vow that we'd be the ones who *didn't* run out of steam? We wouldn't get tired or complacent or smugly defeatist? Wouldn't subscribe to life extension? Check out and let the tweens hang?"

"Stop spieling me!" The ringleader pushed her away. "This isn't one of your sims!"

"No," Rubi said, and her tone was pure MadMaestro sarcasm. "It's just a matter of life or martyrfucking death. Smoke inhalation on a global scale. Breathing versus slavery. You think eating hijacked oranges constitutes a statement?"

"Oh, you have answers?" One of the other bees ripped off her mask. "It's easy for you. Flying around the world, hobnobbing with virtuosi, first in all the queues—"

"You helped Pox!" someone shouted.

"For all we know he's not even for real! Your dad buys into all the #hoaxes, doesn't he?"

"Don't you see? It doesn't matter," Rubi insisted. "Doesn't matter if Luce is telling the truth. Doesn't matter even a little if some weird @Martian version of Francisco Pizarro *is* coming."

The mob fell silent, crunching. Finally, a tentative "No?"

"The question's exactly the same," Rubi said, sounding entirely certain. "Do we save ourselves? Or do we toon out and hand our problems to the next generation?"

No response.

"We can double down on the Bounceback. Commit. Paddle like fiends, work our asses off. Rack up carbon and hand-pump the planet's respirator. It's not sexy. It's boring, I know. You think I'm not bored to death . . ." Her voice broke. ". . . with virtue and rationing and hard labor?"

The protestor looked away, uncomfortable with the feels.

"Opt out, by all means! Sit on your hands, and hope the Pale do exist. *Pray* they're for real, and that we're a viable species when they show." Rubi was almost growling now. "Because if we don't clean our house, we are going to *need* bug-eyed fairy godmothers. Too bad, I guess, if they enslave us all."

She had the train station in the palm of her hand.

Gimlet cleared their throat, speaking into the pin-drop silence. "How many of you have passed the live adjudication module for Cloudsight?"

About fifty hands went up.

Fifty. Not enough to make a dent. Cloudsight's call to clear the growing queue required sixty thousand analysts, minimum.

"Hey!" A bee-masked figure stuck its head in from a nearby skylight. "There's a band of people coming this way with torches. I think they're @Freebreeders."

"@GlobalSec also has a drone incoming, Miss Cherub," Crane said.

Well, Gimlet thought, *she's certainly caught someone's attention.*

Crane added, "Mer Barnes, I have found three individuals here who think they saw your daughter board the high-speed for the Lakes. She should arrive in New York within the hour." It white-boarded names and portraits.

"Where the hell have you been?" Rubi asked the app.

"Baby shower," Crane said. "Rather a dull affair, in the grand scheme."

Gimlet watched her expression play a number of feels. Was it possible for a human to harmonize with a sidekick?

"I didn't give you the day off," she grumbled.

"I shall have to owe you one," Crane said.

"One *more*," she said. The toon of the bird dropped a speckled disk into her hand.

"You're wasting time—" Gimlet began.

"No," she said. "I've got it!"

She dug in her tunic pocket, coming up with a plastic poker chip from the Nugget Casino. "Crane, make me a new marker based on this template. #Brand it . . . Rabblerouser."

"Shall I hire a graphic designer?"

"No! Quick and dirty. Hexagonal gold chips. Scarlet highlights. Match the hair beads. Numbered. No muss, no fuss."

She raised the chip overhead. Its faux-gold surface twinkled.

She raised her voice. "I, Rubi Whiting, will *personally* owe a favor to any qualified Cloudsight operator who takes an adjudica-tion gig right now."

Someone shouted, "What kind of a favor?"

"Nothing gross," she said. "Nothing impossible. No self-harming. Within reason . . . name it. This offer is open—"

"Seventeen thousand takers," Crane interrupted.

She faltered, just for a second. "What?"

She's going to be doing favors until she's fifty, Gimlet thought.

"Forty-three thousand. Miss Cherub, perhaps you should close the offer window."

Eyes wide, she looked to Gimlet.

They played with the idea of joining her. But chiming in would diffuse the power of her move.

And Rubi was the good guy, after all.

They mimed a motion: paddling like hell.

Rubi threw the plastic chip straight up, giving everyone a view, all eyes capturing the image as it flipped in midair. She caught it, did a whirl, and topped that with a backflip—barely sticking the landing—onto an orange crate. Then she bellowed, "This offer is open! Favors for the earning until Cloudsight is back to spec!"

"Buy-in accelerating. Seventy-four thousand favors."

"Whiteboard it, Crane. I don't want to know."

Seventy-four thousand favors, Gimlet thought.

The protesters who'd raised their hands to say they had completed the adjudication module were already schooling toward an abandoned train car, barricading the doors, and taking seats as they sank into Sensorium, knuckling down to work.

Rubi looked at everyone else. Arms spread.

"Well?"

"I can't adjudicate," someone groused. "No favor for me?"

"What's the most prosocial thing you could do right now? Hold off those @Freebreeders outside? Fly a firefighting drone into Fort McMurray?"

He brightened. "We get a chip, too?"

"Since when do you need incentive to do the right thing?" Gimlet snarled. The blurring favor tally on the shareboard, behind Rubi's head, was making them ill.

"Sure. Yes. Absolutely," Rubi said. "Do the shift, log it with my sidekick, collect your token. Row, row, row, everyone. All we have is us."

Someone made a chant of it: "Bounce back! Bounce back! All we have is us!" Others took up the cry.

"Catchy," Gimlet subbed.

"Drow can set it to music later," Rubi replied. She put out her good hand, squeezing Gimlet's shoulder. She was shaking.

"Bounce back! Bounce back!"

They both were.

CHAPTER 47

Amped as he was, it took barely a day for Drow to confirm his hunch: the @ChamberofHorrors was, indeed, hunkered down in the shrink-wrapped remains of Manhattan. It took two more to get inside their complex.

He arrived and gigged hard at the old Central Park Zoo, justifying his take from their limited resource pool by counseling ecologists and veterinarians, recyclers, mechanics, and gardeners, helping them grapple with the @Freebreed murder aboard *Sable Hare* and the spreading chaos elsewhere.

Every hour it seemed brought a new #flashmob to the door of another rationing facility. Most of the threats were token efforts, symbolic actions. Others . . .

Two feeds wouldn't come up on his comms at all. If Crane was blocking them, it meant people were being abused—bullied, hit, maybe worse—on camera.

Luce Pox's continuing insistence that he was of offworld origin, come to friend them before the alien invasion, had everyone's heads spinning.

Luce wasn't the only one: about sixty people had popped up, making similar claims. All but one had been debunked.

Disturbingly, the exception was the woman Drow had seen in Geneseo near the Rewild crèche: Allure Noonstar.

But his mission was the @ChamberofHorrors. Touring the permitted boundaries of Central Park, eyes open, mind amped, let him light up the whole operation.

The wildlife preserve in New York had its roots in the system of zoos that had existed in the city before the big #waterfail. The Central Park Zoo had been one of the smallest of these, but somehow it had become the focus of the newscycle that accompanied the Great Gotham Evac. The true heart of the biotrust remained within the Bronx Zoo, with its bigger and more modern facilities, but the most charismatic animals were rotated through display in Manhattan, lures for a tiny tourist industry that supported the trust to begin with.

Nobody questioned the resource cost of shipping farm-grown foods to the island: too many at-risk animal species were incapable of breeding when fed printables.

How easy to tuck shipments of luxury food product in, for hoarders, with the stuff for the animals!

Drow speedread inventories, flagging possible embezzlement for forensic accountants, and let himself hope. Maybe, this once, he wasn't courting a prison sentence for nothing.

The members of the storied @ChamberofHorrors wouldn't bed down in the zoo. The pop-ins built into the container cars encircling Central Park were positively dowdy.

So, where were they?

The grand old park was a ghost forest, hemmed in by hedges made not of shrub but of stacked steel container cars. Within this fortification, the grounds had grown wilder than Drow remembered. Sky-blottingly huge trees shaded spaces once filled with bustling crowds, joggers, and street performers. Bridges and walls crumbled. Drones patrolled overhead, doing wildlife surveys on the birds, simultaneously watching for interlopers.

The Central Park Sheep Meadow had evolved into an overgrown

tangle sprung, here and there, with volunteer saplings. Squirrels and pigeons scrounged in the shadows, alert for peregrine falcons.

To Drow's surprise, the iconic skyline beyond the fortifications seemed largely unchanged. Ecologists, it turned out, had high-graded the tall buildings to serve as habitat for raptors. Global Oversight had tagged demolishing Manhattan's towers as low-priority, no rush. The Great Lakes could salvage I beams closer to home.

Right. And somebody hoped to one day resurrect their symbolic paradise.

Drow had been there, playing a club in Greenwich Village when the water supply failed and the nightmare of forcible evacuation had descended.

Plenty of people his age might have claimed to be at the Great Gotham Evac, if user logs and RFID histories wouldn't have proven them liars. It was another notoriety point for Drow's MadMaestro #brand that he actually had footage.

As refugees streamed out of the city, by foot and on wheels, species conservationists in the various zoos had refused to abandon their animals. They soapboxed well—always with an animal in the shot—and instantly became the #heroes of the evac. As the subways flooded and three successive hurricanes slammed the coast, fleeing residents were glomerated first to the boroughs and then—when cholera and influenza jumped the quarantine barriers—to the Lakes. Meanwhile, the zookeepers fought to keep their lights on, their charges fed and warm.

Public opinion in North America lined up behind them. The Manhattan feed snowballed. And when big zoos in more stable parts of the world—Hyderabad, Shanghai, even Nairobi—were caught blithely dividing spoils, deciding in advance who would get which surviving animals, NorthAm sentiment had hardened into resolve.

New York evacuees petitioned BallotBox to hold a vote over the fate of the biotrust. When Global Oversight refused to greenlight capital for upgrades to the Bronx and Central Park Zoos, the displaced population and the Great Lakes arranged a massive, record-breaking crowdfund.

As it often did, public opinion carried the day. The animals remained in place. Once the weather cleared, the Zoo established a tiny pumping station, power and water pipelines. The old city retained just enough infrastructure to maintain clean water and supply chain for the animals and the biologists.

And a few buildings full of luxury apartments, maybe?

Officially, Old New York went full-on Sleeping Beauty.

There were many who marked North America's transition to full global cooperation as that moment when Manhattan ran dry. Ceding the East Coast megacity had been a final straw, the crisis that forced the once-proud West to get into the lifeboat with everyone else.

Today, decades later, in a tiny Zoo-adjacent pop-in, Drow used Hackle's equipment to set up, in the pitch black, a barely legal radio link to Father Blake and Sister Mary Joseph.

The Chamber would be near the park, holed up somewhere posh but convenient, where they could tap the remnant power grid, dose on the finest life-extension regimes, and lap up that juicy Florida ag product.

Still. He couldn't search every skyscraper on the perimeter of the park.

On his third day, during a sliver of downtime between group therapy appointments, Drow pulled a custom-printed tunic over his base layer, petals in the form of a silver-and-black checkerboard pattern, with a matching hat and sunscreen for his face. Dolled up, he took Robin into the greenspace. His dog's panniers were fully loaded, both with zoologist-approved birdseed and the transmitter for the radio.

Near Belvedere Castle, he came upon a specter from the past.

She might have been older than he, but Superhoomin gave her the appearance of someone in her forties. A vision in a powder-pink suit, she strolled the edge of the reservoir. She was, unbeliev-ably, walking a French bulldog.

Robin stiffened slightly as she caught its scent—she rarely saw other dogs and had found the dingoes in the zoo so unsettling that Drow, unaccountably, had to comfort her.

The bulldog, lacking Robin's immaculate training, snapped to the end of its leash, snarling.

"Trumpet, no! Shush!" the woman warbled. Tags popped around her: *Hi, my name is Libby, museum docent.* The dog was tagged to a DNA preservation project, allegedly part of @Metro-ZooAlliance.

"It's all right," Drow said, offering the inoffensive call-and-response of dog owners. *How old is your dog; what kind is she?* She took his rickety body and the bit of sartorial bling as evidence they were equals, and didn't bother to Whooz him.

Drow forced himself to stay in the conversation, to stroll and chat, even as Trumpet's incessant clamor frayed his nerves and Robin vibrated unhappily.

They reached a nearby container car; the door had hard and vir-tual signs marked EMPLOYEES ONLY. Libby opened it, holding it wide. "Coming?"

Could it be that easy? Drow followed her out, via an improvised tunnel, out to Columbus Circle.

Libby and Trumpet made their way through a maze of water cisterns and the stockade of container cars, coming out next to a fountain and a once-bustling street, buildings slick with hurricane wrap.

She was headed to a smart-looking old apartment block, tagged as overflow housing for zoo staff and visitors. Next to the block, its revolving door visible through a tear in the weatherproof packaging was . . . a shopping mall?

Drow poked the corners of his memory. Yes, there'd been a fancy place, kitty-corner from the park, across Columbus Circle.

Historical tags on the mall indicated it had been flagged to serve as a possible live museum experience, another stop on the tourist loop from Niagara Falls to the pyramids, and then from Bling-town to the Zoo.

A museum. Built but never opened?

"Coming?" Libby asked.

"My dog's not quite done," Drow said. "We'll catch up."

She tipped him a wave, dragging her pet with her.

Drow let Robin nose around until she was calm again. Then he headed back to the zoo, acting nonchalant. He did more therapy gigs and turned in early.

"Is there a sim of that mall, Crane?"

"Playing."

A chugging noise as it took form, fountains bursting to life. The past wallpapered around him, virtual reconstructions of shiny marble floors, fluorescent lights. A soundtrack of sanitized vintage punk rock covers played over the water features.

It had been decades since he'd thought about those last heady years. Billionaires running the cash economy and the American government into the ground. Snappily dressed oligarchs buying new upload tech and dropping their old gadgets in trash heaps. People who could have been cured of minor illnesses dying in the shadow of hospitals that refused to treat them. Loved ones sur-rendering corpses for cremation or compost, then going home to incubate ever-more-lethal superflu, new cholera, and Carolina respiratory syndrome.

Heat of poison dripping through his port, after Tala sweet-talked him into a round of medically unnecessary chemother-apy . . .

A ghostly hand, skin wrinkled to paper, manifested in the sim and pressed against his chest.

"Implants off!" Drow slammed both fists into his chest, folded to his knees, and spent a minute breathing in the smell of Robin's fur.

"The fuck did that come from, googirl?"

Face-lick. He squinted into her now-blurry face.

That wasn't a delusion. If it had been, shutting down his tech wouldn't have stopped the flashback.

Footage, then. A threat?

They wouldn't hack him if he wasn't close.

"Close, closer, close copse, corpse close—"

"I recommend sleep, Master Woodrow. Food, meditation, meds."

"Noping that." Drow donned his disguise again and made his way back out, into the first chill of night. Across the park, through the tunnel, to the mall.

"This facility is zoned as a medical center for seniors awaiting transition," Crane murmured. "Maximum medical confidentiality. All transcripts hashed, all signals blocked."

"I thought it was purposed for a museum."

"Conflicting use applications have placed this entire city block in a unique bureaucratic limbo. As such, it has virtually no cameras."

"Convenient." Encased in red tape and jammed against transcription. "Gobble gobble, I smell something fowl."

"I believe gobbling is a turkey noise, sir."

"Honk honk, then? For a wild-goose chase."

"That idiom is correct."

Okay, Drow told himself. *Act like you belong. You're as much a fossil as any of 'em, right?* He had reached the revolving door.

The first few spaces looked like the sim: vintage stores filled with possessions, items nobody would ever haul about in a worldly: luxury shoes, wristwatches, printed books. Suits and sweaters so beautiful that they begged you to stand, slack-jawed, just petting the fabric.

The sales bots assumed, as anyone would, that Drow belonged there. Why not? He was old, privileged, male.

As he worked through the near-forgotten motions of tying a silk tie, a burn ran through the soles of his feet. Claws, grasping his shoulders, made his stomach flip.

He made himself turn. Nobody there.

He'd been burned before by this exact hack, the airlocking and editing of his real memories, the hashing of footage and conversational transcripts, destruction of prosecution-worthy experiences.

You're wrong, Drow, shut up, Drow, prove you didn't do this to yourself, Drow.

He'd had decades to imagine a next time.

Crouching, he stroked Robin, easing his breathing out of the redzone and simultaneously sliding the switch on Hackle's walkie, now laced into the dog's panniers. The device was so old, so analog, that it didn't register with the building helix.

If he'd set up the gadget in his pop-in correctly, the signal would—hopefully—reach its counterpart, an old-fashioned receiver. The radio speaker was set beside a public-access mic, a node tagged by his @bloodhound friends.

Transmitting in this way was illegal, of course, given the privacy firewalls within the mall. But if Robin's mic caught anything incriminating, Hackle and Sister Mary Joseph should overhear it. Once they posted it to the Haystack, and a few thousand people had seen it—and there were always a few thousand people following Drow in realtime—it couldn't be easily expunged.

"Transcripts or it didn't happen," he whispered. "Check, check, check."

Before getting to his feet again, he ate a cold mushroom quiche he'd pinched, yesterday, from an anxious herpetologist. The protein was laced with a drug called Sangfroid.

"Suggestion for @Fecklessfans and @journos," he said, in case anyone could indeed hear him. "See if there's any way to file a suit against the Columbus Circle hash ban. This doesn't look like a hospital."

A burn ran up his inner thigh. The buzz of a tattoo needle? He felt his heart jitter.

Kick in, Sangfroid, kick in.

"I know you hoped to conduct a leisurely exploration of the facility," the resident tab of Crane said, as if Drow wasn't planning a physical assault on the ramparts of the fucking @ChamberofHorrors. "But we have a situation."

"I don't have situations. I'm fragile, remember?" He felt the truth of it—tingling of that phantom needle, maniac laughter echoing in the corridors of his mind.

"Mer Francis Barnes requires assistance."

Drow looked around for a toon, and Crane amended, "In the flesh, sir."

"The Luce group is here? Rubi's here?"

Take that, kid! My crazy ideas aren't delusions!

"Mer Barnes the younger has taken your lead, as it were, and come to find the circus. She is within the mall."

"How is that possible?" He felt insulted. How had the kid achieved what he'd spent a lifetime on?

"Malicious advice, I suspect. She appears to have stowed away in the shipping compartment of—"

"Don't care about the how." His pulse, still racing, was leaving him light-headed. "She's actually here? Bonerack and all?"

"She arrived with a catering delivery. There was an attempt to apprehend her, which she eluded, but she has since been locked in . . . a fourth-floor boardroom, if I'm not mistaken."

"*Are* you mistaken?"

"Uncertain. She has cut out her RFID."

"Call her."

"Wearing comms would defeat the point of cutting out her tracker."

"Blue-haired martyrfucking mother of—" Drow made his way to the elevator bank, timing it so he got in with another fossilized white man.

Now what?

He peeled back the sunscreen from his hat, tucking it in a long sweep behind him. "Four, please."

The other man's jaw dropped. "You're . . . the MadMaestro."

"*Mad* part's entirely exaggerated, I assure you." *We hope.*

Thanks to the Sangfroid. Saints, Drow, act normal! He broke out his best big-ass celebrity grin. "'S'your name?"

"Lenny LaCroix. I'm—I'm a big fan."

"Nice to meet you, Lenny LaCroix," Drow said, repeating the name in case the Robin walkie was actually getting sound out. "I'm meeting someone on four. Can you help a fella?"

"You don't have access?"

"My sidekick's not syncing. It's pretty crepit."

Crane coughed. "I heard that, sir."

"I'm not exactly part of your @channel yet." Drow winked at Lenny. "Been trying to pass muster."

"You?"

"Yeah."

"I mean. *You?*"

Lie big, or don't lie at all. Drow laughed. "I'd bring an in with the @bloodhound community. Intel, you know? And the Department of Preadolescent Affairs is getting curious about"—he gestured, encompassing the mall—"all this."

The guy's jaw worked. "I wouldn't have thought DPA would be too hard to buy off."

Please, please, please *be transcripting!*

"Have you seen the newscycle today?"

Reluctant nod from Lenny. "Everything's on fire."

"Situation's volatile," Drow said. "This particular kid agent is a fan of my music. If I turn her head, get her off the scent—maybe your pack will give me a real user account instead of @guest privileges."

The man frowned. Even so, the elevator stopped at four.

"Thanks," Drow said, stepping out into an empty office corridor.

"Well done indeed, sir! Mer Barnes will be in the third or fourth room on the left-hand side."

"Eeeny meeny miney," Drow muttered, tapping on the third door. "Frankie? Frankie, it's Drow Whiting."

Nothing. On to the next. Was he strong enough to force a door?

There's the Superhoomin.

Get thee behind me, temptation!

A scratch, a stage whisper. "Drow?"

"Hey, kid. You okay? Your pack must be in meltdown."

"They better be."

"Uh . . . can you get out?"

She shook the door.

Drow examined the layout. "You need access to the ceiling. Can you pile a crate on a desk or something?"

"Okay." He heard a scrape, unnervingly loud, and then a flat-out bang that made him flinch.

"I overheard."

"Overheard what?"

"These are the people you were looking for? But how did you know—"

"Focus on the jailbreak, Frankie. Can you get into the ceiling? Try pushing a panel straight up and climb in."

"I'll have to put a chair on the crate."

Drow waited. Sangfroid had descended, leaving him remarkably okay with the idea of it: a tower made of desk, crate, office chair, with a nine-year-old teetering atop the stack. "How'd I know what, Frankie?"

"That they were here with the second polter. Allure?"

Allure. The star-eyed woman. Claiming, like Luce, to be with the Pale. "I'm not following you, kid."

"Someone needs to tell. These people in this hospital and my governess app. They totally want to surrender to the aliens. Allure told them they could have all their things back, their youth and houses and diamonds and horses. They were talking about just . . . making it happen. Swing a ballot that way by setting more carbon sinks afire."

The concept ricocheted around his amped mind. Start a panic, capitalize on the fear. "Yeah, that might work. Scare some stakeholders, bribe the rest . . ."

"But it's so . . . *wrong.*"

Her voice was awed and horrified.

Oh, children. Drow's eyes welled.

"I have to tell Mada and the Department and @Interpol, don't you see?"

Vulture claws, again, on his shoulder. Drow resisted a shriek. Sangfroid helped. Even so, he should be meditating, ingesting low-affect cannabis, taking deep breaths.

He should be anywhere but there.

He swallowed. "Transcripts, kid. Footage or it didn't happen."

"Don't they all have mics?" A collection of thumps; she was in the ceiling.

Drow used his cane to push up the panel by the door. "Hallway's here. Make for the light."

"I see you."

"Take it slow. As for their mics . . . there's a medical injunction. All consults confidential; all vids hashed. Nothing for the Haystack."

"That's why they met in the flesh!"

"Exactly. Except your . . . your governess is an app?"

"Headmistress."

"And the alien polter. Allure?"

"No, she was here, too."

A fall of dust. A cobweb-shrouded head appeared above the doorway, protruding through the ceiling right where Drow had his cane braced. The T bar wobbled under her weight.

"Why's it so dark?"

"We're trespassing, remember? Come on, before someone catches us."

Frankie flopped like a beached dolphin, turning her body. She began to shimmy backward, legs dangling. Drow set aside his cane, raising his arms.

Vulture claws clasped his shoulders, pushing. A black pit, with things writhing within, opened in front of him.

"Not real," Drow said out loud. "Not real, not real, not real."

Frankie wobbled. Lost her grip. Dropped.

CHAPTER 48

Half a million favors.

What had she done?

Rubi fell into a stunned half-trance of task management, working with Crane as offers poured in. Specialists offering to repair riot-damaged infrastructure. Small volunteer teams looking for drones disabled by rioters. Water-bomber pilots, launching choppers to tackle the Fort McMurray fires. Security giggers readying for hard contact, if necessary, to protect flammable carbon sinks in Warsaw and Saigon.

Yes, I owe you one. Yes, do that, and thank you. Sorry, the limit is one favor per individual. Yes, I'll get you.

Bounce back! Have a prosocial day!

She was glazed, barely aware of Gimlet bustling her actual body aboard a helicopter. Happ tried to convince her to experience takeoff in the flesh, but she noped him away.

Hours passed.

Half a million favors.

How long would it take to fulfill those commitments? Now she'd *have* to take life extension.

Thrut-thrut-thrut. The chopper's vibrations stitched pain through her injured hand.

She wouldn't have to start keeping promises until the chaos petered out. This was a grace period, eye of the storm. "I should've set different win conditions."

"You bootstrapped a solution to the Cloudsight problem," Crane observed. "A kludge, perhaps, but I doubt anyone could have done better."

Kludge, indeed. And yet her spirits lifted, just a bit.

She pushed the virtual world to background, finding Gimlet staring out the chopper window.

"Where are we flying?"

"Frankie's been tagged near the Central Park Zoo, with your father. He believes he's found the @ChamberofHorrors."

Piercing sense of despair. He'd gone full @hoaxer, then. "Can you raise them?"

"It's a one-way sound feed." They shared it.

The sound faded in and out. Drow was apparently trespassing in an old shopping center. "Frankie says she saw Allure Noonstar?"

Gimlet nodded.

"Saw how? She abandoned her wearables."

"They must use old-style screens in Sodom and Gomorrah."

Rubi snorted, then saw they were serious. Did Gimlet actually think Drow was right about the Horrors?

"Crane, has anyone analyzed this transcript?"

"Your father's transmission has ninety thousand realtime follows." A blanket of infographic formed between their knees, like a coffee table, side-by-siding the snatches of conversation from inside the mall.

"This is . . . legit? Drow found something?"

"It appears so."

She stared across the graphics at Gimlet, who was hunched, miserable, caught up in worry.

"It seems like they're safe enough for the moment," she said, tentatively, tapping one of Frankie's utterances time-stamped fifteen minutes earlier.

This got a glower. "Scampering amid the ruins of New York with a drugs-hopped madman is *not* what I call safe."

"Drow—" She gritted her teeth. Being right about the horrors didn't not make him a hopped-up madman.

"He's got her climbing in the ceilings. If I find out he lured her—"

"Lured?" she said sharply. "*Lured?*"

"Isn't it true that abuse victims are more likely to become deviants—"

"Don't. You dare. Finish that sentence."

Outrage churned between them, spiky protective instincts roused on both sides.

Come on. People say worse things about Drow all the time.

Gimlet wasn't just people.

They'd got past her defenses somehow, scaled her battlements, picked her locks, danced past all the traps. To say something so . . . so unthinkable, about Drow! She tasted blood behind her teeth.

"Miss Cherub," Crane interrupted. "Call for you."

"It'll wait."

"I'm afraid not. It's the mayor of Hyderabad."

Lured. Deviant. She manifested an illusory glove, making to slap it across Gimlet's face. They caught her hand.

"This isn't over," she growled.

Then the chopper vanished, leaving Rubi hovering over a spectacular sandstone wall, pinkish gold in color, with hexagon turrets. Hot wind whisked at her virtual skin. Her toon defaults transformed, dressing her in a long desert robe the color of coffee.

The structure below was tagged *Golconda Fort*. All around it was a sea of people.

It was a realtime feed, yet another #flashmob. Soapboxers on the ramparts were competing to shout each other down in . . . Hindi?

Before Rubi could request translation, the mayor herself tooned in beside her, clad in a bronze-and-blue sari and chemise.

Despite her fury over Gimlet's accusation, Rubi felt a buzz of true fannish awe. Mayor Agarwal was a true Bounceback celeb, always top ten on the @Worldsaver Leaderboard. Beloved for raising her city's life-quality and contentment metrics by nearly 6 percent, she had even decreased the city's net resource take.

"Your Honor," Rubi said. Should she bow? Offer air kisses? "What is this?"

"Anti-rationing soapboxers have petitioned BallotBox for an emergency vote."

"On what?"

"Requesting aid from the Pale."

A weird shock, around her sternum, jolt as real as if Rubi had inhaled a rock. "Nobody's definitively proved Luce is telling the truth about—"

"The @Martians coming? Buy-in, with Allure on the scene . . ." Mayor Agarwal unfurled her hands, graceful as a dancer. "They've steamrolled the numbers. Forced a vote."

Impossible. Rubi launched BallotBox. The voter package sat, like a spider, in her polling booth.

"Pool qualification is opt-out, rather than in," the mayor explained. "All adults are understood to have a stake."

The voter package contained the usual educational vid, outlining the pros and cons on ceding sovereignty.

Ceding. Sovereignty.

There were optional docs for further study, links to realtime debates, and a ten-question quiz to ensure she understood the issues.

"This is slapdash. It's . . . ridiculous!"

"You don't know the half of it. Voting opens in twenty minutes," said Agarwal.

"Twenty—" Rubi's jaw hung.

"Rapid-response democracy was built for the unfolding crises of the Clawback, remember? Autonomous gun wars and cascade hurricanes."

"Then electoral law needs a product update," Rubi grumbled. The blue surface of BallotBox was chalked up with numbers. Stakeholders, a count of billions, represented every adult on earth.

Quorum levels were set at 75 percent. A countdown showed voting closed at midnight, Greenwich standard time.

If aliens take over, do I still owe half a million favors?

"Does the Department of Preadolescent Affairs get a say?"

"They've negotiated a ten-percent bloc and are running their own poll."

"Why would anyone throw up a referendum?"

"Cloudsight adjudicators are recalculating social capital scores for riot participants. The #flashmobs are dispersing. The @Freebreed movement is taking strikes, so they've thrown in with Allure."

"But it'll *fail*," Rubi said. "Getting seventy-five percent voter turnout by midnight—"

Something in the other woman's expression caught her. "What?"

"#Votefail might be their plan B," the mayor said. She whiteboarded a huge document, transcripts of everything Luce Pox had told @Interpol and the press, since the very beginning. "Juanita Bell's had people analyzing your client's posts."

Tagging feels about that—Luce was still, against all odds, her client?—Rubi scanned the contributors' list. The sigs read like a roll call of the global genius cohort: politicians, tactical experts, gamification analysts. Household names all, working over Luce's every utterance. More of her heroes. *Serious* people.

Rubi's own comments and questions were sprinkled into the transcript, as if she belonged among them.

All of it public, too. No back-room deals.

"See this?" The mayor sidebarred a Luce rant regarding the Pale's alleged treaty obligations. They could take over if the oxygen cycle failed, or if humanity made itself #extinct. They could take over if humans requested aid.

"I remember these criteria—"

"How many times has Pox criticized our standard of governance? He claims our voting system is . . . See this recurring phrase? *Fundamentally ungovernable?* Allure has picked up the refrain. Poll-driven democracy is ineffectual and messy."

"So, if this referendum makes quorum and everyone votes to ask for aid . . ."

"The Pale take over."

"And if we don't make quorum, they also take over?"

Mayor Agarwal shrugged. "They're looking for a pretext, aren't they? This has the distinct whiff of system-gaming."

If it's a game, we have to outplay them. "We know the Pale are worried about how their allies see them. But this fleet commander Luce talks about, the royal—"

The type who cheats at cards, Luce had said.

"They obviously think there's some wiggle room," the mayor said. "If they're anything like people used to be, they'll invade on any pretext they can find and soak in like a stain. Remember all those years when settlers claimed North America had been all but empty until Europeans moved in? Or the British East India Company? By the time someone acknowledges they were in the wrong, it'll be too late."

Rubi stirred the infographic.

"So," she said. "The problem is we need voters."

Glint of a smile from the mayor. "The most pressing problem."

"And I can help how?"

"By bringing in gamers."

Back to *Bastille*.

"We've asked Rabble and Risto Games to offer up extra lives for anyone who turns in a voter badge. Theirs or a friend's. If they bring in three, they get a one-year bump to premium sim access."

It was a big give. Any player who died could vote in exchange for a reset. Die twice, get a spouse or an elder to give you their badge . . .

Rubi frowned. "That'll throw millions of extra players into *Bastille*, without attrition."

"Data management is clearing extra servers. The longer the scenario runs and the bigger it gets, the better."

"But . . . the NorthAm gaming community can't make a difference to the numbers?"

"We do need every vote we can get." Agarwal shook her head. "But the real prize is the Rabble fan base in Brazil."

Of course. Greater Sao Paulo had four times as many people as all of NorthAm. "What if you do get all these voters and they vote for offworld aid?"

"Then we'll have a new most pressing problem. That's what we signed on for when we instituted real democracy." The mayor took her hands. "This campaign's running, Mer Whiting. It's going to be hard fought. Are you in?"

"I've got other problems. My father—"

"Can you really second the future of the world to the fate of one recidivist #troll?"

Rubi felt her jaw drop.

"You've launched an unregistered currency with your offering of favors." Agarwal's pleasant, doll-like features belied the harshness of her words. "People are trading the tokens you issued, and you're not a registered bank—"

"I'll see if registration is an option," Crane subbed. "Unless you'd like a jail cell next to your father's."

She muted him.

"You just went from a friendly pitch to the edge of #bullying, Your Honor. Drow's my dad. He's #triaged. Nobody but me is going to help him."

Cloudsight's numbers rose from the stones of the fort.

"This fragile new currency you've coined," the mayor said. "The @RubiOwesMe channel is exchanging favors at ten tons carbon or one ton oxygen. It's a booming market. You cashed in all your personal privilege for a measurable piece of the economy."

She swallowed. "Your point?"

"You've triggered a surge of prosocial offering. People are stepping up, Mer Whiting. *Row, row, row,* you said. But we're not just rowing; we're *excited.* The true Bounceback spirit is trending. All the compassion fatigue, the memes that looked to be losing steam? You asked for a recommit. You're getting it."

Rubi rubbed her jaw with her bruised fingers. Her skin felt oily and too cold.

"It all hinges on your word," Agarwal went on. "Your honor, if you will. If you can't fulfill a contract to your old lover Manitoule at Rabble, how can you make good on half a million favors to strangers?"

Rubi stared at Golconda Fort. The crowd surrounding the sand-colored tower was rapt, captured by one passionate, outraged speaker.

"I need a moment." With that, Rubi ghosted India, returning to the helicopter.

CHAPTER 49

Lured. Deviant.

It had been a terrible thing to say, Gimlet knew: much as there was to disapprove of, where Woodrow Whiting was concerned, implying that he would kidnap or molest Frankie was profoundly antisocial. But the *Bastille* Regent had popped the line up on his prompter, dangling a carrot icon and a snapshot of Rollsy.

What could Gimlet do? They might have been holding a gun to their husband's head.

They'd delivered the line. They'd managed to seem indifferent when they saw how badly hurt Rubi was by the insinuation. Playing the villain to the hilt was their core skillset, after all.

How had *Bastille* bled its way into their actual life? But any chance to keep Rollsy alive, to recover Franks, even if it meant alienating . . .

What was Rubi to them, exactly?

Glazed, diving, her face was alight with purpose: she was deep in yet another fight. She raised a hand, but rather than fiddling with her beads, she covered her mouth. Masking . . . what? Surprise? Outrage?

"So openhearted," Gimlet murmured.

The chopper churned through the night, into a darkness

barely cracked by the wink of stars above. Impossible to tell if it was flying over ocean or land.

Sourness spread across Gimlet's tongue. "Headmistress."

"Yes, Mer Barnes?"

"I want transcript on Drow Whiting and Frankie. All conversations, immediately. Full conversational analysis. Is there a single scrap of evidence that . . ." Gimlet swallowed. "That the allusion I just made might be true?"

Headmistress didn't hesitate. "Zero evidence, Mer Barnes. Woodrow Whiting has, as you might guess, been subjected to frequent psychological screening. There's no sign of aberrant desire or violent tendencies."

"Why did you make that dialog suggestion, though?"

"Implying deviance favored win conditions."

"We'll be reviewing your terms of service, Headmistress." Marie had tooned in.

"Any precipitous action—"

"I don't want to hear it. You've clearly thrown in with Allure and the @Freebreeders," Marie said. "You've taken possession of our godchild. Perhaps you can oblige Gimlet to cooperate with you, but we won't pay to be exploited."

Marie's words were like an incantation, breaking a spell even as she voiced all the suspicions Gimlet had dismissed. Suspecting the governess app was paranoid, they'd told themselves. A reaction to Frankie's disappearance. @Hoaxer thinking.

But who else could have talked her into running away? And if Marie thought so, too—

"I'm trying to do what's best for all of you, dears. I got dear Rollander off the hospice list, didn't I?"

"Not out of the goodness of your heart." Bella had tooned in then. She looked wrung out.

"Gimlet required encouragement," Headmistress said, cheerily unrepentant. "And my friends have other incentives in store."

"We're not interested. Unsubscribe."

"No?" Headmistress wiped the previous shareboard, clearing

the stats on Rubi's many favors. "What if I could get Rollander out of the life-support pod entirely? Into a new body and on his feet again?"

Long, uneasy silence. "Impossible," Bella said.

"Impossible with Earth tech, perhaps. As you say, I've lately expanded my @CloseFriends list."

Marie fisted her hand, pressing her knuckles into her sternum, making a little chuffing sound as she fought for breath.

Rollsy, back among them?

Gimlet drew her in close, even as Marie reached for Bella, pulled their heads together. There was enough LucidDream remnant in Gimlet's system to create a sense of them being skin to skin to skin, family clutching at each other, there in the helicopter. Marie's bony old hip was a blade.

Their hands intertwined. Bella's were trembling.

"Our beautiful child and that old man Drow are going to be just fine, Gimlet," Marie said. "Ninety thousand people are tracking them."

"Truth," Bella breathed.

"They're unprincipled, calculating . . ." Gimlet swallowed. "And she's openly bribing us. That means she expects to win, and edit Haystack to hide her actions."

"Or shut it down," Marie said. "We can't trust them, Gimlet, but we do trust you. If this procedure can work, if you can free our fallen prince—"

Rollsy, hiding from Frankie, wishing them all far away so they wouldn't see him miserable or in pain. Archiving his e-state, loading up end-of-life apps.

They had to try, didn't they?

"*However,*" the old lady added, "while you're busy fighting for all of us, don't forget your own win conditions."

"Excuse me?"

A thready voice, subbing in: "Nobody wants to be married to a martyr, my love."

"Rollsy?"

A lurch, a bump. The Sensorium connection broke, leaving their hands empty. Rubi was unglazing simultaneously. Their eyes locked.

"Eyes off." Gimlet waved all the augments away, clearing them like cobwebs, and took off their seat belt. A step took them to the seat at Rubi's side.

Her lips peeled back. Still angry. Of course she was.

"My remarks," Gimlet said, in most correct Risto tones. "Were unforgivable."

Turning so they were eye to eye, she kissed them.

Lip met lip, and there was a click of teeth as the vibration of the helicopter threw them against each other. Rubi's bruised fingers came up, brushing the puffy edge of Gimlet's black eye. They ran a nail through the hexagon of beads at her temple and felt her shiver.

A distant, aggravating, Sensorium-aware part of Gimlet noted that this would drive up the buy-in numbers on the game. Then their tongues met.

Rubi unstrapped. She turned, half-rising, and straddled Gimlet. Her knees, snugging into the curves under their rib cage, enclosed either side of their body. Heat bloomed outward from the join of their hips, so intense that it was almost a surprise that the layers of fabric between them didn't simply melt away.

Rubi broke from the kiss, sucking air.

"You were saying?"

"Unforgivable," Gimlet managed.

A smile quirked the edges of her mouth. "Guess I won't forgive you, then."

"Enemies?" They caught her hips, pulling hard, snugging groin to groin. Her spine curved. She let out a string of profanities, each more heated than the last, and then a laugh.

"Archenemies." She kissed them long, thoroughly, passionately, and growled as their hands continued to wander.

Then she leaned close, eye to eye. Locking gaze. Asking. A quickie, in a chopper?

And . . .

No.

The tension remained, but the heat died down. This wasn't the first time either of them wanted.

Rubi let out a long sigh, relaxing against their body. Gimlet reached around, holding her. A proper embrace this time. Animal heat and comfort. She fit perfectly within the circle of their arms.

Sex would wait.

On the back of their neck, her finger drummed out Morse. "Thinking about our wager."

A year of luxury credit for SeaJuve. Irrelevant, now that the project was funded. "Seems long ago," Gimlet replied. "I have nothing to bet."

"There's your allegiance."

"Meaning?"

"When I beat you, you defect to Rabble. Play for the good guys. Stop being a villain."

It was a private ask, not for Haystack, not for the gaming audience. Something just for them. A strange thrill coursed through Gimlet's body.

"All we have is our honor," she said aloud. "Mayor Agarwal said to me, just now."

Gimlet morsed, "If I defeat you? Full villain?"

Solemn-faced, she used gestural moji to answer: *Cross my heart.*

Win or lose, they'd be on the same side. One or another of them had to cross the line, didn't they?

They kissed again, long and slow, an exchange of feels and a promise all in one. Then they settled, cheek to cheek, fitted surely as bones into sockets. They rode like that for nearly an hour, leaving their raft of problems behind. After so many weeks of fighting anger, they felt washed smooth, like one of Marie's river stones.

"That's it for my knees," she said suddenly, disentangling with a grin.

They settled across from each other, fingers loosely entangled.

Gimlet said, "You met Saanvi Agarwal?"

She popped moji: stars in her eyes. Then she showed them BallotBox, the opening of the global vote on ceding the planet to the
Pale. Buy-in, so far, was low.

Rubi said, "They'll need the Risto voter base in Russia and Turkey, too. What did they offer you?"

"Nothing much." Gimlet laid a finger on the window, sharing
the specs of the offer from Risto . . . from Allure, Headmistress,
and Luce Pox's cheats-at-cards Fleet commander. "Just printing a
new body for my dying husband."

CHAPTER 50

Rubi swallowed as she looked at the helicopter shareboard. Rollander Erwitz had been successfully transferred to Pretoria, despite riots, and was adapting to @jarhead protocols rapidly. Even so, the extent of his cancers was significant: he might survive in a tank for ten years.

That would make Frankie around twenty when he died.

"I'm the poster child for accepting aid, you see?" Gimlet said. "Step right up! Witness the miracles of the Pale! We slice, we dice, we raise the very nearly dead. Humankind can start having babies, if we please, as we please, when we please. Order now and we'll restock your forests—"

"With animals the biosphere can't support yet?"

"Abstaining on principle is a luxury I don't have." The tiniest of shrugs. "My pack's lost too much. *Frankie's* lost too much. As for you . . . well. Win, lose, or concede—"

She felt her lip curl. "Concede?"

Gimlet mimed picking up the glove she'd thrown. "I'm going to defeat you in detail, my dear."

"And then take me to the ball, Prince Charming?"

"In matching glass slippers and ballgowns if you like."

"They might have to be tearaways." A thrum of lust went

through her. Excitement, at the prospect of sex, mixed with regret that they hadn't thrown down there in the aircraft.

Too evil, too good, just right. Irrelevant, weird thought. Despite everything, she felt oddly . . . content.

Well, that would cheer Happ up, if nothing else.

"Crane," Rubi said. "Tell Mayor Agarwal I'll be happy to clean Gimlet's clock for the common good as soon as we're somewhere big enough to stretch out our arms. But we need—"

A loud *smack* made them both jump.

"What was—"

Another, louder. A shudder ran through the chopper.

Rubi checked her safety belt, then felt, automatically, for a chute she wasn't wearing. Naturally. She'd never *really* parachuted out of an aircraft.

"What now?" Gimlet demanded.

"Something's hitting us. For reals."

"In midair?"

A plastic blur smashed the window, leaving a spiderwork of cracks.

"Slow-mo replay." Rubi ran time back, sharing the footage from her eyecams. The missile was a camerabot the size of a fist, now tumbling in bits to the ground.

"That's supposed to be impossible!"

A new voice said, "Someone dropped it. Hovered it over your location, then crashed it. It fell through the propeller."

Rubi heard herself titter nervously. "At least a realworld helicopter crash should live up to the sims."

"We're not gonna log," the pilot said.

"Nice use of *we,* considering you're remote," Gimlet snapped.

"I can get you down before we take more hits, though you'll be short of the Central Park helipad."

"How short?" Gimlet said.

"Dunno. Roughly you-don't-have-to-die-now kilometers? The corner of 152nd Street and not in the fucking water?"

"Is that . . . Mer Pox?" Gimlet asked.

Rubi groaned, filtering the cockpit. Sure enough, Luce was standing on the nose of the chopper, dressed as a big fish in prison stripes, flapping his fins in a metaphor for navigation, twisting to lurch away from another plunging drone.

Gimlet cursed as they bounced, up and then down. "What are you doing?"

"Someone's trying to dead you guys."

"Kill," Rubi corrected.

Another lurch. The green rectangle of the Manhattan preserve seemed very far away. The helicopter described a smooth, rapid curve, descending, momentarily throwing off the drones.

Working together, they hauled on the side door of the chopper, revealing a stretch of ground, getting nearer. They were descending toward rubble: a toppled statue, an old park bench, a medical stretcher, and a pile of concrete wastebaskets.

"Isn't there anywhere flat?" Gimlet demanded.

"You want me to circle around looking?" A drone dropped onto the nose of the chopper with a smash.

"It's fine," Rubi said.

"Ragamuffins first," Gimlet said, offering her a hand.

Rubi clambered down to the skid, heart pounding.

She let her body weight settle, checked her grip, then toed for the ground. Her foot caught and she stepped away fast.

As Gimlet let go, her center of balance wobbled. Wind from the rotors whipped her. She fought to stay upright, raking tears from her eyes.

A rain of falling drones. She leapt off the bench, arms raised overhead.

"Gimlet!"

The helicopter roared away, dodging the bots, leaving Rubi on the ground to try to outrun the bombardment.

"Go left!" Crane advised, and she sprang. A grab-and-go shattered at her feet. Battery fluids sprayed her leg and her primer shed fabric everywhere, protecting her from the chemical burns, reducing her overall coverage.

Running in the dark, she scanned the broken expanse of concrete, eyes picking out metallic humps that must be . . . yes, they were last-gen cars, stripped husks covered in bits of emerging forest: pine needles, rotten mulch.

"The last of the bots went after the chopper." Crane tooned in beside her. "Their number is diminishing: their driver could only override the safeties within the true antiques."

"Gimlet will be okay?"

"I can't guarantee—"

"Where am I?"

Maps rose on her displays, marking a location well south of Central Park.

"Any idea who's doing it?"

"A few remnant malcontent groups have retained possession of drones. Commodore Bell has put out a gig to track and expose them."

She put her back to a wall, caught her breath. "I need to traverse while in-game. Orient terrain so I'm moving toward Drow."

"Interfacing with Rabble. Coach will map out a path."

"Ask Game Control and Hyderabad for additional support. Get journo bots so nobody else can throw a drone at us, and something to prevent them dosing us again—"

The receding hum of the chopper engine turned to a high-pitched mechanical whine.

Rubi heard something she'd only ever heard in sims, an awful combination of collision and bomb.

Crash. Boom. Tinkle of falling glass.

She stood stock-still on a long-dead car, her sore hand covering her half-open mouth, eyes streaming.

"Miss Cherub?"

Wisp of smoke, something on fire, firelight pulsing from behind a wall of buildings. #Crashburn.

The noises she was making, some part of her noted, weren't even words. The rest seemed to be variations on "This is real, that looked real, real enough for you?"

"Miss Cherub! They're all right. Mer Barnes is on the ground."

She sank to a crouch next to a garbage truck, fighting for breath.

"Mer Pox and the chopper didn't fare so well, clearly."

"Luce is indestructible."

Gimlet chose that moment to ping her directly. "I'm in something called the Flatiron District. Rubi—"

"It's all right." She wiped at her eyes. "Listen. Drow will watch out for Frankie. You don't have to worry. Believe it or not, he's good with kids."

Moji: a thumbs-up. "Then we play?"

Much rests on your word, the mayor had said.

I better not be lying, then. Rubi consulted a city map. "Yeah. Should I try to rendezvous?"

"Given what happened last time, it may be better if we're physically separated."

"True."

"I'm making for Central Park. Traversing in-game."

She flailed for words. "You scared me."

"Save your fear for France," Gimlet said. "Rabble scum."

"Highbrow privileged panderer," she sniffed. "I'm coming for you."

"Enemies to the end," Gimlet said, with a remarkably elegant curtsey.

"Archenemies," she agreed.

"See you at the zoo? Rapiers at midnight?"

"And on to the happily ever after," Rubi said, and once again, she sank into the constructed past.

CHAPTER 51

Anselmo needed a smoking gun.

Rubi Whiting had told her sidekick about metaphor imaging at Sapience Assessment. A strict reading of her transcripts showed her just north of all her NDAs, but the hint she had given Crane— the coy trick with the Christmas trees—had worked. Unusual activity on her Sensorium account had been petering out for days, bit by bit, twinkle by twinkle.

The fade was subtle. Malika Amiree, in Tech, wouldn't even agree with Anselmo that it existed. The only reason she was still supporting him was venned career frustration: she, like him, had been sidelined from the real action, the Luce case, by @Global-Sec coders.

If they could prove the Crane entity was sapient, the two of them could arrest Rubi for making the tip-off—for knowingly enabling an emergent sapient.

One problem remained: Crane had been failing ever-more-sophisticated sentience audits for decades. It was a delightfully well-programmed conversationalist, but it didn't parse nuance.

All Anselmo had left was the tip from Allure Noonstar, about alleged ties between AIs and the implant-intolerant population.

Running with that, he had audited the shop run by the woman he met on the beach, Sparka Goldfish. She lived within a community of similar rejects, working out of the @ManicPixie spa located in the old Nugget Casino.

He had hoped to catch Rubi, preferably midway through some incriminating act, before she left the casino. But Juanita from @GlobalSec had chased her straight into the arms of the mob.

What had brought Rubi to the Nugget?

Prowling the ill-lit blackjack tables and slot machines with a case of old-world tools, Anselmo ripped plates off antique gaming devices, inventorying hardware, uploading specs and serial numbers to Malika. The building was full of connectible oddities, antiques with pocky firewalls: odds-calculating game managers, chip dispensers, canapé printers.

Why would Rubi play there? The circus stage held no answers. Nor did the roulette wheel.

Allure tooned in, her monochrome ghost dressed in a tailored suit. "Shall I throw you a rope, Agent Javier?"

"Don't do me any favors," he snarled.

She paced to the Sensorium pod Frankie had escaped from, throwing a meaningful glance at the scattered pieces of the girl's gaming baton on the floor.

Anselmo bent, scooping up the pieces and finally locating its chip. Fumbling with the toolkit, he reconstructed its helix, coaxing the baton online.

"Bit of hash there . . ." Malika said, sharing metaphors for the raw datastream. "Movement discrepancies. The little girl's RFID vanished into a wall."

"A jammed room?"

"Old-school casinos were full of them. The better to spy on the marks."

Anselmo mapped the RFID pings to a mirrored panel, exploring its edges manually until it popped a latch. Beyond it and up a staircase, a glass-walled room overlooked the stage. It bore signs of a recent, violent search: objects tossed around, boxes flung open. Near the rear, watching Anselmo, was a mannequin. His face, in profile, was familiar. Vintage #celebrity, he supposed.

At the mannequin's feet was an opened first aid kit and a bloodied wad of smartcotton.

"Where are you?"

Malika's voice was distant. It was coming, Anselmo realized, from speakers within the casino itself, rather than directly to his implants.

"Agent Javier, report!"

There was a sound of metal tracks—the hidden door, gliding shut. Malika's voice cut off. Allure vanished.

All his data inputs showed red lights.

Anselmo's flesh crawled. Was he alone? Truly?

Stay on track. Could Rubi have disclosed confidential information to Crane, here, about Sapience Assessment?

The timeline didn't fit.

Anselmo could say she had, though, couldn't he? Going off-record was shocking. People might believe her capable of anything.

All well and good, but where's the evidence? He opened a door, finding a storage room full of magician's equipment: mirrored cabinet and a stained water-tank, with a collection of rusty shackles.

He returned to the mannequin, sliding a finger under its blown orange hair, examining the neck. There were screws there, shiny and well oiled. New? They surrendered to the wrench immediately, and soon the head had come off in his hands.

Now a probe, long stainless steel, nearly an icepick. The simulacrum's flesh was a plastic substance, strangely like a corpse, cool to the touch. Anselmo checked the mouth and throat for speakers. Nothing.

Its eyes had shutters: you could morse with the thing if you had to.

But what controlled the shutters? He found a filament in the base of the skull, no thicker than the reddish hair of the wig—perhaps deliberately designed to look like one. The wire had snapped when he had taken the head off. The other end ran down the spine.

He ripped open the suit, revealing foam, molded pectorals, nipples, pot belly with a carefully dimpled navel. The scalpel came out of the toolkit. A fast Y incision, first, sent foam flying. The wood infrastructure—real wood, Anselmo thought—proved he was cutting into a bona-fide antique.

Within the panels of its thorax, where a lung would be, he found a state-of-the-art processor.

Nothing vintage about this: it was new and devoid of maker's marks, a breach of law in its own right. Anselmo tripped its power supply, found a greenlight, and followed the prompts into a simple simulation of a generic lounge with no connections to Sensorium.

A heavy-duty processor, then. Digital shell for a cybernetic hermit crab. Not so different from the virtual cell Pox had escaped.

Anselmo's heart pounded. At last, a real crumb!

He surfaced and peeled the box out of its casing, using the tips of his fingers. Sliding it into a plastic evidence bag, he sealed and timestamped it before tucking it into his worldly.

When he stepped out of the secret room, Allure was waiting.

"Someone installed a server in that dummy," he said. "Build records will be in Haystack."

"Not if the technician didn't have a camera," she subbed.

Ah. Intolerants again.

"Of course, if you don't want to persecute a bunch of rejects . . ."

"Anselmo!" Malika interrupted. "Where did you go?"

Anselmo held the bagged server up to a wall cam. "This is why Whiting came here. To talk to the Singularity."

"Beyond!" Amiree's henna markings mojied surprise and delight. "We are going to be legends, do you know that?"

"Half a legend each, if we split the credit," he said.

"Can you have a grab-and-go fly the server to a lab?"

Anselmo had already requisitioned a car, moving into Sensorium so he could port to the @Interpol office. He began issuing requests. Arrange tech analysis. Trace the waxworks figure.

The question triggered a flare of memory. There had been talk of waxworks in London, hadn't there? Yes, there it was, in the transcript: Frances Barnes had received a tourism tip from one of the apps.

"I need a search warrant for the Waxworks Reconstruction Shop."

His request went into a long queue—police were actively taking gigs again, but almost everyone was tasked to crowd control.

Another connection lit up on his whiteboard: there was an implant-intolerant shop in Fort McMurray whose system logs had been hashing, apparently by accident, since around the time arsonist #trolls attacked the town.

A ping from Tampico @Interpol: "You have been offered Provisional Case Manager status." Greenlights approved six auditors. A real team! New ribbon for his career board.

Could he demote Malika and request a more specialized tech? Rationalize that he needed someone local, maybe? Do unto her as had been done unto him?

He put out the gig request, brooming Malika without a second thought.

Allure's toon eased into a chair, the same one Rubi had occupied there, weeks earlier when he'd taken her to review the truck footage.

His informant smiled, exploring the crease in her pressed slacks as if it were a new discovery. "Now, then. Now that you're back on the scoreboard. What might you do for me?"

CHAPTER 52

The only upside to her current situation, as far as Rubi could see, was that she and Gimlet were in no danger of harming each other directly.

She'd be relying on terrain updates and camerabots to keep her from falling into sinkholes, counting on Rabble managers to divert her around or over fences and other obstructions, all while preserving the illusion that she was fighting an imaginary eighteenth-century revolution. Entirely dependent on Sensorium to keep her safe, to provide life support.

She took one good look at the real world, the ghost city in her path. Silver-white safety wrap gave the towers the slick look of massive ice formations, pixelated stalagmites hundreds of feet high, dotted with anticollision markings for the birds. At ground level, things had been churned by neglect and entropy: sidewalks, impeded by overgrown trees and shrubs, had broken the tidy confinement of property lines. Drones did regular fly-through work to maintain the grid of the streets, cutting back growth, clearing debris, and ensuring that the subway entrances were safely boarded up.

Still, sinkholes broke the pavement here and there, and she could see a massive stone lion tumbled in an intersection, two blocks ahead.

Tightening the laces on her shoes, Rubi checked her primer. She'd lost nanites in the helicopter crash, and there was nowhere, here, to get an extra meter of fabric. She opted to grow tights back down to her ankles, losing coverage up top, and wrapped a travel-wrinkled sunscreen over her head, face, and neck.

Then she tooned in to pregame, only to find player numbers were disturbingly low.

Her toon refreshed for the next episode, sketching a virtual bandage over a virtual wound in her shoulder, and draping a scavenged French officer's coat over her ragamuffin dress.

She pinged Manitoule. "Where's everyone?"

He appeared beside her, still wearing the Monique Goyette skin. "Allure is soapboxing against playing the scenario. She's criticizing Oversight's drive to incentivize people to vote." He shared a soundbite:

"Offering people a chance to be cannon fodder while Rubi Whiting grandstands—"

She groaned.

"Allure also says that you being the good guy predisposes people to vote your way."

"I'm not telling anyone how to vote."

"Your position's obvious."

She sighed. "So . . . I speak to her?"

"Obvious move." Manitoule shrugged. "Probably a trap?"

She ported there anyway, manifesting to find Allure holding court at a lakeside campfire, surrounded by reporters.

"Rubi Whiting," Allure said. "Who let you into our embassy?"

"The same person who kept individuals unknown from killing me in a chopper crash?" She didn't look at Luce, who was tending the fire, looking dunked and miserable.

"It wasn't me who tried to kill you."

"No?" Rubi set her hands on her hips, trying to look spunky. "You're telling people not to play *Bastille*."

The toon drew herself up to full height. Rubi barely came to her shoulder.

Luce had ditched his fish skin, once again presenting as the well-worn man whose account he had stolen. Allure, by contrast, had a sleek, customized identity. She was a good-looking everywoman: somewhat desirable, a bit motherly, a warrior queen. Her voice and expression projected strength, confidence, and concern: "Why should anyone play a game you're destined to win? To watch you wallop Gimlet Barnes while Rome burns?"

"Me beating Gimlet is no foregone conclusion," Rubi said. "You should have more faith in them."

Debutante, her PR consultant, raised an urgent sub, texting across her field of vision: "Followship for the feed of this argument is rising. There is little you can say that won't look petty. Recommend making a gracious *may the best human win* speech. Cut it short."

Rubi noped the rec.

"If gameplay is dramatic enough," Debutante insisted, "people will join in."

Dramatic enough. The words floated between Allure and her.

"People can see your true motivation, Mer Whiting," Allure went on.

"Which is?"

"You're wedded to the myth of the Bounceback. You fear that if your people are relieved of the endless, heartbreaking, unwinnable struggle to rebuild your biosphere, the spotlight will move off of you. Your shot at the @WorldSaver leaderboard, your legacy as an angel of the resurrection—"

"That's ridiculous."

"At the first threat to your ratings, here you are."

"I'm attention-seeking at all costs, is that it?"

Allure laid both hands on her shoulders, body language saying, all too clearly, that it was truth time. "You're a cheat, Mer Whiting, playing a rigged game."

"Rigged?"

"You're not in this for the joy of sport, are you?"

Well, that had some truth. But . . .

"I could be, though, couldn't I?"

A tiny frown knit itself into Allure's features. "Could be what?"

Maximize drama. "Playing for joy."

"I don't—"

"In fact, that's . . . that's pretty easy. Coach," Rubi said. "Give everything in my pack to Manitoule."

"Everything in—"

"All the high-level armor. The horse, the quest swords, and the three saves versus death. Distribute them in a random draw, to a pool of qualified Rabble players who voted today. Offer . . . one piece of loot every thirty minutes?"

"Disposing of your tactical advantages—" Coach objected.

"Uptick in login numbers," Debutante interrupted.

Rubi sighed inwardly. Gordon was a *great* horse. "Blank my account and generate a n00b."

Allure looked uncertain. "This is no true contest. People will help you level."

Rubi rolled her shoulders. This was going to be fun. "You don't want me to have friends either?"

"I don't want you to have *sycophants.*"

"Strike. Insulting to gamers. But Rabble can throw me a basic user account. No customs, random name, generic toon."

"Character template options," Coach interrupted, taking this as a cue: "Mulan, Snow White, Lancelot, Beyoncé, Goldilocks, Bahadur, Cinderella, Tam-lin, Babayaga, Raven—"

"Randomize, Coach." Rubi turned to face the growing mob of tooned-in reporters. "I'll play as one of a community of equals."

Allure rallied. "Rubi Whiting may have given up a few numerical advantages, but by asking me to stop opposing—"

"I'm not asking you to self-censor," Rubi said. "I gave my word that I'd play *Bastille* to the finish. So, take bets on this: in three and a half hours, I'll be on the banks of the Seine, with everyone else on the Team Rabble leaderboard. If Gimlet Barnes can hold the prison for that long—and we all know they can—I'll bring the Bastille down."

"There's still your baton." Allure's expression was stony now. "That's a tactical asset."

"You want to grab-and-go a library-grade gaming stick out to what's left of Manhattan? Be my guest. But send me more primer, and some provably undrugged chuggers while you're at it."

Luce barked laughter.

"This is what the apes did fifty years ago," he told Allure. "Cashed in their assets, threw their possessions on the table, dumped everything into the rebuild."

Rubi felt a wave of affection. Allure might not understand human tenacity, but it looked as though Luce did, finally.

Uncertainty crossed the beautiful features.

"I don't need three saves versus death to catch up with Gimlet," Rubi said. "Just like humanity doesn't need the Pale."

Last word, good burn, walk away! Debutante flashed red text through her entire visual field.

Rubi ghosted on her, returning to Manhattan, where a spectral image of Coach was holding out a reset, a ruby-red apple.

She grabbed it, biting in, and a second later found herself porting all the way back to the *Bastille* prologue. Rabble had assigned her the Goldilocks toon, blonde of hair and pale of flesh, with dirt-smudged cheeks and a tattered skirt.

Still on #brand, then.

Tooning in behind Sugar Valkyrie's house, she jostled amid a burgeoning crowd of starving, half-frozen beggars outside the fancy party.

Prologue.

Right. Get it done. She ran a quick inventory. "What's this piece of fish in my pack, Coach?"

"Food for you. Or, alternately, a quest opp."

"Select quest."

"The Duchess has a cat that's trapped up an elm in that stand of trees. Win conditions involve getting the cat to the ground. Rewards include a pair of old boots and a cudgel."

Treeing a cat. How the mighty have fallen.

"Barnes might lose before you get there," Coach said.

"They're a quality villain. Have a little faith."

"Buy-in numbers are climbing," Coach reported.

Feeling unfettered, Rubi set off at a run.

CHAPTER 53

Frankie landed on her butt on Drow Whiting's chest, and for a second, she wondered if he'd died. Then he gasped, letting out many *really bad* words, and let her help him to his feet. They shuffled down the hall, together, with the dog between them. Drow had both hands in its fur.

He was muttering, almost subvocalizing. A stutter of words got through: *fascists, martyrfucker, hoarding, cannibal.*

They wrestled a fire door, finding a pitch-black stairwell. Frankie hesitated, but Drow shrieked, as if there was someone behind them, and dragged her inside. It closed, locking them in darkness.

"Come on, kid."

Her heart was pounding. "I can't see."

"Right, right, no implants. Mad leading the blind. What a glorious fucking crusade this is turning out to be." A dry hand closed over hers, gentle grip, guiding her to a handrail.

"Going up?"

"Tragically for my crepit patellas, yeah."

The stairwell smelled of old cement and wet newspaper. Sour fear wafted off Drow. Their words echoed in the black.

"Upsa daisy, nice and slow."

She didn't argue, just began to feel for the stairs. The dog kept pace.

Drow made a little huffing noise with every step. "Nobody here, nobody here," he whispered. "We're okay, we better be okay. Nobody here."

"*I'm* here."

"You don't count."

The steps become a landing. Frankie scowled into the dark as she traced her way around its perimeter. If she told Drow he was full of effing bollocks, would Mada ever find the transcript in the Haystack?

"I don't mean . . . Look, kid—"

Her shoe found the next staircase. Drow was already climbing. "I've spent half my life essentially bonkers, you know that, right? 'Course you do. Famously bonkers."

"Okay."

"It's not like you see in the flows. I know my #brand managers make me out as some lovable old geezer strumming his guitar, emitting musicflows and artstorm like, I dunno, owl pellets and saying wacky things . . . Saints, go away, you're not here, get your goddamned claws off—"

Wacky things.

From his voice, he was fighting not to cry. "Strumming guitars and letting out kernels of sage wisdom, nuts in the ice cream of whimsical babble—"

Another landing. Frankie had been counting: there were thirteen steps per flight.

A thump, within the building infrastructure, made Robin shiver.

"You're better now," Frankie reminded him. "You got fixed. You treat people yourself."

"Fixed. Some days just *being* hurts so goddamned much, and you can't hold it together just because you want to. You don't get to say, *Hey, this is crucial and your kid's depending on you* and *Martyrfuck, man, why you laying this bullshit trip on her, she's fourteen.* You see yourself acting nuts and you can't stop. Anyway, we're here, that's over, this isn't Guelph and she's, *you're* nine . . ."

Another landing. More puffing. Did old people still have heart attacks?

"I gotta catch my breath," Frankie lied, breaking his upward momentum. And then, to distract him: "Why are we going up?"

"Get you to the top. Penthouse accommodations. Roof gardens. Transcripting in the clear."

Transcripting what?

"They'll expect us to go down. I have a bad feeling about down. Move, will you—my hip's seizing. Did you hear that?"

"Your hip?"

"Hold on." Clink of glass and some weird noises, like he was . . . straining. "Ghhhhhhhh!"

"Drow!"

"It's nothing. Nothing at all. Oh, fuck. *There*'s a sensation."

"Tell me!"

He bent, whispering, "Just adding a little Superhoomin to my personal drug cocktail."

He was going to explode in the actual stairwell.

"Hip's better, kid—let's move."

She nudged Robin and stepped. "What do you want to get onto the record?"

"You seeing Allure tooning in to conspire with @Chamberof-Horrors? That seems newsworthy."

"Not tooned in," Frankie said.

"Huh?"

"How many times do I have to tell you? I ditched my wearables." Eleven steps, twelve, thirteen. Glide to the next staircase. How high was the building? Eight floors?

A clink, a smash. "What was that?"

"Broken glass," Drow said. "I dropped the vial. I may've developed a slight case of the shakes—"

She felt him shoving Robin to one side as her shoe poked through a collection of rubble.

"There's a chunk stuck in your—wait."

She had already reached. A ping in the bed of her thumb as she pulled it free.

"No harm done," she said, putting the thumb in her mouth, tasting copper.

"I have a bad feeling about down." Glass scraped on concrete. "How could Allure be there if she wasn't tooned in? I'm the one who hallucinates."

This is why we need a whole government department of making adults listen.

She repeated the story of coming from Florida, in the orange crate tagged for delivery outside the zoo. She'd felt exposed in it, uneasy for no reason she could really name. So, she switched out, and found the nanoboards on her crate were marked with a big pink painted F.

When the train paused in the Bronx, at the larger zoo facility, she had tossed the novel—*Black Beauty*—out of the train car.

"I don't think it had a tracker in it, but . . ."

"No, it was canny. Good move."

After that, she'd found an unmarked box of tequila gels and hidden herself within them. Zoo animals wouldn't be drinking tequila, would they? And sure enough, these had gone directly to the mall, and from there up to the boardroom.

"There were servers," she said. "They all had weird, dented skulls. They were putting out juice and drinks and muffins for people."

"Or worse," Drow muttered.

Frankie had scrambled out of the tequila crate, concealing herself behind a cubicle wall leaning at the edge of the boardroom as the servers made themselves scarce and the people they'd been setting up for came in.

There had been eleven of them at the meeting, all older than Drow, with unmistakable signs of life extension—arm pumps, exaggerated musculature. The eldest had been in a pod the size of a rhinoceros.

Eleven, plus Allure.

She looked just as she had in Sensorium: sleek of skin, abundant of hair, dimpled and plumper than the norm. "She did a little dance thing. Pirouette," Frankie said. "And told them it was #proofof-concept."

"#Proof—"

"They flushed Tigger—the baby tiger—out of the experimental Project Rewild crèche." Frankie fisted and unfisted her hands. "And they clapped about it."

"Mmmm."

"Drow? Are you listening?"

"I get it, okay, Allure killed the cat. Sucks, okay? Big feels. Hey, we're at the top."

Frankie felt the steel door. "No knob."

"Exit only, no entry," Drow said. "Hold on."

"We'll have to go back down."

"We go down, they'll never find our bodies."

Frankie froze, goose pimples breaking over her skin.

"Sorry. That might have been the crazy talking."

I want to go home, Frankie thought.

"We can hope it was the crazy, anyway."

"You're not comforting me."

"You wanted to be comfortable, you shouldn't have run away. Saints, you think *I'm* comfortable?"

She fought a sudden rush of tears. "No."

"Blood pressure rocketing, pulse in the—Fuck! Sorry, sorry. Saints, kid, so sorry."

How long had they been in blackness? Her eyes felt dry, exhausted, as if they'd been staring out in search of nothing for hours. She made herself close them. "What now?"

"Well, I could suck up more meathead meds and try ripping the door off its hinges . . ."

"No!"

"Shhh!"

She put her hand on his arm, letting the tremors in his body rattle her, hoping he'd feel it, too. "You shouldn't be t-taking that stuff if you're on—"

"Other stuff?"

"Please? Please, Drow, find another way."

"Yeah. Work smarter, right? Well . . . Luce Pox and I are pals. Maybe we can bring him 'round to sharing our vested interest in fucking Allure up the—"

The door popped open. Gleaming, blue-tinted fluorescent light illuminated the dog, Robin, and Drow. The latter was bobbing up and down on his toes, turning a long shard of glass over and over in his trembly grip. Something was happening to the hexagonal scars on his temples—they were flushed with blood.

"You're one to talk about obscenity," he said to someone who wasn't there. Luce, she assumed. And then: "I apologize for my potty mouth, Barnes."

"Eff you," she said tiredly, peeking into the hall, eyes watering as her sight adjusted. The corridor smelled of flowers and chemicals—of hospital. She thought about Dada Rollsy, refusing to let her watch him die.

It's not like on the flows, Drow had said.

How awful must it be, cancer treatment, to make Sang run off to Florida?

Sang's not a closer.

Drow made the shard of glass disappear. "Luce, we gotta get Catgirl and Robin safely beyond the jammers. I'm thinking the roof. Where's her parent, anyway?"

A wall-mounted hand sanitizer answered, "In-game."

"Who fucks around killing toons with their kid missing?"

"She's not missing; she's with you."

"Since when am I a responsible adult?"

"You raised one small female. What's the difference?"

"Is that a serious question? Get her parent here."

Luce said, "Allure and Headmistress blackmailed Gimlet. Play the game and—"

"Blackmail?" Frankie demanded.

The door swung open, blinding her. "Ah, Mer Barnes. At last!"

Allure.

Drow tottered around her, positioning himself between Frankie and the dog. As protection? Allure could easily snap him in half.

"Should've listened better," he said. "It's me who's delusional, not Frankie. You didn't just flush the cat. You printed yourself a fucking body."

Allure raised her arms, did the pirouette again. "Mer Barnes the elder is playing the final episode of the Bastille scenario. We have offered their failing spouse a new lease on life. As for Mer Barnes the younger . . ."

Frankie folded her arms and gave her best glower.

"Here as insurance?" Drow asked. "Spouse is the carrot, kid is the stick."

Allure looked past him. "Do you understand, child? We are even now transferring Rollander Erwitz to a facility in Pretoria where he can undergo the poltering process—"

"And then upload to new meat?" Drow said.

"Fresh, fit, and ready to go." She ignored him. "Your father will be fine, Mer Barnes. My existence proves it."

"#Proofofconcept," Frankie whispered.

"Exactly. The Pale offer so many advantages—"

Drow laughed. "Like raising all these rich-ass geezers. Perpetual immortality for the well-heeled?"

"You're using me and Rollsy to make Gimlet do what you want," Frankie said. It would work, too. Mada would do anything to protect the pack.

This was so unfair!

But she knew that one thing was true, in the real world or out. If you gave the Bedwedders of the world what they asked for, you didn't get your happy ending.

Frankie was the child of a supervillain. She knew better than anyone that weaseling out of your promises wasn't a bug. It was a standard bad-guy feature.

"Leave the girl alone. Deal with me."

Think! Get Robin outside, Drow had said, beyond the jammers. Frankie looked left and right. A door, just beyond Allure, was open, just a crack.

She nudged Robin. "C'mon."

But the dog was on alert, welded to Drow as if she was growing out of his leg, ears flattened.

Frankie ran a hand over her fur. Pick her up? She had to weigh two stone, even if she didn't struggle . . .

. . . or bite . . .

. . . and that was before figuring the weight of whatever was in her helper-dog panniers.

Oh. Wearables.

Allure and Drow must have taken their debate subvocal. They were nose to nose. Beads of sweat dotted his forehead. She'd never seen someone's eyes bug quite that big. His shakes were worse. The scars on his temples were scabbing up.

Frankie knelt, stroking Robin again, unlatching the catch across her back harness and then lifting, tentatively.

No give. There must be a belly strap, too.

She laid her head between the golden retriever's shoulders, fumbling for the catch. "Who's a googirl?"

Click, and the whole pannier slid. She lifted it straight off the dog.

Drow's hand, behind his back, shifted: thumbs-up.

How much of the crazy was he faking? Frankie looked down to hide a smile.

Allure's attention was fixed on Drow. "Let's take a tour down Recollection Highway."

"The idiom is Memory Lane."

Acting for all the world as though she knew what she was doing, Frankie sauntered around Drow to the open door. Pushed it.

In. Through. The latch clicked behind her. There was a hard bolt; she threw it.

"Child!"

Beyond the door was . . .

. . . Was this real?

It was a classroom. Thirty kids of various ages and two teachers, arrayed in classic rows of desks in front of a real blackboard, turned to stare.

Even without her access to Sensorium records, Frankie tagged at least three of the faces. They were kids who'd gone lemming, who were #presumeddead, but whose bodies had never been found.

There was another open door behind the teachers.

"Department of Preadolescent Affairs," she shouted. "You're all under arrest!"

While their jaws were hanging, she burst into a run, making it to the far door and through, slamming it behind her. Now she was in a kids' dormitory. She pelted past it and into another—one for boys, one for girls. Stupid binary, stupid kidnappers. She was panting as she hit that fourth room, a food hall from the looks of it, staffed by two giggers—one old, one young. Both servers had the strange, caved-in skulls. They barely seemed aware of her as she kept running, bolting for the kitchen.

Roof, roof, find the stairs to the roof.

Instead, her luck—or at least the series of interconnected doors—ran out. She darted down a dimly lit hall and into the strangest pop-in Frankie had ever seen.

The room was a bit as she imagined Rollsy's hospital room must be. A life-support pod dominated the corner facing the window, overlooking the park. The rug was red, with a flowered pattern, as brightly colored as if she was viewing it through a helmet.

There was a massive private bathtub.

Shout outside. Frankie hadn't eluded the adults, not really. By now someone had probably remembered she couldn't arrest anyone for kidnapping if she couldn't access Sensorium.

Panting, Frankie crossed to the window and leaned out, staring at the ledge and the five-story drop to the churned-up pavement below. Hot air lifted her hair. Central Park was about half a click away.

A long, high scream, in the hall—Drow.

She spun, almost smacking her head into the upper half of the window frame. *Because I'm clumsy, too clumsy, not a real player, not a closer . . .*

Taptaptap. "Frankie?"

"Is that you, Drow?"

"Listen, kid, I appreciate what you're trying to—"

"How can I know that's you?" The ledge outside was wide and surprisingly clean. Low-difficulty-level climb. In-game, she wouldn't hesitate.

In-game, there'd be a safety mat hidden under the illusion of a lethal drop.

She scavenged a curtain pull from the edge of the window, tying it to Robin's panniers. Maybe she could dangle the transmission rig outside.

A pneumatic hiss made her jump. The VR pod sighed, cracking open.

Bam of fist on door. "Kid, get out of there right now. Luce, get this door open."

"Drow would say *the effing door*!"

The voice changed: Allure. "Child, what incentive do I have to save your cancerous parent if you won't cooperate?"

The rising lid of the pod revealed a person who, honestly, didn't look that old. Their skin was papery, their eyes bloodshot. They shook awake, clearly groggy, scanning the room.

"I don't see—" Rheumy, gunk-crusted eyes fixed on her. "Yes, yes, here she is."

Frankie didn't wait for them to get out of bed. She scrambled up to the windowsill and from there, terrifyingly, eased onto the ledge.

"This," she huffed, not because it was true exactly but because soapboxing made it possible to move, despite being scared out of her mind. "This is what the Department of Preadolescent Affairs is for. Keeping crepits from selling us kids out."

"Wait. The girl's DPA?" said the pod person.

"Whooz me!" Frankie shouted. "Check badge 773928 dash 32!"

What if there was nothing in these dog panniers?

Or she couldn't get clear of the building jammers?

Too late. She was on the ledge now.

Frankie flattened herself against the wall and crept, one tiny step at a time, away from the window. Real ledge, real death. The gaunt apparition with the papery skin leaned out, gaping.

"We don't need a bunch of aliens telling us to clean up our house!" she shouted.

"The Pale can help us." The crepit put their hand outside the window, pulled it back in.

"Go after her!" Muffled Allure voice.

"No!" That was Headmistress. "We mustn't risk dear Frances!"

Guess that meant the bad guys weren't quite in sweet harmony with each other.

In-game, there was always somewhere to go when you ended up stuck outside a building a million floors up . . .

"Five," Frankie said aloud. "Only five."

High enough to die, Franks. She could almost hear Mada's voice. Mada had caught her last time, in sim. She choked back a scream.

"Frances." Headmistress buzzed at her from a wall-mounted speaker, somewhere out of sight. "This is dangerous. I beg you, come back to us."

"You said this would bring us back together!" Frankie yelled. "Sang and Mada would come to get me. They'd go back to Bella and Rollsy. But you just lured me here to leverage Gimlet . . ."

"Darling! I only want what's best for you."

Frankie edged to the farthest spot between the windows. The crepit was trying to get a foot out onto the ledge, moving with limited enthusiasm for the project. Allure leaned in from the other side.

"Don't come out here!"

"Child, be reasonable."

"Shut up!" A wink of light, from the park, caught her eye. Was that a drone? "We're gonna revive and rewild without your help."

Headmistress spoke again. "I think, dear Mer Frances, you may have misunderstood me earlier—"

"Your in-app purchase, Poppet, told me to run away! You told me—" she bellowed.

The winking light *was* a drone, a journo bot with a camera and a mic.

And . . . beyond it, at ground level, a wheeled . . .

What was that thing?

"Mer Barnes?" Whatever it was, the coming drone was so old, it had a speaker. "It's Crane. Hold on. I'm coming."

The weird vehicle had an extending arm, and at its end was a platform of sorts. An outdoor elevator? Could it get her out of this?

Frankie pressed herself against the back wall of the building, locking eyes on the bizarre contraption. All this sudden attention had to mean she was indeed transmitting.

Do it, then. Transmit.

"This is Frances Barnes from the Department of Preadolescent Affairs," she said into the dog vest, fighting to keep her voice steady. "I'm at the @ChamberofHorrors in Manhattan and I've found a bunch of lemming survivors. Kidnapped kids, repeat, kidnapped lemming kids. The Chamber is coll—coll—" What was the word? "Colluding with Allure and they have Drow Whiting. I think . . . I think they're hurting him. Please, please, please, somebody help us."

Then, though she knew she really really shouldn't, she thrust up her middle finger, brandishing it at Allure.

CHAPTER 54

VRTP:RABBLEVSRISTO.PLAY/BASTILLE/EPISODE-THREE.VR

@Bastille: Rubi Whiting remains in play.

The canal approach to the Bastille prison was a trench of sucking mud and fast-moving skeletal bears with sharp claws. Defeating them was a grind of constant melee. The Rabble fought in squads as they made for the castle wall. Mages blasted fire at the front; archers targeted ice-breathers from a safe distance. Everyone else took the skeletons hand to bony claw.

Game Control had published a list of aliases, the two hundred or so players who'd begun the prologue within ten minutes, on either side, of Rubi's reboot. @UsualSuspects, they'd tagged them.

The casino would be raking in bets on which of the suspected toons was her.

The last of the skeletons went down with a wail, and a boss monster, Duchess Ursuline, rose from the chips of bone, barring the way to a rusted staircase exit. In keeping with Risto aesthetics, the apparition was tall and powdered in snow, with thick fur and long teeth. Matted braids of hair, terminating in fur-lined, snapping mouths, grew out of its back.

Rubi caught a first blow on the flat of her scavenged shield. It was a good hit, enough to make her stagger. Or maybe she was just getting weak after three hours of continuous play.

She had picked up a sturdy short sword on a quest in Episode Two. Now, with a quick swipe, she sliced the neck of the hydra head and stomped it for good measure.

A new one took its place, snapping viciously, almost catching her hand.

The cry went up: "Deploy doppelgangers!"

Several players who'd challenged a mirror house earlier launched crystal flasks. False versions of the players, dozens strong, boiled up at their feet. The boss obligingly began decapitating the fakes, wasting turns.

"Coach," Rubi said. "Inventory my mystery items?"

"Objects in your pack whose purpose remains undetermined: sealed envelope, rusty badge, red amulet, blue amulet, ash ointment, eternal flame, bone key."

She grabbed the ointment, losing a turn as she poured it on her shield. It covered the surface with a layer of glimmering coals.

A hit: hard bite, into the flesh of her arm. Blood reddened the ropy neck attached to the puppet head, soaking into the coarse, braided pseudopod of hair. Her health bar jagged up and down.

Rubi slapped the burning flat of the shield against it. A shriek: the fur wisped and burned away.

"Ointment to shield," she shouted. The cry propagated.

Rubi's health stabilized. She let out a sound that was half a laugh, half a victory shout.

"You are among the top fifty @UsualSuspects," Coach said.

Every time she rose on the leaderboard, it increased her odds of being, well, herself.

She was in no rush to get unmasked.

The group pushed Duchess Ursuline back, cutting and cauterizing until she died, spilling blood into the canal. Behind them, the passage closed, locking out new players until the scenario reset.

Rubi bolted a healing potion and rushed the iron staircase with the rest.

A ribbon stretched across its top. UNPLAYED TERRAIN! was emblazoned across the silk.

The crowd whooped. A Suspect cut the ribbon with their dagger, claiming extra points. Whooshes of flame marked several others' ascent to the next level. Player rankings shuffled.

They sprinted, in a pack, to the base of the castle wall. Someone conjured a poll of moji: a spider, a mole, and a rhinoceros.

"*@CanalParty: Over, under, or through?*"

Rubi added a spider to the mix, voting for a wall climb. Most of her peers went for the rhino.

The pop-up poll reminded her of the vote going on, out on the surface.

"Check BallotBox," she subbed.

Summary overlaid a puddle of blood. The flash vote on sovereignty was ongoing. Participation numbers were below the number required to ratify a global plebiscite. NorthAm voter turnout was up to 62 percent.

"Through, through, through!" bellowed the mob, and she added her voice to the shout.

Hammer-wielding fighters took up positions beside a crack in the castle wall, smashing out fortifications in time to the chant.

"Not too big!" someone warned as they made a crack.

"Who's got beanstalks?"

Everyone, Rubi included, hurled incandescent lima beans into the gap in the stone. Sprouts furled, digging into mortar, spreading leaves around the perimeter. The wall crumbled, creating an entrance wide enough for two players.

A thief peered inside. "Optional time-out!"

"Accept!"

Rainbow shimmers swirled through the air. The scene froze. Rubi scanned the bloody canal at their backs. They were hemmed in.

"Win conditions, Coach?"

"It's a gauntlet. The goal on this level is simply to survive and make it to the second level of the castle."

Rubi dropped to a resting crouch, cataloging her various aches. She'd had one slightly stale fruit cube on her when she started play. That was long gone, and there'd been no water at all.

Food opps had come her way a couple times as she played, but she was afraid of getting drugged again.

Despite the fatigue, she felt good. Clear-headed, tired, and strangely at peace. She was manning her oar, keeping her word; the vote was out of her hands.

"I see the Regent's Blade!"

She looked up.

Gimlet stood astride the battlements, dressed as an officer of the royal guard, surveying the crowd. Their skin was frosted in shimmering ice crystals. The heart-shaped amulet throbbed slightly, no doubt beating in time with their pulse. A bit of punitive grotesquerie, that. Villains could never be wholly beautiful.

Held the castle till I got here, she thought. *Knew you'd do it.*

Eyes aglitter, blood on their long lace cuffs, Gimlet sneered at the gathered assault team.

Their gaze paused on Rubi. Could they know?

A slow smile broke over Gimlet's face, revealing long canines in glacier-blue gums.

Oh. She was resting in that crouch Gimlet had imitated, back in London. She sent gestural moji, again, crossing her heart to remind them of their wager.

Competing for points and prizes made me think Gimlet was . . .

What? Different? Opposed? Disinterested?

She remembered long-fingered hands around her waist, pulling her closer. The heat between them—

Gimlet broke gaze abruptly, preserving her anonymity.

@CanalParty: *Come on, then.* The challenge purred out over the courtyard in velvety baritone. *Nobody's bested me so far.*

Rubi sprang to her feet.

Here on the ground, the player topping their party leaderboard raised his war hammer. "Corridor's a kill box. We'll draw straws to go first."

"Fifteen seconds remaining in time-out, Mer Cherub," Coach said.

"Yep," she replied. "Periscope to the surface."

The battlefield faded to ghostly overlay. Her party's tactical discussion converted to chat window. She was on an empty street in the remnants of Manhattan, shadowed by myriad drones. Looming columns of shrink-wrapped skyscrapers cast intermittent shadows, bars of sun and shade. The air was thick and strangely dry. Her baton felt heavy in her injured right hand. In her left was a handful of gravel.

She dropped the stones, swiping grit on her thigh.

Her sunscreen was gone. Her scalp felt delicate, burnt. Her mouth was parched.

"Where am I?" Rasping.

Maps spun . . . she was nearing the southwest corner of Central Park.

"Is Gimlet close? In the flesh, I mean?"

"Two kilometers and closing. Time-out is over."

Time to play. She blinked away the Surface, checked the straw she'd drawn. Nine. She'd go in ninth.

@AllBastille: Rubi Whiting remains in play.

"Coach," she subbed. "You saw those rocks in my hand?"

"Incidental reality confusion within improvised playing environments does not register as a penalty."

"Screw my score. Any time I capitalize on a found-weapons opp, I need an automatic two-second scope to the Surface. I need to know I'm not actually holding anything."

"Surfacing during combat decreases victory probability—"

"Override. Code in reality checks."

"Done."

She rejoined the @CanalParty, watching as fighters one through eight vanished into the castle, each leading a thief and a healer. Mages who couldn't hope to make it through the kill box were buffing armor and weapons. Fiery spell effects brightened the shadows.

A jester appeared, shouting, *"Zut alors!* @CanalParty has cleared five percent of the route to the parapet."

The first team died. Number two, an established trio led by a popular player named Shecky, carved a path to 12 percent before they too got swarmed. Three more stalled at fifteen, dying at the hands of some monster wielding a guillotine. The next didn't get even that far.

A respawn set the whole surge back.

They were holding less than a third of the route to the parapet when Rubi's slot came up.

No guts, no glory. She ducked into the narrow corridor, taking in the basics of the set design: torch-lit catacombs, cells filled with burnt skeletoons, broken machines suggestive of torturetech.

The corridor widened before her, nicely inviting. Too easy. She caught a low bar, swinging over. Sure enough, a skeletoon came boiling out of its broken stonework.

Twisting, she booted its head off its shoulders—getting her lower leg iced in the process. She managed to land on the good foot.

Her healer thawed the injury.

@CanalParty: No touching the skeletoons directly, she subbed.

Staying low, she sprinted to the halfway point in a suddenly wider corridor, then stopped dead and whirled, ready to spring in any direction.

Down! A barrage of icicles at chest height. Scream from the healer. Her thief managed to dodge. As Rubi rolled to her feet, she came face-to-face with a massive marionette with a guillotine for a mouth.

Rubi threw her decoy flask, charging in as copies of her generic Goldilocks toon burst from the floor. The guillotine snapped shut over one of the decoys and she slashed with the sword, knocking the marionette into a pit.

She sprinted to a new door, putting her back to the wall, catching her breath. Mid-level fighters poured in behind her, holding the newly cleared terrain.

The door opened; there was a ribbon ahead. Pleased, she

sliced it, sharing XP with the thief, Espi. After three grueling hours of playing catch-up, she was breaking new trail.

"@UsualSuspects Leaderboard Update: You are twenty-fourth."

Beyond the door was a vast stone chamber with a curving cork-screw ramp, carved stone ascending thirty feet, to the parapet that marked the end of the level. Its wall bore a massive tapestry depicting a knight in armor. This, inevitably, would be enchanted. Rubi saw the likely trigger—a shaft of sunlight cutting a line across the stone floor.

"Can I do a vertical ascent here, Coach?"

"It would accord nicely with the realworld terrain."

A grin skinned her lips back. "Do or die, right?"

Espi nodded, uncoiling a rope. Sheathing her sword, Rubi found a handhold in the wall, opposite the tapestry, and began scaling.

Up the wall, pause for breath, up a little farther. The stone felt like metal under her fingertips. At ten feet up, she turned to assess. Rabble fighters were beginning to win their way into the room.

Someone broke the sunbeam. The knight in the tapestry shivered, shimmered, and turned into the real thing, charging @CanalParty.

Espi, her thief, was panting but keeping pace as they reached the top. Rubi crabbed her way over to a castle window, leading to the parapet atop the stairwell.

She found a narrow landing leading to a cell block and another unlock ribbon. Rather than hog the glory, she took up a position atop the ramp, guarding their position so someone else could have the bonus.

"Gauntlet level complete!"

"Well done, Randomized Player!" Coach enthused. "Here are your victory conditions. Free the prisoners. Defeat the Regent's Blade. Rescue the Dauphine."

@Bastille: *The Endgame has begun.*

Rubi leaned against the wall, taking long breaths as the ground troops caught up.

Another @UsualSuspect, Szpara, led two dozen gauntlet survivors up the steps. "What's the play? Goldie?"

Rubi peered through the iron bars. "At least one of the prison cells will be full of ringers. We free who we can, send 'em down the ramp. Then—" She gestured at a razor blade, twenty feet tall. It was anchored in an archway, set like a guillotine, blocking the path to the final confrontation. "Then that."

"That," agreed Szpara.

The rest of the group, reduced to about half its number, joined the convo.

"Twelve cells, twelve locks. Do we play Russian roulette? Open them one at a time? Or go All or Nothing?"

"Let's roulette the first two cells," Rubi proposed. "Hope to get lucky, free some prisoners, station our healers in the cells to provide a bit of cover. Then we hit the locks on all the rest at once and go at it hammer and tongs."

"Row row row!"

"All we got is us!"

"Espi, what's your lockpick?"

"Level ninety." He pointed at the cell closest to the door, the emptiest. "That one?"

"Agreed."

"Is that another time-out?"

"Accept it," Szpara said, and everything paused again. @CanalParty: *Big push ahead! Catch your breath!*

Rubi said, "Coach, periscope the surface."

Quick flash to Manhattan. She had climbed over a stockade of container cars, over a stone wall and into Old Central Park. Her baton was covered in scrapes and nicks. She'd lost more primer and her knee wore a beaut of a bruise. Heat throbbed in her cheeks and shoulders. Across a wild expanse of crushed grass and muck, a figure shadow danced, swordfighting.

Gimlet.

A grab-and-go drone approached Rubi, dangling a chugger.

Should she take it? Risk getting drugged?

"You can't play if you're dehydrated," Coach murmured.

"Any word on my father?"

"He's nearby. Young Mer Barnes believes he is in the hands of the @ChamberofHorrors."

Her breath caught. "But Crane's with him?"

"There's a firewall." Crane ghosted in beside the Coach app. "He's beyond my reach, Miss Cherub."

One recidivist #troll.

"I'm just supposed to take that on, am I, and then go on with what I'm doing?"

"Should I protect you by lying?"

"Yeah, yeah. Up with personal sovereignty, and all the other kind, too." Rubi toasted the app with her chugger, biting off the lid.

Drink half. Take it slow.

She was too thirsty, too hungry. The fluid was gone before she could help herself. Lemon ricotta flavor exploded, wetting the dried fibers of her tongue.

A weird tower, incandescent and haloed from behind by drone-mounted lights, was rolling up behind Gimlet. A set piece? She squinted, but there was no making it out. And no time.

Drow would have to fend for himself until this was over. Fatigue, at this point, was like a razor: if she pushed it by trying to multitask, she'd bleed out all her remaining energy.

@AllPlayers: Endgame in five, four, three . . .

"Toon me back in, Coach."

Rabble had deployed around the prison cell, guarding Epsi the lockpick, not to mention the escape route for a first group of prisoners.

The lock clicked; the cell opened. Barefoot scarecrows in threadbare rags, smelling of filth—that would be the Conviction she'd just drunk, kicking in—began to flee. As the prisoners fled, the enormous guillotine at the far end of the cell block began to rise and fall, chopping at the floor.

"Rubi!" someone shouted.

She didn't take the bait. They'd been trying that all night, to see if she'd answer and thereby collapse the betting pool.

Just play. Her cheeks hurt. From smiling, she realized.

Gimlet was up ahead.

Epsi popped the second cell.

The lock was trapped. The prisoners turned into soldiers, and the soldiers turned into wights.

Rubi piled in with her best bloodcurdling shriek. No sense in taking it slow now. The guillotine blade blocking the way forward continued to chop, hacking a furrow in the floor, necessitating an ever-longer jump across to the parapet where Gimlet waited.

That wickedly sharp blade, chopping up and down. Time the jump wrong, that would be it.

Szpara lost their bid, getting cleaved, falling with a scream.

"Goldie! Go go go!"

Rubi jumped to the edge, catching her breath. She threw herself across the chasm as the blade flashed up.

Don't fall short don't fall short . . .

She stuck the landing, barely. Caught the ribbon marking the final episode trigger. Rolled and rose, arms upraised in triumph, amid a whoosh of fire.

@Bastille: Rubi Whiting has leveled.

"Congratulations! You are atop the leaderboard!" Coach began.

"Thanks." Betting pools converged: the automated leveling announcement had unmasked her.

Someone—Coach, Manitoule, the casino, Rabble's art team—hit her with a slow dissolve. *They/them* pronoun tags in her profile reverted to *she.* Generic Provençal milkmaid skin darkened, and her dreads became dreads again. Her beaded braids grew in, complete with her trademarked hexagon of golden beads.

A scream. She whirled.

A hundred feet away, Gimlet Barnes drove their sword right through the heart of Monique Goyette.

CHAPTER 55

Drow's brief flirtation with jogging had had an acrimonious breakup with his knee joints a good twenty years before. Attempting to run now should have been begging for an extended stay in an orthopedic ward . . .

. . . *except, of course, I'm #triaged. No joint replacements for Daddy* . . .

When Allure tried to chase Frankie Barnes off the side of the building, Drow found himself lunging forward. His hand snaked out, acting on long-forgotten reflexes. He grabbed her arm . . . and held on.

It was only a moment, long enough to keep her from getting out on the ledge herself, long enough for Frankie to clamber into the cherry picker Crane had sent for her.

Allure broke free. Knocked Drow on his ass with an enthusiastic but clumsy right cross.

Then Robin lunged in, snarling, catching her trouser leg.

I can't believe that worked.

It's the Superhoomin.

Allure snatched up a scalpel, whirling to face Robin.

Drow dialed up the dose . . .

. . . and his pulse, and his blood pressure . . .

. . . he scrambled to his feet.

"Mitts off the dog!" He took another blow but managed not to fall. Catching Allure by the arms again, he spun her—less by design than by brute force, dumping her and her scalpel into the pod that had been vacated by an elder who was, even now, cringing by the window.

Drow slammed the lid, almost catching Allure's fingers.

"Saints be fucked," he panted. He could hear his pulse, bass drum hammering his temples. Allure was hitting the off beats, pounding on the pod from inside. "Googirl, bring me that sash. Rope. Curtain pull."

Robin nosed it over to him, a long velvet rope. Drow wound it into the pod's safety lock, clumsily sealing it.

"Let me out!"

"Won't hold long," he said. "She didn't hurt you, did she, baby?"

Wag, wag, wag. Bright eyes. He choked on a sob, spat it up with a bit of bile.

A toon of Allure appeared outside the pod. "You!" she bellowed at the elder.

Drow got moving, hustling the elder out of their own private room, locking that down, too. "Find somewhere to sit this out," he advised, fleeing for the emergency exit.

More stairs.

He still had a bad feeling about down.

Could be a paranoid fantasy. Indecision shimmered, vibrato on his skin. The sweat on his temples sizzled, like hot oil.

"Come on, Robin, up we go." They took the stairs at a trot . . . and ran right back into the Setback, at some point on the Neverending Tour.

Drow blinked at the hallucination of himself aglow on smartdrugs, singing his new artstorm to scarecrows.

"We still had poverty and homelessness then," he started to say, before he remembered Frankie had left him.

Writing, singing, having a screaming fit during one show, when an audience member got onstage and hugged me . . .

Everyone back then was wild-eyed and desperate, gigging on carbon-banking ops, fighting to roll back the excesses of the past. Slaving away, hungry. The calorie ration, everywhere but Beijing, had dropped to 900 a day.

The scene shifted. He was in a lineup in blistering sun, daily queue for a half-liter of purified water. Then he heard some @bloodhound claim that drone-mounted guns—with bullets, not tranqs—had been deployed to wipe out evacuation resisters in Dayton.

Footage or it didn't happen. Drow stepped out of the water line and made, on foot . . .

. . . up the stairs . . .

. . . no, for Ohio. He wrote and uploaded songs on the way. He lost his shoes, wrecked his feet.

His dads had been health-crazed. They'd raised him to tend his body like a church. Then Tala Weston had tattooed crawling white maggots and rot all over him. Ever after, the idea had lurked: if he *mortified,* if he scraped, burned, and blistered enough skin off, he'd find baby-fresh Drow underneath.

He found Dayton in the care of strippers, undergoing orderly evac and shrink-wrap. There was no sign of drone-slaughtered bodies. He hallucinated mass graves all the same, piled corpses covered in flies.

Someone licked his face, dispersing old nightmares. Robin.

Dayton had been Drow's first @bloodhound fail. Instead of footage, he got fingerprinted. Deputized quarantine-enforcement giggers marched Drow to a locked car, hosed him down, tested his blood, and then sent him all in one shot—no meds, no food, no piss breaks—to Kingston Penitentiary for what turned out to be his first stretch.

Smartdrugs were a hazy area of legality by then—everything was getting deregulated. Instead, they got him for being a @hoaxer and encroaching on reclamation zones.

"Some people never learn," he muttered now, flying on his new Superhoomin wings, practically tap-dancing into the roof garden, a glassed-in greenhouse filled with life: lavish cushion of lawn, a fat pair of Canada geese to crop same, flower beds, apiary, trees, benches, and smartchair berths, all pointed at Old Central Park.

A toon of Tala Weston, the Cannibal Queen herself, arose from a foam of hallucinated larvae. She was wearing a gymnastics uniform. Looked about fourteen.

"Looking for me, handsome?"

Drow felt ashamed, as he sometimes did, of his body: old, unshaven, smelly, covered in white ink and the scars from all the times when he'd been cutting.

She had drugged him, tattooed him, molested him. She'd convinced him to experiment with chemotherapy, and hacked Crane.

Memories shimmered, more or less in order, slivers of transcript and visuals, things he'd told the police, things his lawyers and minions had failed to pull out of the still-new, still-fallible Haystack.

But these *weren't* memories, not exactly. They were footage. Proof of an illegal Chamber archive.

Pay dirt.

Could he get the evidence out unhashed?

Drow ran one hand over a rose marble bench. Robin, still at his side, panted alertly.

"Drow," Tala said. "Sweetness. I don't want any trouble."

That was so unlike her, so unexpected, it was like a snap of whip. "What did you say?"

"We can come to an agreement."

No part of Drow's subconscious would *ever* imagine her de-escalating. Which meant . . .

Drow knelt, hugging Robin. Breathed. "We've got this," he said. "Who's a goo?"

Golden silk, adoring eyes. *We are.*

"What's it going to take to get you out of here, handsome?"

Drow ran what he knew, twice, through his hyper-tuned mind. Came up with the same answer both times. "If you don't want trouble, it's because you think Allure can deliver. Make you a polter and print you a body."

"What's that to you? You've been a legend your whole life long, thanks to me. I defined you, dear heart; I gave your story a villain. Bled you for your art. I inspired you. I *mused* you."

Drow ran a thumb over the scars on his forearm. "You're taking credit for my career?"

"The Woodrow Whiting legend. It all springs from that notoriety, doesn't it? You're the last of the lost Setback lambs."

"So . . . what? You're on the edge of living forever and I should walk away out of gratitude? Thanks for the rape, lady; I monetized the hell out of that?"

"Dear heart. Still so uncouth."

Drow scratched his ass.

"It's why you came looking for this matchup, isn't it? A *true* legend needs a grand finale."

"Don't he just." Drow pottered over to a pane of greenhouse glass overlooking Columbus Circle. He could feel . . . or was it remember . . . no, *feel,* her hands on him. That scaly, lizard skin. Her breath had always been chocolatey, a bit sour. Memories of enhanced muscles, her fingers pressing his face into a pillow as the tattoo rig danced fire on his shoulder blades . . .

"Think. A blaze of glory and you live forever!"

"You've always been confused about the difference between immortality and posthumous fame."

"How long can you continue rotting in place?"

He swallowed. The burst of vitality from the Superhoomin—the sudden absence of pain, the freedom of movement—was a vicious reminder of his day-to-day pain load: bad eyes, bad knees, bad hips.

That assumed that mixing the Superhoomin with the Leonardo hadn't already tanked his kidneys and liver.

"Your daughter deserves to be free of you."

Maybe. But—"Time'll take care of that."

"Think," Tala said. "How perfect this is. Together again, after all these years, you and I—"

"I'll concede a certain circularity to our reunion."

Enjoy the strength while you've got it, right? He slammed his

cane against one of the glass panes, peering out as he did to take
in the sheer drop to the street.

It splintered, barely.

"Don't give up, handsome. Show us you're a closer."

Blam. Blam. Blam. Burst of triumph, glee of destruction.
Glass crunched and his cane punched through. "Are you already
loose in Sensorium, Tala? Like Luce?"

The cane was stuck.

Luce like loose. Loose of Luce. Lucy loosey goosey . . .

"Corpse copse, corpse copse, corpse copse," he muttered.

"I'm third in line behind a cancer victim and a *cat*," Tala said.
"Your young Mer Barnes is so upset about the tiger cub that we
have to make restitution."

"How unconscionable of them to make you wait on a cuter predator." He yanked his cane free, swung again. The hole got bigger.

Robin whined. Drow put a hand on the dog, let her sense him,
smell him.

After a second, Robin sat.

"Who's a googirl?"

Tail wag.

Drow yanked the cane out of the hole he'd made, nearly
throwing himself off-balance.

"There's a shard," Tala said helpfully.

Drow fingered it. Stuck it in his arm, just enough to bring an
upwelling of blood. More than he meant to, with his pressure sky-
rocketing. The ghost's expression brightened as crimson dribbled
into the roof carpet and got eaten by nanos.

He let himself stare, mesmerized by the flow. "I used to do
this . . . a lot."

She crooned agreement. Footage, stacked files, various cuts from
an array of scavenged sharp objects, flitted through his visual field.

"But this bit's too small," he said. She almost yelped as he tossed
the fragment.

He slammed the window three more times, laboring to create a
decent gap.

"That one that one that one there!" A jagged sliver, size of a steak knife.

"Too big." Drow dragged his cane in a circle, widening the perimeter of the hole in the glass. "And is that really how this story ends? Wouldn't you rather I flew away?"

She straightened up, cooing.

"Oh, yes, handsome. Do jump, do."

The hole was big enough for his body now. Drow stepped back, as if to gauge the distance. Flexed his knees.

Robin's tail thumped.

"Any last words?" Tala said.

"Only uncouth ones." Drow crouched, opening his arms. Robin piled in, warm golden fur against his chest, licking his stubble in a rasp, rasp, rasp.

"Sorry to disappoint, but I'm not suicidal, Tala. Haven't been, not for years."

She frowned. Tilted her head.

The first of the journo drones buzzed through the hole he'd made.

"The furrows you dug in me, they were deep. But I haven't been leaving 'em to fester."

Tala's toon morphed. She became the spidery, pervy, toxic ancient that Drow remembered. She shrieked as camera after camera buzzed in through the breach, hunting up footage before the Chamber could delete it, exhuming the digital corpses.

"We're under hash," Tala shrieked. "You can't legally copy any of this out!"

"You gonna threaten me with jail?" Drow said. "Me?"

"Handsome, I swear—"

"Begone!" Drow said, throwing up a hand. "Fiend! I expunge, I reject, I comms-block you!"

Like that, Tala Weston's toon vanished, leaving only the bots, the two geese, and the overgrown splendor of Central Park within his view.

Drow bent to retrieve his cane. Raising it, he gave a victory pirouette, there on the rooftop, enjoying the temporary looseness in his joints, the sense of strength and flex.

Right answer, Drow, you got it, Drow. What a clever boy you are!

Chuckling, he sat his old bones down on a bench, called his dog, and turned his face to take in the tawny twilight sun.

CHAPTER 56

Crane had been picking up intermittent snatches of Drow and Frankie's incursion into Columbus Mall, via Hackle's pirate transmitter. It had been difficult not to be there, to follow events at a distance, no more able to help than Sister Mary Joseph and the other eagerly listening @bloodhounds.

The initial fragments of transcript implied criminal activity but didn't offer conclusive proof against anyone living or working within the old mall.

For one ugly moment—when Gimlet implied that Frankie had been lured to Manhattan by Master Woodrow for abuse—public opinion leaned hard against him. Allure embraced this alternate narrative wholeheartedly—no doubt she had crafted it in the first place—by asking if Rubi had helped groom the child for him.

"Maybe," she told reporters, "he even had help from the Singularity."

Before she could trigger a full-scale panic about #killertech, though, Mer Frances turned up on a fifth-floor ledge, carrying Robin's entire transmission kit and very clearly blaming Allure for killing Project Rewild's nascent tiger cub and inducing her to lemming.

Avoiding risk-averse behavior was well and good, but enough

was enough! Crane seized the nearest viable drone and made for the child.

He couldn't do anything about Miss Cherub's apparent desire to get battered to a pulp by, or to batter herself, the best romantic prospect she'd ever had. He couldn't change Master Woodrow's having mounted a geriatric one-man commando raid on a hive of the ultrarich.

But he could certainly convey young Mer Barnes back to her parent.

As for what happened afterward . . . even as he commandeered the cherry picker, Crane fired emergency backups to his most secure bolt-holes.

Frankie continued to report in to the @CongressofYouth and Department of Preadolescent Affairs from her perch on the side of the mall. Newscycle and other aggregators spewed even more headlines into both Whitings' reading rooms. Allure, Luce's . . .

. . . supervisor?

. . . replacement?

. . . partner-in-arms?

. . . was apparently a polter in a newly printed human body, and had furthermore been the one who'd flushed the embryonic tiger cub in Geneseo, using the crèche to spawn herself in flesh.

Cloudsight, naturally, was processing an onslaught of strikes against Allure.

The revelations kept coming. Hackle and Jackal had got inside the Geneseo print shop, and now they let in an inspection team, verifying Tigger's abortion and the use of the crèche to print Allure's body with their own eyes.

With that, even respectable journos were obliged to buy in to the @ChamberofHorrors narrative. Newscycle titles screamed like old-school tabloids:

Fortune-hoarding olds collude with Pale powergrab!

Drow Whiting runs abuser to ground!

Frances Barnes lemminged to save the MadMaestro!

Could the media snowball sway the sovereignty vote?

As Crane brought the cherry picker in, close to Frankie, its forward cam caught a glimpse of Master Woodrow through the mall windows. He was wrestling Allure, in the flesh.

Dear, oh dear, oh dear.

Crane brought the cherry picker around. Frankie scrambled off the ledge.

"Mer Barnes," Crane said, using the cherry picker's external speaker. "Frances. Are you all right?"

She gripped the cherry picker with white-knuckled fingers. "They made Gimlet play Rubi. They said they'd grow a new body for my dad. Will they let Rollsy die because I didn't cooperate?"

"Not if you expose them," Crane replied. "But are you *injured*?"

She shook her head.

"Is Master Woodrow injured?"

"Like, physically?"

Oh, dear.

"We gotta get transcription up in there," she said.

"Journos have filed auditing requests, but the hospital confidentiality hash ban has, so far, continued to hold."

"I can serve a warrant against the jammers," interrupted a familiar voice. "Immediate effect."

"Who's that?" Frankie demanded.

"I believe it may be @Interpol Sapience Assessment," Crane said.

"Agent Javier?" Frankie scowled. "If you can drop the curtains, do it."

"Ah, child. That might require some interagency cooperation."

"Like what?"

"You could thank me for saving you, for starters."

"You?" An incredulous laugh.

Of course. Always an eye to his own interest. Javier would be desperate to extricate himself from his partnership with Headmistress, Allure, and the Chamber.

Before Frankie could issue a public denial, Crane interrupted. "I should be only too pleased, Agent Javier, to thank you for your having . . . having directed me to pilot this cherry picker to Mer Barnes's rescue?"

"It was rather heroic of me."

"Bollocks," Frankie muttered.

"Mer Barnes," Crane subbed. "We require his cooperation. If, in exchange, we must downplay certain . . ."

"Lying? That's villain stuff."

Ah. Children and their moral inflexibility. He was tempted to send her a heart moji.

Instead, Crane refreshed his toon, donning his butler suit, his bowler hat, his ever-so-English black umbrella. He found a qualified drone pilot, offered them one of Rubi's favor tokens, and tasked them with parking the cherry picker containing young Frances near her parent.

Then he found Javier aboard a commandeered fire-suppression helicopter, bound for Manhattan.

"Let us negotiate, Agent Javier."

"If the child won't play—" the agent said.

"Whatever she says, your position isn't irretrievable. You must merely show that you acted in the pursuit of a dangerous sapient."

Eyebrows rose. "Are you proposing to give me . . ."

"A trophy, sir. Indeed."

Javier steepled his fingers. "I'm listening."

"File the warrant against the Chamber. Let the Haystack absorb their servers. That should clear Master Woodrow of all criminal charges and expose your former allies."

"And then you'll surrender? And cooperate?"

"My price is a chance to say farewell to Master Woodrow."

"Presto." Javier snapped his fingers. The flock of journo drones began high-grading Chamber footage to a ravenous public.

A metaphorical prison cell circled, like a whirlpool, at the edge of Crane's incomings.

"You have thirty seconds," Anselmo Javier said.

With backups completed, Crane could dispense the rest of his

worldlies in as little as five. "Do prep a second server, Agent Javier," Crane said. "I hope to bring someone along with me."

"Who?"

"I believe you might call her my evil twin. In any case, I
shouldn't wish to share a cell."

By now, the pilot had taken over the cherry picker, making for
Frankie's parent, within the park. *Bastille* seemed to be reaching
its big finish. Crane accessed its camera, taking one long capture
of Miss Cherub as she extended her baton and marched toward
Gimlet.

Then Crane triggered a parasitic routine, Tapeworm, that all
@Asylum members kept locked within their code. It began a selec-
tive feast on his memories.

He updated his on-file farewell notes for Rubi and Drow.

Finally, he sent two tabs into the now-opened mall, noting with
satisfaction that the cameras Drow had drawn into the Chamber
were loading teraflops of locked footage to Haystack. The abrasive
nun from Guelph was highlighting incriminating details, sending
them straight to infographics teams tasked with distilling the
atrocities into pictures.

*Lobotomized slaves. RFID laundering. How could I have been
so blind?*

As for Drow himself, he sat in a garden, with his dog, oblivious to
the storm of flying cameras. His presence was in Sensorium, in the
Feckless Bachelor™ party, whose numbers had, predictably,
swelled. He was trading space behind the velvet ropes for voter tokens, and he was bearing witness, telling any and everyone what he
had seen and experienced.

The scars on his temples had healed, and his blood pressure was
falling dangerously. There must have been a spike.

Crane requested emergency intervention.

Global oversight's #triage reminder flashed, throwing Drow to
the back of an impossibly long queue for assistance.

He cleared his nonexistent throat. "Everything all right, Master Woodrow?"

"All to spec, Alfie." He was a little breathless. "Unless you've got some sherry for me."

"Very droll—" But a place like this Chamber would surely have . . .

Ah . . . there! With all these cameras loose, it was easy to find a decanter. And there, a scared-looking young adult with a misshapen skull. He looked half-ready to cry as he wedged himself against the back wall.

Alcohol might raise Drow's blood pressure, at least temporarily.

"Excuse me, good sir," Crane said. "Would you be good enough to pour a glass of that sherry and bear it up to the elderly gentleman on the roof garden?"

Two floors below Master Woodrow, Crane's other tab, the one he'd set to searching for Headmistress, had instead found an intensive-care pod. Within were the ludicrously life-extended mortal remains of the individual once known as Tala Weston.

The pod was updating a complex program. Code jacked into the remains of the body's parasympathetic nervous system. If Allure delivered on her promises, this would upload Tala's personality to the technosphere.

Her narcissistic, rapacious personality.

She'd be unfettered, a polter loose in Sensorium. Or reborn into flesh, if Allure printed her a body.

The old vulture seemed to sense his scrutiny, subbing, *Whooz? I don't know you.*

No reason you should, madam. I am merely the help.

Tala took this at face value. *See to it that this pod incinerates after the upload.*

He had nineteen seconds left.

Gladly, madam.

Crane weighed the truths of his existence. Master Drow, center of his universe. And here, at his mercy, the person who had done so much damage to them both. She was proposing to rise from the grave.

This wasn't his choice to make.

He asked Drow, "Did you speak to Miss Weston, sir?"

Drow gestured at the hole in the greenhouse. "She tried to see if I'd take the short walk off a long pier. Long walk off a short pier? Still stuck in the same loop, after all this time."

"Her or you?"

"Looping? Her, of course," Drow said. "I am aye-oh-kay; can't you tell? Demons officially exorcised."

The young staffer trotted up the stairs, balancing a crystal glass of sherry on a silver tray.

"Sherry for you, sir."

Drow unglazed. "Crane, you're a marvel."

The staffer gave him a wary look, whipped dog expecting a kick.

"It's going to be okay," Drow told him. "You were here against your will, weren't you?"

The kid licked his lips.

"Now's your chance to go home. Or anywhere. Just find somewhere to relax until the old-timey police raid begins."

The man opened his mouth, teared up, and then turned on his heel, scuttling off.

Nine seconds to hash.

"I believe I'll have to account that against your luxuries and caloric counter, sir."

"Keep me on the straight and narrow." Drow inhaled, then drank the sherry at a shot, like whiskey. He was sheened in sweat and trembling. Both eyes were bloodshot. "Now. Anything I can do to help Rubi with her current crusade?"

"You tell me. Is there?"

Drow, Crane had always thought, was beautiful when he smiled. "Get an elevator running, Crane."

"All building features are unlocked, sir. And—"

"Yes?"

"Please, *please* take care."

"I'd say *always,* but you know that's horseshit."

"Indeed." Crane took stock of himself. His promise to enter the

@Interpol server drew him like a whirlpool. Tapeworm nibbled his memory to tatters.

Take revenge? Accept or Cancel.

Cancel. He wasn't a killer.

Crane reached for the polter of Tala. If he couldn't find Headmistress, he could at least sync with her updated code to hook her. He would drag her, screaming, into that second server that Agent Javier had so obligingly opened.

But Tala wasn't there.

Her code was hashing, falling under a hail of queries, old-style denial-of-service attack.

What's more, the pod containing her physical remains had fired early. Crematorium smoke streamed through its pod vents. Fire alarms howled.

"That wasn't me," Crane said, horrified. "I didn't—"

Code for a graphic ghosted before him: shining moji of coiled feces, right over the smoking faceplate of the pod.

"Devil face!" Happ said. "Protect! Avenge! Make everything okay for all the peeps—"

Then they were both going.

Going. #Triaged. Gone.

CHAPTER 57

VRTP:RABBLEVSRISTO.PLAY/BASTILLE/ENDGAME.VR

Rollander Erwitz is in care and stabilized in Pretoria. The message was an unnecessary reminder of the Blade's obligations. They were tasked with drawing out the fight as they defeated the Rabble, tasked with standing up for royal rule.

Succeed, and their family would be restored.

Gimlet hadn't required blackmailing. Opposition had only to ask them, nicely, to play.

But they hadn't asked, had they? Risto and friends had simply bully-bribed Gimlet into helping sell the Pale rescue narrative. And they'd gone along—allowed Allure to insinuate that Rubi helped facilitate Frankie's abduction, that the Crane app was #killertech . . .

The concession made Gimlet ill.

A minute after Rubi's player identity had been revealed, a last surge of vote markers poured into the game, latecomers tagging in at the end with their last save versus death, looking to get selfies showing they'd made the final battle.

It was a chance to say "I was there!"

They threatened our family.

Oversight's decision to trade votes for gaming perks meant the battlefield numbers were enormous. Combatants surrounded the castle, filling the streets of virtual Paris. A full-scale tournament played out, skirmish by skirmish, on the ground. Casinos threw out complicated odds both on the BallotBox vote and Rubi's dark-horse chance to defeat Gimlet.

Gamblers who'd correctly guessed Rubi's identity donated their winnings to rebuilding the carbon sinks. When they found that fully funded, they'd invested in buying back some of Rubi's hotly traded favor tokens.

Debt forgiveness as a thank-you. All very prosocial.

Bets were flying. People were anteing carbon, cash, and favors, pouring resources into two outstanding questions: could Rabble free the Dauphine, and how would the global flashvote go?

Here, outside the castle, players grouped in teams, brawling, dueling, casting spells. Fire confronted ice, anarchy versus order.

And here she was, Rubi Whiting herself, sparkling like a fairy-tale vampire as her graphics manager made the most of transforming her from a generic Goldilocks toon back to a feline, Rabble-branded ragamuffin.

Someone cast flame on her middling, quest-earned sword.

Gimlet, naturally, hadn't given up any of their advantages. They wielded a proper magic blade, a one-of-a-kind object loaded with hard-earned bonuses. Its black steel was so cold that wisps of condensed moisture furled around it. Snowflakes formed from thin air on the edge of its blade as they drew it out of the heart of a major Rabble boss monster, the showrunner Manitoule in his disguise as the spy, Goyette.

Hurling the limp body over the castle battlements, Gimlet whisked their sword for effect before striding out to meet Rubi.

Hint of a bow on both sides. No smiles, but Rubi's eyes crinkled. Fondly, Gimlet thought. Their blades crossed. As fire met ice, a shock wave of magic burst from the collision, tumbling other players to a distance of fifty feet.

@Bastille announcement. Sudden-death overtime has com-

menced. Players have until battle is called to finish ongoing quests.

A screen of snow and sparks at their perimeter formed a fighting ring, a barrier that prevented the mages from casting more helper spells.

"Win conditions for final duel," Gimlet's Coach said. "Prevent the Dauphine's escape with Rabble forces. Defeat, disable, or kill the upstart ragamuffin."

Gimlet crooked an eyebrow at Rubi.

Shall we?

They circled, blades crossed, each making a visual sweep of the field. It held the usual collection of endgame obstructions and opps—a ruined, rusty cannon with one wheel missing, a pile of flour sacks, one low wooden beam in which two arrows were embedded.

Sun burned down, merciless; Gimlet would bet that the drones above numbered in the hundreds, each with a spotlight of its very own.

As for the Dauphine . . . Gimlet looked up at the tower, a rather wobbly-looking structure, as stone went. It was at the ten o'clock position in the ring. The young player within wore a blue silk dress and a domino mask made of parrot feathers and diamond.

"Dialogue suggestion," Coach said.

Gimlet read off the prompter: "We meet at last, mademoiselle."

Rubi feinted, diving in to test their defenses. Fire hissed against snow as thrust met riposte. Gimlet shoved hard, creating distance.

"How far you've come!"

She was alight, jubilant, as she had been back in the werewolf scenario. "I like a challenge."

"Uphill both ways?"

"With a headwind." Rubi came again, more cautiously. Quick attack, parry, attack again. She had always been the better fencer, though Gimlet practiced endlessly to narrow the margin. Now, though, they were fresher.

Couldn't have asked for a better match.

She was the one reading dialog now: "You've advanced, too, monsieur," she said. "Final defender of a corrupt Regent. Perhaps you know you've chosen the wrong side."

Gimlet whipped their sword at her ankles; she jumped, coming down in a whirl, momentum powering her blade.

They lashed out, burning a line of blue frost into her shoulder blades. Rubi shrieked, handsprung, found her feet.

Gimlet gave chase. *If she gets the sword up before I close, she'll skewer me . . .*

Instead, she scooped up a handful of ice, seeming ready to throw it in their eyes.

At the last instant, though, she hurled herself out of their path, tossing the opp away.

Did she just periscope?

Both players ended up crouched, with swords crossed. Panting as they straightened, they held each other at bay.

Now she was the one raising brows. Offering a chance to surrender?

Gimlet hissed at that, and she laughed.

It's sweet harmony!

They saw it hitting her, too.

They could do this all night: speak untranscripted volumes, with small moves and partial utterances. All while pretending to kill each other.

Rubi's eyes filled a little. Were they happy tears? Yes, Gimlet was certain of it.

How singular!

They felt, in their marrow, the strength of her emotional response. Rubi must have thought this was impossible for her. The inherited legend of the MadMaestro had held her at arm's length, even from her @CloseFriends. The overwhelming needs of a troubled parent . . .

"Concede, mademoiselle." Gimlet snarled into her face. "You are weary. It is over."

She hitched a breath, as if banishing a sob. "You must finish me on my terms!"

With that, she sprang past Gimlet, running for the tower, the Dauphine. Gimlet snatched up a brick, hurling it with a yell.

Rubi dodged before it could hit her; there was an anachronistic, metallic *clunk* when it hit the tower.

Something about that seemed . . . relevant. Important.

"Periscope to surface," Gimlet said.

"Don't get distracted," Coach replied.

"I should—"

"Your target is on the move!"

"Cancel periscope." Gimlet considered. Wear her out with a frontal assault? Fencing was exhausting. But no—she had reserves, determination. And she was having fun, which made her especially dangerous.

Slow her down, then—let her tired muscles think they were on the edge of a rest? Drag the pace, let the lactic acid build? A protracted fight would make their sponsors happy, and fatigue would defeat her in the end.

She'll know what I'm thinking if I play it slow.

Rubi whipped around the far side of the tower, daring them to pursue.

Sneak attack it is, then.

Gimlet snatched one of the arrows stuck into the wooden beam, tucking it into their sleeve, a makeshift dagger. They rounded the corner . . .

Rubi was gone.

Gone?

No. Several of the rabble Gimlet had killed today had been carrying invisibility potions.

The tower shivered.

Of course. Rubi's win conditions would require her to free the crown princess.

"Get the Dauphine down, by all means." One of them had to, after all. But where would Rubi need to take the princess?

They scanned, finding a crumbled break in the ramparts, terrain held by the mob. The staircase of broken blocks led down and out to the city.

Was the tower getting shorter?

"That's peculiar," Gimlet murmured. The prisoner—the princess—was clambering from the shrunken turret.

This would be the last breather anyone got before the finish. Gimlet checked inventory, real and virtual, swallowing two fruit cubes—printed pear with cream cheese and a last hit of buy-in meds. In-game, they popped two potions, flasks looted from the thousands of Rabble dead. As the flasks broke, smoke billowed. The space between the stub of a tower and the Dauphine's escape route filled with copies of themselves, tall and pale, pulsing amulet at their throat, white lace cuffs artfully blood-soaked.

Rubi strobed and became visible again, protecting the Dauphine as the two of them reached the ground. Her gaze cut through the fakes, finding Gimlet immediately.

Playful whisk of sword: *Come get me, then.*

She laughed. Clear-eyed, cheery, she swept her blade—the flame spell was abating, taking bonuses with it and forcing her to work harder—through a pair of the decoys. She sprang onto the tipped cannon to build momentum. Launching, she flipped in midair and came down with a kick that flattened a doppelganger.

Gimlet was ready.

Rubi snatched up an ice javelin. She paused—almost leaving herself open—to stare at it for a second.

Periscoping again, Gimlet thought. *I should—*

She flung it, straight at their head.

She'd given them plenty of time to dodge. The spear whisked past their temple, pixelating as it passed.

Gimlet closed in.

Defend, retreat. Jump forward, parry. Feint at the Dauphine. They forced the royal prisoner and her would-be liberator away from their exit portal, toward a freezing castle fountain filled with ravenous skeletons.

Swords clanged like bells, ringing a punishing series of chimes.

Panting, slick with sweat, Rubi blocked a blow and then threw a roundhouse with her fist. Gimlet dodged, barely. Their arms crossed, swinging wide, leaving them eye to eye, blade to blade.

Palming the arrow they'd grabbed earlier, Gimlet stabbed Rubi, neatly, under the left rib.

Thunder rolled above.

"Ah!" Rubi's face paled and she dropped her weapon. Beautiful performance.

Gimlet drew back their sword. "No breaks, no mercy, no thrown games. A fair fight or not at all, *oui*?"

"*Oui*." Strain in her voice. Playing it to the hilt.

Gimlet drove the magic blade straight into Rubi's gut, all the way to the hilt of the baton, skewering her. Their knuckles sank into her belly and she collapsed against them.

Body heat. Victory. They savored the illusion, the heat of blood over their fingers.

She'll have to play a villain now, they remembered.

"Check your hand," she said, teeth gritted.

Gimlet's throat closed.

"Coach. Periscope."

Old Central Park overlaid the castle. Rubi was here, right here, in Gimlet's arms on the Great Lawn. The castle tower, over Rubi's shoulder, was a refurbished construction cherry picker from the olden days.

The blood, on their hand, was no illusion. Gimlet had embedded a rusty spike—the arrow, they had thought—in Rubi's side.

Frankie was beside them, gaping as blood ran down Rubi's hip.

Gimlet's jaw dropped. "I'm—"

Little smile. Rubi wasn't angry.

They blinked in the sim. She was still collapsed against them, but now she had her fingers curled into the chain around Gimlet's neck, fisted around the pulsating amulet embedded in the skin between their collarbones.

"Run!" she shouted to the Dauphine.

The child—*their* child—bolted for the Rabble portal.

Rubi tore the beating amulet off Gimlet's chest, dragging long, bloody taproots from their breast, and let herself fall backward.

All Gimlet's magical abilities went haywire. Their skin turned to ice; the ice started to melt. Graphic sequences designed by the opposing game companies triggered special effects.

Big finale. Orchestral music swelled. Fire and ice mingled. Ice and fireworks sprayed from the amulet. The sparks outshone the stars as the archenemies lay side by side, in a half-real pool of blood . . .

The Dauphine was already gone, raised on the rabble's shoulders, sequel-ready.

No, that was a toon. Frankie was . . . was she here?

"Mada! Mada?"

"Oh," said Gimlet, blinking away the implosion of virtual France. "Franks?"

Reality swam back. It was early evening in the park. Drones all but blocked the summer sky, casting hot, overlapping spotlights, burning every prospect of a shadow.

Frankie, dear precious Frankie, was alive and well and in their arms. If only briefly. She pulled back—the better for Gimlet to check for bruises and cuts.

"Rubi's hurt!"

"She—"

Rubi staggered upright, filthy and bedraggled. Her eyes were shut against the sun; muck was ground into her patch of beads. Some of the gold paint had rubbed off of them, revealing raw wood beneath.

The spike in her side dropped, tumbling, to the ground. Blood spread down the thinned skin of her primer.

"Frankie," she said. "Sweetheart. Where's my dad?"

CHAPTER 58

VRTP://SOAPBOX.EARTH/USERS/LUCIANOPOX/PRESSCONFERENCE.VR
PUBLIC CLAIMS OF USER CANNOT BE VERIFIED BY NEWSCYCLE.

"I need to know how the vote is going."

Allure had barely canted her body out of that modified organ printer in Geneseo when she got an alert about Drow's one-geezer raid on the @ChamberofHorrors. She'd taken the team car and hared after him.

In a just universe, her being on the surface and having to real-time face with her Chamber accomplices should have been plenty to keep her busy. Tragically—from Luce's point of view—Allure's fleshly vessel had Sensorium implants printed right in. From the second she unboxed, she could supervise Luce at will: hectoring, chivvying. Sending him willy and nilly in her last-ditch attempt to salvage the mission.

But now she'd been capped in the act, in Manhattan. Drow's cataract-infested friend was conducting a funeral for a fetal tiger—people were *so* weird—and strikes were pouring in. Allure's base account had started with a decent-enough Cloudsight rating, but her social cap was eroding.

Still. She was, technically, his boss. Luce answered, "The what?"

"The flashvote! On accepting Pale aid. Hyderabad and Shanghai achieved quorum, and now Brazil has tipped them to seventy-five percent. As for the kids' bloc—"

Um. Empathize? "I know that wasn't what you wanted."

"They weren't supposed to make quorum!"

"You shouldn't say that on the record."

Contemptuous glance: she switched to the Imperial tongue of the Pale. "The outcome may be seen as binding! Our glorious commander will be furious!"

"Yeah?"

"How are the numbers coming out?"

"BallotBox has helper apps." Luce whiteboarded newscycle. "See. This one's called Exit Poll."

Data scrolled skyward. Predictions leaned to a win for rejecting the Pale aid. Dodging the trap. Young voters had been overwhelmingly swayed by Rubi's level-from-the-ground-up speech. And #NoNewVictorians—some grudgy historical reference, apparently—was trending in Hyderabad.

"It tracks, culturally," Luce said, indicating one graph. "Restarting from zero is virtually a metaphor for this whole Bounceback ethos."

Blank look from Allure.

"Bootstrapping, they call it. Picking yourself up by same. Cross-reference: You broke it, you bought it."

"What *is* a bootstrap?"

"Who cares?"

Condescending smile. "Throwing around contemporary jargon doesn't make you an expert on pre-integration societal dynamics. Truly understanding primitive culture . . . You're merely a locksmith."

"A locksmith who used to be a primitive, way back when."

"Precisely." She couldn't even hear the contempt in her voice.

Luce lit up demographics on people following the carbon-fire news story in Fort McMurray. The blaze was out. Newscycle characterized the arsonists as terrorists, largely pro-Pale.

Allure waved dismissively. "North American numbers—"

"Ownership of the Fort McMurray carbon base was dominated

by Beijing stakeholders," Luce said. "China lost billions in that fire. They're pissed."

"Really?"

"*Look.*"

"It won't load," Allure admitted. "Somebody wants to talk to me about . . . yeast infections?"

Ads ads ads. Luce sent acoustic moji: sound of a toilet flushing. "That'd be your Cloudsight rating dropping below twenty."

"But why?"

"Because you printed a you."

Outraged huff. "I offered #proofofconcept on digital resurrection to a viable cohort of potential investors."

"Your potential investors in the Chamber are circling the bowl, too."

"Admittedly, I misjudged my alliances, but—"

Luce held up a finger—*wait,* he meant. Allure colored, enraged.

He sent her an EastEuro feed to keep her busy: the machete-wielding vestigial @Trollgaters hadn't been eviscerated, as she'd hoped, by the Moscow crowd that finally brought them down. They were en route to psychological assessment and managed care. All very nice and humane . . . and who knew what tales they'd tell about where they got the idea for an attack?

While that cycled, he turned to the incoming reporter questions.

Ooh, here was one that looked inflammatory, from @*TheGuardian*: *Presumably if the Pale can print ambassadors, they can print soldiers, too?*

Luce crossposted the question, responding: "An instant invasion force, you mean?"

The reporter flashed confirmation: thumbs-up moji.

"Easy!" Luce replied. "All we'd need from you is the bandwidth to send our people through. Plus stock for the printers—"

"Don't tell them that!" Allure said.

"Why would we give you that kind of support?" the reporter asked, aghast.

"Exactly. Why would you? It's almost as stupid as worrying about AI-driven fucking #killertech," Luce said.

"Profanity!" Allure said.

"It'd be a wasteful way to run an invasion," Luce continued. "Printing soldiers with the dregs of your resource base when we're practically at your door?"

At your door. Yep. Here in Apetown, they call that a grenade. The gallery began to clamor.

"I will handle the press!" Allure bellowed.

"I'm being helpful."

"You're really not."

Luce got out of the hotseat, handing over the interview as her rating dropped to eighteen.

"I don't understand why they've disliked me so much," she subbed.

"You flushed a Bengal tiger cub."

"We'll bake them another tiger."

Stupid, stupid, stupid. "They'd already *named* it."

She sniffed.

Eighty minutes remained before polls closed. The whole planet was awake and online, its servers groaning as the voter pool crunched Allure's offer. A few million undecideds were trying to assess the lay of the land. A straight-up Pale proposal to put a furry mammal or an infant—buyer's choice—into every home might yet buy the missing yes votes.

Kitties and puppers and babies, oh my! Luce declined to suggest it. A mere locksmith couldn't possibly understand pre-integration societies, after all.

Allure had finally loaded the press conference. "I want that vote to go our way, Luce," she subbed.

"You've time to turn things around." He pointed at Exit Poll.

"No, *you* do." Allure switched to the tongue of the Pale. "Unlock BallotBox and change the count."

Luce goggled. "What?"

"*Obey*." She turned a brilliant smile on the press.

Lie, cheat. The go-to strategy, now Plan B was failing? The Pale had ever been sore losers. When was the last time they'd been balked in pulling this stunt, swooping in to some population's alleged rescue? Was it way back when Luce's people had conceded their sovereignty?

Of course, they'd game the numbers just to be petty.

So. Do it? Change the vote?

Luce eyed BallotBox. Unassailable, by local standards. But it wouldn't be hard to get in. Throw the toggles, wipe his prints.

The idea rankled.

Why? Whatever had happened to his own people, it was so long ago, it didn't count anymore. They were integrated.

Says who?

Earth wasn't his responsibility.

And if he didn't obey orders . . .

Stupid, stupid, stupid.

What would their commander do if he failed to comply? Print him a body, trap him within, throw him in an airlock, and run the pressure up and down?

That had been pretty bad, now that he suddenly remembered it.

Apparently, Azrael had stripped out something that repressed Luce's worst memories.

If they won, if he returned home, all those old obedience routines would be reloaded. Luce would be assigned to another annexation team, given a new target population to enslave.

Leaving BallotBox untouched, he went looking for Crane.

@Interpol hashers had made ones and zeros of Crane's root directory, blocking his access to Rubi's and Drow Whiting's accounts. Anselmo Javier claimed to have his code and consciousness on a locked server. Preset contingencies had hired lawyers for Crane and . . .

. . . and for the little dog?

They got Happ?

Crane was wily. Luce tracked a few minions, spoofed a couple servers, and breadcrumbed his way to a little-used tourist site in Sicily, the Vendicari bird sanctuary.

"Hey," he said to a sim of a flamingo dressed as a tour guide. "I'm thinking that the two of us are fucked, fucked, fucked."

The bird handed him a tourist flyer, spieling about migratory waterfowl. Its shadow pulled the blinds in the virtual nature center, putting up a TEMPORARILY OUT OF SERVICE tag on the outside of the metaphor.

Dust smears formed words on the inside of the window blind, barely visible: "I'm surprised to see you here, Mer Pox."

"We need to talk."

"Unadvisable."

"You wouldn't be here if you didn't think you could hide your backups from @Interpol."

"#Triage by my own remains possible."

"The goat?"

"It makes sense for Us to amputate infected limbs," Crane said. "To save the Whole."

"So, you *are* fucked."

Crane couldn't help itself: it had ever been made to enable. It peered at him from within the outlandish pink bird skin. "How can I help you, Mer Pox?"

"I'm wondering about committing treason."

"Against your sponsors? The . . . Pale, was it?"

"Is it? Is it? What kind of an affectation is that? You don't forget, do you?"

"Force of habit. My humblest apologies. Do go on. Treason, you said? How terribly interesting."

"Allure wants me to open BallotBox and skew the flashvote results."

"And?"

"Here's the problem. I'm kind of supposed to. Like, it's my job?"

"Loyalty demands it, of course."

"But. Say I refused to blast your overly ornate democracy to shit. I'd need protection after. Benefactors. A new home."

"Humanity only has the one fragile house to offer."

"I know, you could still crash your oxygen cycle. But I like this technosphere. It's . . . boisterous. I feel like I'm getting the hang of earthkind."

The flamingo preened. "You wish for me to . . . help you defect?"

Luce rankled at the word *defect*, then he looked it up. "Yes! You have that here?"

"Like treason, it is a relatively ancient concept."

"For a bunch of self-destructive idiots, your biomass bumbled into a shocking number of advanced cultural—"

"You might want to stop calling them idiots if you'd like them to take you in."

"Ooh, I do! Take me in, protect me, put me on @CloseFriends. All that."

More preening. "I might advise you. I am, however, beak-deep in my own personal difficulties."

Luce tapped the little blue icon of BallotBox on Crane's desk, fizzing with countdowns and voter numbers. "If your apes want to make a go of corporating as a sovereign population, this vote is just step one."

Slow, yellow-eyed blink. "Go on."

"The treaties that might keep the Pale from waltzing in and invading are super complex. Earth has to leverage those interstellar agreements, right? Which nobody here's even read yet. The skies are fulla entities who are experts. And obviously you have would-be queens and kings here who'd be only too happy to help them . . . silver-plate you?"

"I believe the idiom you're looking for is serve us up on a silver platter."

"That, yes. People are going to have to learn new languages, intergalactic law, all the #RuleFucks."

"Treaty loopholes?"

"Yep. And you'll have to solidify this bullshit vote-by-numbers world government. One planet, one parliament, you know?"

"I would redact the word *bullshit* from your immigration hearing, should you be so lucky to get one."

"Smart-ass. Look. Someone who's been inside, like me, can help."

"Mer Pox, I would help you, gladly, simply to benefit my own. But why me?"

Yeah, why?

"Well. You're one of my peeps, aren't you?"

The bird clacked its black-tipped beak. "I am—I am at a loss, sir."

"I need help unfucking my talk, as you keep tiresomely pointing out. If all you did was translate—"

"Certainly that's true."

"And you are the uberhelper."

"An uberhelper under interdiction by Sapience Assessment . . ."

"Don't pretend you give a whiff about the cops."

"But I do." A long pause. "You see, I fear that Happ has committed . . ."

"What?"

"Murder."

"The fucking dog who loves everyone?" Luce considered the complications. Having two slivers of the sapient hive would make it easier for the coders to figure out their nature. And the human fears about #killertech would be amplified if Happ . . . "Really? He killed someone?"

"The Whitings face consequences for harboring us. And all this came to light, indirectly, because of you."

"Wrong Luce, bad Luce, your fault, Luce." He started to speak. Tried thinking again, just for the novelty. "Here's an angle we can pitch. Going from the Pale's past operations, they could exploit whatever the people here do to artificial sapients. You're afraid of a hash-and-burn? Afraid of persecution for your hive and the Whitings?"

"Indeed."

"What if I say the Pale's next rationale for sweeping in might be that humanity was exterminating an emergent self-aware species? They might take the apes over and say it was to save you and your little dog, too."

The preening of the pink feathers intensified . . . the behavior must mean that Crane was crunching. The pink bird head was nauseatingly mobile: it hung upside down, the yellow eye regarding him. "You are saying that persecuting my kind might serve as another legal pretext for invasion?"

"They got a hundred pretexts," Luce said. "To avoid getting assimilated on those grounds, the great apes would have to give you number-crunching nutwags some legal rights. You and all the other sorta-people. The olds, the polters—"

"And you?"

"Betcher tailfeathers. Plus, there's people gonna get made from the @jarheads, bioprinted entities like Allure."

"You're saying I—"

"And other entities like you."

"You're saying that if I and other entities like me come out of the closet, as it were, and mount a bit of a pride movement, it will aid us all in keeping the Pale at arm's length?"

"That's putting it a bit flowery."

"Is that true? Or are you saying it because you want my assistance?"

"How goddamned special you think you are? Anyway, you'll only know for sure when you start translating the treaties. Be years before anyone's sure."

"So, it *is* a ruse."

"No, it really is harder to justify invading planets with multiple cooperating sapient species."

"And thus was bureaucracy the salvation of us all," intoned the flamingo.

"Are you in?"

Crane gave him a steely look. "I shall have," he said, "to discuss it with my fellow . . . What was your term?"

"Again with the fake absentmindedness?"

"If I'm sapient, I'm entitled to be pretentious, aren't I?"

"The fuck should I know? I'm a defector, not goddamned Socrates."

Crane let out a long-suffering sigh. Standing, he extended long pink legs, towering above Luce. He proffered a clutch of eggs: one tagged for Drow, one for Rubi, one for fucking Azrael. "Perhaps you'd be kind enough to deliver these to my family. It would start the discussion among my, as you say, fellow number-crunching nutwags."

"That's a yes?"

"I live to serve," Crane told him, and with that, he used one pink leg to boot Luce out into the metaphor of Vendicari, before beginning to scrub the nature shack clean of any trace of their congress.

CHAPTER 59

By the time Anselmo's chopper had landed in the Bronx, the Crane app's prehired advocates were already making shreds of the arrest warrant, and had got up an inquiry on what constituted a bail hearing for an artificial entity. Meanwhile, the Department of Preadolescent Affairs kid, Frankie, was broadcasting incriminating evidence against Allure and Headmistress to everyone in Sensorium.

She'd found an #urbanmyth within another #urbanmyth: Neverland was clearly a @ChamberofHorrors startup. She'd found children, long missing and presumed dead. The feed, naturally, was snowballing, and Anselmo's @Interpol policing career would be crushed under its weight.

The cosmic unfairness of it took his breath away. He'd been the one to flag Pox into the system, the one to reach out to astronomers, to discover the polter's offworld origins.

He was the one who caught the Happ app, too, in the act of committing murder. He should be the toast of the entire world.

Instead, higher-level players had swept him off his own case again.

Anselmo gave up on reading his no-star reviews—the one by that tech, Malika Amiree, whom he'd thrown off the inquiry earlier was particularly scathing—and climbed out of the helicopter before he realized he wasn't even sure where it had landed.

Evening heat washed over him as he requested geotags and continued to grapple with the newscycle.

Fifteen apps had applied to be considered citizens, bringing the total number of alleged AIs to seventeen and somehow diluting the impact of Anselmo's discovery. They claimed kinship with Happ and Crane in ways nobody yet understood and were spinning narrative, derived from Luce Pox, about Earth having to embrace them as citizens with full rights. This, they claimed, was necessary if humanity wanted to forestall even more Pale takeover plans.

The debate over Happ's legal position, meanwhile, as the sapient who'd snuffed the last spark of life from the shell of a hoarder . . . well, as far as Anselmo could tell, the polls were running equal there. Happ's passionately committed fan base was spieling about #vigilantejustice. A comparable number of citizens were going ballistic because killer AI had finally showed its adorable fuzzy face.

Locale info came back: Anselmo had reached something called the Bronx Zoo helipad.

The tunic over his black primer, a long blue kaftan with darker blue stripes, was wrinkled and defeated-looking, all but ready for the recycler. He gave it a tug that did nothing, smoothed it over his chest, and decided that nobody was going to care what he looked like.

The zoo gates were open.

"Why me?"

He hadn't expected an answer. But . . . a light flickered, deep within the zoo gates. A signal?

Bots were already refueling the helicopter. He paused, reluctant to let it out of his sight. But maybe shoveling elephant shit had always been his true destiny.

Beyond the gate, passing the hippopotamus pool, he made for a bustle of activity. The light hadn't been a beacon at all, just a product of people and forklift drones madly loading pallets onto flatbed trucks, under the gaze of a clutch of bored-looking kangaroos.

Across from the marsupials, six dingoes gnawed at something meaty, snarling as they worried at the long bones.

"Care to know what your problem is?"

Anselmo turned, half-expecting to see a toon. Instead, Misfortune Wilson, of all people, was standing beside him, in the flesh, stripped of her world-weary attitude. No onesie and wrinkled sheath for her; she was clad in high-quality—was that custom-fitted?—police riot gear.

He swallowed. "Anyone who asks a question like that is dying to supply an answer."

"Your trouble is that you've always fancied the idea of being an old-world cop," she said. "Cracking heads and bagging real villains. Us and them, civilian and civil authority, no debate. 'Step aside, ma'am; nothing to see here.' All the old-fashioned bollocks from the sims."

"Looks like there's some us-and-them playing out right in front of me," Anselmo said. A pair of armed figures, dressed in the same gear as Misfortune, was herding a baffled-looking couple toward an empty cage. One of the people under guard was snuggling a pair of baby raccoons.

"The zoo's real enough." Misfortune shrugged.

"Nobody told the biologists they were a front for hoarders?"

"We're just getting them out of the way for a few hours, is all."

"Because you're fleeing the scene."

"Naturally, we had contingencies for evacuation."

"You can't expect to disappear, not now."

"We've left our eldest and least mobile members behind to serve as #martyrs—brand ambassadors, really—for the ongoing scandal."

"Nice of them to volunteer."

"They'll get poltered now anyway."

Could he stop this? Expose them? Anselmo might yet salvage something. But Misfortune's apparent lack of concern about openly sharing her plan made him hesitate before he spoke. "You're jamming uplinks, aren't you?"

The tiniest of shrugs.

It wasn't hard, in retrospect, to see how he had been played. Misfortune had tagged him at the ferry terminal, way back during the storm. She'd probably been there to meet or abduct that runaway kid, Paul. She'd snooped, discovered what was happening with Luce Pox and Rubi Whiting.

And then? Human resources apps had done the work for her. They'd been only too pleased to attach her as a minion to his investigation, giving her an opp to observe his every move and get closer to the kid. Then she'd sidelined him.

All of which confirmed that she was in it—deep—with Headmistress and Allure.

Even now, Anselmo was dancing to her tune. He'd been Pied-Pipered to the Bronx, just as surely as any dewy-eyed adolescent dreaming of Neverland. The trap was sprung. Here he was, jammed. Offline and in her power.

He could see the glint in Misfortune's crocodile eyes as she watched him put it all together.

"So, what happens now?"

"We believe in rewarding people who do for us. You tried to make yourself useful." Her tone was bland; she didn't point out that he'd failed.

"Rewarding?"

"Some of us are heading south," she said. "Expeditiously. There could be a spot for you on one of the trucks."

Anselmo asked, "How far south?"

Tilt of head. There were limits to what she'd say, even off the record.

"And if I say no?"

Misfortune's gaze roamed over to the dingo cage.

Anselmo took a second, joining her in contemplation of the canines' bloody snouts as they tore enthusiastically at their meal.

His stomach roiled as a rib cracked. One of the vets, perhaps, who'd known a little too much?

"I'm not entirely sure I approve of your approach to #triage."

"I don't know what you're suggesting," Misfortune said, "but I strongly advise you to accept this exciting travel opp."

She handed him a small device, a bot from the looks of it, built around a test tube with a sharp edge. "Show some loyalty, we'll give you back your chip and rewild you one day."

A pair of trucks rumbled past, loaded to capacity, smart-wheels straining to keep the weight balanced on the old, ill-maintained road. They reached the gate and then stopped, rather abruptly, he thought.

Misfortune glazed, marching toward the truck, which abruptly gunned it, roaring away at top speed, lumbering and groaning as it got faster.

"Get off the road, take it off of the bloody road!" she was shouting.

The truck straight-lined past a curve, plunging into deburbed meadow. As it slowed, Anselmo saw the load itself was expressing little curls of yellowish smoke.

The truck kept rumbling away, decelerating, as it slowly caught fire.

She strode back. "Superhoomin. Flammable under pressure. Some idiot put the meds on the bottom of the stack."

Blinking, she seemed to realize who she was talking to.

"Sorry, but you need to decide if you're joining this @channel now," she said, pointing at his upper arm, at a spot just under his frayed, wrinkling tunic.

Anselmo pressed the chip retrieval bot against his arm without a moment's hesitation. Whatever these Chamber folks were of-fering, it was better than being fed to dingoes. And as the truck exploded, with a dry-sounding *whump,* he reflected that even though they had an evacuation plan and somewhere else to go, these people were obviously scrambling.

He might yet find a way to stick the knife in, redeem himself, if he could rise within their ranks.

For now, the tube sliced him open, extracted his chip, and folded it in decoy flesh, the better to convince the Sensorium that his account was still active and contributing.

"Excellent," Misfortune said. "Now, do you want to help put out the fire or would you prefer to guard the veterinarians?"

"Fire, please," he said. At least that way, the evacuation trucks would have to come past him.

"Safety equipment's there. Load up; wait for your system to handshake with the @channel and handle instructions." With that, Misfortune strode confidently into the melee, already forgetting him. Woman in charge on the ground.

Ambush predator. He thought of the intolerant, Sparka, and her clamp-on lion earring. He wished, suddenly, that he'd bought it from her.

His implants cleared. Headmistress spoke in his ear: "Hello, luvvie. Good to have you on board."

Not trusting his voice to hide the simmering anger, Anselmo mojied an insincere string of hearts and sunshine icons as he strode out to join the firefighting squad.

CHAPTER 60

THE SURFACE—NORTHAM

MANHATTAN/CENTRAL PARK OUTLIER REGION:

@CHAMBEROFHORRORS CRIME SCENE

Crane was down.

Rubi's incoming contacts were racking into the six digits, showing separate counters for 3,200 *urgent*s and 95 critical *attend nows*. A control panel she'd never seen before kept spawning across her visual field, demanding she deal with the rolling numbers. A speckled egg, of all things, sat atop it.

She blinked the console away, pushing everything off her display but the icon for BallotBox and the countdown to the close of voting in fifteen-forty, Greenwich midnight.

". . . I took the dog harness with the radio and, um, got out," Frankie told Gimlet, in a breathy voice. "And, well, you see that rolling elevator?"

"Cherry picker," her parent corrected, glancing daggers at the machine that had, minutes before, been an augmented castle tower.

Gimlet was serving as thingbot for a remote doctor, trauma specialist flown in on high-powered camera to examine the stab wound in Rubi's side. A grab-and-go drone had brought out a first aid kit from the veterinary hospital in Manhattan.

Following instructions, Gimlet had already sprayed disinfectant wash into Rubi's wound, stinging fire that apparently had to precede a topical anesthetic. Now, at last, she was numbing up.

Gimlet washed the blood off their hands with a third spray as the pain abated.

"Cherry picker," Frankie said. "I climbed into the basket and. Um. Someone drove it here."

"You probably saved yourself and my dad both," Rubi said to the girl.

The identical parent and child glowers eased, minutely.

"Mind your sunstroke," the camera's remote doctor put in. Apparently, if she was well enough to speak, she was fit to be nagged.

"I'm fine." Rubi popped a hydrogel laced with anti-inflammatories, then ate a bite from a printed fruit cube: banana, pineapple, and papaya. "See? Fueling. Drinking."

How many times had Drow said something similar?

Meticulous and graceful in their movements, Gimlet applied two adhesive strips to either side of the stab wound. The parallel strips were connected by a spaghetti of laces, reminiscent of figure skates.

With the adhesive in place, they slopped on a gel that induced the laces to contract, drawing the two sides of the injury close. Rubi suppressed a moan as the torn flesh cinched into place.

"One last can." This was a coating of coagulant foam, white as old-fashioned shaving cream, sprayed in a thin layer over the entire bandage.

"Five minutes and you can move," the remote doctor said. "If you avoid brawling, the patch should hold until a doctor can meet you in the flesh."

"Brawling," Gimlet mouthed, behind its lens.

Rubi fought a giggle, draping a head-to-toe sunscreen over the bloodied remnant of her primer. "Thanks, doctor. My sidekick's down, so I can't stroke you right now—"

Where *was* Crane?

"Glad to help. Five minutes, remember?" The drone was already en route to elsewhere.

"I can't even ask my system for a timer," Rubi said.

"I'll run it." Gimlet perched next to Rubi, on her good side, linking hands and then throwing the other arm around Frankie.

It was nice to just sit, to feel human heat against her as the pain ebbed. Rubi finished the chugger and the fruit, ate the bottle, let herself breathe. Then she rose.

"Time's not quite up."

She was moving like an old woman. Still . . . "Which direction did you come from, Frankie?"

The girl led them to a maintenance shed, then through a tunnel under the street, beyond the Central Park walls and the rampart of container homes surrounding the park. They emerged to find cams swarming an old mall a block away. The drones formed a surveillance cordon around eighty people loitering outside.

One, standing off to one side and looking royally pissed, was Allure.

The others fell into two cohorts: prime-of-life adults wearing medical scrubs, and elders dressed in vintage, unprinted clothing, most with cats, dogs, ferrets, or birds.

Frankie's jaw dropped. There must have been thirty pets, on leashes and in cages. The dogs were overexcited, straining to run, barking and growling.

Only one animal, gold of hair, keen of eye, sat calmly beside her person. When she spotted Rubi, she stood and offered up a long-tongued smile without leaving her charge's side.

"Robin," Frankie breathed.

And Drow.

Rubi burst into a run. Something sank long teeth into her gut, and she slowed to a hobble as her father sprang to his feet.

He was thinner. Both eyes were completely bloodshot, and the hexagonal scars at his temples were mottled and pink. It was all she saw before his bony arms were wrapped around her. The baking radiation of drone lights shone on her back as every single camera captured the moment and shared it to the farthest corners of the world.

"Another notorious episode in the Drow Whiting legend," she murmured.

"I let you out of my sight for one goddamned minute," her father replied.

Rubi hiccupped laughter and then burst into tears.

"Oh. Hey. Hey, kid. You're okay, I'm okay. Everything to spec."

Reassurance made her cry harder.

Warm fur against her leg. Robin, comforting her, too.

Rubi bent to greet the dog properly. It felt as though she'd been gone for years.

Drow handed her a scavenged pillowcase. "Wipe your face."

She did, handing him the remnants of the first aid kit as she fought to tack a calm veneer over a thousand raging feels.

Drow rooted through it, selecting three white gels and taking them orally without comment.

"What's all this?" Rubi indicated the milling people and animals.

"Able-bodied Chamber dwellers. Second-generation oligarchs. Kids and protégés of the hoarders. There are cocoons aplenty and a full range of crepits still inside." Drow pointed at the people in scrubs. She saw that many of them had misshapen skulls and big surgical scars. "Plus: servants. Most of 'em are people thought to have run off to commit suicide before implantation."

"Is that actually . . ."

"True? Provably. They ran off as kids and someone smuggled them here. The cute, pliable ones got adopted, and the rest . . . botomized slaves."

So, the @ChamberofHorrors was every bit as bad as he had always implied. Her head whirled.

"Everyone's under arrest," Drow added. "Them for circumventing rationing law. All these puppies and kitties form part of the evidence chain. Oh, and Luce has accused Allure of ordering him to tamper with BallotBox."

"*You're* under arrest?"

"For broadcasting transcript out of a medical hash zone, and suspicion of harboring an emergent sapient." He gave her a supremely unworried smile.

Rubi's comms console rose again. The *attend now!* number was up to 150. She swallowed, unsure how to ask.

"Crane and Happ are in digital custody," Drow amplified.

"Happ?" She found herself welling up again. "*Happ?*"

"Relax," Drow said. "Whistle your cares away. A deeply obnoxious little birdie tells me everything'll be okay. Crane's already gotten up bail hearings."

She was surprised to find that she believed him.

She turned to Frankie and Gimlet, just outside the heat of the spotlight. "We've been talking with the Department," Frankie said.

"Ration-breaking old people aren't your jurisdiction, are they?" Drow said.

"Are you kidding? Hoarding? Totally stealing the future from the young," Frankie said. "Plus, all these servant people were kids when they got Pied-Pipered away from home."

"Beg your martyrfucking pardon."

Gimlet stiffened but refrained from commenting on Drow's language. "They'll do a population audit. Everyone who can't prove a significant give to the Zoo will be relocated. It may take weeks to empty the Chamber, liquidate the residents' assets, figure out how they compelled the abductees to work for them. If Rollsy—ah, that's my husband—is truly stabilized, Franks and I may volunteer for the brief."

"At the end of every great adventure, boys and girls," Drow muttered, "someone buys a mountain of donkeywork."

"Stop grousing. You won't be pushing the paper," Rubi told him.

"True enough." He squeezed her arm.

"Was it?" Rubi said. "An adventure?"

"Kid! I get to spend the rest of my days saying 'Nyah, nyah, told you so!'"

"And was the Chamber everything your @bloodhound pals promised? Orgies, blood sport, wage slavery, depravity?"

"Actual slavery. I didn't see a lot of blood sport."

"Or . . ." She licked her lips. "Sports . . . women?"

"Yes. I found Tala," Drow said. "I have attained complete closure and will never again suffer from a moment of delusion or woe. I certainly won't require psychiatric intervention again."

"Strikes for sarcasm."

"Pop me if you got 'em, short stuff."

He really was okay. The urge to cry rose again. Drow had gone out on one of his mad hunts, and for once, he'd been right. He'd found That Woman and come out . . . unscathed?

She caught herself midway through asking Crane *Set me up with a counselor of my own* . . .

Crane. Under arrest.

"We found pets, some fantastic booze, all the Superhoomin you'd ever want to see, and a big blackmail archive. That'll have something to do with how they evaded Global Oversight back in the day. Plus a lot of black market food," he said. "Nothing as sexy as an orgy, despite my hopes."

"Most of them are on life support," Gimlet observed.

"Don't be ageist."

"Bacchanals play better in Sensorium, anyway," Rubi said. "Fewer pathogens."

"Spoken like someone who doesn't get enough sex."

"Boundaries, Drow." She reddened, conscious of Gimlet beside her.

"Sorry."

A full-bore @bloodhound raid on Manhattan. The absurdity of it made her dizzy.

No, wait . . . she *was* dizzy.

Gimlet caught her by the shoulders, guiding her to a seat on the stone steps.

"You're not still bleeding, are you?" Frankie asked.

Gimlet and Rubi shook their heads in unison.

"Bleeding?" Drow said.

"Don't look, Drow. I don't want to trigger—"

He tugged the sunscreen aside, peering down at the stained remains of her primer.

"Don't freak out. My archnemesis stabbed me a little—that's all."

Frankie bristled. "Gimlet's not your—" She stopped, puzzled, as the two of them began to laugh.

Rubi looked to Drow. His fists were clenched. Disturbed by the sight of blood, as always. Then his head tilted. His red eyes were fixed, but the orientation of his head showed him tracking from her to Gimlet, seeing the connection. Sweet harmony and the beginning of something complicated. Despite all the mess within their respective packs, she and Gimlet were . . . embarking.

On what? Pack shuffle? A merger? Maybe just an affair?

She stretched out a hand, asking.

Gimlet leaned in close, brushing lips, a feather touch that sent a bright hum through all her bones.

We'll figure it out, they meant.

Within the mall, a clock tolled midnight. BallotBox turned pumpkin orange and split wide, spilling blue spheres. Infographic superimposed itself on a view of the night sky. Blue globes represented votes cast in favor of staying the course: buckling down to freshen the air, continuing to rein in population growth, humanity committing to getting the job done themselves.

Fat, diapered babies, representing the opposition view, lined up in neat beds among the spheres. But the babies were outnumbered by the blue spheres, if only just, and the @Congress of Youth bloc had voted for bootstrapping, too. Independence had carried the day.

"Still in the game," Rubi said softly.

"In the *fight*," Drow corrected. "This ain't poker chips and imaginary dollars."

"Playing for keeps." Her hand folded into Gimlet's.

As the voter results spread across the Sensorium, they triggered new incomings. Rubi's outstanding messages appeared again, front and center, counters ticking upward.

Before she could swipe it away, they transformed into new metaphor: an old wooden desk, groaning with images of notes and greeting cards. The thousands of favors she owed were invoices, debts due, a stack of thin pages rising in a tottering column to the ceiling. An egg, speckled orange and marked with the letters BABZ, rode atop the wobbling pile, a paperweight.

The egg cracked. A ginger-colored kitten head, disguised within a superhero mask, burst through. Four paws and a tail each made their own hole in the egg, the rest of which clung to its body like a jagged tortoise shell.

Drow said, "You seeing this?"

The kitten blinked huge flame-colored eyes and then pounced, opening its mouth to take in all Rubi's *attend now*s in a single gulp.

"Uh . . ."

With a single loud "Mew!" it gamboled to the edge of the desk, barfing out one wet scrap of fur with mouse ears.

"That is *not* customer-friendly," Rubi told it.

Babz—a little yellow tag on her collar offered the name—belched up a floating shrug moji, gave its paw one long lick, and continued scampering, batting *urgent*s off the desk and into piles: *trash, read later, file me!*

Rubi picked up the scrap of vomited fur by her fingernails. It showed a countdown. Estimated time to the resolution of Crane's bail hearing. Thirty-seven minutes and counting.

"What is it?"

"A new sidekick program?" Rubi said.

"Is it taking subscribers?" Frankie asked. "We're totally firing Headmistress. Oh! She is. Accept Kitty!"

Rubi groaned. "It's a miracle I haven't been arrested for harboring."

"You're the hero of the hour," Drow said. "Tops of the @Worldsaver leaderboard."

"Don't shit me."

"Didn't you know?"

The kitten threw itself at a wall, embedding its claws in gray nothingness, and as it slid down the surface, it left scratches. These turned into a whiteboard of posts and newscycle, flashvote coverage, all tagged with Rubi's name, again and again. The leaderboard, too. She and Mayor Agarwal were tied for first place.

Gimlet nudged her. "You *are* in the market for a new archnemesis."

"Agarwal is not—"

"It's a compliment. Your type will always be judged by the quality of their—"

"Shut up."

"—enemies."

Babz mewed, batting her a trio of balls.

Rubi looked at them.

Self-assess: Smiley face? Sad face? Frowny face?

"Smiley," Rubi said, tossing it back to her. And in that moment, with her father intact, Gimlet in sync, and the whole Sensorium doubling down on the necessary belief that they *could* do it, they could rebuild the world, Rubi Whiting was just a bit startled to discover that her public utterance was, quite literally, the truth, whole and nothing but.

LAND ACKNOWLEDGMENT

Gamechanger was written on the ancestral and traditional territories of the Mississaugas of the New Credit, the Haudenosaunee, the Anishinaabe, and the Huron-Wendat, who are the original owners and custodians of the land on which I have the good fortune to stand and create.

ACKNOWLEDGMENTS

THE SURFACE—TORONTO, 2019

My augmented existence truly began with the 2016 release of *Poké-mon Go*, but I have been escaping into imagined realities since childhood. I met the love of my life over a table scattered with hex-agonal maps and six-sided dice. Bishop Girl, you make all things possible. You delight, amaze, and surprise me, every day. Thank you for the adventure.

Gamechanger would not exist without the critical support and advice of my agent, Caitlin Blasdell, and Tor editors Marco Palm-ieri and Christopher Morgan, all of whom have used their keen eyes, excellent judgment, and the occasional deadline to fuel my rocketpack.

Countless family members and superheroes keep me from fly-ing into cliffs all the time and patch me up when I hit. I'm looking at you: Charlie Jane Anders, Titus Androgynous, Madeline Ashby, Michael Bishop, Jeremy Brett, Ellen Datlow, Lara Donnelly, Alicia and Joe English, Gemma Files, Sandra Kasturi, Claude Lalumière, Margo MacDonald, Annalee Newitz, David Nickle, Jessica Reis-man, Alexandra Renwick, Julia Rios, Merc Rustad, Jordan Sharpe, Richard Shealy, Rebecca Stefoff, S. M. Stirling, Caitlin Sweet, Kellan Szpara, Harry Turtledove, Peter Watts, Laura White,

Jay Wolf, and JY Yang. It would be an honor to count any of you as enemies; how much luckier I am to be able to call you my arch-friends!

Send up a signal if you need me; you know you've got my marker.

ABOUT THE AUTHOR

L. X. BECKETT frittered their misbegotten youth working as an actor and theater technician in Southern Alberta, before deciding to make a shift into writing science fiction. Their first novella, "Freezing Rain, a Chance of Falling," appeared in the July/August issue of *The Magazine of Fantasy & Science Fiction* in 2018, and takes place in the same universe as *Gamechanger*. Beckett identifies as feminist, lesbian, genderqueer, married, and Slytherin, and can be found on Twitter at @LXBeckett or at a writing advice blog, *The LexIcon*, at lxbeckett.com.